Durham County Council Libraries, Learning and Culture	
C0 2 72 49327 8E	
Askews & Holts	
AF	

© Copyright 2006 Marion Wehmeyer.
All rights reserved. No part of this publication may be reproduced, stored in a retrieval system, or transmitted, in any form or by any means, electronic, mechanical, photocopying, recording, or otherwise, without the written prior permission of the author.

Note for Librarians: A cataloguing record for this book is available from Library and Archives Canada at www.collectionscanada.ca/amicus/index-e.html
ISBN 1-4122-0069-5

Printed on paper with minimum 30% recycled fibre. Trafford's print shop runs on "green energy" from solar, wind and other environmentally-friendly power sources.

TRAFFORD
PUBLISHING

Offices in Canada, USA, Ireland and UK
This book was published *on-demand* in cooperation with Trafford Publishing. On-demand publishing is a unique process and service of making a book available for retail sale to the public taking advantage of on-demand manufacturing and Internet marketing. On-demand publishing includes promotions, retail sales, manufacturing, order fulfilment, accounting and collecting royalties on behalf of the author.

Book sales for North America and international:
Trafford Publishing, 6E–2333 Government St.,
Victoria, BC V8T 4P4 CANADA
phone 250 383 6864 (toll-free 1 888 232 4444)
fax 250 383 6804; email to orders@trafford.com
Book sales in Europe:
Trafford Publishing (UK) Limited, 9 Park End Street, 2nd Floor
Oxford, UK OX1 1HH UNITED KINGDOM
phone 44 (0)1865 722 113 (local rate 0845 230 9601)
facsimile 44 (0)1865 722 868; info.uk@trafford.com
Order online at:
trafford.com/05-2794

10 9 8 7 6 5 4 3 2

BABYBOOM DOOM

LOSS OF INOCENCE

We were children,
Patriotic, brave children,
Innocence of honor.

All too soon
We were forced to grow up,
To face danger and bloodshed,
Terrors real and imagined,
Waited there in the dark.
But grimly determined,
We stood our ground,
Though the reason got lost,
In the fight.

And we were proud!
Then we came home,
Some of us whole and some of us not,
And no one cared.

All those years we've stumbled along,
Bewildered and lost, remembering,
And lonely.

Scorned, ridiculed and ignored,
For something out of control.

And now we're men,
Hardened and inside ourselves.
But it's not too late,
Won't you try to understand,

We were just children.

Anonymous

BABYBOOM

The following is based on a true story with special attention given to historical accuracy. The character's names have been changed to protect the innocent.

CONTENTS

CHAPTER ONE

    INNOCENCE..12

        The Park..13

        Grandma..22

        The Change..26

CHAPTER TWO

    ELEMENTARY DAYS..36

        The Pond..45

        The Threat..52

        The Forest..55

        Segregation..61

CHAPTER THREE

    TEENAGER..63

        Early Friends..64

        High school..74

        Work..76

CHAPTER FOUR
MARINE CORPS..................79
- Basic Training..................88
- Infantry Training..................90
- Military MOS..................97
- L.A. International Airport..................102
- Containment Policy..................108

CHAPTER FIVE
VIETNAM..................115
- Chu Lai..................122
- Da Nang..................130
- Base Life..................132
- The Fights..................137

CHAPTER SIX
OKINAWA..................175
- Jungle Training..................180
- Liberty..................187
- The Return..................198

CHAPTER SEVEN
VIETNAM II..................192
- The Fights II..................200
- Hong Kong..................230

    Coming Home..................242

CHAPTER EIGHT
    CAMP LEJEUNE..................245
        Stateside Duty..................249
        Med Training..................251
        BLT 2/2..................254

CHAPTER NINE
    ROCK OF GIBRATER..................256
        The Town..................259

CHAPTER TEN
    SPAIN..................260
        Barcelona..................261
        The Dance..................262

CHAPTER ELEVEN
    FRANCE..................268
        Toulon..................268
        Corsica..................276

CHAPTER TWELVE
    ITALY..................280

  Sardinia I..................280

  Naples..................282

  Rome..................288

  Sardinia II..................296

CHAPTER THIRTEEN

 COLD WAR TENSIONS..................298

  Russian Trawlers..................298

  Harassment..................300

  North Koreans..................246

  Babyboom Doom..................302

CHAPTER FOURTEEN

 THE ATLANTIC..................304

  The Storm..................305

  PTSD Behavior..................311

  The Final Landing..................313

CHAPTER FIFTEEN

 CAMP LEJEUNE II..................315

  Reserve Training..................315

  Test Program..................316

  Undecided About Reenlistment..................325

CHAPTER SIXTEEN
CIVILIAN LIFE..............................329
The Trip Home......................330
Baytown, TX........................333

CHAPTER SEVENTEEN
PTSD DEFINED..........................337
The Symptoms Begin................287
College...............................245
SCUBA................................348

CHAPTER EIGHTEEN
FREE SPIRIT..............................358
Truck Driving......................365
Success..............................412

CHAPTER NINETEEN
SURVIVAL................................414
Washington DC....................419
Epilogue............................424

CHAPTER TWENTY
REFLECTIONS...........................427

SELECT BIBIOGRAPHY................428

CHRONOLOGY..........................432

INDEX....................................448

INTRODUCTION

There are millions of stories concerning the *Babyboom* generation. This is a story about one baby-boomer who was raised in the innocence of rural America, who went to war, survived, then suffered the humiliation of being a part of the chaotic period connected with the Vietnam War.

After many years of suffering symptoms later called by psychiatrist, *Post Traumatic Stress Disorder* (PTSD), the main character, Casey, takes you from his very simple upbringing, to the very complicated emotional whirlwind he experienced throughout his life, as he tried to come to terms with his war experience.

Like many ordinary soldiers, Casey denies his problems associated with war at first, and he refused to talk about his experience of combat with others. He kept the horrors he experienced to himself for so long, he began to accept his condition as *normal*, when in fact he was very troubled.

Casey takes you through his many failed relationships, and his inability to keep work, as he struggles with adjusting to the civilian life style he no longer understands. His *live for today* attitude is emphasized by his maverick lifestyle, and his unwillingness to except that any of it is *his* fault.

Easily bored, Casey masters one job after another, only to seek peace elsewhere. His search for peace, love, and joy takes you through a journey full of ups and downs . It takes years for Casey to recognize that he has a problem, and the love of a special person who gives him a reason to seek recovery.

Casey has to change his wild ways! He decides to focus on his problems by first praying to God for answers! God tells him to go home, to stop wandering, and to settle down. Confessing his sins openly to the night stars from the truck cab of an eighteen wheeler, he decides to go home and to seek forgiveness, by excepting Christ as his savior.

At church God delivers Casey that very special person who was conditioned by Him, to be the one person to love and care for Casey unconditionally. When Beth enters Casey's life, he seriously begins to seek recovery, both because of his love for Beth, and for his need to survive the past!

Casey seeks professional help through the Veterans Administration *Trauma Recovery Program* (TRP) , and learns ways to cope with his *anxiety* disability. Through his experience, he explains what PTSD is, and how recovery is possible for anyone who *seeks* it.

Casey systematically changes his earlier behavior, and finds peace through his adopted family, his Bible, and his family of God at church. Casey explains how he found that peace in his senior years, and how he is rewarded with a fulfilled life. With the support of the TRP, he discovers the potential for a fulfilling life, and *finally* a happy marriage.

After following Casey's journey through a Babyboom history, you will embrace your own experiences, and come away with a refreshed awareness of your own past. Since you cannot forget your past, you are left with making peace with it, and of becoming free of the quilt and shame that has prevented you from enjoying love, joy, and peace.

Babyboom Doom is a stirring testimony of the life of a soldier, whose attitude was shaped by the historical events of his time. The war doomed many of his generation to a life of unsolicited self discovery. After war, Casey seemingly is forever doomed to a life of failures, but with true grit and fortitude, he struggles on to become a survivor of the Babyboom Doom.

BABYBOOM DOOM

CHAPTER ONE

Innocence

It was 1946. World War II had ended just months before. The returning men of war produced the largest baby boom in the history of the US. From 1946 to 1964 seventy-six million babies were born. They were affectionately known as *Babyboomers*. Casey knows, because Casey is a Babyboomers. This is his story.

It was early spring, March 1949, when *Casey Lee Trainer* first started to remember things. He was a young blue eyed, white haired boy, with very fair skin typical of German and English decent, just three years old. Like many all-American boys, his ancestors were from Europe.

Casey was full of curiosity as most young innocent children are. The day was bright and sunny with bluebonnets and Indian paintbrushes that covered the field nearby. Casey was especially attracted to the buttercups that seemed to be everywhere. These flowers are common to the Texas hillsides. Casey lived in a small government apartment complex that was just a short walk to downtown Brenham, Texas. His life journey begins in the innocence of this twentieth century, rural countryside community. It is a journey full of emotional ups and downs and dangerous forlorn adventure!

The Park

One beautiful sun shiny day Casey's mother, Mary Lee took him to a small park. It was known as *Fireman's Park* and it was a delight to small children for many years in Brenham. The central attraction was the glamorous antique carrousel horses that paraded in a circle as they moved up and down to the sound of cheerful music.

The first thing that Casey saw that he was not afraid of, were the swings that swayed in a rhythmic dance with the breeze. They seemed to beckon him to come to them. He also, almost at the same time, saw the slides. He ran as fast as he could, sort of stumbling, as if he could not decide where to go or what to focus on. He ran through the flowers unconsciously screaming with delight! "Look! Something very colorful is fluttering to each flower." "What is it?" He wanted to catch it but it flew away. The flowers had a sweet smell that drew you near them. They were full of bright colors; pink, blue, red, yellow, white, and black! How marvelous to see and experience these sweet smells and bright colors for the very first time!

Casey ran to the swings. He screamed, "Look mom, it moves, it moves!" The swings did move as if something magical was happening. With his mom's help, he climbed aboard the swing not knowing what to expect. His mom ever so gently pushed him back causing him to swing. The swing began to swish him from side to side. He was amazed and surprised all at the same time! It was a sensation he had never felt before. He felt excited but he didn't understand why. He felt energized and he just wanted to keep going. Casey hollered with delight while he indicated to mom that he wanted down. As soon as his feet hit the ground he began to run. He ran through all the swings several times making them crash into each other, first one direction, and then the other. Then he laid in the middle of one swing, on his stomach, and he saw the ground move as if he was lying still and the ground was moving in all directions beneath his eyes. Casey could not believe that he was having so much fun in this new place of discovery. By now he had fallen down several times and his tee shirt and trousers showed the wear of his exploits by becoming soiled with the dirt and occasional grass stain, in addition to an abrasion or two that mysteriously appeared on his elbows and hands. Casey was not feeling any pain though because he was so excited to be running and enjoying the outdoors. As his mom tried to keep him under control he ran around and around until he spotted something else.

"What's this?" Casey wondered. He walked around the object until he saw the ladder that looked like something he could grab onto. He had never seen such a device. The ladder led upward to a small slide that angled toward the ground. Next to the small slide was a much higher slide. He looked at them both and instinctively chose the small slide to investigate. He slowly climbed up the ladder. His mother screamed in disbelief! He struggled to position himself at the top. He let go of the support bars and down he went propelled toward the ground at a speed that seemed much too fast for him to understand. As he reached the end of the slide, he suddenly felt that he was falling from the sky. To his surprise, very swiftly Casey hit the ground with a loud sudden thump. His mother was there to safe guard him from falling wrong. Shaken and out of breath from the impact, Casey got up to brush himself off. He was confused about what had just happened, but he was willing to do it again. Much later in life he would know that life is full of confusion, much like that, going so fast it can't always be understood!

After becoming unafraid of the small slide, having tried it successfully several times, Casey ran to the tall slide. It was at least twice as big as the little slide. He started up the ladder. His mother, very concerned, ran toward him to try to stop him from climbing up that high. She was protesting his attempt to climb that high of a ladder. A fall from the top would easily have caused a very bad injury. Casey had no concept of broken bones or how a fall from way up could hurt him. About halfway up he began to loose his nerve because his mother was trying to reach him before something happened. Casey didn't know what was going on. He became afraid, not only because his mother was yelling, but because he was so high he didn't know what to do! Casey cried as fear took its unfamiliar hold on him. "Help, I'm stuck," he cried. He was almost to the slide part, but he could not bring himself to sit at the top. His mom shouted, "Casey Lee, you come down here!" She called him *Casey Lee* instead of just Casey, when she really meant for him to obey her. Casey's pale skin was as light as his white hair by now. With his blue eyes opened wide he began to shake. Casey thought he must go up higher and sit down, but he just could not move. It was as if his ability to move his arms and legs had suddenly stopped! He did not know or understand what was happening as fear had its surprising grip on his body. Casey struggled to reach the top. He started to cry louder for help as his mom neared the top of the ladder to help him. She was nearly in a state of panic by now. She could just see Casey falling any second. "Mommy please help me," He cried again! Casey's three-year-old cousin Tom stood at the bottom of the slide, wondering what would happen next. Shrouded in fear and unable to move Casey just wanted to get down.

As Casey's mom reached for him he got the courage to move away to the top to sit down, but he was afraid to let go of the support bars. Why he was hanging on so tight he did not know. He had let go earlier without any concern! Suddenly Casey let go of the support bars just as his mom reached to grab him. He did not want her to stop him!

Timidly and very unsure of his actions, Casey inched toward the slide. He slid down so fast that before he realized what was happening, he crashed into Tom who was standing at the end of the slide. They both tumbled to the ground. Casey didn't know what was going on. He was so excited, crying, yelling, laughing, and tumbling. His mother picked him up and she yelled, "Are you alright?" She checked him and Tom to see if they had been injured. They both were stunned but they were OK. They were just excited about life. Then they both started running, looking for their next adventure. It came right away!

The carrousel had many hand painted wooden horses that seemed to gallop right toward Casey and then momentarily disappear as he watched nearby. The galloping horses seemed to keep coming endlessly as they went round and round. Casey and Tom wanted to ride the horses! Their mothers' said no at first, but they soon held them on top of the wooden horses as they rode. They did not want to stop when their mother's finally said that they needed to stop. The boys protested with their screams but they soon forgot what they were upset about. Their mothers took their hands and they walked toward home. It was the highlight of a fun filled adventurous day, full of innocent lessons and joy.

Casey's cousin Tom and he were about the same age. They were born just two months apart. Tom lived in the apartment across from Casey. They played together a lot. Being typical boys they would fight over almost anything. They would wrestle each other and get into fistfights and yell a lot. They would play like they were cowboys and Casey would be the sheriff and Tom would be the bad guy or they would switch roles and Casey would be the bad guy and Tom would be the good guy. Western mythology was everywhere as they grew up.

Casey ended up in a fight with Tom. They were playing in the field next to their apartments when they came upon a big hole in the ground. It was a pretty day, sun shining, birds chirping loudly. Casey could not remember ever seeing the hole. He wondered, "Where did it come from?" "How did it get there?" Tom said it was his and Casey said it was his. They started to wrestle over it. All of a sudden Casey found himself inside the big hole in the ground. Tom had pushed him and Casey fell into the hole with a loud thud. Casey then pulled Tom in. They both managed to climb out and to fight over whom would remain on top. Casey got real mad and hit Tom hard with a toy pistol, knocking Tom's cowboy hat off his head as they twisted and turned about in the dirt pile that lined the hole. Tom got so mad he hit Casey in the nose with his fist. The fight was getting really rough. Casey ran away across the field and Tom chased him picking up rocks as he ran, throwing them at Casey. Casey made it to his apartment without being hit, but just as he climbed to the top of the stairs that led to the entrance of the apartment, Tom, still furious that Casey had hit him with the medal pistol , threw a hammer he found on the ground at Casey. The hammer slammed into Casey's right ankle. A burning sensation began to follow the blow. It hurt, but Casey's pride was hurt even more because Tom had gotten the best of him in the end.

The boys seemed to always make up after a fight. Each new day began anew. A few years later Casey was to learn that the hole they were fighting about was the beginning of the community swimming pool and their apartment complex was scheduled to be destroyed as part of the project.

Each morning began with a sound that Casey found comforting. He would see in the bluebonnet field, birds that ran along the ground. They made a soothing cooing sound. This sound he began to always associate with the beginning of a new day. One day he tried to catch one of the birds just to know what it was like. But the bird would run away before he could get near it. The morning doves were music to his ears. He always looked forward to hearing them.

Casey also discovered morning dew! He would sit on the ground in the morning and it would be wet. It had a fresh smell, a distinct smell that energized him the first thing in the morning. Casey would run in it, stop quickly, and then slide for what seemed like a long ways. So he would run and stop. Run and stop. Run and stop, to slide in the moist grass. He would be wet from head to toe. But he loved the experience. My gosh what an adventure for a three year old!

Casey was just beginning to experience life. He discovered all kinds of birds and animals and spiders and snakes and plants. Each day brought forth a new adventure. Like the time Casey found a hole in the ground where a big spider lived. It had furry legs and ran fast across the ground. Casey later learned that these large, fast spiders were tarantulas that were common in the area. The grown-ups used to pour hot water down the tarantulas' holes to make them run away. Casey was very scared of the monstrous looking creatures. Someone had told Casey that the bite of a spider could make you very sick or maybe even kill you. But Casey and Tom played in the fields where they lived and they saw the spiders quiet often. There was a certain sound they made as they scurried through the grass. Casey thought the spiders looked very, very big then. Every thing is big and exciting when you are just three years old.

One day Tom and Casey discovered matches! If you rubbed the end of this stick against something rough, it would erupt into a hot bright flame. They tried it again and again. Wow what amazement! And if you placed the flame against something else, it too would erupt into a flame. Casey and Tom were outside experimenting with their new discovery. They found paper and it would *burn*. They found dead grass and it would burn. They went to great lengths to prevent their moms from knowing what they were doing. They could make light with these things and that allowed them to see well. Casey's mother discovered the bad habit one day in a way that no one could have predicted.

Tom said, "Casey let's see what is down this black hole." Casey lit the match and placed it in the black hole to see what was there. All of a sudden he was lifted off his feet and thrown several feet backwards. He smelled an awful smell, and he felt an awful pressure. Then for what seemed to be a long time, but was really only a fraction of a second, he heard a loud noise, then silence. His mother came running from across the courtyard, grabbed him and shook him. Casey had been knocked momentarily unconscious! After a few moments he awoke and cried, "What happened?" "What did I do?" Hysterically, his mom grabbed him by his arm and began spanking his behind! "Why is mom spanking me?" thought Casey. He started crying and shaking and thrashing all about. It all happened so fast.

"Just wait until your dad gets home," she screamed. Casey's hand and his hair had been burned badly and his fun had suddenly turned into a very bad experience. "Why?" "What had *he* done?"

Casey's dad was not too happy when he came home from work. Casey's mom always threatened him that way. She would have Casey's dad spank him when he came home, if Casey did not mind her during the day. Casey had been hurt, but he was even more scared that his dad was going to spank him for sure. Casey's mom was still acting mad. She wanted his dad to punish him for playing with matches. Casey learned later that his mom was just *very* frightened over what had happened.

Casey's dad learned that the backend of his car had been destroyed from the gasoline explosion. Casey's mom told his dad that Casey had stuck a match into the car's gas tank! Casey was still confused. He knew he had done something very bad because everyone was upset, but he really did not understand what he had actually done. He just knew that he never saw what was in that black hole. It took years before he understood what had happened. Life is like that!

Casey loved to help his mom with the chores. She would wash the family clothes using an old scrub board that helped to get the grit out. The board had tin ruffles that made a thumping noise as the clothes were passed over them. She would soak the clothes in a tub before the scrubbing began. Casey would wring them by hand to get the water out. It was as if he was wrestling the clothes each time he tried a different piece of clothing. Casey considered himself a he-man when he succeeded to get the water out; a real Captain Marvel or maybe even as strong as Superman. Casey would twist those cloths to the very last drop of water was forced out. Then he would help her hang them on the clothesline out behind the apartment. The clothes would blow in the breeze all day and make kind of a flapping noise that proved relaxing in a simple way. The sun would give them an unusual hue that shined brightly until the clothes were completely dry. When the clothes were dry, they were ready to be brought in. Casey enjoyed getting them off the clothesline and putting them in a basket. He would then carry the basket to the apartment. There were stairs that led up to the small porch where the front screen door was. One day he was carrying the clothes up the stairs. Casey had so many clothes wrapped around both arms that he could not see in front of him. Casey struggled up the steps, step by step until he reached the top. He shuffled over to the screen door. The door handle was on the right side of the door, so he moved to the side to open the door. The door had to swing toward him to open. When he stepped to the side to open the screen door, he stepped off the porch. Casey fell about five feet right on top of a gas meter! The pain was excruciating! His mom ran over to him screaming at the top of her lungs, "Are you hurt?" "Are you OK?" Casey was hurting and scared and crying. She carried him to the bed where she examined him. She thought his leg and foot was broken or that his tiny testicles were injured, but as it turned out he was only bruised and battered. Casey was beginning to learn that you have to be tough to live in this world!

The next day Casey awoke to hear the morning doves. That glorious sound that gave a peaceful beginning to each new day. By the time he was four years old, Casey had discovered flowers, dew, black holes, spiders, the park, and all sorts of other adventures.

Grandma

Casey began to learn about grandma, his mother's mother, whom he called *Grandma Dorothy*. Her name was Dorothy Davis before she married an Oklahoma man named Leslie Swain Stevens. Grandpa Stevens, Casey's mom always said, was part *Native American Cherokee Indian*. Casey's mom would say that in an almost shameful way, because being part Indian in a predominately white European culture, at that time was considered subhuman. Casey never knew him well because his grandpa died when Casey was only about three, although his grandma and mom always talked about him a lot when Casey was growing up.

Grandpa Stevens traveled a lot because he worked as a track welder for the railroad. He was adored by all because he obviously loved Casey's grandma and the family. They lived in Somerville, Texas where Casey's mom and dad often visited them, by making a road trip from Baytown, Texas. The road trip led right through the tall pine tree forest of East Texas to the rolling hills of Brenham, Texas. The pastures would be plush with green grass and the cattle would be fat from the fresh feed. The Brazos River, running swiftly to the south, was an awesome site to behold beneath the steel braced bridge that took them across the river. During the spring the bluebonnets would cover the fields as far as one could see, nourished by the spring rain that also swelled the river high. Casey loved all the flowers that could be seen as they crowded the small two-way road that led to his grandma's house.

Grandma Dorothy's place was very much like a typical home in East Texas in the late 1800's. Every big room had a wood-burning heater with a stack that went up towards a very high ceiling. The kitchen had a wood-burning stove. In one corner there was a box. Ice was placed in it to keep foodstuffs cool. Casey always looked forward to seeing the iceman bring those huge chunks of ice that he would put in grandma Dorothy's icebox. Then the milkman would come and place one or two bottles of milk at the door. Grandma Dorothy would tell Casey to get the milk and put it in the icebox. He always did and he liked the rich milk given to him for his efforts. It was a very rich tasting kind of milk, the kind that only comes fresh from a well fed cow. The milk was brought in a strange looking wagon pulled by a horse. Casey watched the horse pull the wagon slowly down the dirt path for as long as he could see it. Casey smelled the aroma of the smoke coming from the chimneys of the other homes as the wagon disappeared from his view. He could hear the roosters crowing and the sounds of the doves. He could smell the wood burning and the food being cooked. Grandma would say, "Casey Lee, go fetch us some firewood." Casey would go through some grass that was sharp as a razor to get to the woodpile and bring in one or two pieces of wood to be put in the stove. He learned to hate that grass. It would cut his legs and his legs would burn like fire when he walked into it.

Casey could smell the kerosene. Kerosene was used in the lanterns and to start the wood to burn. It was kept in a special metal container that always smelled very strong. Casey didn't like how it smelled, but it sure got the fire started in a hurry.

Grandma Dorothy had a special way of cooking. She made

homemade bread and churned cheese and many other homemade foodstuffs. Her pecan pie was Casey's favorite. It was made with the sweetest of syrup, the kind that just oozed with the right thickness. The pecans were gotten from the back yard. Casey liked picking them up from the ground and putting them in a small tin pale that he carried along. He liked to crack the pecan shells. He used pliers and hammers and rocks and all sorts of devices to crack them open. Casey put about as many pecans in his mouth as he placed in the bowl for Grandma Dorothy. He always thinks of Grandma Dorothy when he eats pecan pie. It seems that nowhere has Casey ever found better pecan pie than that pie that grandma used to make.

Casey also loved Grandma Dorothy's fried chicken. Grandma Dorothy had live chickens all around her yard. They scratched and pecked at the ground as they cackled. Casey watched the chickens and spent many mornings feeding them. It was very exciting to him to have all of that activity right in the back yard. Casey also gathered the chicken's eggs to bring them to his grandma. She rewarded him with a hug and a kiss and said that he was such a nice young man. Her fried chicken just melted in his mouth. It was the best- fried chicken he ever had!

It did get confusing to Casey when he had to catch the chickens and wring their necks in order to kill them for food. Blood spurted everywhere as the beheaded chickens body flopped around the yard until it died. Casey did not enjoy ringing the chicken's neck or the plucking of the feathers. He hated the awful smell of the wet feathers as he cleaned the chickens. Casey enjoyed feeding and caring for them. He felt that he was doing something wrong when he chased them for food. But Casey was to find out that life itself gets so very confusing, no matter what the age.

Casey became four years old in 1951. His existing world was about to change. He woke up one morning to find his parents putting everything they owned into the car. Casey got ready and went outside to play like he had always done. He loved to run! Casey ran here, and then he ran there, always exploring new adventures. This morning it was very cold. Ice covered the ground in late January. The ground was hard and cold and Casey kept slipping and falling down. He had a sleigh that his dad had built for him out of wood to slide down the hill. He was playing with it when suddenly his dad came to say it is time for us to go. Go? Go where? This was Casey's whole world, the only place he had ever known. Grandma Dorothy's house, Tom, the park, and other friends that he had come to know. He started to cry. He started to scream really, "No, no, no! I don't want to go. *Please* no!" He thrashed about, a tiny little person, with no power to stop the awful senseless act.

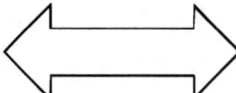

The Change

    Casey's parents had decided to move from the rural country in Brenham, Texas to another rural area in Texas called Baytown. Baytown, in the early 50's, was a piney forest area of East Texas. Various bays surround it near the Gulf of Mexico. It is a suburb of Houston. The main industries were Humble Oil and Refinery (later to become Exxon-Mobil), rice farming, fishing and foresting. Casey's family lived in this area. His dad and mom decided to move to the area to be with relatives and to find work. He was to learn that moving is a way of life. His dad worked construction jobs mostly. In Brenham he would make 90 cents an hour. In Baytown he could make 2 dollars an hour!

    The trip was made in his dad's 1941 Chevrolet. There was no air conditioner and the heater made them sweat a lot. They all smelled like musk or something like that and they all seemed to be a little irritated. The windows had to be down at times and the noise was deafening. That night it started to rain. Casey made his dad mad at him when he turned on the windshield wipers after he had told him to leave that knob alone at least three different times. The windshield wipers worked off the vacuum of the engine. The car engine actually lulled when the wipers were on. They were not too efficient; the wipers smeared the windshield with road mud and no one could see where they were going. Mom said, "Stop the car!" "Stop the car!" Casey jumped to the back seat. His dad swerved the car from side to side and rolled down the window and stuck his head out in the rain so that he could see where he was going and to regain control of the car. He finally found a safe place to stop the car so he could wipe the windshield with a cloth. Casey heard his dad mumbling some indescribable words with a scowled look on his wet face; the kind of look that scares even a mad dog. Casey just knew that those wipers would allow them to see. He had seen them wipe the glass before. He did not understand about road dirt and oil that can mix with the rain. They stopped in the rain to wipe the windshield. The smear did not go away. Casey's dad was not too happy about the delay. His clothes were all wet. His windshield was smeared with road oil. Casey's mom was giving instructions. Casey was curled up in the back seat. He was a little scared but he was also excited about doing what he thought was right. He could not understand what all the fuss was about.

The roads were two-way and narrow then and one had to go through little towns to travel. Although just a small boy of four years, Casey found it was exciting to see the hustle and bustle of the towns. They had to drive right through Houston. There were trains that whistled and bridges that crossed bayous way below. Cars drove on roads made of bricks. They were red. Casey had a thousand questions about all that was going on. Where are the trains going? Why is that truck carrying trees? Why was that building so big? Why was the bridge so high? Is there fish in the water below the bridge? How many horses are there here? Do Houston people have chickens, big spiders, or doves?

On the east side of Houston they came upon more water than

Casey had ever seen. It was the Houston ship channel and bay, but he did not know that. They were going along near the bay on a street named "Market Street" when he heard this thump, thump, thump. Casey's dad pulled off the road. He had a flat tire. Casey didn't know what a flat was, but he could see him fixing something. Tubes were used then. The tube was inside of the tire and the tube had to be patched or replaced. Not an easy thing to do. Casey's dad started the repair.

Casey saw the water. His dad had said to stay in the car. Casey was too excited and curious so he opened the back door and he jumped out of the car to see what was going on. Casey saw the water! He saw his dad working on the car. His mom was standing by him. The next thing he knew he was burning with pain! He didn't know what was happening. He started crying and screaming. His mom was there in an instant! She slapped his legs and jerked him from the ground. His dad stopped what he was doing and ran over to them both. "What's wrong?" "What's going on?" Casey's mom said, "Casey jumped right into that ant bed. He's covered with big red fire ants! Help me brush him off!" Casey screamed, his mom was delirious; his dad was just trying to fix the flat. Casey's legs were red with blisters as the ants crawled away. His legs continued to hurt for a long, long time. He thought they would never get to where they were going. Casey wanted to go back to Brenham. He wanted to go home. He wanted grandma and Tom and the park. He cried for a long time. He wished he had listened to his dad when he said to stay in the car.

The first house Casey's family lived in was located on Magnolia Street in old Baytown. It had a funny looking tank in the back. It was a water tower made of wood that looked like a big barrel setting high up on stilts. It reminded Casey of a flying saucer that had landed in the back yard. The object really fascinated him. It made hissing and roaring sounds as the water rushed in and out of the tank. Casey was both afraid of it and fascinated with it at the same time. He did not know what it was. At first when he wanted to play outside Casey ran to the other side of the house to avoid going near it. The tank rumbled and shook the ground with such force that it frightened Casey to the point that he ran faster than he'd ever run. He ran away from it very scared that it was about to capture him. Eventually , Casey began to gain confidence by slowly sneaking up to it. It would hiss and Casey would jump so high his feet began moving before he hit the ground to run away and hide. Casey peaked around from where he was hiding just to watch it. He shook uncontrollably from the adrenaline his body had produced in response to his fear. In all his four years, he had never seen such a thing. It must be some kind of monster, he thought. Or maybe some kind of space ship. Maybe there are creatures inside of it. Maybe they want to get control of the world and destroy everything and everybody. Casey shook for years whenever he heard similar sounds, real or imagined anywhere he was.

 That night Casey woke up in bed thinking that the creatures were trying to get him. He had had a bad dream. Every shadow was terrifying! He imagined all sorts of things. A shadow on the wall from the movement of a tree branch made Casey think that a creature just ran by his room. "What was that noise?" thought Casey. "Did you see that? What was that?" Casey always slept with the windows open because air conditioning was not yet available. The hot humid Texas summers were the worst, especially the sounds of the night. Casey was used to the hums of the mosquitoes. They were taken for granted, but he was still learning about the night sounds of other insects and animals. The night sounds made him feel uneasy. He sweat from both the heat and the fear until his sheets were damp. He stared into the night where the moonlight played tricks on his imagination. A cat ran by and all he could see was the shadow. The tree branch made a squeaking sound so he covered his head with the sheet. A roach scurried through the wall where the sound was magnified beyond reason. Casey focused on *every* sound and sight; intense, fearful sounds and sights. He imagined the figures on the walls, which danced right in front of him, were creatures from the unknown. He began to say his prayers over and over again. Through prayer he began to feel that he was stronger than the monsters and that they had better not try to get him. "God will protect me", he thought. "I'll punch them in the nose! I'll kick them and make them run away. They are not going to get me! God will punish them if they even tried! Casey ran to his parents bedroom crying, afraid of the night. They comforted him but he wanted to not be afraid anymore.

    Casey learned about his Grandpa and Grandma Trainer on his dad's side. His grandpa was born in Port Lavaca, Texas at the turn of the 20th century. He died when Casey was ten years old. On his death bed his grandpa held Casey's hand to tell him, with a weakened voice, to grow up to be a good boy.

    Casey never forgot the promise he made to his grandpa. Casey took that moment, from the heart of a dying man, very seriously. He promised his grandpa that he would be a good boy. It was an oath of truth! He often thought of the promise as he struggled to grow up in his inherited world, a world full of trails and tribulations. Especially whenever he did something he thought he should not have done.

    Grandma Trainer was born in very rustic Brenham, Texas 1898. She became the apple of grandpa's adoring eye. They obviously loved each other. They had nine children, five fine boys and four girls. Casey had many aunts and uncles who often played games with him, teaching him right from wrong. He grew up with many cousins who often came over to grandma's house too. It was fun to play outdoors at Grandma Trainers house. Everyone enjoyed the yard play so much they looked forward to doing it often.

Casey's dad had a brother named Herman. Herman was born in 1915, two years before Casey's dad. He died in 1927 when he was only twelve years old. Dad Trainer remembers that Herman stepped on a splintered board while playing in the horse barn. The wound was cleaned and treated. The wound healed over but became infected inside. When Herman complained that his foot was hurting and that he did not feel well, the doctor was called to the farm. The doctor examined Herman's foot. A large splinter was discovered deep inside the foot. It was swollen with infection. The infection had already spread throughout his body. It was too late to reverse the effect of the toxin. At ten years old Casey's dad cared for his older brother at his bedside.

Dad Trainer loved Herman! They had played together, laughed together, and worked together. He had taken up for Dad Trainer when their parents tried to discipline them. He had lifted the heavy pales of milk for Casey's dad when they needed to be carried from the barn to the house. He had carried wood and fetched water from the well. He was looked up to by Casey's dad. He was *his* big brother!

Dad Trainer watched as his brother's muscles around his face twitched and tightened from the toxin. He watched as the fever increased and his brother's body poured with sweat. He watched as Herman's jaws locked into a tight gridlock. He tried to give him water and food, but Herman was too sick to eat or drink. He watched as his brother's life slipped away. Herman died of tetanus before the dawn!

BABYBOOM DOOM

Casey's Dad, Walter Trainer blamed his parents for the loss. He felt that Herman should have seen a doctor sooner. He also blamed himself. Casey could tell that the loss of his brother affected his dad all of his life. Tears would well up in his eyes whenever he talked about the circumstances surrounding his brother's death. He never stopped feeling that the loss of his brother was a tragic unnecessary loss. In 1927 however, it was common to lose loved ones over lack of immediate medical attention.

Cousin Katy was the same age as Casey. She was a very cute little girl that could run as fast as Casey. Casey was determined to run faster than she did. Casey often chased her and she would chase Casey for all sorts of reasons. Then there was Carol, who was Katy's sister. Casey always thought she was a pretty little girl. She was a little younger than Katy and Casey, but she was a lot of fun to play with.

Katy and Casey sometimes sneaked between the buildings to kiss each other like they saw their parents do. They hugged each other tight and played like they were man and wife. Carol would run to tell her mother what they were doing. Katy and Casey both got mad at Carol. Mom Trainer told them that they could not do that any more, so instead they played cowboy and Indians. Casey knew about cowboys and Indians from the *radio*. Television was not yet available to everyone. The radio stories were very exciting to Casey. Casey came into the house just to listen to the radio programs. There was "The Lone Ranger" and "The Red Rider." There was "Amos and Andy" and "The Life of Riley," but Casey usually played like he was a cowboy or an Indians. He always looked forward to sitting on the floor in the living room to listen to the radio programs. But mostly, Casey played outside and explored every rock, limb, and creature he could find. Playing and being outside was quite an adventure for him!

With mud pies, sticks, and rocks he could make almost anything to play with. When Cousin Lane came along, he was good at throwing rocks and things. Later that manifested into him being a good baseball player.

When Casey grew a little older, he learned about Uncle Herschel, nick named *Buddy*. He was a strong lad in his youth. He did not have any formal education but he had a strong back. He always worked hard. He was the youngest brother, the one that the others always teased and had fun with. Herschel started drinking beer at a young age. Later in life he was addicted to it! Mom Trainer did not like anyone who drank beer and got drunk, so she did not allow him to come over to her house very often. Casey lost touch with him as a result. Casey had little to do with them as he grew up. He felt ashamed of his alcoholic relatives.

The year Casey was five years old, he was moved again! His new home was a garage apartment. The apartment was located in the old Baytown section of town off a street called *Market*. Baytown was formed from a combination of three little towns. There was the old Goose Creek area, another area called Pelly, and another area called Baytown. All three merged to form the city of Baytown. Casey eventually lived in all of the different areas as he grew up.

The main street of *Old Baytown* was called *Market Street*. A theater was across the street, which was called *Bay Theater*. There was an old military surplus store a little farther down, the post office, and a Wieners clothing store. There was a small corner grocery store nearby and Humble Oil & Refinery within site of downtown. Baytown Elementary and Baytown Junior High were close by. There was another elementary school very near Casey's apartment. It was called San Jacinto Elementary located on Virginia Street. Casey could walk to any of the stores because everything was so close to his place. Casey loved to play in a sandbox in front of his house every evening. He loved to play, but there was no one his age to play with at the new place. Casey played alone making him less dependent on others.

Casey used to run everywhere. One day he found a nickel so Casey decided to run to the corner store to get a popular soda drink called Coke-A-Cola. It was sprinkling that day so he wanted to run fast. When Casey came to the bad intersection he had to wait for a car to pass. When it passed he started to run across the street. When he was about halfway across, Casey saw another car coming. He quickly turned around and ran back to where he started. But he was now scared to cross the street. That other car with that mean stranger in it had almost run over him. Casey was so frightened that the only thing he could think of was to run home as quickly as he could. Casey's heart was pumping so fast and he did not fully understand the feeling. Casey was scared to a state of confusion. He waited for the intersection to clear. There was very little auto traffic but he thought it was, in his frightened state. When Casey saw a car in the distance he exclaimed, "What's taking so long? Why won't the cars stop so I can go home? When are they going to stop?" The delay somehow increased his fright. He felt an urgent need to get home right away, to where he was safe and secure. Casey waited for what seemed like a long time to try again, although only seconds had really passed. "Oh no, it's still not clear! Now! Now run! Run fast!" Casey started across the street as fast he could run. About halfway across he tripped on something and almost fell down. But he didn't fall down so he kept going as fast as he could. "What's that on my foot? It's all red and wet! Where did that come from? What happened to my foot?" screamed Casey. Casey kept running until he got to the bottom of the stairs leading up to the garage apartment. There was a trail of blood following him. Mom Trainer screamed, "What happened to your foot? What happened?" Casey was so scared he did not know what had happened. He didn't know his foot was cut and bleeding badly until he got home to his mom.

Casey later figured out what had happened that fateful day when he ventured out to the store. He had started across the street with his soda. The coming car had so scared him, he turned to run back. He dropped the soda bottle in the middle of the street but he did not know it. It broke in half and left a sharp piece of jagged glass there. Casey was so frightened from seeing the coming car he forgot he even had the soda. When Casey finally got the courage to run across the street again, he stepped on the broken bottle. The bottom half of the bottle lay flat on the street, while the sharp jagged edges pointed straight up! The entire weight of Casey's foot came crashing down directly on top of the sharp glass as he ran through the intersection. Casey had slashed the bottom of his foot wide open, but he just ran faster. Still afraid, Casey didn't even stop to see what had happened. All that he knew was that his foot was hurting and feeling strange when he tried to run and that he was limping as he tried to keep going.

It took a long time for Casey's foot to heal but it did heal with his mothers care. Going to the doctor for injuries in those days was not as common as it is now. Casey's foot was cut to the bone. Adventures can end up that way!

Casey was too young to know that his injury had made his dad think of his lost brother. Dad Trainer was concerned for some time weather or not Casey's foot had healed properly .

CHAPTER TWO

Elementary Days

When Casey became six years and ten months old, He started school. The school year ran from September, 1953 to May, 1954. This was September, 1953 and segregation was the political state of mind. Most of the kids at school were white. Some were of Mexican decent. No Black people were there. Casey did not even know there were black people then. There were none where he lived until he became older. Korea was a new word to Casey. What is an Oriental? Where in the world is Korea?

At almost seven years old he obviously was not fully aware of the political circumstances that shaped the world's events. Casey knew some things of international importance were happening because his parents and older relatives would talk about that sort of thing. In 1950, the North Koreans attacked the South Koreans. The U.S. came to the aid of South Korea as the chief non-Communist power. The Chinese Communist joined forces with the North Koreans. The Soviet Union supported the establishment of any Communist regime and therefore gave support to the North Koreans. Additionally the Soviet Union did not give independence to the Eastern states of Europe after WWII. With the balance of world power at stake, the Korean war raged on until 1953. The Korean war was about to end in a stalemate with no clear cut of victory for either side. After the Korean war, the economic war and military positioning between the non-Communist and the Communist continued. It became known as the *Cold War*. The Cold War between the U.S. and the Communists was really heating up. Propaganda about the Communists was everywhere; radio, newspapers, magazines, and later TV. Adults were always comparing the Democratic system to the Communist system. Casey just knew the U.S. schools had to be better than those old Communist schools!

The school was about a quarter of a mile away, so Casey walked or ran to school every day. All that he remembered about that first year in school was that he met a lot of different kids. Some he perceived as good and others he did not understand.

At school Casey learned that he could take care of himself physically. He seemed to excel at the play-yard games and he was not afraid of anyone his size. On the way home from school one day, a boy, about Casey's age, and Casey got into a fight. It was a territorial dispute of the route home. The boy called Casey a name and said he didn't like him. Casey then said that he didn't care. The boy yelled, "You have a sissy's name. You can't go home this way. "I go home this way all the time," retorted Casey. The boy pushed Casey and Casey pushed him back. They began to wrestle until they both fell to the ground. Casey climbed on top of the boy and started banging his head against the concrete and swinging at his face. The boys were both scared but they reacted with the primitive instincts they both possessed to survive. Casey's mother saw what was happening from the house and yelled at the boys to stop fighting. They did, but from then on Casey was sensitive about other people's perception of him. In defiance, he continued along the path of life getting a little tougher each day.

Casey continued to use the same route home and the other kid never bothered him again. Isn't it funny how the little things that happen early in life, long ago, actually change how we react to people and things in the present? Casey also realized that day, that when other people are involved, sometimes you have to fight for what you believe.

About halfway through his first year of school, Casey's parents moved again. This time it was to the part of Baytown known as Pelly, a wooded area near the bay built as a result of the nearby oil fields. Casey could not run home from San Jacinto Elementary any more because his new place was too far away. After school everyday, he would wait for his dad to pick him up. He would sit on the high part of the steps and wait for his dad to pull up in his 1950 pickup truck.

Casey's dad always drove. His mom didn't even know how. This was an age when the man worked for a living outside of the home, and the women stayed home to take care of it and her children. So Casey's dad is who he looked for. There were no cell telephones to just call up a friend. As a matter of fact, Casey's home had no phone of any sort. The only contact with others was with those who were immediately around you. Casey's parents had no other electronic devices like TV, or computers. It was a very innocent time. They did listen to the radio a lot, after dinner.

Casey was beginning to realize that the moving around every year was preventing him from having long term friends. Every time his parents moved, he had to adjust to different people, a different neighborhood, a different house, a different bedroom, a different school, with a different group of officials, and a different set of rules, and he had to adjust to conflicting attitudes about everything. This

BABYBOOM DOOM

soon was to define his entire life for many, many, years.

Pelly was an old neighborhood, but Casey could find a lot of adventure there. He made new friends. He started second grade at school. The Elementary School was called *Anson Jones*. He started the school year of 54'-55' with all the excitement of a new adventure.

Casey learned to ride his new bike that his dad bought for him. He would run along side of the bike, jump on, go a few feet, and then both the bike and he would fall down. He'd get up and try again, bruised and sore, but determined to go a little farther the next time. Finally Casey could go the length of the street that ran in front of the house. But his mom would not let him ride it to school because Casey still lacked the necessary skill to sustain the balance for very long. The other boys at school didn't understand his obedience.

Casey often walked to school. At first he was afraid to go because there were three boys that were much bigger than him who always yelled at him when he came to the schoolyard. They would yell and throw rocks at him and call him distasteful names. He didn't understand why they were treating him that way. He did not know them and he had never done anything to them to cause them to treat him mean. Casey would just run away from them. But everyday they would look for him to chase and taunt. Casey was scared and unsure of what was going on. After a few days of this, he decided that he wasn't going to take it anymore. So one day on the way to school, Casey picked up a lot of rocks and put them in his pockets. Sure enough the three boys that Casey was so afraid of started calling him names, like "Momma's boy! Sissy!" *On this day Casey wasn't going to run away*! This day his fear of them would be faced. This day he was going to risk being hurt. He wasn't going to be pushed around anymore! So to the mean boy's surprise when they ran towards him,

Casey just stood his ground. They stopped, yelled, and bent over to pick up more rocks to throw at Casey. When they reached for the rocks Casey started running towards them! He started yelling and screaming anything that came to his incensed mind. "You stinking bullies, come here!" Casey unloaded a hand full of big rocks at them. "Take that you creeps!" Casey screamed loudly, yelling a growling sound, like that of a big mean bear. To his complete surprise, the three mean boys broke ranks and ran from him! They ran from *him*! Casey did not stop when they fled. He chased them around the schoolyard and the school building, throwing rocks and just hoping he could catch one to fight. He was still too mad to be scared of the thought. Casey chased one away one direction, and then turned on another to hit. They were very scared of Casey this day, because he was a person possessed. After that day, Casey always knew that if he had to stand up for himself he could do so. He was no longer afraid to go to school alone. Mean boys never bothered him again!

    Casey was sick a lot when he started third grade for the 55'-56' school year. He missed a lot of school. Casey's grades were bad as a result. He was going through a lot; bleeding nose, head infections, and coughs with fever. Doctors were not as available then. Casey never went to the doctor for anything when he was growing up. He just did whatever his mom wanted him to do; hot chicken soup, orange juice, rest, maybe an aspirin. Somehow Casey would start to feel better.

    When Casey felt good, he would climb and jump off the buildings in the neighborhood. He would jump from the roof at one height, and then the next time he would climb higher and jump from there. Casey would keep this up until he reached a height that hurt too much to jump. Casey was trying to discover his physical limitations. Luckily, he always knew when to quit to keep from seriously injuring himself.

On a beautiful day, when the flowers were blooming, and the sun was out, Casey explored what was in the grass. He discovered bees! He figured out how to catch them by hand without being stung. He would just cup them in his hands. They would just buzz around in there. Casey enjoyed going outside at school to the clover fields. He would catch the bees and run over to the girls to show them his prize. They would say, "Let me see." He would open his hand and the bee would fly out, their stingers still stuck in the palm of his hand. The girls would scream and run away. Sometimes they would ask him to catch one for *them*. Casey liked the attention from the girls.

Casey loved to wrestle the other boys during the class breaks. He could tumble and stretch into any position possible to gain the advantage over his opponent. The boys always returned to class with grass stains and dirt all over their clothes. The teacher acted like they were doing something wrong! She got mad at them just for being boys. Casey's mom always said," Boys will be boys!" He figured that meant he could wrestle and play rough if he wanted to!

Casey liked to try to catch one of the neighborhood squirrels. One was running all over the place. Casey liked to run too, so he would chase it to see if he could catch it, or to see if he could run faster than it could. The squirrel would run up a tree most of the time. Casey tried to climb the tree to get it but he could tell it was much faster than he was when it came to climbing trees. This day he managed to chase it under the car. Casey thought, "I've got you now!" He reached for it and grabbed it by the tail. It swung around and bit Casey's thumb right at the nail, you know, where the nail meets the skin at the top. Casey let go of the squirrel, and it just chattered as if it were laughing right out loud at him. Casey's thumb bled and hurt badly. His mom said, "Let me kiss it. There it's all better." Casey wasn't so sure because it really hurt badly for days. Lucky for him the squirrel was healthy! Rabies was common to animals in the woods.

One day Casey's dad brought home a funny looking box that had a round piece of glass in front of it. He set it in the living room. He took a wire and plugged it into a socket. The box came alive with sound and wavy lines that rolled up and down. The light was bright. It looked like snow at times. The box would make a hissing noise. Very faintly, almost visible, were people moving and talking within this box. Casey's dad would turn a knob, first one way, and then another. Finally the hissing would be less, the sound of people talking would be heard for a moment; the wavy lines would show a black and white figure moving around. His Dad would move some wire sticks that looked like rabbit ears several different ways to get a picture to show in the big round glass. Casey would jump up and try to get a picture by turning the knobs. Casey's dad would tell him to sit down and let him do it. But he would give up eventually, so Casey would fix it himself.

The box was a TV, short for television. Casey only liked the cartoons and the westerns. The cartoons would only come on once a week, usually on Saturday. The *westerns* were about cowboys who wore white hats if they were good and black hats if they weren't. There were only two channels that showed any resemblance of a picture. It was so difficult to keep the TV picture, Casey preferred to play outside or to just listen to the radio. He figured someday the picture would be better, but he figured it would be a long, long, time before that happened.

Casey's parents moved again. This time they moved to an area of Baytown that was heavily wooded near present day Garth Road. He had to ride a bus for the first time to school, but he was still in *Anson Jones Elementary* in the third grade for the 55'-56 classes.

One day Casey missed the bus at school because he got confused which bus was his. When he realized that no more busses were coming, he had no choice but to walk the five miles home. Casey's dad was at work and his mom did not have a phone. It would be hours before they could come for him. Casey didn't know he could have asked someone to take him home, but by the time he realized he missed his bus, everyone had left the school anyway. Casey walked until he came to the wooded section of road that led to his house. He crossed Goose Creek where the cattle slaughter house was located. That made him sure that he was going the right way. The stench from the pens and the mooing of the cattle made Casey feel uneasy as he walked by the creek. Casey then walked at the edge of the woods that bordered the road when a pickup truck came to a stop a short distance from him. The passenger door flew open and a strange man whom Casey did not know hollered for him to come over and to get into the truck. Casey said no and just stood still! The big man kept insisting, almost begging Casey to get in. Casey's mom had always told him not to talk to strangers. Casey was afraid of the big man who smelled badly and who acted and looked mean. The man got out of the truck and started toward Casey. Casey started running fast! The big fat man became exhausted and soon gave up the chase, returning to his truck. Casey ran all the way home reaching safety, much to everyone's surprise after they found out what he had done. Casey's mother knew the man Casey refused to ride with, but Casey still didn't like him when he met him. Later that week the same man and truck was found upside down on the side of the road near the wood line where he wanted to pick Casey up. The big man always smelled of alcohol because he drank a lot. Casey felt vindicated although he did not know then that the feeling he felt was called that.

The house Casey lived in was made of solid stone. It was off the beaten path, set back in the tall piney woods. You could say that they lived like the backwoods stone age people did. At least, Casey thought so!

When you are a young nine or ten year old person each change is a lifetime forming experience. Although they did not move far, each move *seemed* far to Casey. There was no media influence to shape his thinking like developed much later. His surroundings and his environment was his entire world.

Each time Casey moved his whole world was unraveled. He would have to adjust to new people and to new surroundings when he was still trying to figure out where he fit into his previous surroundings. Casey always seemed to make up for the adjustment by finding adventure anywhere he could.

The Pond

    Down the dirt road that ran by Casey's all stone house in the woods, maybe a hundred yards down the road, there was a pond. The pond had a number of creatures that lived around it, many of which Casey had only seen for the first time. There were ducks, snakes, frogs, fish, rodents, and all kinds of new and intriguing insects. Some of the insects flew in large numbers. Many insects seemed to be able to walk on the surface of the water. Insects of all shapes and sizes flourished around the pond. The mix of insects intrigued Casey. They would buzz around him in seemingly disarray. Sometimes Casey captured some of the insects and put them in a bottle. He punched holes in the lid of the bottle so that the insects inside the bottle could breath. Casey watched them in the bottle for hours so he could see up close what they looked like, and how they moved. After his curiosity was satisfied and his study complete, he let them go.

    Casey often saw the water snakes slither away as he approached the pond. His mom had said the snakes were dangerous, so he was very careful around them. He always looked for them as he walked. Casey found one snake slivering along the ground. He observed it from a distance, always ready to run away should the snake move toward him. As he got braver, He would capture a snake by using a small tree branch as a stick. He enjoyed watching their tongue move in and out of their mouth. It would move so fast Casey could barely see it. He wondered how the snake could move so fast without any feet. He often saw them slide into the water and swim, creating a wave pattern across the top of the water that traveled outward from the snakes head. Casey caught a glimpse of one type of snake moving through the grass. He chased after it just to watch it move. He was fascinated with the different colors. His mom often told him, "Red, Yellow, Black, Get Back!" Casey did not know she was talking about the very poisonous Coral snake at the time. He just stayed back from *all* snakes no matter what the color. He knew not to let one bite him. In spite of the danger, Casey's curiosity often got the best of him. He went looking for the poisonous snakes anyway.

There were all kinds of snakes, some about three to four feet long. Water Moccasins thrived at the pond. It's a pit viper; a dangerous venomous snake abundant on the U.S. Gulf Coast. Casey was afraid of it because it looked so mean, with its dark colored skin and fat midsection. Another pit viper Casey saw was the Copperhead. Casey guessed it got its name from the copper like bands of color around its body. Casey was told by his parents that if that snake were to bite him, it would make him very sick, or it could even kill him.

The other pit viper venomous snake Casey saw a lot of was the Rattlesnake! It preferred the dry land area of the cattle fields. It raised its tale in defiance when Casey came near it, rattle the segments of its tale, and coil up to strike if Casey did not back off. Since he saw all the snakes often, he figured they would get him if he couldn't run away fast enough. So Casey snuck up on them, hollered, threw something at them to make them slither, and then just ran away as fast as he could. He slid to a stop, and looked to see if the snake was coming after him. Sometimes he just *thought* it was still coming after him, so he ran way up the road to get away. He even found the snake in the weeds where he looked for berries. They seemed to be everywhere. Reaching for a berry one day, Casey felt a sting on his hand. Had he been bitten by a poisonous snake? It turned out to be a sticker on a vine but he could have been bitten at any time.

There were several different kinds of birds where Casey grew up. One of the birds was called an Egret. It was a bright white bird that had a long beak and long stick-like legs. It would walk around the cattle to pick insects from the grass. A member of the Heron family it would walk around in the water and search for food. Well, this was new and fascinating to Casey. How could these birds walk and behave like that? Casey sit quietly and watched them for a long time. The Heron caught snakes, little fish, and bugs of all sorts. It used its beak to pluck at its own feathers and twist its long neck all kinds of ways. Eventually Casey threw a rock at it just to make it stop what it was doing. Often it would fly away. Later he would see it right back there in the pond.

Sometimes Casey walked in the mud near the water's edge. There he found a funny looking mountain of dirt, sort of piled up in a circle, with a hole in the middle of it. These mud holes were everywhere. Inside was a crawling creature with funny looking eyes that looked like a lobster, but was smaller. In Texas they were called crawdads. Casey took a stick and poked at it to find out what it would do. The crawdad threw up its front legs in defiance and just dared him to try to get it. After awhile Casey worked up enough courage to catch it. Casey pushed it into a jar with a stick, put the lid on it, and hurried to find someone to show what he had found. Casey learned that crawdads are good eating when prepared with just the right kind of spices. Unknown to Casey his first hand experience with his environment was preparing him for a hot war not yet begun in a similar environment far away.

The house he lived in was made of concrete blocks and stone. Wood was not used for the walls or for siding. It was damp a lot but at his young age it was adventurous to live in the woods near the pond. There were a couple of other houses down the dirt trail that ran through the woods. Casey had some other kids his age to play with at times. He rode his bike down the dirt trail to their house sometimes. When he got taller he traded his small bicycle for a larger one with one of the smaller kid's dad. Casey had a dog named "Snowball" which always went where Casey rode his bike.

Most of the other kids were not allowed to go down to the pond. If Casey tried to get someone to go with him they would not go because their parents would get upset. Casey sometimes got into trouble with the grownups just for *asking* one of their kids to go with him. Casey didn't understand then, because he enjoyed the pond so much.

Casey's mom got into a fight with a neighbor over something that occurred between Casey and one of the other kids. She was always there to rescue him with her fiery temperament when Casey was young. She probably did not know how often he ran off to the pond to sooth his own inherited temperament.

The frogs around the pond would jump around when he came near them. Sometimes several would jump into the pond at the same time, creating a moment of excitement for him. He wanted to know how far they could jump and he wanted to know if they would try to jump on him. He was delighted when he discovered they just wanted to get away, that they did not want to harm him. Casey could catch one to have fun with for hours. He did not want to harm it. He just wanted to watch its throat as it moved and how it moved its eyes. How could it jump so far? It could also open its mouth so wide! Casey was told that frogs would cause warts to form on his hands, so he always washed his hands to be safe.

Casey enjoyed the sounds of the pond as the chorus echoed through the forest to where their stone house was located. At night the frogs would croak. Later, although he did not know it yet, he would hear that same type of croaking twelve thousand miles from home, in a place called Vietnam. It would serve to remind him of his youth and of the good times he had lost forever.

Casey's parents moved again! This time they moved to an area of town that was near the bay off a road called Bay way Drive. He attended Burnett Elementary for the fourth and fifth grades. The school had one building built in 1896 which was used as a music room. The rest of the school was located by a gully that led to the bay. Casey was naturally attracted to the gully. The gully exposed several different kinds of shells and other marine animals to explore.

Casey moved again within the same area to a house on John A Street while he was still in the fifth grade. During his eleventh and twelfth years of age, he discovered his sports abilities. Casey was very coordinated and good at most physical activities, something he began to take pride in.

Casey often explored the bay. Sometimes he saw a big ship go by. He wondered where it came from and wondered where it was going. Is it from some foreign, mystic land, where people are a lot different from him? What kind of cargo is it carrying? Are there animals aboard? He wondered if he would ever get to ride on a big ship like that. He was growing up to face his inherited world.

BABYBOOM DOOM

The waves rushed toward the shore as the ship went by. The wave washed over the sand. There in the sand he became interested in what he saw; all kinds of creatures. There were crabs that scurried across the sand. Some had only one claw. Others ran into holes in the mud. Sometimes he shot at them with a BB gun, they would run faster, and they would all run at once. Casey was becoming an expert shot by just carrying his BB gun with him all the time. Other weapons were used during other times to manage his environment.

There were also funny looking shells, most of them broken by the action of the surf. Some presented a surprise. Inside were some kind of living animal that would quickly scurry out of the shell as soon as he picked it up. Others retreated deep into the shell as if to say, "Get me if you can." Casey sometimes collected them and brought them home, put them in his room, looked at them, tossed them from hand to hand, stacked them, made patterns with them, and showed them to his friends and relatives. Things of nature were always very interesting to Casey.

Casey found driftwood that remind him of different things. One looked like a fish or maybe a mermaid. One looked like a spider. Another looked like a wave or a rock. Casey tried to make other things out of driftwood that was fun to look at. He picked sea grass and placed it in the driftwood as if it was growing there all by itself. He placed sand on and around it. The imagination of a kid is truly endless.

Casey saw big houses along the bay. Some of his school friends lived right next to the water. Would the water ever rise to get in the house? Would a big wave wash them away? How was he to know that in just a few short years a hurricane would do just that? Most of those houses were completely destroyed in 1961. But he still had some growing to do before then.

During 1956, Casey discovered Elvis, who became the *King of Rock and Roll* singing his version of rhythm and blues. Casey saw his release of "Jailhouse Rock" at the Brunson Theater in downtown Baytown and became an enthusiastic fan of the Elvis style; a style that represented a *freedom* of spirit. Casey was ten years old and he became a lifetime fan. In 1957 he bought Elvis' "Hound Dog" song as soon as he could find it.

Casey worked as a stocker in the local store nearby to earn some spending money. He was there after school everyday. It was hard for a ten year old to *have* to work, but Casey always worked very hard as a youngster. It made him tough and free to do many things he enjoyed.

The Threat

Casey enjoyed the innocence of the fifties. With no air conditioning he slept with the windows open so that he could remain cool. The night sounds could be clearly heard. The house was never locked and he never feared that anyone would invade the house.

The fifties were an exciting time. In school Casey learned about reading, writing, arithmetic, and the Communist threat. The kids played sports and games outside in the schoolyard. Part of Casey knew that the world was recovering from World War II. It seemed everyone was afraid of that country called the *Soviet Union*. The Soviet Union had put an artificial moon in orbit around the earth in 1957. They called it *Sputnik*. They had developed big rockets that could possibly fly all the way to the United States. Casey's mom thought that God would not approve of the artificial moon. His dad and his friends, World War II veterans all, were concerned and worried that the Soviet Union was now more scientifically advanced than the United States. The radios and TV's were all saying that this event was a surprise to everyone in the U.S. How could the Russians do that when the U.S. could not? Was the U.S. an inferior people in an inferior country? Hadn't the U.S. won World War II? Besides that, their whole system of government was different than the U.S. They called it *Communism*. All Casey knew was that it was supposed to be bad because people who lived under a Communist government could not do a lot of the things that Americans could do living under a *democratic* type of government. People in the U.S. had freedom of choice. At school the teachers made Casey hide under his desk with alarm. At times all would hurry to the hallway, get next to the wall, and cover their heads with their arms. This was supposed to help keep everyone safe if a bomb fell on the school. At home people prepared *bomb* shelters. Extra water and food was kept in storage. Casey knew the Chinese had a Communist government, and that some of our soldiers had fought the North Koreans because they had a Communist government. A wall that was called the "Iron Curtain" divided Berlin. The Communists were on one side, the democrats were on the other. People talked about war. The "Cold War" was getting worse, they said. Casey knew that the Communists were bad for the U.S. Americans owned property and had human rights as established by law. Communist could not own property and they were prisoners in their own country with their so called *socialistic* state!

    The TV showed spy stories, good versus evil type of stories. One show was even called "I Spy." The adults talked about what they would have to do to survive if the Communist tried to invade their country. They always said, "We should stop them before they take over the world." Casey took that very personal. It seemed everyone was afraid of the Communist. So Casey continued to explore his world, but he knew he had to be strong for the coming fight with the Communist! Casey just knew the Communists were coming! He set in the school library to study how much of the world had been taken over by the Communists. He was just learning about his world. Casey did not want it to end because of those evil Communists.

    In the United States, a congressman named McCarthy claimed that the Communist had infiltrated the U.S. government and that they were scattered all over the country in leadership positions. He attempted to purge the suspected Communist from the U.S. government by claiming that many people were Communist when there was no proof of such activities. Eventually he lost his position in the government. The media however had managed to create more tension about the evil Communist. Casey just knew he had to fight the Communist someday!

Casey was moved again when his dad relocated nearer his construction job! The house was much like many others he had lived in, except it had two separate bedrooms. Most of the houses he lived in had one bedroom and one bathroom. The wood homes were built high on blocks for a foundation. That placed it high enough to keep the flooded yard from entering the house. The living area was always a part of the kitchen. Casey would usually sleep in the living room on a military cot that folded up during the day to make room.

The next area was near Goose Creek, a shallow winding creek that ran through the woods of Baytown. Many of Casey's relatives lived near by. He remembered the street was named Airhart Drive. Casey went to Baytown Elementary for the 58'-59' school year. He was twelve. He began to have interest in girls. His first girl friend was discovered there. Her name was *Mary*. Casey's heart fluttered every time he saw her. He was still too immature to nurture a relationship, but he flirted with her a lot while at school and enjoyed showing off around her. Casey would do anything to get her attention.

Since Casey had no brothers or sisters, his cousins were the next best things. They all lived near the woods. There was Rubin and his brother Hart, who they all called Sonny. Sonny was the oldest, kind of broad at the shoulders and narrow at the hips. He was big and strong. Everyone thought he was supernatural or something. He liked to box all comers. He could lift anything and out work most anybody. Sonny's brother Rubin was also older and stronger than was Casey. Casey was about twelve years old now and Rubin was about seventeen. Sonny was about nineteen.

The Forest

Casey often went over to Rubin's house. They ran around together after school. They loved to go into the woods and explore the unknown. They found a possum one day, a little baby one. They brought it home to show everyone. It squirmed in Casey's hand as it tried to find food. Rubin found a rabbit and chased it. Rabbit stew taste good when your hungry. One day Rubin put on a screen looking cloth over his head. He told Casey they were going into the woods. "Why do you have that on?" Casey asked. Rubin said, "We are going after some bee honey." Bee honey? Rubin always seemed to know where things were in the woods. Casey and Rubin traveled for what seemed to be an hour or so, deep into the woods. Casey listened for all kinds of sounds. The bugs made sounds, the rodents made sounds, and the birds made sounds. The trick was to hear the sound, identify the source, and to know where everything was that was making the sounds. This skill would serve him well in the future!

Rubin pointed to the tree trunk. "There!" he said. Casey knew the bees must be in that tree trunk because he could here the buzzing sound. "But how are we going to get the honey with all those bees there?" asked Casey. Surely Rubin must be crazy! Casey stood back as Rubin climbed up the tree truck to where the hole was. Rubin looked into the hole. He could see the bees and the honey. He reached into the hole and grabbed a big hand full of wax soaked with honey. The bees started swarming everywhere. Casey ran a short distance and hid behind a tree. Rubin got some more wax soaked in honey. After awhile he had a big bag of wax and honey. He moved away from the tree, having been stung several times. The bees were going nuts. Casey was nervous and a little frightened but he wanted to see if he could get some. Casey wrapped a cloth around his head and climbed up the tree trunk to take a quick look. Rubin had gotten most of the honey. Casey grabbed a small piece for himself. Then they carried the honey wrapped in cloth through the woods to Rubin's house. There they put the honey, along with the wax into jars. Casey had honey on his hands, between his fingers, in his hair, on his head, on his clothes, and all on the outside of the jars. Casey put a chunk of honey wax into his mouth and sucked the honey from the wax comb. The pure sweetness of the nectar melted into his mouth convincing Casey it was worth the adventure to get it. To be sure , it was a sticky mess but it sure tasted sweet! Their parents could not believe that Rubin and Casey salvaged the honey from the woods. They were thrilled over the honey and their adventurous boys. Casey, Rubin and their parents had honey for breakfast many times after that.

    At Rubin's house another meal from the woods was rabbit stew. Casey wasn't sure about eating the wild animals. The rabbits came from the woods. The honey came from the woods. The eggs came from the woods. The squirrels came from the woods. Casey enjoyed the food, but he enjoyed the adventures more.

    Casey and Rubin often went into the woods together. Rubin pulled a flower off of a honey suckle vine. He smelled it, pulled the central stem from the flower and put it in his mouth, then he pulled the stem out. Rubin wanted Casey to try it. Casey was dubious at first because he never had eaten wild flowers before. Seeing that Rubin was suffering no ill affects, Casey cautiously tried it. He touched it to his tongue. It was delicious. It was very sweet!

Rubin and Casey walked through the woods, sucked on the flowers, talked about the communist, school, their parents and friends. They talked about what they wanted to do when they grew up. Casey wanted to travel and to see the world. He was fascinated with the world beneath the sea. He wanted to learn how to SCUBA dive so he could venture deep beneath the vast sea. Rubin wanted to join the army and to get married. Casey looked up to Rubin. Rubin was his closest friend, his older brother in effect. They talked about what had happened the day before or just talked about anything that came to their minds. They would forge waterways and just keep walking and talking. Sometimes Rubin would deliberately run away to hide from Casey. Casey searched the woods for him. Rubin would try to surprise Casey. At first Casey could not find Rubin. It scared him to be alone in the woods, lost and abandoned. Overcoming his fear, Casey learned to find Rubin after awhile. It was not easy to ambush Casey after such antics.

Casey and Rubin decided to take a watermelon from the large garden that grew in the yard a few yards from the old wooden house that Rubin's parents owned. The watermelon was plump with its juice and large enough to require a strong back to lift it. They stopped long enough to eat it. The next thing Casey knew, Rubin threw a large chunk of melon rind at him. Casey retaliated by throwing a large chunk towards Rubin. A full fledge watermelon fight ensued. Watermelon was coming from all directions it seemed!

A piece of melon landed right between Rubin's eyes when

about the same time his melon hit Casey in the jaw. Both boys laughed and ran around throwing the melon rinds at each other until they both were exhausted.

Casey and Rubin enjoyed going into the woods. They liked to look for the creatures that lived in the woods. The Texas armadillo was one strange looking animal to Casey. It had a hard shell-like armor covering its body. It made a rustling noise as it poked around under the brush. About a foot long and maybe six inches high it scurried beneath branches that protected it from predators and curious boys like Casey and Rubin. Still through creative positioning they captured it just to look at it. With their curiosity satisfied they let it go. But the chase through the woods was fun to Casey. They would also observe the snakes, but they were careful not to get too careless around them. Rubin whispered, "look at the snakes." Casey whispered back, "Where?" The snakes scurried into the water as soon as the boys approached the waterways.

To catch a possum the boys used scare tactics. The possum just sort of froze when they got near it. One would think that it had died of fright. But of course it was only using that technique to fool them. The boys tried to outlast the possum by just being still themselves. The possum always outlasted the boys because Casey could not be still for very long.

Casey learned to play a lot of games at Rubin's house. The men played dominoes, usually forty-two. The women sometimes played dominoes with them, but most of the time they just sat around and talked. Rubin and Casey liked to play cards with each other along with friends their age. They usually played poker. Rarely was there any money involved. Match sticks made a good substitute and Casey delighted at winning his share.

Sometimes Casey and Rubin watched professional wrestling on TV. They were not sure if the sport was *real* wrestling because of the way the wrestlers hit each other. When Casey and Rubin hit each other, it hurt!

Boxing was always fun to do. Rubin and Casey put on the gloves and boxed until they were exhausted. Arm wrestling proved who was the strongest. Casey was not yet matured, so he usually got beat at arm wrestling. Tricks were always played on everyone. The puzzle of the day was usually tried. Outside they would play football with the neighborhood friends. They often met in the evenings to play football. They played real hard tackle football with no equipment for protection. This experience served Casey well in school when he played football with pads. Casey and Rubin had fun but times were changing.

Casey moved again. It was another two bedroom house. Two bedrooms, wow! Casey felt like he was moving up in the world because he now had a room all to himself. Like the others his new house was made of wood. It too set high on cement blocks with no bricks for the sides. The house still had a very small kitchen and only one bathroom, but it was located in a better neighborhood than Casey was used to. The house was located in the old Pelly oilfield.

The Pelly district consisted of a large oilfield, while Old Baytown had the Humble Oil and Refinery which was used to process the oil. Downtown Goose Creek consisted of the various merchants that kept the oil men in supplies while Citizens Bank financed most of the community needs. Casey was beginning to understand his inherited environment in the forest of East Texas surrounded by the bays of the Gulf of Mexico.

One corner of the house began to sink because the oil well in the yard pumped out too much oil, leaving a vacuum in the cavern of the well! The ground gave way. The house tilted on one side. The well was eventually capped, and Dad Trainer leveled the house to repair the damage. It would become his home throughout the rest of his teenage days, from 1960 to 1965.

Casey finished the seventh grade at Baytown Junior High in 1960. He was fourteen. He started Horace Mann Junior High for the eighth grade and remained there through the ninth grade. There he made new friends and played football for the Goslins.

Rubin went into the army during the early sixties. The largest hurricane to hit the Baytown area, Hurricane Carla in 1961, greeted Casey soon after he moved to Pelly. Brownwood, an area near the bay, close to where Casey used to live, was completely destroyed. All the houses were leveled. Casey's new house only suffered some slight roof damage from the high wind. He was depressed about the weather, having had to make the move, and now Rubin was gone. Casey missed him and all the fun they had. Like always Casey had to start over with new friends in a different neighborhood.

Casey's new neighborhood was not directly in the woods, although the woods were not far away, a quarter of a mile maybe. The trees of the subdivision were cut down to build the homes. All the houses were close to each other. They were built after World War II for the oil field workers. Cement blocks were used for the foundation so that the hard tropical rains so familiar on the Gulf Coast only flooded the yards and not the house. The wooded area extended to the bay just past the neighborhood.

Air conditioning was becoming available but was not yet affordable to everyone. Hugh attic fans were being used to cool the homes. People slept with the windows open to keep cool. The mosquitoes were terrible because of the water and the nearby woods. Casey rode his bike or walked to school. Buses were not available for the neighborhood. This was Casey's new home for his teenage life.

Segregation

There were no black people in Casey's neighborhood. They lived in their own neighborhoods completely separate from white neighborhoods. This was the early sixties, and segregation was still the politics of the time. Fortunately things were changing but the injustices still existed.

Casey had seen black people from a distance. He had seen the signs *No Coloreds Served* or *Whites Only* that excluded black people from the town stores. He did not understand any of it the way older people did.

Black people could not use the same restrooms that white people used. The restrooms were labeled, *Colored Restroom* or *White Restroom*! There were even different fountains for Black, and White people. They couldn't even stay in a hotel that white people stayed in!

Black people were called *Nigger's*! Casey had heard the childhood chants, "Guess what, another nigger got shot!" "Nigger" was, and still is, a very offensive term to black people. It was so offensive because it was used to insult or belittle anyone that had dark skin. It took many years before it was eventually controlled by law, and removed from social terminology as being a *politically incorrect* term. Casey heard how older people thought and he could not see why? He was just trying to understand his world!

Black people even attended different schools in Baytown. They did not attend Robert E. Lee High School. Black people attended Carver High School. Until the Equal Rights Act of 1965 blacks attended different schools at all levels. So, no blacks attended the same schools Casey attended. They did not even associate with white people unless it was to render service. At this time in history, the two races were truly segregated from each other. To most whites the black schools were considered to be inferior to the white schools. No whites wanted to attend the black schools. So Casey did not know much about black people as a young boy. He was to learn later that society had placed an unnecessary burden on all of them, both black and white. This was Casey's environment, the only place he knew. Casey was growing up during these difficult times, while the world events turned without much concern about Casey or rural East Texas.

CHAPTER THREE
Teenager

Casey was changing as he entered his teenage years. A full compliment of hormones flowed through his blood exciting every muscle in his body. He was getting very restless at home. He wanted to venture out. He wanted to meet girls and to see the world.

Casey's parents enjoyed staying at home and watching TV together. This bored Casey to tears. His parents smoked a lot and Casey resented how it was destroying his parent's health, much less his. The tiny living room filled with smoke attaching itself to everything, including Casey's clothing. Casey's eyes burned while his nostrils drained its protective fluids and everything smelled of nicotine. He decided right then and there that he would never smoke *his* health away!

Casey hated to stay at home and to choke on the acrid smoke. He could not sit still for very long anyway because his energy was in overdrive. He felt stifled at home. He knew he had to get away from home but he was still very young and dependent on his parents financial support for the basics of life, like food, clothing, and shelter.

Emotionally Casey was becoming more and more independent. With each new day Casey was changing from his age of innocence into a young adult full of dreams and promise. He did not know how he was going to get away, but he knew he must figure out a way. He wanted to become independent and to make his own way.

Early Friends

Casey was still too young to legally drive but he always wanted to leave to be with his friends in the neighborhood. There were several kids Casey's age in the neighborhood. There was Mickey. Mickey was slender and had blue eyes, the kind of eyes that seemed to look right through you. They would seem to illuminate a brighter blue the longer he stared at someone. The girls at school thought him to be very good looking. Casey and Mickey studied a lot together, usually over at his house. His mom and dad were a little skeptical of Casey at first. He never dressed well. His clothes were usually old fashioned. As he grew his clothes did not fit right so that they were too tight for his size. But when Mickey's parents saw that Mickey and he were serious about making good grades, they allowed Casey to come over in the evenings. Casey and Mickey sort of competed for the best grades on test day. Usually Casey made a little higher grade because he felt the need to do so. Mickey had a younger sister who Casey was not attracted to. He never got to know her at all. Her mom was very protective of her.

Mickey's dad worked for Humble Oil & Refinery, later to become Exxon-Mobil. So Mickey always had the better material things, since the oil company paid about the highest wages in town. When Mickey got a scooter, a sort of automatic driven motorcycle, Casey for the first time in his life realized that he was not from a privileged family. Casey tried, begged really, for his dad to get him one. His dad said no! Casey found it really hard to understand why Mickey could have things while he could not.

Mickey was kind to Casey. He always let Casey ride with him on the back of the scooter to school. Casey enjoyed the smell of the morning dew as the breeze rushed by his pimpled face. At times Mickey let Casey ride the scooter alone. The sense of freedom and of being in control excited Casey. He decided that one day he would have his own motorcycle. It seemed an unattainable wish at the time. So for about two years Casey and Mickey rode the scooter to school whenever they could. It was a lot faster and more fun than riding a gearless bicycle and it made them feel like they were somebody. They both were in the eighth grade and they enjoyed the attention received from the other kids who just road their bikes. The enjoyment of the adrenaline rush and of riding free hooked Casey from then on to motorcycles.

A boy named Lewis lived about two houses down the street from Casey. He was half-Mexican and half-White. His hair was a shiny black. He usually wore it long for the times, sort of like Elvis Presley wore his. He had brown skin that looked like he always had a good tan. His teeth were even and straight and about as white as teeth can be. Lewis' smile could melt even the most stern of a parent or girl friend. He could have his way with almost anyone. That made him a natural leader in the neighborhood. Mickey and Casey liked to go over to Lewis' house most of the time. Lewis' father worked for a tug boat company. He made better than average wages and tended to give Lewis what he wanted. Since Casey's dad never gave him anything he wanted without him having to work for it, Casey was a little jealous and envious of Lewis' situation.

Lewis had two sisters. There was Loretta who was about two years older than Lewis and there was Charlotte who was one year younger. Lewis was lean but his two sisters were chunky. Loretta had large features and pretty hands. Her teeth were like Lewis' and her smile radiated the same kind of energy. Charlotte had very smooth white skin. Her complexion was perfectly smooth without even the hint of a blemish. Her eyes were dark brown and kind of round. She was built much like her older sister; she too had large features.

The Johnson brothers lived farther down the street almost directly across the street from Mickey. They were a lot less adventurous than the rest of the neighborhood kids. They tended to stay home a lot. They were into the ham radio media. With the ham radio one could talk with someone on the other side of the world. From time to time Casey would visit them. The radio preceded cell telephones that later became popular toward the end of the 20th century. Casey learned to talk on the radio which served him well later on in the military.

The Heists lived in the circle area down the street. Casey could see them as he passed by on his bike. They were older than was Casey so he never ran with them as a teenager. He did get to know them later in life.

Casey was into football at school, but most of his immediate friends in the neighborhood were not. Casey was serious about being a good player. He organized a gym at his house with the state of the art equipment available at the time. He spent hour after hour doing all sorts of exercises trying to bulk up for football. Casey was very strong for his size, but he felt he was a little small for football. Casey weighed about 140 pounds then. He was lanky and very well coordinated. This served him well in sports, although he still had some growing to do. Mickey and Lewis came over to exercise with him from time to time. They gained a lot of respect for Casey's physical strength. The kids in the neighborhood thought he could whip anyone in school that dared to challenge him. They knew Casey had boxed with his cousins before, he played football and did all that it required, he was strong and hard bodied because of the weight lifting, and he worked construction with his dad. All this combined to make him very physically fit. Additionally, Casey was very adventurous, and the guys enjoyed being with him.

One day Casey fell off of Mickey's scooter while they were riding around in the neighborhood. Mickey hit a bump in the road that helped to catapult Casey right off the back of the bike. He hit the concrete pavement so hard, it knocked the wind out of him and momentarily stopped his heart. Casey tried to take a breathe, but he could not. His lungs felt like they were in a vice that only tightened as he tried to breath. He struggled to get up but only staggered as he fainted toward the pavement. The chest pain numbed his body to a stiff contraction and he laid there momentarily paralyzed and unconscious. Mickey turned the motorbike around and rode it to where Casey lay. Casey was scraped up considerably. His raw skin on his face, his hands, his arms, his sides, and stomach revealed the result of the impact on the rough concrete. Casey lay motionless as the blood oozed from his skin. Mickey did not know what to do. He thought Casey was dead.

When Casey finally got his breath, he staggered to the side of the road semi-conscious unsure of what had just happened. He always knew that if he crashed or fell from the motor scooter he could be badly hurt. A couple of friends he knew were killed and another badly maimed from motorcycle accidents. He was shocked at the extreme pain from falling off the motorcycle at just 30 MPH. After a few terrifying moments Casey told Mickey he was OK. He was not really OK, having suffered a concussion and badly burned skin, but his pride would not allow him to admit that he was hurt and bruised. He was the neighborhood tough guy and he did not want to show weakness by crying or whining. Although in a lot of pain, Casey brushed himself off and got back on the motorcycle to prove he was not afraid of a little adversity.

Casey had to miss school the next day. He was exceptionally disappointed because that day was the designated *play-day* at school. On that day various physical contests, such as running relays, tug of rope, jumping, and throwing tested ones physical abilities. Casey knew he was more physically fit for all the contests that could be entered and he was sure that he could have won several ribbons. But he was badly injured so he could not go. Mickey was real sorry the mishap had happened. He wanted to make it up to Casey somehow. He agreed to take Casey's plastic model cars that Casey had collected since childhood up to the school, for the model car contest. After school, Mickey brought Casey's cars back. He showed Casey the ribbons that he had won during the day, and handed Casey a ribbon. He said, "This one is for you. Your model cars won first place!"

Casey felt proud that his childhood hobby had won him first place, but he was even more proud of Mickey for giving him the ribbon. Casey hid his anger and disappointment as best he could when he saw the ribbons Mickey had won. He felt he had been denied the opportunity to be recognized by his peers at school for his physical prowess. He had worked out in his home gym for months to gain a physical edge. Not to be recognized hurt him more than the abrasive burns that covered his body.

In the ninth grade Casey started to take an interest in Lewis' sister. Loretta was not the prettiest girl he had ever seen, but she seemed to be responsible beyond her years. She talked to Casey about her personal feelings. She could drive her daddy's car because she was sixteen! Lewis and Casey were only fourteen. She often got her daddy's car on the weekends, and they all went to the football game on Friday nights and then they cruised around town afterwards. Although they weren't old enough to have a drivers license, the guys took turns driving. When Lewis drove, Loretta and Casey got in the back seat. Casey experienced instant excitement every time he got near her, although neither one of them had ever had sex before. Casey enjoyed being in the back seat almost as much as driving.

After the game they drove through their favorite hamburger place, called *Trainers* where all the other kids hung out. They yelled through the car windows at each other, sometimes leaning out of the window to wave and just laugh and holler. Everyone knew that "Trainers" was the place to be. There a carhop took your order. She would have on tight shorts and a sweater that emphasized her assets. The energy and the feelings going through Casey's body was almost overwhelming. He would only hold Loretta's hand at first, but later on in the evening Casey snuggled up closer. There was something about her breath that seemed to keep Casey excited the entire evening. Eventually Casey experienced his first kiss. Loretta kissed in a way that was completely uninhibited. When the evening was over, Casey left the car completely light headed and exhausted.

At times Lewis' parents went out of town for the weekend. Mickey, Lewis, Loretta, Charlotte, and Scott, a friend from school, would get some of the other kids from school to come over to Lewis' house. There the party began where everyone listened to music, danced, and drank beer. Loretta and Casey by now were kissing a lot and constantly with each other. The guys liked to show off to the girls. They challenged each other in all kinds of ways; pushups, setups, arm wrestling, kick boxing. The girls just laughed and giggled at the humorous antics. Casey liked to challenge Lewis or Mickey to a show of physical strength. He knew he was stronger than the other guys and the girls presented him with an opportunity to prove his primitive dominance and perhaps win their favor from such a display. The girls rarely admitted that they found it exciting to see the boys shirtless, with their muscle definition displayed, but the boys somehow knew it excited the girls, not to mention that it also established the dominant male of the group. He that defeated all contestants was the man that won the girl's favor!

Mickey's cousin, Willy played the guitar and the group liked to sing the songs of the day. Willy became part of a band that gained some local notoriety later on. The band had many gigs. Casey went with the kids of the neighborhood when the band had one of their gigs around town. Afterwards the group cruised around town for awhile until they eventually gathered for a house party.

At the house parties, after awhile the boys paired off with their favorite girl. Everyone went to various areas in the house to be alone. After one party when everyone had left, Loretta and Casey kept talking. They talked until they got tired and they went to the bedroom. There they began to kiss and pet. The next thing Casey knew he was so hot he began taking his clothes off! Casey began to experience irresistible feelings for sex. He was only fourteen, Loretta was sixteen, and they had been running around with each other for months. On this particular night, caught up in the excitement of the moment, they could not stop if they wanted to. It seemed so natural, the two of them being together, as if they had no control of the forces of nature moving them into the unknown. On this night they felt something that neither of them had ever felt before, or so Casey thought at the time. Casey lost his virginity that night and he liked it! Loretta however was sweet on Mickey.

The next morning Casey was scared and confused. He was unsure of what had happened the night before. He started his work out in his home gym both excited and confused. "Ahab the Arab" by Ray Stevens was a popular song of the day. It was playing on the radio. Casey's mom was trying to talk to him but Casey's mind was on the last evening. He had used protection! He thought, "Did it work? Am I going to be a father? I can't be! I'm only fourteen! I must find another job! I've got to finish school. What will the guys on the football team think of me? Oh my, I have really messed up. I'm too young to be a father!" Having sex before marriage was against all Casey had been taught. He was really ashamed of himself. He hoped he could make everything OK.

He couldn't wait to see Loretta. When he did, she put his mind at ease. "Everything is going to be OK," she said. They talked about how they cared for each other. They talked about being together forever. They talked about how great it felt to be together. They even talked about getting married some day when they were older and more capable of supporting themselves. From then on they did everything together. Their physical relationship continued every chance they got. They would stay up late to wait for Loretta's parents to go to sleep so they could be alone with each other. *Their elementary days were defiantly over!* A new dawn had arrived. Casey was becoming an adult and life seemed great.

After Casey's parents went to bed, Casey sneaked out through his bedroom window to go see Loretta. At first he just went over to her house to be with her. Her parents were usually there, so they found a reason to leave. Eventually, they needed transportation. Casey did not have a driver's license yet, but he could drive a car. Since he did not have a car, Casey figured out a way to use his dad's. Casey's dad felt Casey was still too young to drive so he would not consider letting Casey use his. Casey therefore, quietly pushed the car out of the driveway onto the street. Casey pushed the car to a distance far enough, where the engine could not be heard. He quickly disconnected the speedometer, hot wired his dad's 1958 Pontiac, started the engine, picked up Loretta, and off they'd go for a ride. Sometimes they went to the Decker Drive Inn Theater to see a movie. Since they had no money, at times they would drive into the theater from the exit. Once they got caught entering the theater that way and the guard told them to leave. Loretta told Casey that they shouldn't do that anymore, so they never did go into the exit again. Hiding in the car trunk to go to the drive-in was a part of growing up. Most kids tried it at least once; less tried to go into the exit but it was fun to try. Once inside the theater many never saw the movie for all the other things going on.

    Later Casey returned the car by shutting off the engine just before he entered the driveway. Casey let the car coast to a stop. He always replaced the fuel that was used so that there was no clue that the car had been driven. He reconnect the speedometer and left everything exactly how he found it, right down to the exact spot he had left from, to the position of the steering wheel. Casey had no telephone at his house, so it was not as easy to communicate then as it became later. If someone saw them, they just assumed Casey had permission to be out. He always drove safely so they were never stopped by the police. How they ever did it for so long without being caught is still a mystery.

Casey's dad never did find out that he took the car many times. Casey eventually stopped borrowing his dad's car since Loretta had permission to use her family's car more often. When Casey became old enough to get his driver's license, he bought his own car. He and Loretta went everywhere in *his* car after that. His juvenile behavior remained a secret for decades, until one day he told his dad about it. His dad thought that he was joking!

High School

Casey was aware of world events even as a small boy since his dad talked about the enemies he had fought.

The Communists were up to their tricks again. It was 1962. Casey was sixteen years old, almost seventeen. American spy planes discovered that the Soviet Union was placing offensive nuclear weapons in Fidel Castro's Cuba, just ninety miles from the United States mainland. These weapons were missiles equipped with *nuclear* warheads. These missiles were ready for use and they were capable of destroying several major American cities within minutes. Soviet ships were shipping more missiles as Casey learned about it. If war started, he would be at the age necessary to go into the military soon.

The United States responded by placing a military naval blockade around Cuba and by putting its military on full alert, including its entire nuclear arsenal! *It looked very much like the end of the world was imminent.* If a nuclear exchange took place between the United States and the Soviet Union, life as Casey knew it would definitely end. The earth would most likely be covered with a radioactive cloud and a new ice age would soon begin. In the unlikely event that Casey was to survive the initial nuclear blast there would not be anything left for him but a slow death of radioactive misery and disease. This was on Casey's mind!

With Armageddon in the balance, for thirteen days Casey watched the news media severely frightened of it all. The Soviet ships were on their way to Cuba loaded with offensive missiles! If they tried to run the blockade the U.S. war ships were ordered to sink them. The Soviet Union would consider it an act of war. Didn't the Soviets have a right to ship on the high seas? Was WWIII about to start?

Loretta and Casey tried to go on with their lives as usual. It wasn't easy for them. They wondered if the bombs were to be dropped, who if any would be spared. Would the Soviet Union bomb a little town like Baytown? Is oil *that* important? Casey wondered!

Houston is only thirty miles from Baytown. The Houston ship channel leads to one of the major ports of the Southwest. Is Houston a likely target? Doesn't the Houston area and the entire Gulf of Mexico region provide the fuel that helps run the whole economy and the military, with its petrochemical industry?

Casey was frightened and very worried. He realized that the area that he was growing up in could be *ground zero* for nuclear destruction. Casey believed his days were numbered for sure. Loretta and Casey thought, "If we must die let it be in each other's arms, embraced, oblivious to the whole outside world." Fortunately, the Soviet ships *did* turn back, the missiles were removed from Cuba, and World War III was avoided.

The thought of being a target never left Casey. He began to prepare himself for a revengeful battle with the Communists.

Life at school continued. Casey was in the tenth grade now and attending Robert E. Lee High School. The High School was the pride of Baytown society. Loretta and Casey were an item there. Casey played football and continued to exercise at home. His strength had increased and he now weighed one hundred and sixty pounds. Casey was still a little light for football, but he was growing tough.

His body was getting harder and larger. Casey also had a dark tan. He was physically ready for the tough challenges of life. If only he could get away from the small town he felt was stifling him. Little did he know that he would be getting the chance very soon.

Work

On the weekends and after school, Casey helped his dad work construction jobs. Home construction was his main source of income. It is hard physical work, especially in the hot humid weather of the Southwest. Casey had thick hard calluses on his hands.

During the summer break from school Casey also worked as a landscaper. The extra work allowed him to make enough money to pay for his truck that he had bought a few months before. It was a used 1954 Ford pickup truck. With his dad's help Casey paid three hundred dollars for it. Most of the time he barely had enough money to buy gas for it. It was his first set of wheels and it was his pride and joy.

Casey worked hard to get a few bucks. He liked to tinker with the V-8 engine to make it go faster. The first improvement for performance was to put a four-barrel carburetor on the old Ford. Casey also tinkered with the valves and cam. When the engine started burning oil, he replaced the engine with another and later overhauled it with new piston rings. He used a tree limb to attach the chain lift. Casey painted the body of the truck in his backyard. It was a gray-blue color that was ahead of it's time. It seemed that he was always doing something to his truck. He installed a stereo with back speakers, unheard of at the time. He covered the seats with a special cloth. Casey even put red lights under the dash so that the floorboards would have a red hue. He installed a toolbox that his dad made of wood and placed it in the back of the truck bed.

Casey's obsession with the truck began to affect his school attendance. He needed work to pay for the truck repairs and he needed the truck to get to school. Casey began to skip class to work on the truck. Only a day here or there. It was obvious that he wasn't making enough money to continue school full time. His grades were starting to suffer. He had to go to summer school to get enough credits to stay on track to graduate.

His junior year at high school was a transformation year for Casey. He had to do something to change the situation. He enrolled in an apprenticeship program at school that allowed him to get credits for work related subjects. So Casey worked as an air conditioner repair apprentice for half a day, and went to school for half a day. He went through spring practice for football, but his heart was no longer in it. He couldn't work and play football too, he reasoned. Loretta and Casey were now serious about getting married. He sold the truck and bought a 1952 Ford car for a hundred dollars from his friend Mickey. He kept it until he graduated from school.

Part of Casey felt like a failure because he started doing other things instead of staying in football. He was one hundred and seventy-five pounds now, very physically fit and tough as nails. His coaches wanted him to play, but he was overwhelmed with needing the money to finish school and to support his relationship with Loretta. Loretta graduated from high school and she began working as a telephone operator to help make ends meet.

Casey began to resent Loretta's brother and the way he behaved. Lewis dropped out of high school and became more and more wild. He built hotrods and wrecked them all. He ran around with a gang-like attitude with his friends. Later his group began to carry guns. He had wild parties and wild women around all the time. Casey wanted to work and to be responsible and to raise a family. Loretta and Casey were serious about that. Loretta loved her brother and wanted to be there for him. Casey wanted no part of what was going on with Lewis although he was a very likeable fellow.

Casey missed his friends he used to play football with. He had no encouragement from his closest friends in his neighborhood to play football. They did not deliberately discourage him, but they weren't involved in football so they did not influence Casey to play either. He missed his other friends. He began to think that his life was heading the wrong direction. He wanted out! He wanted out of Baytown, out of the neighborhood that Lewis flourished in!

Casey's senior year was long and dull. Casey thought his senior year would never end. At the very least football would have given him a connection with the school. Without it he had no real connection with others at school. He was working half a day as an air conditioner repair person and he went to school half a day just to finish the requirements. He was losing interest in school. He couldn't wait for each class to be over. Later, he often wondered what difference his interest in school would have been if he had not quit football? Wouldn't his life be more carefree? He wondered about that for many years. Still, Casey needed to get away from the dull life he now had. He was eighteen and just itching for adventure. He made very little money and Loretta was the only good he felt for the future. Casey wanted adventure! He missed the adventures that Rubin and he had had in the woods as kids.

CHAPTER FOUR

Marine Corps

It was March 1965. Casey was eighteen years old and very bored. He joined the U.S. Marines Corps while he was still in his senior year at high school believing that he could find real exciting adventure. Casey stayed in the reserves until he graduated from high school in May. He was scheduled to go into active service July 1, 1965. Loretta was unsure of his decision. What would happen to their relationship? Would she ever see Casey again? Casey put her at ease by agreeing to get married after his basic training was over and that gave them both something to look forward to.

Casey was very serious about serving his country. His dad was a World War II hero! He had served in the Pacific theater. His unit had helped to open the Burma Road to China. Casey wanted to serve his country too.

During WWII the Japanese occupied Indochina (Vietnam) and cut off supplies from the seaports to China. China was a U.S. ally then, before the Communist took them over in 1949, and the Burma Road was essential to getting supplies to China. The Burma road was a jungle infested treacherous road through the Himalayan mountain range. Casey had heard about the hardships that his dad and others like him had endured fighting for the country. Casey felt that he owed all his way of life to his dad and the men like him who had fought for a system of government that allowed freedom of choice. The *least* Casey could do was to carry on the tradition. The Marine Corps was much tougher than the Army, so he felt, therefore he would be better than his dad or Rubin, because he joined an even tougher outfit. He was trying to live up to his dad's standards and to do better than his relatives before him. Ego and pride is a fallacy of youth, and Casey was eaten up with it!

Casey started training for the Marine Corps as soon as he joined the reserves. He increased his weight lifting routines at home. He started running in the evenings. He ran at the high school stadium steps, up and then down, like he used to do in football. He climbed ropes that hung from the top rafter in back of the stadium. He made obstacles out of stadium cross members to jump over and climb around. All during the spring and summer of '65, Casey road his bike to the school stadium early in the morning to begin his training routine. He did pushups, chin-ups, sit-ups, jumping jacks, and all kinds of tumbling and running exercises. He wrestled, practiced judo, boxed, and practiced shooting. Casey weighed one hundred and seventy-five pounds. There was not an ounce of fat on him. By July, he was about as physically fit as one could be. Casey, having worked very hard, was physically and mentally ready to meet the high standards of Marine Corps training! He was ready for the adventure he longed for!

Casey had no clue how his life was about to be forever changed. In July a Marine Corps recruiter drove to his house and picked him up in a government car. The recruiter introduced himself as Gunny Sergeant Bill "Bulldog" Able. Bulldog was tall and thin, his jaw was square, and he carried himself upright in a way that showed he had all the confidence in the world of his abilities, the least of which was to intimidate whoever he wished. His jaw set like a solid rock, he began to talk to Casey. The airport was about 30 miles from Casey's house. Bulldog talked all the way to Hobby Airport, located in Houston, Texas. There Casey was to catch a plane to the Marine Corps Recruit depot in San Diego, California. The recruiter said, "So you want to be a Marine, huh?" Casey said, "Yes sir, I do." The leather tough sergeant didn't know that being a Marine was all that Casey had thought about for months and that for the last several months Casey had been preparing himself to be a marine. They talked small talk for awhile. He asked, "Do you have any brothers or sisters?" Where were you born? Do you have a girl friend? Do you think you are good enough to be a Marine?" Casey answered his questions but his mind was on other things. He was thinking about Loretta and his Mom and Dad. "Would Loretta forget all about me and start dating other guys while I am gone? Would Mom and Dad be angry with me for joining the Marine Corps and leaving them after they had raised me?" Casey was thinking, "this is actually for real! He was actually leaving Baytown. He was on his way to a new and exciting adventure. He was on his way to California, the mountains, and the Pacific Ocean. He would see mountains for the first time!" Casey was excited about becoming a U.S. Marine. He was ready to see the world! He was also about to have an anxiety attack!

    Casey was a little in awe of this man, this warrior in his uniform next to him, and he was bashful for a kid anyway. Casey sincerely respected all the Marine next to him stood for, and he shook in his presence. After all, Casey was so, so young and Bulldog was so experienced. Bulldog began to prepare Casey mentally for what Casey was about to get into. He said, "How would you like to shoot a man, and just stand there and watch him die? How would you like to see his *guts* all over the ground? See him bleeding and squirming?" Casey didn't know what to say! He knew he wouldn't *enjoy* that. Was he supposed to *enjoy* killing someone to be a good marine? Casey said that he did not think that he'd enjoy that. Sergeant Able said that people die in a war and that the Marine Corps soldier should make sure it is the other soldier that dies. Casey suspected that the Gunny was just testing him. Casey did not take him too seriously, although he was shaking by his unabashed questions! Casey decided that he didn't like Gunny Sergeant "Bulldog" Able. The ride to the airport seemed exceptionally long. Casey could not wait to get to the airport.

They arrived at the airport on time. Casey was still shaking from their conversation. "Maybe I *have* made a mistake!" though Casey. "Maybe I should go back home?" The plane arrived on time. The old crusty Gunny Sergeant stood at parade rest as Casey boarded the plane. Casey sat in a seat next to a window. He just kept staring out of the window as if he was staring into the great beyond. The plane lifted off the runway. Casey sat there stunned. He could not talk.

A really attractive young girl sat in the seat next to Casey. Casey froze. She was really pretty and friendly, but he was thinking of Loretta and the commitment he had with her. He was naturally shy around strangers anyway. She tried to talk to him, but Casey could not talk. He was getting uncomfortable because he was really emotionally confused about what he was doing. He had not prepared himself mentally for the departure! It was the defining moment of his commitment to be a Marine. He had heard that to be a marine you had to be tough. He was tough physically. Was he tough enough?

Casey began to quiver as he stared out of the window. Tears began to escape as he attempted self-control. They were sad, slow , painful tears that flowed silently down his cheeks in a way that nobody likely noticed. Casey put his hand over his eyes to give a subtle wipe as he hid his face.

The plane lifted higher into the air. Casey continued to use all of his emotional control to hide his tears. He watched the buildings swish by as long as he could until the plane climbed into the clouds and the buildings disappeared; the scene reflecting the loss of the known and the beginning of the unknown.

The girl that had sat by Casey continually talked to Casey about *something*, but he was far away into his thoughts. He heard her, but as if she was talking in the background in a subliminal way. Casey was never really listening to her as she attempted to have a normal conversation. Eventually, she recognized Casey was not listening to her and that he seemed to be upset. She excused herself to go sit by someone else. Casey was really struggling with his emotions.

Casey struggled to understand how his eighteen year old life was about to change. He felt so alone. His parents were not there to comfort him; to see him off. Loretta was there on the ground but she could not comfort him there. He was sad and excited all at the same time. What will become of him now?

After awhile Casey began to focus on the world he was about to enter. The Marine Corps was looking for "A few Good Men" a recruiting slogan that caught on later. This was the moment of truth. Was Casey really good enough to meet the rigorous standards of Marine Corps training? At that moment, with his confused emotions, he was not so sure.

Casey spoke to no one the rest of the trip. The plane landed at San Diego airport a few hours later. There Casey saw for the first time that there were mountains in the distance with houses that were perilously perched high on the edge of them. Casey thought, "How do they get those houses way up there?" The houses looked as if they could fall right off the side of the mountain! Casey could see the blue Pacific Ocean in the distance and a long, white beach that disappeared into the horizon as the plane came to a stop on the runway. He was in awe! The plane seemed to take forever to roll to a complete stop. The military bus was waiting for him.

People were everywhere; more people than Casey had ever seen in one place before. They talked different than what Casey was used to. The sound of their words seemed shorter and quicker. They went in and out of tall buildings that looked a lot more elaborate than what he was used to. Cars whizzed around on a multi-laned highway that appeared to be at the bottom of the mountains. Casey had never seen a highway with so many lanes and with so many cars going in one direction.

In Baytown and Brenham, the two places Casey was most familiar with, there were narrow gravel roads made of crushed oyster shells, or black topped roads that ran along side of rice paddies, or cow pastures, or trails that simply cut through the middle of the forest. The cars would go in either direction on those undeveloped roads back home. Dust would billow out from the back of the cars. Sometimes the driver had to dodge a tractor or hay wagon.

There was no forest surrounding this new place, and there were no refineries billowing smoke from their chimneys. But the air from the car exhausts stung the eyes, and it did not smell fresh. Dust was also in the air from the winds that blew through the mountains. A steady, cool dry breeze blew from the ocean that day. It mixed with the wind coming from the mountains to chill the summer day.

The bus went through town and got on the freeway that led to Camp Pendleton. It was strangely quite on the bus. No one said much of anything; just sort of stared at the surroundings. Perhaps they were thinking about many of the same things that Casey was. The bus went through a guard gate to enter the base. The security guard was dressed in the dress blue uniform that was the standard issue for U.S marines in 1965. He saluted as the bus went through the gate. Casey felt his freedom was being threatened with all the appearances of the security. It frightened him a little.

The bus stopped near a building. The door opened. Two mean tough looking sergeants jumped hurriedly aboard the bus as if they were hijacking it. They stated that they were "drill instructors," and they immediately started yelling at the new recruits. One drill instructor yelled, "You young stupid people belong to me now!" The other drill instructor yelled obscenities and stated, "No *maggots* are allowed on my bus! You maggots get off my clean bus before you stink it up any more than what you already have!" The recruits were told that they, the drill instructors, hence forth were to be their momma's from now own! Therefore, there would be no crying home to momma!

The drill instructors yelled at the recruits from all directions, using language far more colorful than Casey had ever heard before. There was no doubt left among the recruits that they belonged to the drill instructors. If Casey doubted that they meant business before, at that very instant he was rudely made aware that they did. The Marine Corps is no boy scout outfit!

Everyone very hurriedly filed off the bus. As they stepped off the bus there were yellow painted footsteps on the pavement. The drill instructors in charge started hollering, some right into the recruits face, to step on those (expletive deleted) footsteps! "Match your feet's position with the position of the painted footsteps," yelled the drill instructors. The recruits placed their feet exactly into those painted footsteps, heels together, and toes at a forty-five degree angle. They stood up straight, eyes to the front, chin up, hands along their sides. They were told to *shut up* and to listen and to not move a muscle. The drill instructors again yelled that they were now the recruits mothers and fathers and that anything they said, anything, was to be, regardless of what the recruits thought about it. They called the recruits all sorts of demeaning names to strip them of their individuality. They shouted using *profane* language in a loud husky voice that made the schoolyard profanity pale by comparison. When one drill instructor was through with his instructions another one would start yelling *his* instructions to the recruits. Casey was to find out that this was to be true throughout his basic training. Finally the recruits were marched into a building where they were told to run to a bunk. The bunks were two tier bunks that had medal frames and wire cross members. A hard flat mattress covered the wire. Some small springs were attached to the medal frames and the wire. This allowed the mattress to sink a little when one lay in the bunk. Casey was assigned the bottom bunk.

    The next morning Casey and the other recruits were marched to the Marine Corps' version of a barbershop. Several men with hair clippers stood by the barber chairs liked vultures after fresh meat. They ran the clippers through their hair as fast as they could, cutting the hair down to the skin. Everyone looked really bad with their "skin heads" and they felt even worse. Casey felt really demoralized as a result, losing his sacred personal fashion and all. Everyone was hygienically cleansed with showers, issued clothing, and marched to their new quarters. The buildings, called "quanson huts" were made of wood and curved metal . They were systematically aligned in rows. Each hut had a door at each end and a window at each end. The only things in the huts were the bunk beds known as "racks" and a wooden box called a "footlocker." The huts were to be the new recruits sleeping quarters for the next twelve weeks.

The huts looked and smelled old. They had been hastily built during WWII to provide shelter for training troops. Several generations of troops had trained there. Their ghosts haunted the huts each night. Veterans of the battles of Iwo Jima and Guadalcanal, and other Pacific island campaigns. Casey knew that he was following their tradition. This somehow made the quarters and the training more bearable since he was carrying on the tradition of the Marines that had preceded him. Casey was ready to start his basic training.

Basic Training

Most of Casey's initial training consisted of a great deal of physical exercise along with a shouting dialog that was designed to strip him of his individuality. He and the other recruits were severely tested both physically and mentally each day by the individuals known as DI's, or "drill instructors." The harder the recruits, also know as *boots*, tried to comply with the drill instructors orders, the more the drill instructors would insist that they were not complying. Each boot was to comply with their orders without question. They were to react, and then think later! A soldier that lacked discipline was a *dead* soldier and the cause of the death of a fellow soldier. Discipline, discipline, discipline, all designed to make them a fighting unit that depended on each other. No individual mavericks would be tolerated! If one person in the unit failed to comply, all the people in the unit failed to comply, and therefore were punished as well as the individual. The marine had to function as part of an overall unit to survive.

Casey learned to use a variety of standard Marine Corps weapons. Every Marine is a rifleman; every rifleman is a Marine, in the Marine Corps. The main weapon is the rifle! Casey's weapon was his rifle; his (expletive deleted) was his gun. "This is my rifle (rifle), this is my gun (expletive deleted). This (rifle) is for shooting, this (expletive deleted) is for fun." *A Marine never calls his rifle a gun!* The standard rifle issued in 1965 was the M-14. It fired a 7.62mm round. It weighed approximately 9.3 pounds and could be made into an automatic with a device called a *selector*. It was very accurate at distances up to a thousand yards; 500 yards without a scope. The boots slept with their rifles, they exercised with their rifles, they drilled with their rifles, and they marched everywhere with their rifles. Each recruit had to shoot for score on qualification day at the rifle range. Not to qualify with the rifle was a major failure. Those who failed would be severely punished by both the drill instructors and the entire platoon. Casey quickly became an expert rifleman. He scored expert on a variety of courses designed to both challenge him, and to measure his efficiency.

Casey had to take a final physical test in order to graduate. During his training, he had run day after day through the hills. He had done hundreds of pushups. He had conquered numerous obstacle courses. He had fought the other recruits hand to hand. He had exercised his body every way imaginable. He had been shot at while crawling through barbed wire. He had crawled through the mud and dirt. He had been pushed, hollered at, and hurried every step of the way. He had been stressed way beyond any reasonable normal human endurance. He had been inspected numerous times. He was ready! Casey scored the highest expected score in every category. He was ready to graduate from Marine Corps basic training.

For twelve weeks Casey looked forward to graduating from the basic training. He was inspected a final time, and he and the other graduates paraded in front of their superiors on the parade ground. *One of the proudest moments in his life was when the Marine Corps Band struck up the Marine Corps Hymn as he marched by the commanding officers. Casey felt ten feet tall!* He had done it! He had met every challenge with flying colors. He was now a United States Marine!

Infantry Training

After basic training, there followed two more months of combat training. Casey learned to assault towns where he removed the enemy from the buildings.

He played war games day and night. He shot flame-throwers, grenade launchers, rockets, threw grenades, fired a variety of machine guns, pistols, and flares. He attacked pop up targets as one member of four marines who made up a fire team. A fire team used live ammo with locked and loaded M-1 rifles. The fire team advanced through an area and fired upon any target that popped out of the bush. Casey's fire team got the highest score in the company. Since he was one of the fire team members that got the highest score, he was convinced he was becoming the best he could be. The fire team was rewarded with a five minute break under a shade tree!

Casey welcomed the break, because the summer temperatures in the California hills where he was training exceeded one hundred degrees day after day. He was hot, sweaty, and exhausted from the relentless training. Sweat dripped from Casey's eyebrows and ran into his eyes. His eyes burned and momentarily blurred from the salt and minerals draining from his body. Casey's rifle became slick with sweat as he tried to keep it within his grasp. The sun caused him to see heat waves rising from the ground like some strange ghost dancing in the wind. The water in his canteens became warm as hot coffee.

Casey's team got the highest score while marching toward a rendezvous point. They were high on a hill and the shade tree was far below. They didn't care. As soon as they were told they could sit under the tree for being the best, they bolted into a full run down the hill and across the plain to that tree yelling and screaming at the top of their lungs. Exhausted but very proud Casey savored the moment!

At night fatigue played tricks on Casey's mind and he imagined all sorts of things. "What's that shadow?" Casey imagined. "What's that noise?" Flares shot up into the night sky to help him to see. An eerie *shadow dance* developed that increased Casey's anxiety. Every object seemed capable of moving. A bush shifted left to right, right to left, as the flare suspended from its little parachute, rocked back and forth with the breeze. Rocks seemed to be in motion. Images appeared out of the night reflected only in Casey's imagination. Battles of gunfire erupted to erase the shadows that danced. Tracers lit up the cool damp sky with streaks of red lines. Silence followed. Sweat dripped off of Casey's forehead from the strain of intense awareness. The next morning brought a well-deserved reprieve. Casey and the other trainees were exhausted but they were glad to see the daylight brought forth by the mercy of God.

After marching from one training area to another Casey's feet felt like every muscle was pulling his foot bones from different directions. Casey's feet needed some relief but he knew he could not stop. This day was not to be the day for any such relief. As Casey approached the base of the hill, he was looking forward to a rest. Instead he was mercilessly ordered to climb the hill as fast as he could! "You have got to be kidding," Casey screamed to himself! "This is not possible! I'll never make it!" Casey turned to a companion next to him hoping to voice his complaint, but the man,

BABYBOOM DOOM

sweat pouring from his body just like it was pouring from Casey's, just kept going up the hill silently hurting without a word.

Casey started up the hill along with the other Marines. Casey grunted and snorted like a bull after his first cow. He pawed the earth with his hands as his feet pounded the earth like pistons of a mighty engine forcing him up and up toward the summit of the hill. The steep almost vertical ascent caused his legs to burn with tremendous pain as he struggled to make each step. It was as if Casey was wearing lead boots as he struggled with each step.

No one dared to stop! Tempers flared within the ranks but only one serious fight broke out. By now the whole platoon was on all fours clinging to the side of the hill with every ounce of strength available. Everyone was ordered to remain in the pushup position while the two at combat cursed and shouted at each other with each blow. The combatants rolled over and over in a cloud of dust. The tension from the stress caused Casey to want to join the fight. The fighters kept rolling over and over. Casey wanted to jump up from his position to kick both of them for breaking ranks. He wanted to take his pain and frustration out on them, like they were taking their frustration out on each other. Casey knew he must hold his position or the DI's would also come down on him all the rest of the day. Although his muscles flinched for action each time he thought about entering the fight, Casey clung to the hillside "I'll get them for this," Casey grunted!

The DI's stood over the two fighters yelling at them without mercy. The two fighters, totally exhausted from their efforts, slowed their fighting and just lay in each others grasp, neither capable of hurting the other and each oblivious to the DI's commands. The combatants would pay for their insolence, as well as the platoon.

The drill instructors lifted the marines off of each other and pushed the fighters to continue the hill climb, even though the marines could barely move, much less walk. They crawled on up the hill inch by inch, rock by rock, until they reached the top. The DI's were waiting for them. They did not let up on them all day. The message was clear to all of the recruits. A lack of *discipline* would not be tolerated!

All day Casey marched up one hill then another. The two who had broken ranks to fight each other were now fighting to survive. They had to run *around* the platoon in a circle while the platoon ran at double time forward. With the temperature near 100 degrees and the distance to run much farther, the task before them was unbearable, but they continued determined to meet the challenge. If one stopped for any reason the DI was right on top of him to force him onward. It takes guts to keep going when every muscle in your body cries for relief! The undisciplined marines learned *discipline* the hard way that day. They did, on guts alone, show the determination necessary to be a U.S. Marine. Casey respected that! All marines learn that discipline does mean the difference between life and death in a combat situation. It takes unimaginable guts to be a marine. Casey was very glad it wasn't him who had disobeyed the DI's that day.

The temperature remained near 100° for most of the day. It seemed the day would never end. When the daylight did finally end, the Marines were up all night attacking bunker positions with a variety of assault formations. Blanks were used during the bunker assaults, but the sound of rifle fire and set-piece explosions made Casey *feel* that this was his last day on earth. Trip flares wired into the bushes for booby traps exploded without warning. Many explosions went off as the Marines ran toward the objective. High flying flares filled the night sky and the flashes of rifle fire could be seen up the hill as the *enemy* fired into the assaulting Marines.

Casey assaulted the hill as he maneuvered through the maze, firing at the rifle flashes with his M-1 rifle. He wasn't sure the enemy could be dislodged from the hill with the frontal assault he was a part of. He just kept moving forward toward the bunkers.

The bunkers were located all along the perimeter of the hill, camouflaged by a blanket of cool mountainous fog, and the shroud of darkness brought on by the misty night. The Marines manning the defensive positions fired relentlessly into the assaulting troops. Hand to hand combat began as soon as the assaulting Marines reached the top of the hill. It got so rough it was sometimes very difficult to remember that the war *exercise* was just training!

The hill taken, the objective complete, the marines then switched roles where the assaulting troops were now the defensive troops. To defend the hill was just as difficult as attacking it as the shadows of the attacking men could be seen approaching the defensive positions. The battle was as real as it gets for infantry training; flares, booby traps, rifle fire, explosions, obstacles of razor sharp wire, orders being hollered over the noise, wounded being cared for as they called for the corpsman. With the light of the next day, the exhausting sleepless night over, the marines regrouped to prepare for the next day. Casey was now *trained* to attack or to defend a position as dictated by the circumstances on the battlefield.

The next day Casey climbed under barbed wire and over other obstacles while live machine gun bullets was being fired just over his head. Casey had no problem with discipline there! He knew he had to hug the ground to stay down below the machine gun fire; he had to stay down and crawl the distance or die! Casey didn't know the importance of the training, or that he was to be even more severely tested later in a place called Vietnam! He just trained hard for the present.

The loud explosions throughout the course rattled Casey's bones while the full combat gear he wore weighed him down as he crawled on his belly. He crawled through the hard dry dusty ditches toward the objective several hundred yards ahead. The dust choked his lungs and the relentless heat drained his body of all of his strength. The physical and mental stress took its toll on Casey as he became angry, irritable, quick tempered and hard to get along with.

Casey had reached that point where he was acting on instinct. He was becoming a hardened Marine, reacting without much thought of the danger to himself. As he approached the sharp barbed wire obstacle, he paused to size up the situation. Machine gun fire continued overhead so he knew he could not go over the wire. Casey flipped over on his back to craw through the barbed wire. He placed his rifle on his chest and used it to push the wire off of his clothing. To have his clothing snagged by the wire meant likely death from the entanglement in a combat situation. Casey knew he had to be careful as he crawled around large rocks and around logs while he squirmed along under the wire. The deafening noise and the rat-tat-tat of the machine gun shook his nerves to the breaking point. Forward he crawled inch by inch. His objective was to make it to the trenches ahead and to take up a defensive position that helped to form a perimeter. Once the mission was accomplished it just meant that he now had to take another hill, take another town, or take to the bush again. Attack! Attack! Attack! Carry the wounded to safety! Pick up more ammo, reload and attack. Casey was undaunted by the challenge as he gained the confidence necessary for combat duty.

The night brought more attacks on the hills. Live ammo was being used. Every fifth round fired at night was a tracer. Tracer rounds leave a red line all the way to the target. When everyone fired at once, a blanket of red lines formed that looked much like a red spider web just above the ground. The smell of gunpowder filled the air and smoke became thick as fog. The sounds of explosions, gunfire, and people yelling, created an eerie state of euphoria. Once intoxicated with the sounds of war, one just reacted almost mechanically to it all. Fear disappeared, replaced by a relentless and timeless courage.

Casey marched to his next objective! Orders were shouted by the team leaders. Use the M-79 to blowup that fire team! Throw that grenade! Take that bunker! Capture the enemy! Attack! Attack! Attack!

Casey mused, " This is pure hell! Surely the real thing could not be worse than this training." Casey was wrong!

Military Occupational Specialty

Casey's training was not over. After infantry combat training, he began to train in a specialty area of combat otherwise known as Military Occupational Specialty or MOS. He was assigned to an armored battalion for his next phase of training. The armored personnel carrier of the day was an amphibious vehicle called an LVTA1-P5. It weighed 65,563 pounds! It was 141.30 inches wide, 358.10 inches long and 115.7 inches high. It was a monstrous machine that could be heavily armed with a variety of assault weapons. Casey thought it looked like a *floating coffin* with caterpillar like tracks. Casey shuttered because it looked to him as if there was no way the thing could float in water.

It did float although only about two feet of it was above the water. Inside there was storage for all kinds of equipment and enough room to carry approximately thirty-four combat equipped marines plus a crew of three. A V-12 gasoline engine that roared to life powered it. Four hundred fifty-six gallons of gasoline fuel, supplied by twelve fuel cells located at the bottom section of the vehicle, could be stored for use by the massive engine. The cruising range was about 185 miles. Its maximum speed was 28 MPH. The LVTA1-P5 could go almost anywhere on land and could go from shore to ship or from ship to shore with its payload.

Casey began his training somewhat skeptical at first. His initial training consisted of half a day of classroom each day to orient him about the main features and capabilities of the vehicle. The other half of the day consisted of actual operations with the vehicle. The name most often used to refer to the LVTA1-P5 was *amtrac*, which was an acronym for *amphibious tractor*. It was often referred to as an *amphibious tank*. Some were equipped with 105 Hollitzer canons! Casey studied the technical material every day. Casey asked, " How fast will this vehicle run on land? How fast will it run in the water? How many troops will it hold? Is the vehicle tough enough to withstand combat conditions?" Casey asked the instructors question after question. He soon gained confidence in the vehicle and he was proud to finish academically first in his class!

    Casey found the amtrac to be a lot of fun in spite of the hard work necessary to keep it going. The amtrac required daily maintenance to repair the steel tracks and suspension. The oils had to be maintained and changed often. The suspension had to be greased after each use, and retainer pins that were used to hold the sections of track together, had to be continuously replaced. Olive drab green paint was used as camouflage and it seemed Casey was always painting. The engine had to be kept in a constant state of readiness. This included cleaning the fuel filters which accumulated moisture from sweating inside the huge cylinders that held the filters. The filters had to be switched periodically to keep the engine running smoothly. The marines challenged the machine, while the amtrac challenged the marine's driving skills. Casey drove the amtrac through the sand dunes and up steep hills that made the massive amtrac roar loudly as it climbed almost straight up the incline. He drove the amtrac with the skill of a well trained fighter pilot as he steered up, then down the narrow ridges of the mountains, fearlessly peering the valleys below. Casey shouted to the instructor, "This is more fun than a turkey shoot!" "Yeah, it kind of grows on you after awhile. Wait till we enter the surf head-on, right into the waves! You'll really get a "kick" out of that!" said the instructor.

It was challenging, but fun to crash through the surf and to float through the huge swells of the Pacific Ocean. The instructor was right! Casey *did* get a kick out of that! The amtrac clawed through the cold water at about five miles an hour bobbing up and down like a cork in a washing machine. The ship loomed into the distance offshore appearing to Casey to be but a small spec of black on the horizon. The mother ship was called an *LSD*, or *Landing Ship Dock*. Precise steering was necessary to guide the amtrac onto the ship. A miscalculation sent the amtrac crashing into the side of the receiving ship, turning the amtrac sideways and out of control into the surf that rushed into the bowls of the ship. After entering the ship the amtrac was steered to turn the vehicle around 180º. Casey knew that the maneuver must be done correctly or the whole loading procedure would be jammed as the amtracs entered one after the other. Casey carefully steered the amtrac around and into its docking position so that the front of the amtrac faced the rear of the ship for a quick exit later. The sailors looked on in awe as Casey and his fellow marines precisely loaded the amtracs onto the ship. Some sailors shouted instructions while others just stared in marvelous disbelief. Each amtrac came to rest in formation on the deck of the ship like individual soldiers lined up for battle.

Casey also practiced using the *LST*, or *Landing Ship Tank* of WWII vintage. The marines entered the ship via a special ramp in the front of the ship that led into the ship's hold. The LSD had its entry ramp at the *stern*, or rear of the ship whereas the LST had its entry ramp at the *bow*, or front of the ship. The ship then closed the ramp to pump the water out of its hold. The marines chained the amtracs to the deck of the ship to prevent them from sliding. To secure the amtrac to the deck, Casey used large swivel clamps and chains that weighed as much as he did.

Casey practiced various assault formations from ship to shore. First he entered into a formation of a circle of other amtracs as he left the ship. Then he spread out in line with the other amtracs to form a straight line. One by one each amtrac left the circle to spread out into the straight line. Upon a predetermined signal, each driver floor boarded the accelerators and headed in as straight a line as possible for the landing on shore. Explosions to create chaos and confusion were often used during the landings to make it as close to the real thing as possible. Once on shore, the amtrac crew dropped the front ramp of the amtrac. The Marine assault troops rushed out of the amtrac to take their positions on the beach. A simulated firefight began! The battle lasted until the beachhead was secured. The marines maneuvered across the beach, established a beachhead, then they moved inland.

Casey joined the other amtrac crews to load supplies into the amtracs used to support the assaulting marines. The amtracs usually followed the assault in battle formation with other armored vehicles; tanks, minesweepers, and ontos, all moved inland carrying troops.

The marines practiced driving through the hills, through rivers that seemed very willing to push them off course with their strong currents, through forests, and onto roads of all types. Up and down the hills Casey drove. Day and night the marines practiced. Casey began to feel invincible as he became more and more skilled to wage amphibious warfare.

The crew consisted of three men. One man was the driver. He controlled the amtrac's direction by sitting behind mechanical controls on the left front side of the amtrac. On the right front side of the amtrac sat a second man who was the crew chief. The crew chief was responsible for the entire operation of the amtrac. The third crewman was a Gunner. His responsibility was to operate the weapons system. At night Casey slept inside the amtrac storage compartment. Each crewman had a fold-up cot that could be unfolded and placed side by side inside the main compartment of the amtrac. They had a first class *camper* equipped with machine guns, rifles, rockets, canons, and armor plate. One just naturally felt safe in the field at night with the amtrac for protection. When it rained, Casey could go inside. When it was hot he could make shade along side of it. After infantry combat training, Casey felt lucky to be assigned to the amtrac battalion. He liked his MOS very much.

Although training in the United States Marine Corps is a continuous experience, Casey's initial training was over. He was ready to take his place as a well-trained and highly qualified U.S. Marine. After six months of continuous training, Casey got his first leave.

L.A. International Airport

The trip from Camp Pendleton to Los Angeles was surreal. Casey had been training for months under a very restricted regimen. All focus was on mastering a vast array of military equipment and machines. He went everywhere using military equipment and machines. Now he was in an ordinary car owned by one of the camp instructors, en route from San Diego California to Los Angeles. He felt like he was doing something wrong!

Highway 1 runs along the Pacific west coast. The coastal mountains were dotted with lights that flickered in the night air. Casey could see the waves crashing inland off shore and the vast expanse of the Pacific Ocean as it disappeared into the night horizon. Somewhere across that vast ocean was his destiny. He was doomed from the very beginning of his life to fulfill his destiny. *It was called Vietnam.* The communist were over there! Casey was trained and ready to fight them. It was something he had always expected to do from childhood.

During the trip to the Los Angeles airport Casey felt very strange. It was as if he was in a dream. All that was happening seemed strangely unreal. He saw strange looking cars. He saw people that he felt were somehow much different than he. They were in fact much different! Casey had changed during his training although he didn't really know it at the time. The things that he related to before seemed so juvenile now. Casey felt self righteous, proud, and important. *He had taken the oath to defend his country.* He was *earning* his right to be an American!

Casey was a little angry the people walking around outside on the streets of L.A. were not showing any desire to earn their rights. The privileges they enjoyed, it seemed at that moment, were being taken for granted. There was no hint of being responsible towards this great nation of ours or even of being concerned that the Communist might someday try to take all of Americas privileges away if Americans refused to stand up to them. Didn't anyone care? Casey thought that it is better to fight them over there than to fight them in the U.S. He was going to do his part to ensure that the human rights of the people of America was protected. He was willing to fight over there in Vietnam. He was willing to fight in the U.S. against terrorist. He was willing to fight in Germany against the Soviet Union. He was willing to sacrifice himself in the Cold War against the Communist anywhere. *Freedom* to chose meant sacrifices had to be made and Casey was conditioned to do his part!

Casey boarded the commercial airliner to fly back to Houston, Texas. Everything was different now. Casey felt he did not have long to live, and that feeling surpassed any desire to have fun because his mind was preoccupied with only a desire to survive the next few months. Casey was both scared and excited!

He wondered what was going to happen in Vietnam. Was this great adventure going to be his last? Was he doing the right thing for mankind? Where was his boyhood desires now? Had he lost his way? Had he gone mad to give up the creature comforts of home and to venture into harms way? Somehow Casey knew that destiny was in charge and that his life had been shaped by God's will and that what was to be was really up to Him and not up to Casey. Casey put his faith in God's will to comfort his confusing thoughts. The political circumstances and Cold War alignments were already in place before

Casey had been born. His Babyboom doom a forlorn conclusion.

Casey went home for thirty days. It was the Christmas holiday season. Loretta and he followed through with their plans to get married. It was a simple affair. They were married at Liberty, TX by a Justice of the Peace that he did not know. Casey's mother and dad were the only ones with them when they took the vows. They had been with each other all of their teen years. Now they were married. Casey was nineteen, Loretta was twenty-one. They had no honeymoon. They just enjoyed the experience of being with each other after being apart for what seemed then like a long, long time.

Casey and Loretta went to Somerville to visit his grandma. She was thrilled to see them anytime. They also went to Brenham to visit his cousins. Tom was impressed with Casey's physical presence. Casey was in the best shape of his life and he looked great in his uniform. Casey's military training had transformed him into a much more mature person. He was now married. He looked forward to a good future.

After Casey's first leave, he was ordered to report to Fleet Marine Force Pacific for additional training and for staging for his overseas assignment.

Additional training as a combatant began as soon as Casey returned to Camp Pendleton in California. Many forced marches took place in the hills and several rifle ranges later Casey was fine tuned for combat.

Instead of being shipped overseas right away, Casey was assigned to work as a *mess duty* private. This meant peeling potatoes, cleaning tables, and washing pots and pans. Casey did not like the assignment at all, but did what was expected anyway. He was required to get up each morning at 3:00 AM and to work past 10:00 PM. After a few weeks he was getting very irritable from lack of sleep and the non-stop work. Casey was soon put in charge of making sure the seating area was cleaned and prepared for service. He had to serve the officers while on his feet hour after hour just because they had been to college and he had not. *This infuriated him to the point that he decided right then and there that one day he would go to college to make up for the humiliation.* The spoon fed rich kids got to be officers while the hard working blue collar kids had to work their way up the chain of command through trial and error. Casey was learning the cruel facts of life.

After each meal Casey had to cleanup the mess. If the mess was not cleaned fast enough the senior NCOs or officers in charge would exercise their authority over him. Soon Casey got real upset with the other marines when they did not carry their load. Since he was in charge he expected the work to be done! Casey did not like being *chewed out* by the officers.

One marine was not doing his job! Casey told him several times to clean the tables. Instead the marine in question went outside to smoke while the work was left undone. Casey tried to get him to help several times before Casey began to lose his cool. Each time the lazy marine ignored Casey's orders. He went to the *head*, a Marine term for restroom, obviously to hide from the work. So after several days of this Casey followed him into the *head* and confronted him. Casey told him he had to straighten up or he was going to pay. Lazy said, "Give it your best shot!" He shoved Casey and put his hands in the fighting position. That set Casey off! He immediately stepped back, took aim and kicked the marine square in the groin! The marine bent over at the waist and was going down on his knees as Casey furiously karate chopped him at the back of his head. Within a split second before the marine collapsed, Casey's right hand lifted him off his feet, followed by Casey's left, then his right. The marine was out cold! Casey hollered at him to get up, but he was unable to move. Casey, now in a full blown rage, slung the door of the *head* open and threw the broom clear across the mess mall.

When confronted by the others, Casey told them the marine had been goofing off for days. "You don't do that as a Marine," exclaimed Casey! The other marines immediately went back to work and they never gave him any lip after that. The unfortunate combatant was taken to the hospital on a stretcher. Casey thought for sure that he would be busted and sent to the brig, but fortunately for him no one had seen what had happened. No charges were ever filed and the incident passed. *Casey knew that as a Marine you had to fight,* you had to be tough, and yes you had to be down right mean at times to survive in the Corps day by day. It would not be the last time Casey would be challenged to a fight!

Loretta came to see Casey while he was on leave for five days in California just before he was to be shipped overseas. She got a motel room in Oceanside and they stayed there during the night. During the day they explored California. They rented a car and drove to Anaheim to Disneyland! It was childhood dreams come true! Casey especially enjoyed the jungle river trip and the sky rides through the castle. It was a wonderful week. After she left Casey's life was to be changed forever.

It was January 1966. The Communists were at it again. This time it was a place called *Vietnam*. At that time Casey had little knowledge of Vietnam. He knew there was a South Vietnam and a North Vietnam. He knew the Communist wanted South Vietnam and that the United States did not want that to happen. Casey knew it was his duty as a soldier to do what he could to stop the Communists from advancing any further into any other countries. Casey was in the best shape of his life. He was a United States Marine! *It was his sworn duty to uphold the U.S. policy to stop the Communist from taking over the world.* To him, it was just another hot spot in the *Cold War* with the Communist!

In 1949 China had become a Communist state. In 1950 the U.S. had fought the Communist in Korea. The Soviet Union and China were strong powerful allies of North Vietnam and supported the Communist doctrine of world domination. The U.S. had come to the brink of nuclear war over missiles the Soviet Union had placed in Cuba in 1962. "We Americans stood up to them then. We must stand up to them now," Casey reasoned! Casey was going to Vietnam to fight the Communists as a United States Marine and more importantly as a very loyal patriot! He was ready to do his duty. The *Containment Policy* was the reason why. It would prove to be much more complicated than that!

The Containment Policy

In his address to Congress on March 12, 1947, President Harry Truman stated: "If we falter in our leadership, we may endanger the peace of the world and we shall surely endanger the welfare of this nation." On that day in March the *Truman Doctrine* of containment officially declared war on Soviet expansionism in Europe.

The U.S. *Containment Policy* as a doctrine had gained potency from the historical lesson American policymakers had learned from pre WWII. The U.S. had learned that appeasement of aggression merely fueled increasingly more strident and unreasonable demands from dictators. Hitler and Stalin had shown the world in Europe that appeasements did not matter as they continued to demand more. It was better to *contain* Communism than to appease it. The U.S. was also concerned that if the Communist gained Southeast Asia, that the fall of one country, would lead to the fall of other countries in a chain like reaction the Eisenhower administration called the *Domino Theory*.

A *Flexible Response* strategy suggested to our enemies that the U.S. might not risk nuclear war to defend its interest in Western Europe or Asia! Aware of this policy the Communist in Southeast Asia reasoned they could win a war in Asia by simply out lasting the U.S. through a war of attrition. The Communist believed that the American people would grow impatient with a long drawn out war. The U.S. believed it must contain the Communist in Vietnam to the Northern sector above the 17th parallel that divided North Vietnam from South Vietnam. The U.S. policy makers had to stop or at least challenge Communist expansionism in the Pacific basin of world trade.

The U.S used *Containment and Flexible Response,* policies that meant we would use any means *short of nuclear war,* by forming bases near its adversaries and spying in every conceivable way. The ideological confrontation included economic pressure on U.S. adversaries, diplomatic confrontations, and an unprecedented arms race. The G.I. or common soldier would have to bear the burden of manning the basses on the front lines of defense.

This *Forward Collective Defense* strategy would include the bases near our adversaries of China and the Soviet Union, use of *coalition* forces from other countries, and the *limited fighting* of a conventional war instead of a nuclear war. Vietnam was one such base!

The Communist had their opening! Their Mao Ts Tong inspired guerrilla wars, also called the *Peoples Revolutionary War for World Order,* gained momentum. The U.S. viewed all such nationalistic revolutionary wars as orchestrated from the Soviet Union and China. The Asia conflicts behind the *Bamboo Curtain* included conflicts in China, Southeast Asia, and Korea.

Examples of the U.S. *Cold War* containment policy included many verbal and propaganda filled conflicts with the Soviet Union. Spying on each other manifested many conflicts in Eastern Europe; Germany, Czechoslovakia, Yugoslavia, Greece, Albania, Austria, the southern flank of the Mediterranean Sea, and the northern flank of the artic are but some of the examples of U.S. face offs behind the Iron Curtain and beyond.

The *Iron Curtain* was a boundary that separated U.S. allies from the Soviet Union that stretched from the Baltic to the Adriatic

Sea. British Prime Minister Winston Churchill stated on March 6, 1946 in a speech at Westminster College in Fulton, Mo that an "Iron Curtain" stretched across the European Continent separating the two dominant ideologies of Democracy versus Communism.

After WWII the *Marshall plan* was designed to provide economic aid to Western Europe to contain the Soviet threat. The Soviet Union would be less likely to attack a strong West Germany backed by U.S. allies.

In April 1949, NATO, the North Atlantic Treaty Organization, was formed to place military personnel in strategic areas around Europe to *contain* Soviet Communism to Eastern Europe. Several events occurred during and after WWII that shaped *Casey's* commitment to be an honorable patriot as he grew up. These events doomed Casey's evolution as a Baby boomer. For example:

During WWII President Franklin D. Roosevelt favored independence for France's Indochina colonies, after the Japanese occupation was defeated. France did not!

In 1945, after Southeast Asia was liberated from the Japanese, the *French wanted to retain Vietnam as their colony.*

In 1946 French forces attacked Haiphong Harbor in November. The French attack on North Vietnam sparked the war of resistance against all colonial powers. *Casey was less than one month old!*

In 1948, the *Berlin airlift* worked to stop the Soviets from dominating Berlin, Germany.

After 1949, when China became Communist, the US refused to recognize the Peoples Republic of China for many years. Only after negotiations that took place during the Vietnam War did the U.S.

open the lines of communication. President Nixon signed trade agreements between the U.S. and China. The U.S. later gave official recognition to the China regime in 1979.

In 1950-1953, the U.S. fought the Korean War to stop the Asian Communist from dominating South Korea because our *Forward Collective Defense* strategy dictated the need to defend this base of operations for U.S. interests. The idea was to fight the enemy overseas, at distant locations, instead of the U.S. mainland.

Post WWII American leaders supported French colonialism because France was a key component of NATO and the U.S. needed France's help to restrain Soviet expansion in Europe. The U.S. began helping France in 1950 to defeat Ho Chi Minh's nationalist Communist movement in Southeast Asia.

In 1954, the French were militarily defeated by the Viet Minh, later called Viet Cong, or simply VC. As a result of the 1954 Geneva Convention Vietnam was divided at the 17th Parallel into a South Vietnam and a North Vietnam. The Communist officially controlled North Vietnam, but immediately fought for unification of the North with the South.

In 1955 SETO, the "Southeast Treaty Organization" was formed to contain Communist expansion. If any member of SETO were attacked, all the other members were to resist. The USA, Britain, and France were the main members trying to protect Vietnam, Thailand, Cambodia, Burma, Laos, and the surrounding Pacific basin of Indonesia and Malaysia.

In 1956 the USA began seriously training the South Vietnamese as a conventional army copied after the US Military.

In 1957 the North Vietnamese Communist increased its

insurgency into the South. The US was becoming more involved with Vietnam with each passing year.

The Soviet Union had launched the first artificial satellite in 1959 called *Sputnik*, giving credence that they could scientifically dominate the world with their brand of Communism. Their support for North Vietnam was one more step toward world domination. *Casey was personally shook up by both prospects!*

In 1962, President Kennedy's administration went to Decon 2, and alert status just short of nuclear war with the Soviet Union, over the Cuba Missile Crisis. If Soviet ships caring missiles to Cuba chose to run through a U.S. naval block aid around Cuba, the U.S. was prepared to sink them and attack the Soviet Union with nuclear weapons.

When the U.S. discovered that the Soviet Union was placing offensive missiles with nuclear capability in Cuba, the use of a U.S Naval block aid around the island of Cuba was the only hope of *preventing* all out war. The U.S. could not afford to have offensive nuclear weapons from opposing forces so close to its mainland. The missiles had to be removed! A U.S. invasion of Cuba seemed imminent. A U.S. invasion of Cuba meant a confrontation with the Soviet Union that would start WWIII!

This confrontation of the two most powerful nations on earth brought the world to the brink of destruction. *The world stood on the edge of all-out-war as the two most powerful nations in history decided the fate of mankind over a Cold War issue.* Fortunately, a political agreement between the two forces ended the world crisis.

In 1963, President Kennedy was assassinated! Lyndon Banes Johnson became president. LBJ would greatly escalate the U.S.

commitment to the *hot spot* in the *Cold War* known as Vietnam. Many referred to the war that came as *LBJ's War*. LBJ referred to it as that "*piss ant* war in Southeast Asia."

By 1964, the stage was set for the U.S. to commit its conventional military to defend South Vietnam from the North Vietnam insurgency into the South; advisors and special forces were no longer enough support for the South Vietnamese government to survive.

On March 8, 1965, LBJ sent the first large troop deployment into South Vietnam. The 9th Marine Expeditionary Force of the 3rd Marine Division landed at Da Nang. *Casey graduated from high school that year and immediately joined the Marine Corps on active duty.*

Kennedy had stated in one of his speeches, "*Ask not what your country can do for you, but what you can do for your country!*" Casey was inspired to do his part to answer his countries call! Now he was going to be one of 200,000 American combat troops established mainly along the coastal area of South Vietnam. Things were heating up the Cold War!

By 1966, Casey's year to arrive in South Vietnam, the number of U.S. troops had nearly reached 400,000 by the end of the year, and 500,000 by the end of the following year. American troops started counteroffensive operations on a large scale. Casey was now on the front lines of a *Hot War* in a *Cold War* political environment!

BABYBOOM DOOM

VIETNAM

CHAPTER FIVE

Vietnam

On March 8, 1965 the 9th Expeditionary Brigade splashed ashore on *Red Beach* at Da Nang Bay. Their initial objective was to establish a foothold in Vietnam. Then they were to establish a defense for the airfield at Da Nang. Casey was to be sent to Vietnam as a replacement.

It was January 1966 the beginning of the New Year. It would be the year that would have the most profound effect on Casey's entire life! After 1966 he would be forever changed although he did not know it then. Casey could not even imagine how.

After a short leave with his family during Christmas, Casey returned to Camp Pendleton at San Diego, California for *Staging* to go overseas.

In February 1966 he boarded a bus that would take him to the Marine Air Base at El Toro. That night the marines boarded the 707 military jets to fly to Hawaii. Casey's mind raced with the fear of the unknown. There were no windows to look out of the plane. The seats were placed with their backs facing the front of the plane. The noise was deafening and Casey was feeling a little sick. The hours were longer it seemed than normal. No one said much. Casey tried to sleep but only managed to doze from time to time. His thoughts were of Loretta, home, his life, and friends. Was Casey destined to die in a foreign land even before his adult life began? "If I must die, *so be it*," Casey thought! "At least I can die with honor! Who cares anyway!"

Somehow Casey took comfort in the perception that he was better trained and equipped than was the enemy. "If I must die, then I will make sure that I die only after I have killed at least ten of my enemy!" reasoned Casey. Casey got comfort from believing that if, as a warrior he was able to make his enemy suffer more for their cause than he suffered for his cause, he would then at least have an honorable death. Casey's duty to his country would be undeniably fulfilled. The rights and freedoms of his country's people preserved. The might and power of the U.S. unquestioned. *God's will to prevail!*

It was very strange flying backwards in that plane with no windows to clue you where you were. Casey wondered if they really were going to where they said they were going. Were they on some secret *Cold War* mission instead?

The air transport landed about five hours later on the island of Oahu, Hawaii. It was good to step out into the breeze and to feel its soothing caress against Casey's damp skin. The smell of the sea filled his nostrils in a way that was as refreshing as a dew filled morning. Casey felt that he had emerged from some cocoon to be reborn again. The open space flooded his soul with the relief of freedom. "What a beautiful place," Casey softly mumbled.

Since the marines had arrived in Hawaii early in the morning, the sun was just about to peak above the volcanic formed mountains. It appeared to be somehow majestic as the sun's rays danced through the misty clouds. Casey wondered if the sky was as beautiful that morning the Japanese flew their planes from the sea, over the mountains to attack Pearl Harbor at the Hawaii Islands on that fateful day December 7, 1941. As Casey looked over the horizon he could only imagine the frightful sight of hundreds of Japanese planes swarming toward him. He shook with the excitement caused by the adrenalin rush he had unintentionally aroused.

The marines departed the plane and walked across the runway to a military looking grey building. Casey sat in one of the chairs that were arranged for a meeting. A female officer stepped into the room. Female officers were very uncommon in the sixties. Some of the men whistled, hooted, and hollered at her. She was a tall white woman with blond hair and a good figure. She was very sexy looking in her uniform and the marines were young with their full compliment of male hormones making them behave accordingly. The male officers quickly came to her aid. They reminded the marines in typical military fashion, that she was a military officer due the respect of such ranking. Everyone quieted to listen to the officers. The men exchanged glances at each other to indicate that to them she was a fine woman. The drift was that she certainly was not fit for combat situations, a common belief of the time about women in the military. She was certainly an attractive *woman*! There were many who wished they could be with her, if only for just a few minutes. Casey just sat and stared in amazement.

The female officer, a captain by rank, explained that the marines were at a military base in Hawaii and that they were going to stay there until the next day. Then they would fly to Okinawa, Japan where they would be flown to Vietnam, Southeast Asia. She explained that the Communist had control of most of the South Vietnamese villages and that they were called Viet Cong, a slang contraction for Viet Cong San, *Vietnamese Communist*.

The Viet Cong were very well trained and motivated by the North Vietnamese Army, NVA for short, and the rebellious PLAF *Peoples Liberation Armed Forces of South Vietnam*. Both the army of the north, also known as the PAVN, *Peoples Army of Vietnam* and the

PLAF of the south, confronted the ARVN, *Army of the Republic of Vietnam*. The ARVN was fighting for the independence of South Vietnam from North Vietnam and was in support of the South Vietnamese government headed by President Nguyen Cao Ky. The US had helped to develop the ARVN and was also in support of the Ky regime, although the Ky regime was a dictatorship, unstable and largely disliked by many of the South Vietnamese.

The Communist movement was spearheaded by the NLF, *National Liberation Front*, formed on 12/20/60. The NLF was determined to stop *any* colonial rule of Vietnam and to unite North and South Vietnam under a Communist regime. The captain said the Viet Cong were in violation of the 1954 Geneva convention which prohibited armed incursions from the north beyond the 17th Parallel, which separated the north from the south. She said the South Vietnamese had a right to form their own government, separate from the North Vietnamese Communist government headed by Ho Chi Minh. "Your duty, as Marines, is to uphold the Geneva convention and to stop the invaders from the north." The marines were told that the Viet Cong often came into a village to execute the village chief. They would then take control of the village against the villager's will and dictate policy. *The Viet Cong would stop at nothing to gain control and would kill anyone who resisted their authority.* The captain made it clear that as Marines they were going to *war*, even though congress had not declared war against North Vietnam. "The Viet Cong and the NVA must be stopped now or South Vietnam will fall to the Communist," explained the captain. Most policy makers were sure that if South Vietnam fell to the Communist the entire Pacific basin was in danger of Communist rule. This was unacceptable to the United States of America. The islands of the Pacific, which included

Indonesia, Malaysia, and the Philippines, had been *liberated* from the Japanese during WWII by the United States and her allies. To allow the *Communist* to gain control of the area without a fight was considered a security risk for the future of the United States. The U.S. government had to have a show of force from the U.S. military to show the Communist that continued aggression in Southeast Asia or the Pacific basin would be met and deterred by the U.S..

Early the next morning, the marines boarded the plane, it having been refueled and checked out, for the trip to Okinawa, Japan. "We're back in the noisy tomato can," Casey blurted out. Last night in a beautiful tropical paradise the marines smelled the fresh air of civilized freedom as it blew through the green volcanic mountains. They watched the sun dance from the glistening Pacific waves one last time as the plane swept them away from their dream place. It somehow made Casey feel very sad that he had to face the war and that he had to just forget about the prospect of a good time. Casey's mind raced with conflicting thoughts and he noticed that everyone else was quietly thinking. The silence spoke volumes! It was just that it was hard to let go of the good feelings from Hawaii as the cold, hard, reality of what was happening settled next to their restless souls.

After about two hours of flight the platoon leaders explained that there was a problem with one of the plane's jet engines so the pilots had to make an emergency landing on a small island in the middle of the Pacific Ocean. Casey knew they had not flown long enough to reach Okinawa. Eventually the plane landed hard on a tiny airstrip on *Wake Island*, truly a mere speck of land in the middle of the Pacific Ocean! Casey was very suspicious at first because his imagination had run wild while he was cooped up in that tin shaped tomato can they called a military jet. Where were they, really?

The marines were asked to silently leave the plane. Repairs had to be made to the jet engine; something about oil pressure. When Casey stepped out, he could see the ocean water all around them, within walking distance since the place was so tiny. Soon Casey realized that they were on Wake Island for sure. He knew from history that a fierce battle had taken place there during WWII for possession of the airfield they now had landed on. As a testimony to the fact a small monument was erected to those who had made the supreme sacrifice. Many of the damaged WWII machines remained where they had been destroyed like some creepy ghosts of the past. Casey stared in disbelief at the ruins and in his own way gave tribute to those that had fought there. After a few hours the plane was repaired and the pilots set a heading for Okinawa, Japan.

Casey arrived at Kadena Airfield in Okinawa the next day via the military transport plane. It was a 707 jet that had no windows, and the seats faced the rear of the plane! It was obvious that the plane had been designed to quickly transport troops and their equipment, without much concern about the comfort of the troops. They were military soldiers en-route to a war where comfort gives way to other priorities, such as survival. Casey was scared, but he was determined to do his duty. No amount of discomfort was going to bother him.

The marines were given leave their first evening at Okinawa. Casey did not want to get into any trouble his very first night in this strange place, so he stayed behind when most of the other guys went out. Casey understood that most everyone was out to get high and to get laid. He was not interested in doing either. Casey slept in an entirely empty barracks that night. One by one the guys drifted into the barracks. Most were drunk from *Sake*, a kind of rice vodka, or from some other form of intoxicant. Some came in singing and staggering from one side of the room to the other. Many had a great deal of trouble finding where their bunk was. As more and more of the troops drifted in, all kinds of strange sounds echoed through the barracks. Casey heard moaning, a high pitched eerie sound that sent chills down one's spine, coming from one direction. A sick marine was sprawled out in his bunk, his shirt tail hanging out and the rest of his clothes in disarray. He smelled terrible! A mixture of vomit and booze covered his chest. He was moaning and thrashing about uncontrollably as if the devil was trying to demonize him. He was obviously hurting from too much Sake and other unmentionables.

Then from farther down the roll of bunks there was some eerie mumbling, as if someone was carrying on a conversation with someone, although no one was there but one semi-conscious marine. The smell of alcohol and cigarette smoke filled the room. One or two marines came into the barracks at a time throughout the night. Some talked about how they loved their girl back home, while others seemed to be just looking for someone to fight. Others snored loudly as if nothing in the world mattered. Casey dozed in and out of sleep several times but he never really felt like he could sleep soundly under the circumstances. Casey was glad when morning came.

The marines boarded the plane for their flight to Vietnam early the next morning. No one talked all that much. They all still seemed to be in some sort of strange trance. Some were still hung over from the night before. Others, like Casey, were just wondering if they would ever return home alive.

The plane landed in Da Nang, Vietnam early in the afternoon, February 15, 1966. The first thing that Casey noticed was how hot it was. Stepping off the plane was like stepping into a hot furnace. The air hit your face like a blast of hot air from the exhaust of a jet engine. The air was not only hot but it smelled like ammonia or rotten soil, like the swamp gas areas of Louisiana or Southeast Texas.

A few Vietnamese were standing around the tarmac. Casey was strangely curious about them, how they looked, how they reacted to the new arrivals coming there. The Vietnamese had dark brown skin. It seemed to be rough and wrinkled from the harshness of the environment. Everyone Casey noticed was short in stature compared to their American counterpart. Their hands were formed into knotted knuckles swollen in disproportion to the size of their short arms. Their hair was a very shiny dark black, short on the men and very long and straight on the women. The clothing flowed in the breeze as they scurried about. The pajama like clothing looked to be made of black silk. The upper clothing of the women was either black or white silk. It fit loosely, yet formed to the body of the women as if to properly accent their virtues. There was no fat on their bodies. The muscles were well defined like a well tuned athlete on both the men and the women. Their eyes were slightly slanted while their lips seemed somewhat puffy. The children wore only underwear with no shirt or nothing at all. The Vietnamese seemed very disinterested in what we were doing as they continued their tasks.

Chu Lai

Casey's plane flew to Chu Lai, a coastal city in the southern part of Vietnam, in the Province of Quang Tin. Chu Lai was located in the military zone of *I Corps*, about 100 Kilometers (klicks) south of Da Nang. When the marines arrived, the transport trucks were waiting for them. Casey and his fellow marines quickly climbed aboard for the trip to the base.

Casey, along with the others boarded the troop transport trucks and started south on highway 1. Casey was very uneasy about being in a war zone with no armored escort. He was also very suspicious of everyone! It was a little surreal riding along the highway and seeing these strange looking people for the first time. Casey was mentally locked and loaded fearing the worst. He was trying to watch everyone at once but after awhile he realized that the only thing he could do was to react to whatever was going to happen, so he just continued to ride with a subdued sort of nervousness.

When Casey arrived at the Marine base, it consisted of only a few tents right on the beach area where the marines had landed just a few months before. Casey learned that he was one of the replacements for the guys that had fought the first major battle of the war involving the Marine Corps. The battle was a great victory for the U.S. The operation was named *Starlight*. During the battle, the Viet Cong 1st Regiment had ambushed an armored column of Marine amtracs. The Marines counterattacked with infantry and air support, and won the most decisive battle to that day.

Casey felt so green, so new, and so afraid when he heard the stories of how the Viet Cong had attacked the column with their hit and run tactics. The marines involved said the VC were a lot better fighters than expected. The Viet Cong attacked (hit), then they just disappeared (ran); they seemed to vanish like ghost. They had unknown underground tunnels every where! Casey immediately began to feel that this was a very determined enemy, one that was not afraid to attack a superior force, or to die for their cause. He could see that the morale of the Marine unit was very good though. The victory gave the military leaders hope that the war would be over quickly.

Casey did not sleep the entire night that first night. He felt so vulnerable in the tent, and it seemed the enemy could come at them from any direction. Casey heard every sound! The movement of what he learned later to be giant lizards in the bush, the buzzing of insects through the air, and their collisions into the tent. The insect collisions echoed with a loud exaggerated thumping noise that seemed to make him want to look on one side of the tent then the other. All the sounds of the rain forest created an uneasy fear of the unknown. Casey could not figure out if the fear of the noises was worst than the pounding of his heart. With a full adrenaline charge going, there was no relaxing on this night!

Casey felt the urgent need to relieve himself. He was so nervous and afraid to go out alone he chose to lay and suffer until his bladder was about to pop. Finally he got the courage to venture a short distance from the tent. He just knew he was going to be surprised by the enemy while he nervously stood there. The sounds of the night were greatly amplified while Casey tried to relieve himself. "What's that? Who's there? Lord help me now! Come on, Come on, finish!" It seemed as if it took a long, *long, long* time, although it was only for a few seconds. Casey stopped short of completely emptying his bladder so that he could hurry back to his rack in the imagined safety of the tent. Still, Casey felt as if he had just survived his first major battle. In a way he had, because to gain courage he *had* to face his fears head on.

Casey was so glad when morning arrived. He now had a chance to see where he was. He walked around the small compound to get familiar with the area. He found the amtracs! Casey just wanted to be assigned to his amtrac as soon as possible. Casey met up with the platoon sergeant. He was a short man with good muscular conditioning, kind of stocky, with a no nonsense attitude about him. The platoon sergeant gruffly said, "This amtrac is your responsibility. Guard it with your life!" "That's about as true of a statement I'll ever hear," mused Casey. Just to see those big beautiful machines somehow gave Casey comfort! Perhaps it was because the amtrac was his weapon for fighting for freedom. Or perhaps it was because he finally *belonged* to an outfit. Either way, the long trip was over and he was really in Vietnam.

Casey began to know who was there with him, to meet the guys that he would serve with. They were all just like him, young and spirited, trying to come to terms with there doomed situation. They were Babyboomers all, who were about to very quickly lose their innocence as the war raged on. Each one somehow knew that by the end of the war, all that they would have left was each other. The primary objective for each one of Casey's new *brotherhood* was to help each other to survive. The brotherhood is all there was!

The sound of the waves from the nearby surf added a strange peace to the area. The Marines were there to wage war, and yet the beach made them feel like they were on a vacation in some far away land, where you could surf and swim and just have a great time. Some of the guys did not even carry their weapons with them everywhere they went because the beach seduced them into thinking they were safe. Most wore no shirts while working in the hot sun and some swam in the surf for relaxation.

Casey just could not feel comfortable without his M-14 and it was always strapped on his shoulder everywhere he went. Some of the guys called him "Slingshot" because they never saw Casey without his rifle. Slingshot may have appeared foolish to some, but *all* soon learned that there was no such thing as a safe haven anywhere in Vietnam, especially the bases that invited VC attacks.

At night one of the amtracs was positioned on the beach to guard the base flank. Casey "Slingshot" Trainer stood guard there, near the surf, the sky clear as it could be, with its full compliment of sparkling stars. Some shooting star would flash across the sky. Slingshot made a wish as it whisked across the immense dark sky filled with those sparks of the unknown. It made him think of loved ones and happy times. The surf crashed against the beach and for a few brief moments the war was far away.

Slingshot often thought of Loretta and how they were there for each other as they grew up. Slingshot remembered how he had spent almost all of his free time with Loretta and how they made excuses to be together every chance they had. Slingshot thought about how they soon became an item, and how over the years they fell in love with each other. Slingshot remembered how they first made love, and how it was the beginning of a long meaningful relationship that allowed them both to grow up.

Loretta was always on Slingshot's mind in Vietnam. He wrote her every chance he got. He worried about her welfare, while rarely being concerned about his own, even though he was the one the *Viet Cong* (VC) was trying to kill everyday. Slingshot often times fantasized about their sexual relationship. It helped him to hold on to some form of sanity about what life is really like outside of warfare.

So it was that when night fell, when the surf greeted the shore with its sensuous sound, or the frogs sang a chorus in the moonlight of the rice fields, Casey "Slingshot" Trainer would think of home, and specifically of Loretta. She was his teenage sweetheart, his first love. He often wondered, if by chance, that should he survive the war, would Loretta still be there for him, or would they both be so different that they would not know each other. It would be years before Slingshot would know the answer!

Most of the days at Chu Lai were spent working on the amtracs, truly a maintenance challenge because something had to be done everyday, either to the engine, a whopping 12 cylinder gas guzzling monster, or the track and suspension system, which always needed a section repaired. When the vehicle was running, Slingshot used it to go after supplies from the nearby airfield while the marines waited for orders about their next patrol or mission.

Slingshot's next orders came after only a short stay at Chu Lai. The NVA and the Vietcong were infiltrating the south from Laos into the Quang Tri, Thua Thien, and Quang Nam Provinces, near the DMZ, and threatening the airfield located at Da Nang. Da Nang is near the coast in the Quang Nam Province north of Chu Lai. His new orders were to join an advanced party to establish a Marine Corps base just twelve miles southwest of the airfield. One hill near their area of operation was called "Hill 55." Another hill was called "Marble Mountain." The Vu Gia River flowed below the new base, and the Truong Son Mountain Range was visible from the west.

In February 1966, about the time Slingshot arrived into Vietnam, General Westmoreland, commander of US forces, told President Johnson and South Vietnam's Premier Ky, that if he were NVA General Vo Nguyen Giap, he would strike into Quang Tri to annihilate the ARVN 1ST Division to seek a quick victory. Some of the favorite entry points of the NVA were through the "A Shau Valley" from the Ho Chi Min Trail, the "Hai Van Pass" between

Quang Nam and Thua Thien, and areas around the DMZ. Marine commanders speculated that the 324B NVA Regiment forming in the area was bait to lure the Marine's limited forces away from their successful "Clear and Hold" pacification efforts near Da Nang, perhaps to bog them down indefinitely in a static *defense* of the DMZ. Although trained for assaults, General Walt's Marines were never-the-less soon deployed north by General Westmoreland. Eventually the military leaders decided to call this northern deployment, *Operation Hastings*, and later the second phase of it, *Operation Prairie*.

To complicate the already difficult situation in 1966, the Buddhist rebelled against their cruel treatment by the South Vietnamese government run by Premier Ky. An uprising began in Da Nang against the ARVN. Later it was called the *Buddhist Crisis*. They rebelled against Nguyen Cao Ky and General Nguyen Van Thieu. U.S. Marines were sent to intervene between the two combatants. The crisis ended when the ARVN, with Martine logistical support, put down the rebellion and regained control of Da Nang.

The Buddhist Crisis hastened the USMC deployment north. A large force of U.S. Marines *needed* to be positioned between the VC and Da Nang. It was felt by the commanders that the VC was sure to take advantage of the confusion and chaos in Da Nang.

With an advance party, Slingshot left Chu Lai via a C-130 Hercules transport plane in March 1966. As he lifted up from the air field, he felt like a small fly in a large soda can. The C-130 was designed to carry military cargo. It had a large open area in the rear of the fuselage. Straps hung from the ceiling and protruded from the walls. The walls seemed to vibrate the straps in a way that caused the medal buckles and hooks to sing an unnatural chorus against the fuselage walls. It was a very noisy tin can with only human cargo to claim as it flew through time and space.

Although the windows were small, the view of Vietnam from the air at low altitude seemed to put the marines in an era from three thousand years before. The powerful prop engines roared and vibrated the plane and its human cargo, while the tiny people below seemed unaware that they were there. The rice paddies covered great portions of the land, like a checker board, with it rows and rows of planted rice, with the small channels of water glistening in the sun. The rice paddy farmers had their black pajama pants legs rolled up high while they walked through the fields, like tiny ants on narrow trails. They wore a pointed conical straw hat that acted like a portable building over their head to protect them from the very intense, hot tropical sun. Over their shoulder rested a curved flat piece of wood designed to carry a basket on each end. Some were using water buffalo to plow the wet prepared rows. Others rode the water buffalo in a slow rhythm like stroll through the field. The Vietnamese's dark brown skin revealed that they were use to the sun, and that a shirt was not really needed, but it was sometimes worn anyway. The beautiful serene picture below looked like a picture from National Geographic, with no hint of it being a war zone.

Slingshot was a little uneasy as they flew over the landscape in that thin shell of a plane. He was concerned that someone down there was going to *shoot* at him, and that the plane would crash into a field, carrying him to a fiery death. After what seemed like a long flight, but really was only about 60 miles, the advance party of marines arrived at Da Nang.

Da Nang

There were only a few marines aboard the plane. The rest of the company would follow soon. As the plane approached Da Nang airfield, Slingshot could see rocket booster assisted Phantom F-4 jet fighters taking off to a mission. The roar was deafening as the booster rocket lifted the plane directly into the sky. Slingshot wondered if they were on their way to a routine patrol, or were they on their way to rescue a platoon engaged in a firefight with the enemy. Slingshot wondered if he was needed as a replacement of the wounded in the field, or was he really going to be used to help establish a base camp twelve miles southwest of Da Nang.

The plane came to a halt at the end of the runway and taxied to a building at one end of the field. After a few moments the back ramp of the plane slowly opened; it came to rest on the tarmac of the airfield runway. Slingshot was startled to see Vietnamese all around. It made him uncomfortable, although he knew that these were "supposed" to be friendly people. The moment he stepped from the plane, a hot blast of wind nearly took his breath away. Slingshot was already soaked with sweat and dust. His eyes burned from the salty dew all over his face. His heart pounded as the adrenaline gave him that rush that he was going to become very familiar with throughout the coming months. Slingshot was excited, but he was also very tense because he was entering a world unknown to him, a strange and different world from the one he had known in Baytown, Texas. The air smelled and felt strange. It was like stepping from the plane into a receiving oven where he was about to be roasted.

The airfield was bustling with activity. Trucks and planes were being loaded and unloaded. Planes were landing with a loud screech of the tires, and engines roared as the planes took to the skies. Military equipment was everywhere. The people scurried around, each having a task to do, although one just stepping off the plane could not really understand or comprehend the necessity of all the commotion.

Slingshot sat around the outside of the building waiting for a six-by truck to pick him up for the journey to the field. Some marines smoked as they waited, while others tried to catch a wink or two. Slingshot was much too excited to sleep and he did not smoke. He just kept his eyes moving, watching everyone, especially the Vietnamese. They looked so strange to him. They had that kind of a hard, mean look that comes only from hard times.

Some young woman kept digging into the trash bin and finding items that she would remove, and then she would leave with them and then return for something else. Some prisoners with blind folds had their hands tied with rope and were sitting in a squatted position.

Slingshot wondered how they could remain in what looked like a very uncomfortable position for so long. One American soldier watched over them. The wind blew the hot dust about as if some mystical force was beckoning Slingshot to take notice. Slingshot expected the prisoners to make a break for it. He wondered what he would do if they did. Should he shoot them! Slingshot had just gotten off the plane. Was it really his business? Slingshot learned very quickly that in 'Nam you just reacted to a situation so that you could live to think about it later.

Base Life

The six-by trucks finally arrived to take the advanced party of Marines to the hill that they would eventually turn into a major Marine Corps base. They traveled down Highway 1, named by the French as *Street Without Joy*. There were numerous VC attacks on those who dared to travel it. The marines traveled around the hills on dirt roads where the dust that bellowed from beneath the truck covered everything in a blanket of dirty stench. Their objective was to get to an area about twelve miles southwest of Da Nang. Highway 1 connects the port cities along the coast. Highway 1 had to remain open for supplies to reach the troops being deployed into the area. Marines were being used to keep the road open and to protect the Da Nang airfield.

Casey "Slingshot" Trainer was from the Texas east coast, where the land was flat, and the dirt was called *black gumbo*. He had never seen such *red* dirt before; the landscape was even a rusty red. Had he gone to Mars to visit the red planet or was the scene jus a bad dream? The wind took liberty with the dirt, blowing it into a red cloud as they traveled down the road. It filled Slingshot's nostrils with a mud like coating and covered his mouth to be baked in the sun into a flaky mud cake that stuck to his sweaty skin. The dust settled all over his wet, sweaty body, where it seemed to stick like glue to his clothes. His eyes protruded from the mix like some monster's hidden lumps featured in a horror movie. Some of the marines seemed real relaxed as they joked with each other. Others, like Slingshot, were real quiet, somewhat up tight about traveling through this hostile land so exposed to ambush. Vietnamese people walked along the road, some suddenly stopped, lifted their pants leg, and urinated right where they were. Slingshot began to understand the reason for the acrid smell in the air. He was very concerned about a possible ambush. The marines arrived at the base location without incident, although Slingshot had been expecting anything but a trip without incident. Casey "Slingshot" Trainer was relieved to be off the truck!

A quick overview of the area reminded Slingshot of the cattle fields back home, except there were no cattle. The ground was hard as cement from the 100 degree temperature. The bushes that covered the hills and valleys seemed to be an evergreen variety. Even the bushes had to be tough to survive the extreme heat and harsh conditions.

The marines located an area that seemed just right to pitch the large tents. The tents were the heavy green canvass type that used central wood poles to establish the anchor points in the center of the tent. Ropes were used to tie the sides to stakes. It was next to impossible to drive the steel stake poles into the soil. The sun had baked the soil into a layer of solid brick. Each strike of the stake with a 16 pound sledge hammer was like hitting solid rock. The jar from the strike of the sledge hammer radiated a shocking pain through the muscles with each blow. The sweat pored out of the marine's bodies. Several sledge hammers were broken. All of the young marines worked very hard for several days. They strung concertina wire, dug fox holes, filled sandbags, established latrines, and brought in equipment and supplies from the air field. Slingshot was finding out that a lot of a war effort is just plain hard work!

After about two weeks the rest of Slingshot's unit from the **1st Platoon, Company A, 1st Amtrac Battalion, Fleet Marine Force**

Pacific (FMFP), 3rd Marine Division, joined them. His platoon of amtracs came from Chu Lai via an LST. They landed in Da Nang and drove the amtracs to the base the advance party had started. The platoon brought along a great deal of very much needed supplies. Casey was back with his unit now.

Soon the marines built the NCO Club where they could drink beer, have barbeques, play dominoes or cards, play sports such as basketball on a makeshift court, or play tackle football without the pads. Kids must play! Gambling with dice or playing poker with the MPC paper money, the U.S. Government military certificate of pay, was the favorite pass time of many. This was serious play because hundreds of dollars changed hands at the games. The excitement relieved the reality of the war. It made the marines forget about the hell hole they were in for a brief time. It also kept them from going in sane after each mission.

A mess hall was built to feed the marines in an organized way. It was built by the marines as tents at first. The Seabees, Navy construction teams, eventually replaced the tents with plywood huts. The marines used WWII surplus medal plates, forks and knives, and their medal mess gear cups to drink Kool Aid or water. The water they drank was from the Vu Gia River so the Kool Aid helped to make it taste better. Base food was much better than the C-Rations the marines ate while in the field. It *resembled* a cooked meal back home and the mess hall food was a nice change from the field food.

To wash the mess gear, a drum was cut in half and fuel oil was piped under it to heat the water. At times the flame was so high that the marines were burnt trying to wash their gear, either from the boiling water or the raging fire.

Showers were made from jet fuel tanks or 55 gallon drums. River water was dumped by hand from 5 gallon cans into the larger tank. The showers were outside with a makeshift wall of canvas waist high surrounding the shower head. Pallets were used to stand on and the sun was used to heat the water. A shower made one feel renewed although many times Slingshot was just too exhausted to walk up the hill to take a shower. It was not uncommon for the marines to go for weeks without a shower.

The medical tent provided a place where medication could be cooled by a refrigerator driven by a diesel fueled generator. The generator provided enough electricity to provide a single light bulb in each tent as well. *Penicillin was a mainstay*! A few military bunks were provided for the wounded and the sick not fit for combat duty.

Eventually the base was staffed with Vietnamese civilians to provide laundry care, haircuts, and cleaning duties. It was a great temptation for the marines to make out with the women, *being young, dumb, and full of hormones*! Although hormone driven and greatly tempted, Slingshot stayed away from the women because he feared them as much as the enemy. Slingshot had known of marines who were infected with a strain of gonorrhea that was extremely resistant to penicillin. The venereal diseases could take months to cure which could prevent one from returning to the states until pronounced safe. Additionally the women were used as booby traps! Grenades or other explosives were used on the marine while he was in the compromising position. The VC women also placed razor blades in their vagina via a tube device to severely cut the soldier, rendering him unfit for combat duty! The experience of others was enough for Slingshot to stay away from all Vietnamese women. Many were beautiful girls that at least caused dreams, and at the most a night of homesickness. Guard duty had its moments!

Outhouses were provided by digging a deep trench and placing a crate over the hole to sit on. The Seabees provided a better structure later. The outhouses had to be cleaned and the hole sterilized with fire. For a marine to do his business was an exercise of breath holding, because the stench was so bad it literally took his breath away. Slingshot dreaded the experience. Many of the outhouses had a playboy or two there until the officials found out about them. It was their policy not to have them there but the magazines kept showing up, much to the delight of many, and the disgruntlement of others.

All the mechanical devices on base had to be maintained so it was routine to be fixing something. The generator needed to be refueled or repaired, the tents had to be restocked, the trenches refitted with ammo and the weapons cleaned. The showers had to be refilled, and so on. Everyone did their share to keep the base functional as well as making it as comfortable as it could be. After awhile the base resembled a small town as the marines strove to Americanize the area.

The base routine was much too boring for Slingshot! The only exception was going on a patrol. *Slingshot got to where he looked forward to being in the field to be part of the action of battle.* His morale was high because he knew that the Marines were sending a message to the Communist that they would stand and fight for what they believed in. Their job was to make the Communist pay for their small revolutionary wars of expansion, and they did make them pay dearly!

The Fights

First Platoon was soon deployed into the field. Their mission was to conduct various search and destroy missions and to provide armored support to the infantry in the field. Their amphibious tractors were well suited to carry troops and supplies. They could go just about anywhere on land and they had no problem crossing rivers.

The Viet Cong were particularly strong between Chu Lai and Da Nang in the Phuoc Ha Valley. First Platoon patrolled widely throughout *I Corps* and gave support to the 1st, 3rd, and 5th Marine divisions of *I Corps*. The primary objective was to protect all routes to Da Nang. This included not only the Phuoc Ha Valley, but also the heavily VC infested An Hoa Valley and Que Son Valley. Eventually the Marine firebases stretched from Da Nang's Monkey and Marble mountains, west to hill 55, and then onto An Hoa Basin's "Arizona Territory." First Platoon patrolled the Vu Gia River and the Thu Bon River with their amphibious tracked vehicles to seek out the VC supply lines, and to find the enemy villages that supported the VC. There were many villages that Slingshot never even cared to know the name of at the time. The First Platoon methodically searched them and then moved out for the next one. The VC controlled the "Truong Son Mountains" just four miles to the west of Da Nang. Those mountain ridges that loomed in the distance with an eerie presence invoked an uneasy restlessness in Slingshot. He knew the beast hungered there!

Several bases were soon to be in place near the DMZ. The

base of *Khe Sanh*, which consisted of an airfield that supplied the U.S. troops in the area, was under constant attack by the VC and NVA. The battle for Khe Sanh would become legendary by 1969. The battle for the city of *Hue*, the imperial capitol of Vietnam would reach epic proportions. The *Rock Pile*, a firebase south of Khe Sanh, received its share of assaults. The *A Shau Valley* was a main entry point for the VC coming down the Ho Chi Minh trail from Laos. The Marine patrols often ran into the NVA patrols. The Marine base near Dai Loc, about 25 klicks north of An Hoa where Slingshots unit often re-supplied for field operations, was constantly harassed by the enemy.

Over the next few days the marines prepared their vehicles for what became routine patrols. The patrols took them to villages that seemed to exist in some kind of time warp. Thatched huts, made of bamboo poles and grass roofs, the kind that have existed for thousands of years in Vietnam in the jungle mountain terrain, aligned each side of a jungle trail, as if they were totally unaffected by the advancement of modern civilization. Pigs either roamed the village at will, or gathered in a pin made of bamboo poles. Chickens fluttered their wings to escape the patrol advance. The pigs squealed as if they were warning the villagers to beware! Slingshot was surprised to find many villages without defense.

The marines drove their Amtracs through the village, stopping only long enough for the infantry to dismount. The infantry then proceeded to search the village for any evidence of VC activity, while the amtracs formed a perimeter outside of the village. All Vietnamese that approached the perimeter had to be stopped before they were allowed to enter the village.

Other times the amtrac crew did a walking patrol without

their amtracs. Slingshot entered each hut, knowing he was very vulnerable himself. Scared but determined, Slingshot searched the rooms for weapons of war, and he searched each villager for any evidence of supporting the VC. Slingshot was more concerned about booby traps than actual VC contact.

The most obvious thing he noticed as he approached a village was that there were very few young men around. The village usually had a few old women, and maybe a few very young kids who huddled close to the elderly. At first Slingshot was looking for a fight, but he soon realized that those he wanted to fight had disappeared from the face of the earth. He learned that anyone that even could be suspected of being a VC had gone literally under ground. Booby traps became the terror of such a search! The enemy had left the area, but their ability to harm was under every basket, door entry, or path in the form of booby traps, or handmade bombs. In 1966 in Vietnam, at least 1000 deaths per year resulted from VC booby traps alone!

Sometimes the platoon went out to the field of operations to find the villagers to provide humanitarian aid, part of the Marines overall strategy of *Pacification*. Troops that occupied and provided aid to the villagers, were there to disallow VC control of the villages. The most common way of providing aid was to provide the Vietnamese transport via the amtracs to a hospital tent that had been hastily provided in the field. The villagers were gathered up from various villages, transported to the hospital tent, treated for a variety of ailments, fed, clothed, and then returned to their homes. *This was an attempt to win the heart and minds of the common folks.* The leaders of the military named one such operation *County Fair*. It is doubtful that these operations did what they were intended to do. The VC recruitments remained high throughout the war in spite of every effort to stop it. Slingshot doubted that the villagers felt very comfortable about being forced by gunpoint to leave their villages, regardless of what the Marines true intent was.

One of First Platoon's early assignments involved guarding a South Vietnam village. The amtrac crew became an infantry platoon for this duty. In other words, they dismounted their amtracs and boarded six-by trucks for their journey down Highway 1. They started on their journey late in the afternoon. About two-thirds of the way to their final destination, they decided to stay with another outfit that had a field base near Highway 1. It was getting dark as First Platoon approached the compound. The compound consisted of tents that looked as if they had been hastily built. About a 3 foot sandbag wall surrounded the compound. Beyond was a field full of brush.

To sleep for the night, the platoon was given a tent that contained no bunks. The tent did have a plywood floor that resembled a small scale roller coaster platform. In other words, the floor was very uneven. The entire First Platoon, about thirty-nine Marines, was crowded into the small tent. There was not any space in the whole tent that was not occupied. Everyone laid beside each other in kind of awkward positions. Backpacks were used as pillows and backrests. Rifles were lying every which way, but remained at the marine's side for quick access.

Slingshot felt very uneasy in this situation. It was that *one grenade will get you all complex*! The wall outside the tent seemed to be all there was between the platoon and certain enemy destruction. With an uneasy feeling, and his senses on high alert, Slingshot found it very difficult to sleep. He was crunched up between the other marines next to him with hardly room enough to turn over from side to side. To make matters worse, a low spot in the floor collected rain leaking from the top of the tent that kept him wet no matter how he moved.

Suddenly an explosion occurred in the tent next to his. Two marines scrambled to the outside to determine the source. "Incoming" was hollered loudly! Everyone thought they were under attack, so they quickly scrambled to the sandbag wall. Then word came back that a marine in the next tent had accidentally discharged his own grenade, and that he and two others were badly injured. The marines never found out if it was really an "accident" or a deliberant "Fragging" of an officer. After the initial terror, they resumed their uneasy rest while the dust-off helicopter arrived for medical evacuation of the wounded to a field hospital near Da Nang.

With virtually no sleep during the night, Slingshot was delighted when the blessed morning arrived. He had survived another dreadful night! He washed and shaved his face with the water from his canteen. He ate some WWII dated C-Rations. The order came down to board the trucks to continue the journey to the outlying village. First Platoon boarded the trucks and arrived near the village without incident.

After dismounting the trucks, First Platoon walked in column formation to the village. Slingshot was always alert when he approached what to him was an unknown village. Even though it was supposed to be a *friendly* village, he did not trust any Vietnamese with his life, not even the ones that were supposed to be the ones that were helping. In his mind, anyone of them was a VC until proven other wise.

The village was located about 25 klicks southwest of the port city of Hoi An. Slingshot didn't remember the exact name of the village. It was a large village complex south of the *Thu Bon River* just west of Highway 1. Someone said it was the Village of Que Son. The Annam Cordillera Mountain Range could be seen in the distance covered by a shroud of early morning mist that increased the intrigue. The village had several buildings that were made of masonry material full of rifle shot, holes from previous fire fights. Many of the thatched huts so common in the country side of Vietnam stood there just like they had been for a thousand years. Now the perimeter was surrounded by bunkers, made from sand bags, rice paddy mud, and straw. The bunkers faced open fields, each about one hundred yards from the tree line of the jungle. For some reason, high command valued the strategic location of the village, probably to ensure that Highway 1 remained open as a supply route. The word was that First Platoon was deployed to protect the village for just one night until another unit would come and occupy the village the next day. Intelligence believed that there was a high risk of a VC attack during the night. The VC was known to be particularly active in the nearby *Que Son Valley*.

Slingshot helped man a bunker that was farthest from the village. There were three marines in the bunker. They were more experienced than Slingshot and were far less concerned. Slingshot was very concerned, to the point of being a little jittery. A pending attack was supposed to be the reason they were so quickly deployed, not as an armored tracked vehicle platoon, but as an infantry platoon.

When night fell, the moon was not very bright. The frogs started their nightly chorus, while the insects joined in with their harmony. The field that was directly in front of the bunkers was littered with brush and small trees. Although Slingshot had not slept the night before, he could not sleep this night either, even if he wanted to. His senses were on overdrive! Every sound and every shadow cast by the dimly lit night-time sky was etched in Slingshot's memory as the hours passed by. The more nervous he got, the more prepared he tried to become. Slingshot checked his rifle. Was it properly loaded? He checked his additional ammo. Was it where he could easily get to it? "If they shoot a rocket into the bunker, will I even have a chance to use my weapon?" Casey nervously imagined. "What if they use mortars or grenades on us? Where are *my* grenades? Do we have enough flares? What about my bayonet?" Slingshot mounted his bayonet to the end of his M-14 rifle as the night progressed to the likely time of the attack. The others joked with him as they could sense his nervousness. Slingshot actually jumped so quickly when one of his mates hollered, that he almost stuck himself with his own bayonet! They kept Slingshot tense by saying such things as: "I wonder when they are going to attack? What's that? Did you see that? Over there, I saw something?" A dog was slowly crossing their line of fire. At first they did not know what it was. It looked like a black shadow inching along. Slingshot started to shoot it, because he was not sure at first what it was. When he realized it was a dog, he actually was a little disappointed. He thought the battle was about to start, and by now he was so tense he just wanted to get it over!

Night passed without any enemy probing of the lines. When daylight arrived, the villagers visited the bunker. Some merchants had arrived trying to sell their wares. The Vietnamese parents chanted in their native tongue. Slingshot could not understand what they were saying, but their body language indicated that they wanted him to buy their children some clothes. They energetically held up the individual pieces of clothing to show him what they were.

Every piece of clothing was made of a light material, mostly all white or all black, and designed for practical use versus style. The children ran around laughing and giggling as they played. A grown woman waved the clothing in front of Slingshot. She appeared to him to be about 40 years old, although everyone looked older than their years in Vietnam. She had long black hair. Her body was thin but well toned. Her lips were full like the typical Vietnamese. Her face looked tanned with high cheek bones lifting her strong chin. One child ran up to Slingshot, a young girl of about six years old, but small in size. Slingshot reached down to pick her up. She accepted his kindness, so he lifted her and set her into the curve of his arm. Someone took a picture of him as he talked to the group. He knew they did not understand his language, but he attempted to express his concern for their well being. Slingshot did not buy anything, although he was temped to give aid. He just was not sure that the merchants were legitimate. He thought that maybe they were trying to put something over on him. Slingshot suspected that the older women were relatives of the younger women and that the clothes already belonged to them. He suspected they just wanted money. At any rate he showed warmth and kindness to the best of his suspicious self. The Vietnamese offered him a coke. Slingshot accepted the coke and acted like he was going to drink it. He never did drink any as he talked. He had been told by the veterans that the VC was known to have placed glass in cokes or some other substance to poison Americans. Slingshot had decided to never drink or eat anything in Vietnam that was not provided by Marine Corps logistics. Incidentally, the marines were also told not to have sex with Vietnamese woman because drugs were ineffective against the strong disease strains. Casey never cared to take the chance.

  The ARVN, *Army of the Republic of Vietnam*, troops arrived to relieve First Platoon. First Platoon had stayed in their bunkers until dawn. The WWII C-Rations were provided for breakfast. The date on Slingshot's box was 1942. This was 1966! The C-Rats tasted quite stale, especially the small green canned bread. After Slingshot ate, he wandered into the village with the others, where he explored some of the buildings, and waited for the trucks to arrive to take them back to the main base. After a while, the word was passed that the trucks were not coming. First Platoon prepared to walk back.

Orders were given to form up into a column in spread formation. The column of marines started their journey. It was a least 100 degrees. Slingshot's body was drenched with sweat and dirt, their odor was a result of not bathing for two or three days. The equipment Slingshot had, weighed at least fifty pounds and the noise it made as he walked somehow gave noticed that he was not well prepared to carry it a long way. The platoon had walked several miles along Highway 1 when the heat started to have its eventual drain on the men. Some of the guys started bunching up as a result of the fatigue. One marine private in front of Slingshot kept falling behind the marine in front of him, so Slingshot kept urging him to step it up. He got so upset with Slingshot after awhile that he turned around and threatened him with his M-14. Slingshot told him to just keep up, and he would shut up! It took most of the afternoon to walk back to the main base. The base was on a hill that had to be climbed before First Platoon reached the defense wire. Just as they worked their way through their own defense wires, and cleared it at the top of the hill, the same private that had had trouble keeping up directly in front of Slingshot, reached toward his belt as if he was struggling to grab a grenade.

The platoon sergeant grabbed at the private, a struggle

ensued, and the sergeant hollered, "grenade!" Everyone scattered. Slingshot ran so fast he forgot to count the seconds it took for a grenade to explode. When he thought the time was up, he hit the ground while unconsciously throwing his rifle down to cover his head with both hands. Slingshot reasoned that if he was not far enough away, the shrapnel would hit him in the back if he did not hit the ground. He wondered if he had run far enough to be out of range. Others had run far past him! "Have I run far enough? Am I too close? Am I about to die from this stupid private?"

    Slingshot expected the shrapnel to hit his feet at any moment. He rotated his ankles to flatten his feet to the ground. "My soles will catch some of the shrapnel, but my feet will still be hurt," Slingshot feared. His back muscles quivered from the strain of tightening his skin, as if the harder he strained, the better it would shield him from the coming harm. Slingshot tried to cover his entire head and neck with his hands, moving them first to one spot, then to the other. He waited, his breath gone, his heart pounding, his adrenaline sending him into that unexplained shock that numbs one's mind and body when it faces eminent danger. The sergeant wrestled the private until the grenade fell to the ground. Slingshot could *feel* the shrapnel about to hit his feet as he tensed his muscles even more! The only shrapnel Slingshot *truly* felt was the fallout of his self induced fear. With the private disarmed, the danger had passed. Still shaking, Slingshot slowly picked himself up when the all clear was sounded. The other marines that had run past Slingshot were still over the ridge of the hill. Standing like some monuments of triumph his fellow marines peered down from the ridge at the shaking marines, then they slowly began to make their way back down the hill. The platoon had finished the mission with a moment of sheer terror and they were glad to just be alive for one more day.

The next day the order was given for the platoon to fall out! "First squad, prepare for night patrol," commanded the platoon sergeant! Slingshot fell out with his M-14, flak jacket, helmet, water, and ammo. Tired and dirty from working all day it would be a long night! The marines had to protect their new base by having patrols every night. They left the base as a patrol, and then they set up an ambush for the enemy patrol. At times they left just before dark.

While passing by a rice paddy, Slingshot noticed three kids were leading a large water buffalo through the rice paddy. He watched them closely because he did not trust anyone in Vietnam. When he had gotten within a few feet of the kids, the water buffalo quickly began snorting its nose and shaking its head while pawing the ground with its feet. It charged forward about four or five feet. Slingshot swung his M-14 around and clicked the safety off all in the same motion. The kids immediately jumped on the water buffalo's neck screaming something in a high pitch tone that Slingshot guessed meant don't shoot. The water buffalo shook its head, but the kids forced its nose toward the ground. The water buffalo then came to a sudden stop while the kids continued their desperate chatter. Slingshot watched it all as he passed within about 15 yards of the animal. He maintained the ready to blow it away if it resumed its charge. The kids struggled to save the water buffalo from being shot as the column slowly passed. Slingshot kept his eye on the commotion looking over his shoulder several times as he walked away.

On patrol the marines had to be aware of animals, snakes, insects, civilians, terrain changes, smells, sounds, feelings, instinctual signs, booby traps, noise, and quietness from insects, birds flying, and each other, as well as the enemy. Sometimes the enemy patrol on the other side of the hill was spotted as they were trying to find an ambush position. The leaders of the squad disagreed on what to do next. Should the marines attack, wait, call for support, or move out.

Slingshot carried the radio! It was a large square radio mounted on a backpack that required quite an effort to hump through the bush. Slingshot was needed near the squad leader when he carried the radio. It allowed him to immediately know what decisions were being made by headquarters. He liked that. Headquarters was informed of the VC activity spotted across the valley on the ridge of the hill.

The night patrols were especially spooky. Every sound could be heard from the insects. The frogs echoed their chorus as if they were croaking in harmony. Every clank from the equipment, the slush from the water in the canteens, the slap of a rifle sling in the breeze, could be heard unless a big effort was made to reader them silent. Even the marine's dog tags were silenced with rubber covers. Slingshot's senses were honed to perfection as he listened for any sign of the enemy that he hunted. No talking, sneezing, coughing, or slapping of misquotes was allowed. Even the slightest noise could give their position away. That meant the difference between living and dying that night! So the marines stalked the enemy with the stealthiest of the wild animals they had become.

This night was especially dark and still. After the squad of marines had walked several miles around the base perimeter the patrol set up in an ambush position. No enemy activity could be detected in the valley area except for the VC patrol spotted earlier. After a couple of hours had passed, the word was passed to move to another position. Slingshot was the next to last guy in the formation. When they moved out, Slingshot noticed that the last man had disappeared from behind him. Slingshot was very nervous, and yes even scared to see the others in the squad moving away without notice. He passed the word for the patrol to stop its advance because they were missing one man. They had moved about a hundred yards from their ambush site. It was pitch black and Slingshot could not see very far into the distance. They knelt into their holding position for what seemed like an eternity hoping to see their missing man appear. When he did not appear Slingshot decided to back track to their previous position to see if he could find him. The squad held its position while he began to look for the missing marine.

    Slingshot felt like he stuck out like a sore thumb because he was all alone, but he knew how to advance through the bush quietly. He probed each bush cautiously, expecting to be attacked any moment. Suddenly, he spotted a shadowy figure in a bush just across the valley field. Is it a VC, or is it the missing squad member? He had already removed his safety from his rifle that allowed him to fire it instantly. He could not see the other squad members although he knew they were up ahead waiting for him. He now took up all the slack in the trigger mechanism of his M-14 rifle to be able to fire it even if he was hit! He slowly worked his way toward the shadowy figure without giving away his position. It was so dark he could not see the uniform characteristics of the shadowy figure. He got close enough to see a slumped figure of a man, his face covered by the brush, nestled deep within the bush. Was he the missing man or the first of many VC waiting in the bush? It was Slingshot's job at that moment to find out! He could see he had the element of surprise as he pointed his rifle very quietly within inches of his throat! He was trying to watch the man and at the same time watch everything around him. He could hear his heart pounding so hard and loud that he thought its very sound and movement was going to give his position away. "Was the man dead? Am I next? Is it our guy or the enemy?" The thoughts ran wild in Slingshot's mind. He felt that at any moment the first of many VC AK-47 rounds was going to strike his spine, and that he would be cut in half by enemy fire!

Slingshot's adrenaline rush had forced his mind and body into a cold numbness. He took his rifle and placed it ever so gently under the chin of the man, took all free play out of the trigger, and was about to blow his head off! Still coiled like a Texas rattle snake to strike, Slingshot whispered softly, "Hey!" The man did not move or respond! "I must shoot him now, or he will kill me," Slingshot thought, as his body became tense and the cold sweat trickled down his face! A sense of urgency seemed to overwhelm him! Time stood still as a few seconds became an eternity. Still tense he said, "Hey, Hey man!" No answer!

The startled man then looked up to see Slingshot's M-14 pointed within an inch of his mouth! Slingshot then recognized him to be the missing squad man! Was he injured? He was relieved to find that he had not been killed or wounded but had fallen asleep from battle fatigue! Slingshot said very little, just motioned for him to move out by pointing his rifle in the direction he had to go. They were all exhausted from lack of sleep because they fought for days both day and night. Slingshot understood because he was a walking zombie himself. He was running on the adrenaline of the moment. It seemed to drug him without mercy.

Slingshot slowly led the marine back to where the squad was waiting and once again they continued their hunt. It had been a typical scary night, although on this night not a single shot had been fired, yet. In the distance they heard the ever present sounds of the war as flares shot up into the night sky. The crack of gunfire echoed through the air, reminding them that *Charley* was awake and well. They never knew what to expect from Charley, but they were ready to expect anything! The beast was out there and Slingshot knew it!

The squad was crossing a rice paddy to gain position, when they received incoming fire. Slingshot was caught in the open as the firefight began. He could see the bullets hitting, first to his left. He moved to the right, then the bullets were hitting to his right, so Slingshot moved to the left. The bullets followed to the left! Back and forth he jumped for what seemed like an eternity, although it lasted for only a few seconds. His adrenaline was in complete control now as he dodged the incoming bullets, bullets that were sent by the enemy with the sole intent of ending his life. Bullets that were hitting all around him as he witnessed their evil intent. He was now very numb from his aerobic dance for life. The incoming rounds stopped for a brief moment, probably so the enemy could reload. He now had no idea which way to go, because the bullets were not hitting around him to guide his direction. *Slingshot seemed to freeze for a moment in an upright position!* Was he standing there in defiance waiting for the enemy to fire at him again so he could locate his position, or was he just scared stiff for the moment? He wondered why he had not been hit, fully *expecting* in this brief moment to be hit! He literally *mentally felt* a bullet hit his chest! He became weak in the knees and he could not move. "It'll be over quickly," he thought. "I'm about to collapse from the impact of a burst of bullets at any second!" He was not being fired upon during this trance like state. He was just standing there in the open unable to move! He believed that maybe the enemy could not see him in the dark if he just did not move. When he was dodging the bullets just moments before, the enemy had a target they could see as he moved back and forth. Why he was not hit at this moment of fear induced indecision he'll never know. Corporal Hasty shouted, "Get down!" He jumped up and grabbed at Slingshot's shoulder to bring him down. It was all it took for Slingshot to snap out of his fear induced shock. He hit the ground to his right and he fell behind a rice paddy dike. Immediately the incoming began again. The movement had revealed his location. The bullets were hitting just inches in front of him tracking left and right. As the rounds hit within inches of his face, he calmly, as if in a *methodically controlled trance*, very slowly, like it was all a dream, located the mussel flashes of the incoming rounds. The incoming rounds seemed to be zeroed in on him alone, as he began to fight back!

    Slingshot knew that everyone else was under fire at the same time, but that somehow did not change the focus of fear he felt for himself. He could see the other members of the squad firing their weapons but he could not fully hear the commotion. In his trance, he waited for the distance flashes to erupt again. The black night covered the enemy in its protective wrapping of shadows and brush. The enemy was well concealed. Slingshot took very deliberate aim as he watched exactly where the flashes were, and he timed his shots, first on one flash, then on another. Each time he did this the opposing fire stopped. Everyone else seemed to be firing randomly. Slingshot was shooting from a trance like state, one round at a time. When his rifle jammed, he calmly unjammed it, and fired again, one round at a time, one flash at a time.

    When the firefight stopped, Slingshot expected the squad to go see what was left of the enemy, but to his surprise the order was given to return to the base. They had been lucky! No one had been hit. To pursue into the night would only invite the casualties they had narrowly escaped. The firefight had alerted the base. Therefore their mission as a patrol had accomplished its goal. They returned to the base without further incident and braced themselves for debriefing.

The confused state of mind Slingshot experienced that night was the same fear experienced by WWI soldiers. It was called *Shell Shock*. In WWII the fear for life induced by the *traumatic* circumstances was termed *Battle Fatigue*. After Vietnam the accumulated abnormal emotional effects of the war would be termed *PTSD or Post Traumatic Stress Disorder*. *Slingshot began to believe that he was going to die in the rice paddies of Vietnam, if not today, tomorrow, if not tomorrow, some other day soon!*

Ironically he began to also believe that God had provided him with a guardian angel that night and that just maybe, just maybe, he *could* survive with His help. "Life or death situations would be the will of God," he figured. "Was my destiny, my purpose for life to die or to live?" The question could not be answered then of course, so it was easier for him to accept death as a constant companion. *Living in constant fear of death gave Slingshot many emotional problems after the war.* His abnormal PTSD behavior became normal behavior for him! He did not understand the non-inflicted personalities of civilians, and civilians did not understand his PTSD inflicted behavior. He began to emotionally isolate himself from his marine companions as the war continued, and he continued to act distant later to civilians.

The war continued around the main base as usual. Life around the main base consisted of many routine tasks; digging fox holes, cleaning outhouses, performing mechanical repairs, and building showers from old 55 gallon drums, or damaged airplane fuel tanks. Slingshot disliked being at the main base.

To gather water, a detail would be assigned to go to the river for the water. Slingshot felt very uncomfortable when he was required to do this, but someone needed to get the water. They gathered oil and other parts for their LVT'S, washed clothes, picked up cigarette buts, filled sand bags, laid and repaired constantine wire, set up claymore mines, built and maintained bunkers, and all the while the Marines were dodging sniper rounds, mortars, or rockets.

Many times the routine around the base was interrupted to pursue the snipers. Slingshot checked the peasant's ID's many times. The VC disguised themselves as peasants there to work, to pick up trash, or to cut the grass. Slingshot was sure their real mission was to evaluate the Marine defenses for future attacks. The night and day patrols were always necessary to control VC intrusion.

Cleaning machine guns and rifles, and making trips to the Da Nang Airfield to gather supplies provided additional responsibilities. Several of the marines climbed into the back of a six-by to make the trip from the base to Da Nang via highway 1. Highway 1 was the main coastal route that traveled from South Vietnam to North Vietnam. It was designated as a secure supply route, but the route could be attacked by the VC anytime they chose to. Slingshot was constantly on alert when he traveled anywhere in Vietnam. His weapons were always clean and ready for action, especially on Highway 1!

One task that was hated by all was to be on *mess duty* which basically meant that you washed pots and pans. During one of the morning musters, Slingshot was ordered to be on mess duty from July 30 to August 30. He hated being assigned on such a task because he felt that his duty required him to be with his unit out in the field. He vehemently protested the assignment but to no avail. It was his turn for the detail and there was nothing he could do about it. Each day he washed pots and pans for the cooks and each day he hated every minute of it.

Slingshot should have realized that the base was not a safe haven free from attack! That realization became clear just two weeks after being stationed there!

The Marine main base grew to include tanks, ontos, and artillery. Each day the firebase became stronger. The stronger the firebase became, the more it was capable of giving the troops in the field support. They were the first line of defense for the airfield in Da Nang. The base also became a prime VC target!

Within their firebase lay a number of graves that the Vietnamese claimed should be removed. To Slingshot's astonishment, the brass allowed a detail of Vietnamese men to come into the base to dig up the graves for removal of the bodies to a different location somewhere outside of the base. The Vietnamese customarily performed a religious act of exhuming and reburying the bodies of dead relatives. The family would locate the bones, wash them, and rebury them. This custom was called *Cai Tang*. As the men worked, they dug the holes, and they constantly talked in Vietnamese. They looked like VC to Casey. He did not trust them. He had to walk by the field of dug out graves everyday to get to his sleeping quarters. He always approached them with caution.

One day Slingshot walked over to the grave site where some men were, to observe what they were doing. They had a cloth sack that they were using, to place the bones of the dead into. One man handed Slingshot a bone from the grave as if to assure him that all they were doing was digging to remove the bones. Slingshot kept one eye on the men, while he examined the bone from the grave he held in his hand. The Vietnamese man appeared agitated and spoke in a way that convinced Slingshot he was disliked by him. Another Vietnamese man shook his fist at Slingshot as he walked away. Slingshot could not help but to believe that the men were VC. He felt they were there to map the base, and to observe the daily routines so their snipers and attack squads could attack with precision. Slingshot thought the brass was crazy to allow them to be on base.

On August 15, 1966 while on *Operation County Fair* a friend of Slingshot's was *wasted* while handing out candy. He was shot in the back by a woman! The marines were beginning to believe that to die in Vietnam was a *wasted* effort. When someone was killed, they were *wasted*! U.S. policies would not allow the Marines to capture North Vietnam to end the fighting.

Another marine was lost when he wondered a short distance from the unit to take a bowel movement. The VC grabbed him, tortured him for information, and then shot him twelve times. His mutilated body was found stripped naked in a grass hut.

Another friend of Slingshot's from Colorado was killed when he was *fragged* over a whore. Two other marines were lost during a firefight. Slingshot was beginning to hate *Charley (VC)* over the frustration of the lost men. He wanted vengeance! He could not wait to get back in the field.

It was about 2:00 AM on August 16, 1966. Slingshot was asleep in his bunk when all hell broke lose. The first rounds came whistling in. Mortars were flying into the base camp thick as flies. The safe secure area, the area that was out of harms way, was under attack! Slingshot jumped out of the sleeping rack, grabbed his trousers and quickly put them on, and then he jumped into his boots without putting on his socks or tying the boot strings. In a dream like daze he grabbed his rifle and his cartridge belt, and flung on a flack jacket after scrambling for it in the dark.

The dark night was lit up only by the flashes of light caused by the terror of the explosions that rained down on the marines. As the shadows danced from the momentary flickers of the light, Slingshot ran zig zagging out of the sleeping hut, jumped the stairs that led out of the hut, and ran down the small hill that led past the company office. Everyone was running around in a confused manner, some to their assigned fox holes that surrounded the sleeping huts, and others to the amtracs neatly parked in a roll on top of the hill. *Slingshot ran across an open field toward a ditch that he knew would provide cover.* Mortars were dropping all around. The VC knew precisely where to attack! The mortars hit the sleeping area Slingshot had just ran from, and they chased him as he dove into the ditch. Not three seconds after Slingshot hit the ditch, a mortar round hit dead center into the path he had taken! The explosive round hit only about ten yards from where Slingshot was, spraying gravel, shrapnel, and dirt into his hole as he quickly covered his head with his hands and arms. "That was much too close for comfort," screamed Slingshot! Mortars were dropping everywhere into the company area. Three seconds slower and Slingshot would not be alive at all! He had run faster than was possible, like he was being *pushed* by an unknown force. *Guardian angels work that way!* Slingshot *was* spared at that moment to become what he was meant to be, although he wasn't even aware of that then.

When Slingshot dove into the ditch, he landed on two cooks who had also found refuge there. He then realized that there was machine gun and rifle fire coming from the perimeter where his amtrac was parked. He could hear the firefight taking place on the hill. Slingshot told the two guys with him that the VC was attacking the base from the hill where they had the fuel depot. "We must get over there," Slingshot screamed! "We're not going anywhere," they hollered. "I'm going up on that hill in the direction of the firefight," Slingshot yelled over the loud explosions. After he got his boots tied, Slingshot got out of the ditch, and he started running toward the fight to counterattack the VC. His guardian angels regrouped.

Slingshot ran to the amtracs where all the explosions and shots were coming from. Machine gun fire seemed everywhere and his amtrac was right in the middle of the action. He could see shadowy figures running everywhere! Under the cover and confusion of the mortar attack, the VC had breached the wire and they were now inside the firebase perimeter. Slingshot felt he had to reach his amtrac to remove it from the danger zone.

Bullets were flying everywhere and Slingshot was very scared, too scared to be afraid, too numb to feel anything. He climbed to the top of his amtrac in a very low stoop and opened the entrance hatch. The inside was dark, but from the light of the night flares that were being fired into the sky, he could see the inside was a mess. He noticed that the escape hatch located on the side of the vehicle was blown off. All he could see was that it was gone! Was the VC inside the vehicle? Had they popped the hatch from the inside? In between the light of the flares he could see that the tool box was opened and overturned, with the tools spread all over the deck. When the flares went out, it was pitch black inside the amtrac. If the VC was there, and Slingshot was to jump inside, he would be killed instantly! Slingshot was scared, but he was also determined to move his amtrac from the attack zone and into a counterattack position.

The VC had used Chinese made RPG 7 Rockets and

mortars to knock out the main perimeter bunker, post #5, silencing the machine gun. Two marines were dead that had defended the position. During the time that Post #5 was pinned down, the VC blew a hole in the barbed wire and came right through the wire past the bunker. Three marines were wounded and another marine was scared stiff, but he was unharmed. More marines got into the bunker and got the machine gun going. Eight VC were killed.

Tanks and ontos were parked on a hill next to the amtracs. They were hit hard also. A VC mortar hit dead center on the major's tent, killing him instantly. Six other marines were wounded.

Slingshot worked his way to his amtrac, LVT-12. He could see that the VC had blown up the supply tent. Its blaze lit up the area. The VC had also killed the occupants of the bunkers on the perimeter, and had attacked all the amtracs in an attempt to destroy them, by throwing satchel charges under them. They had attempted to blow up the fuel depot, but their dead bodies were proof that they had failed. They had attempted to kill as many marines as they could with the mortars and rockets, primarily to cause confusion. As the mortars landed on their mark, the VC poured into the base. One VC ran toward Slingshot's amtrac to throw his satchel charge under it. When he saw Slingshot running toward the fight, the VC turned and ran from Slingshot's amtrac toward the perimeter wire. Slingshot gave chase. He raised his rifle to shoot the VC as he ran through the wire toward the brush just outside of the perimeter. The VC fell as two other marines also fired at him. Slingshot saw the VC hit the ground hard. The VC curled up into the fetal position as Slingshot watched him die!

Slingshot remembered what the recruit sergeant had asked that first day he picked Slingshot up to take him to the airport. He asked, "How would you like to watch someone die?" Slingshot remembered how revoking that sounded then. Suddenly he knew for what the crazy gunnery sergeant was trying to prepare him! Slingshot had just watched someone curl up and die from wounds he helped to inflict! Slingshot knew that in this crazy war the dead VC would not be the last to die. He had to deal with it, like it or not. To deal with it however, had to wait until another time because there just was not enough time to *comprehend* the present horror; no time to digest all the life threatening events. With conflicting emotions, Slingshot had no choice but to just continue on. War is like that!

    While the fight continued, Slingshot decided to move his amtrac off line into a position on the perimeter to defend the base. He had to enter the amtrac to start it! He pulled out his knife. Scared, but determined, he opened the steel hatch. It was pitch black inside the amtrac. He jumped into the darkness of the opening that led to the inside of his amtrac controls. As his feet hit the deck in total darkness he swung in a 360 degree circle to slash or engage any VC that might be waiting for him inside. It was very, very dark in the cold steel machine, but he knew where the controls were. In the blinding dark he felt his way along the wall until he reached the control center. Slingshot felt for the switches that controlled the lights. While the firefight continued outside, his fingers recognized the proper switch. *Slingshot's hands were sweating from the bite of the adrenaline rush that now drove his movements.* It felt like he was once again in a trance and everything was happening in slow motion. He flipped the light switch and the controls came into view. He found the starter switch quickly. He immediately cut the lights off and pressed the starter switch. The massive engine roared to life. Slingshot threw the transmission into reverse and backed away from the fire that was burning directly in front of his position. He slammed the transmission into forward gear and after a hard right turn, the vehicle surged forward through the explosions. He headed for the perimeter wire to place his vehicle between the perimeter wire and the fuel depot. Once he was in position to defend the fuel depot from any attack from outside of the perimeter, he tried to find the tripod of the machine gun to set it up on top of the amtrac. Everything was so chaotic he had trouble finding everything necessary to assemble the machine gun. The firefight continued all around with flares popping every few seconds. Helicopter gun ships arrived with their support. A couple of amtracs roared to the outside of the perimeter to pursue the VC. Firefights erupted all around the base and the sound of war could be heard throughout the area. The bunker next to Slingshot cut down two VC that were running for the opening in the barbed wire. One caught a burst in the face and the other was hit in the groin area. Another VC trying to reach the precious fuel depot with a satchel charge was cut down by another bunker position. Other VC were killed outside of the perimeter and their bodies were dragged away by their fleeing comrades.

Slingshot found the parts and the ammo needed and he mounted the machine gun on top of the turret. From behind the sandbags stacked there for such firefights, Slingshot opened up with the machine gun. He could only see shadows as he fired. He stopped firing after he could not see anyone moving. Fully expecting a second wave of the enemy to attack, he waited to almost daylight before he realized the attack was over, and that no second attack was coming. He was a little disappointed that they did not attack again because he was itching to cut loose on them with the machine gun. As dawn arrived, all was quite. With the night over, exhausted from the fight, Slingshot decided to leave the battlefield to return to the mess hall to start the new day. The body count found was twenty-two enemy dead.

On August 31, 1966 Slingshot received his Purple Heart medal for the wounds he received on the battlefield back in June. The commanding officer called a company formation for the ceremony. Slingshot, along with several other Marines, formally received their medals. He was honored to receive the oldest award offered by the U.S. military. He stuck out his chest as the colonel pinned it on his shirt, and then he shook his hand. It was a solemn affair, but he was proud to be among the heroes. Slingshot had now been in Vietnam for six months. It seemed like a long time ago since he was just Casey from East Texas.

Slingshot was removed from mess duty. His new orders were to help complete the repairs on the disabled amtracs at the firebase. Five of the platoons ten amtracs were dead lined because of the raid. Slingshot was to help complete the repairs, and then go back into the field for operations at 1/1 (1st Battalion/1st Marine Division).

He began to work on the amtracs that needed the repair shortly after the night the firebase had been attacked. He now knew that the VC controlled the country, and that no place was safe from attack. Since the VC had failed to destroy the fuel supply, he expected another attack soon. Slingshot was jumpy as hell! He jumped at every noise he heard. He soon received some other bad news!

While on patrol September 9, 1966 his platoon was ambushed during a night operation. The amtrac #17 that he would have been driving had he not been on base duty, struck a mine. It was the second amtrac lost in one week. The fuel cells exploded causing the whole thing to burst into flames. His crew chief fell into the flames, probably unconscious, and was being consumed by the flames. While the confusion raged, the VC attacked the helpless crew and began to shoot them down. One member of the platoon ran over to pull the flame engulfed crew chief from the rubble, and while under fire from the enemy, dragged the wounded marine into the rice paddy water to douse the flames. The marines returned fire, and the enemy, having accomplished its goal, broke off contact, and fled into the night. Slingshot's crew chief, L/Cpl Brown died later that day! He was the closest friend Slingshot had in the whole platoon. Pvt Dan, Sgt Laverne, and Pvt Ben also suffered several burns.

When he heard of the battle, of what had happened, Slingshot was devastated. The man that had taken him under his wing when he first arrived in Vietnam, the man that had taught him to drive in the field, the man he had driven for on previous patrols, was dead! Slingshot felt at the time that he should have been driving that night, that somehow it was his fault because he was left behind at the base! Why? At least one enraged sergeant thought Slingshot should be the one to identify the charred remains. Slingshot said that he would do so, but that he did not volunteer for base duty. In fact, he explained that he had protested vehemently to the platoon leaders about the assignment, right up to headquarters.

Slingshot was later told that he would be on mess duty for only a short while, because he was needed to refit two amtracs at the base. They needed mechanical repairs to the engines. It was important to get the armored vehicles back into the field to support the search and destroy missions. The first sergeant told the platoon sergeant that he would identify the crew chief and that Slingshot did not need to be the one to do that.

Slingshot felt really confused about the events. He discovered what *guilt* felt like! It was a gnawing feeling believing that his friend's death was somehow *his* fought. He felt he should have been there for him. "Was it fate that I was spared that patrol, or was it *Devine* intervention? Was I not safe back at the base while my platoon was in harms way?" Slingshot painfully thought. He felt *guilty* to be alive! He had forgotten that just three weeks before *he* had been attacked. He had barely survived the attack that night on the base. Yet he felt responsible for his crew chiefs death.

Slingshot helped the mechanics refit two amtracs that needed repair. It was his duty to deliver the two amtracs to the platoon that was operating in the field. He knew it was a hazardous mission, two amtracs alone, but he was honored to be able to rejoin his outfit in the field. He knew the way to them from previous patrols he had done. It meant traveling through mine fields, rivers that slowed the amtracs to a crawl, past Marble Mountain, and possible other ambush sites. It meant risking a breakdown and being isolated from the platoon after dark. It meant certain ambush and death if he failed to reach the platoon before dark.

It was an all day journey that September 14, 1966 to where the platoon had established the firebase designated as 1/1. First Platoon used the base to refuel and to repair the amtracs while in the field of operation. When Slingshot reached the platoon, it was just before dark. The amtracs were delivered for operations on schedule. The others were both surprised that they had made it, and grateful for the effort it took to provide the additional support. Slingshot was glad to be in the field where he felt he belonged. He was especially grateful that he had made it! He had managed to live another day!

From the firebase the marines launched many unsung operations. Although some marine encounters were labeled as distinct operations, the fighting was more or less continuous and was designed to trap the VC or NVA soldiers. On May 23, 1966, a major operation, part of the preparations for *Operation Hastings*, took place consisting of three columns of armored vehicles. It was a typical marine operation in which the marines attempted to defend the *I Corps* tactical zone from large concentrations of enemy troops. Twenty amtracs, all loaded with infantry, along with numerous tanks, conducted such *search and destroy* missions from one end of *I Corps* to the other. Most of the sweeps were either south of the demilitarized zone, or southwest of Da Nang around the remote area of the Que Son Valley. An unknown number of villages were either destroyed or made useless for enemy use, and many of the enemy was captured.

Although there were several operations throughout the year, there were three major operations that required deployment north. They stand out in Slingshot's mind: "Operation Hastings" which officially took place between 7/7/66 and 8/3/66, "Operation Prairie" which took place between 8/3/66 and 1/31/67, and "Operation Prairie II," which took place between 2/1/67 and 3/18/67. Slingshot's unit, part of the 3rd Marine Division, received the coveted *Presidential Unit Citation* for its exceptional performance under fire on the missions. Such unit service must be comparable to a *Navy Cross* that is awarded to an individual.

Sometimes the amtracs were used as a blocking force while the infantry swept the area for the enemy and forced them toward the armored wall; the iron and anvil approach. Once the VC came toward the blockade the marines either captured them for interrogation or they killed them if necessary. The marines also went on operations that kept them in unknown areas for days. There were so many places they went Slingshot cannot even remember them all; villages that had no name, river routes that took them away from known routes, companies that they joined on operations and then left to support other companies and operations, each of which had a name, but which were so much alike that the name became meaningless in the field. There were airfields and LZs that the marines went to, to pick up supplies and troops to support one group or another.

Slingshot seemed to go everywhere, and everywhere he went, he found the enemy was able to attack his unit on their terms. Land mines, designed to destroy armored vehicles, and personnel mines, designed to kill or maim infantry personnel, took a heavy toll on operations. Every armored vehicle, from tanks which often accompanied the armored personnel carriers, to ontos and trucks, were hit by the enemy via land mines. Later Slingshot learned that 70% of the armor used in Vietnam was damaged or destroyed by well paced VC land mines. That was unquestionably hazardous duty!

The marines were often attacked at night when they desperately needed sleep. *The enemy was relentless with its nightly attacks.* They generally attacked at night and disappeared into their underground bases during the day. They shot at Slingshot even though his unit had tremendous superiority in terms of firepower. Hit and run was a routine tactic for the VC, and because Slingshot moved around so much he seemed to always run into the enemy. His amtrac platoon worked with all the infantry companies. Companies A, B, C, and D all operated in "I Corps" with amtracs in armored support.

On May 22, 1966 third platoon was mortared by determined VC who were located in a nearby village. The furious marines called in artillery. When it was over they had all but destroyed the VC village. Slingshot could hear the people screaming and hollering as the village burned. The experience would haunt

Slingshot forever in the silence of his nightmares.

The *grunts* or *foot soldiers* better know as infantry, always treated the LVT guys with disdain. One remarked, "I don't know about you LVT guys. I got a million miles on my feet, and all you've got is calluses on your ass!"

The grunts gave Slingshot hell but what they did not know is that he and the amtrac crews were also grunts at times. Many patrols were conducted on foot! When the amtrac crews were not walking on some patrol they were working on the LVT. When Slingshot's amtrac blew a fan-angle-drive while on an armored patrol, he had to climb into the radiator compartment where the temperature was about 200 degrees and work on it for most of the day. When a tract was thrown the amtrac crews worked with sledge hammers and crowbars to put it back together. Supplies such as boxes of ammo, grenades, mortars, flares, C-Rats, and all other supplies were loaded and unloaded day after day by the LVT guy! They were extended grunts with a flare. While on the ground, they were among the approximately 33% of infantry casualties caused by anti-personnel mines.

It was getting harder to get any sleep. On July 6, 1966 no sooner did Slingshot hit the rack then all hell broke lose. Rounds started coming in from everywhere. The VC hit his unit from both flanks! The marines opened up on them with 30 cal machine gun fire and their M-14s. The tanks fired their 50 cal guns and their 90MM canons into the attacking VC. The ARVN shot flares into the air that lit up the sky like the "Fourth of July." Slingshot was caught in the open before he found a foxhole to jump in. *Slingshot began to realize that he was going to be a nervous wreck before he got home.* It was beginning to be a habit biting dirt!

BABYBOOM DOOM

Efforts in the field, while productive, were also very costly. On July 3, 1966, amtrac A-05 struck a land mine wounding three marines. On July 10, 1966 A-22 was struck. July 11, 1966 A-07 was sunk in Song Cau Do River. On July 21, 1966 A-08 was damaged by a land mine with one marine wounded. July 28, 1966 A-26 struck a land mine wounding two marines while operating in the *Arizona Territory*, so named by the marines because of the expanse of desert like sand in their field of operation and because they were under fire a lot from the VC. August 1, 1966 it was A-47's time. On August 18, 1966 A-22 was struck. The next A Company Amtrac, A-40, was struck by a mine on September 4, 1966. On September 9, 1966 A-17 was completely destroyed by a mine and the resulting fire. Slingshot's friend was killed and three other Marines were wounded. The patrols were very dangerous as the marines extensively sought to seek and destroy the enemy. Marine casualties continue to mount. On October 6, 1966 it was A-43 with four wounded. On October 9, 1966 A-44 was struck with three wounded in action. Then on October 16, 1966 A-26 was struck wounding one Marine. Amtrac A-05 was again struck with three more marines wounded on November 9, 1966. Soon after November 12, 1966 A-26 was attacked with one wounded. The next amtrac victims wounded were on A-21 when it was struck by a mine on December 10, 1966. On the next day, December 11, 1966 two more marines were wounded on A-28. Another marine was wounded December 30, 1966 while operating the new A-17. Amtrac A-14 struck a land mine on January 9, 1967 wounding one and then the very next day struck another mine wounding three more marines. Soon after on 16 January 1967 A-10 was completely destroyed, wounding four. February 18, 1967 three more were wounded aboard A-43. After A-44 had been replaced, it was struck three days later on February 21. On February 26 it was A-49. Then on March 1, 1967

A-18 was damaged. Three more Marines were wounded on March 3 when A-19 was hit. On March 5, 1967 five more marines were wounded aboard A-12. Amtrac A-28 was hit by a RPG and sunk, killing two and wounding four. On March 9 it was amtrac A-48. On March 14 another marine was wounded aboard A-35. On April 1, 1967 A-23 was struck wounding two more. *April fool's day wasn't too funny!* Two day's later on April 3, 1967 A-33 was damaged by the enemy. Then on April 10, 1967 A-46 was destroyed from Third Amtracs with four wounded. The next day brought four more wounded aboard A-38. On April 15, 1967 A-32 was damaged. On 20 April 1967, the other new A-17 was struck by a mine.

These A Company amtracs were mostly from the 1st Amtrac Battalion and the 3rd Amtrac Battalion which operated in the I Corps area of Vietnam. From June 1966 to April 1967 at least 36 amtracs were damaged or destroyed by enemy action. That's an average of approximately three amtracs per month. Company B also suffered a similar fate with many of their amtracs destroyed or damaged which caused many casualties as well. Subsequent years did not fair any better as the VC targeted the amtracs with a variety of weapons.

In addition to damage caused by enemy action, amtracs A-10, A-14, A-18, and A-17, as well as others not mentioned here from 1st Platoon suffered mechanical failures. Every one of the amtracs were damaged by enemy attacks! Some were completely destroyed, while others suffered track damage or some other mechanical failure. On July 10, 1966 amtrac A-16 was almost lost because it ran out of gas! Maintenance and mechanical repair was a daily requirement for the already stressed-out marines!

It was not uncommon for a vehicle to hit a mine, burst into flame, bodies to be thrown every which way, and rescue efforts to come under attack. The marines always tried to recover the damaged vehicle to keep the enemy from using any part of it against them. At times they conducted operations without their amtracs by simply becoming infantry. Later because amtrac crews walked on many operations, amtrac personnel were eventually called *Am grunts*.

It was June 12, 1966! While operating in the *Arizona Territory*, First Platoon got a call that an ontos, an anti tank tracked vehicle that used six mounted 106 Howitzers as weapons, had been destroyed by a mine. Slingshot's crew was ordered to recover the bodies and to protect the recovery team from attack.

Slingshot drove the second amtrac in a column of two. They reached the attack site without incident. The commanding officer of First Platoon helped to make arrangements for the bodies to be recovered. When the decision was made to return to the field base, the command amtrac took the lead, and Slingshot followed it's tracks close behind.

Slingshot knew he was operating in a heavily mined area, but he had no idea where the minefield ended. As he left the area, he started up a rice paddy dike, a sort of hump in the ground to hold water in its place. The lead amtrac had just gone over it. As Slingshot started up the dike, he suddenly felt a tremendous tearing pressure of power that seemed to push and pull him in every direction at once! His testicles felt like they had just exploded, and his head and face slammed hard into the steel hull of the amtrac he was driving.

Slingshot was wearing a shrapnel absorbing flak jacket. He was also wearing a helicopter helmet, which had padded ear muffs designed to allow him to hear the radio over the noise of machinery. The flak jacket saved his life as it caught most of the shrapnel, while the special helmet protected his head and ears from the tremendous blast and noise that followed. Although he was knocked unconscious when his head hit the top of the amtrac, he was still alive!

Slingshot regained consciousness to find that his amtrac had been hit by a land mine! His face was a bloody mess, blood flowing from his mouth, nose and ears, and his head and groin area was burning with pain. The front of the amtrac was badly damaged, a 3 foot split in the ramp, but the amtrac engine was still running since it was located to the rear of the amtrac. The track had not been damaged. Slingshot knew that there are 450 gallons of gasoline used to fuel an amtrac. His first thought was that the gasoline was about to explode, and the amtrac was about to be engulfed in fire. He grabbed his rifle and jumped off of the amtrac. His body hit the dirt hard in an uncoordinated way. He clumsily rolled into the very hole the bomb had just created.

Slingshot immediately took aim at the tree line on his right, fully expecting an attack from the VC. He waited and watched for evidence that the VC were there. Nothing was happening from the tree line. The captain, lieutenant, and the platoon sergeant were running toward Slingshot from the other amtrac. As they neared him, Slingshot crawled out of the hole to stand. *He was in shock, confused, and out on his feet!* His face was a bloody mess, shrapnel was in his hands, upper chest, and arms. His dizzy, disoriented head was hurting badly from the concussion. His testicles were intact, but they had received the full blast from below making it very difficult for him to stand. Fortunately, the steel seat he was sitting on had stopped enough shrapnel to prevent complete castration!

His ears were ringing, his senses were dulled, and he was just reacting, not thinking, about what had just happened.

The captain grabbed Slingshot by the shoulder, got right into his face, and yelled, "Are you OK marine?" "Are you OK?" Slingshot did not respond. "Marine! Talk to me!" He asked Slingshot several more times if he was OK and shook him trying desperately to get him to respond. Slingshot *was* out on his feet! Of course he wasn't OK! He had just been blown right out of his driver's seat onto the top of the amtrac by a tremendous blast. Slingshot was still trying to react to an ambush and watching out for that, even as the captain was asking him if he was OK. Finally, the captain saw in Slingshot's eyes that he was not OK, turned to the platoon lieutenant, and told him to write Slingshot up for a purple heart and to get him a corpsman! It was later determined that the mine was a 155mm shell with a pressure device.

Still dazed, Slingshot climbed back into the damaged amtrac. Although only semi-conscious, he quickly assessed the damage caused by the explosion. He saw that the sandbags were blown off the deck and sand was trickling into the crevice created by the bomb. The hot metal smoldered with smoke as the sand smothered out the fire that would have caused the fuel cells to explode into a fiery death for Slingshot! The presence of sandbags on the amtrac deck had literally saved Slingshot's life. The smell was acrid, typical of hot metal and it made Slingshot afraid that the fuel cells might *still* explode! He found that the amtrac was still drivable. The massive engine in the rear of the amtrac continued to run. In his confused state, he wondered why none of the gauges worked! The other people aboard the vehicle were basically OK, except that their ear drums had been blown out, and blood was trickling from their ears. The steel helmet that they were wearing had not protected their ears in the way that the helicopter helmet had protected Slingshot's ears. Slingshot shouted at the other crewman, "Are you OK?" They could not hear him so they pointed toward their ears indicating their loss of hearing. The crew used hand signals to communicate with each other and Slingshot could see that none of the crew were *fatally* wounded.

Slingshot *had* to climb back into the Amtrac to drive it. He had to prove to himself that he was not afraid to drive the vehicle after the traumatic experience of having just been blown out of it! Although hurting all over, he bravely climbed into the driver's compartment, took the controls in his hands and began driving the damaged amtrac back to the field camp. The corpsman treated Slingshot in the field-camp medical tent. They gave him something for pain, cleaned him up, and released him for duty.

Slingshot, still very shaky and weak returned to his amtrac. He stepped to the rear of it and started throwing up from the shock. He hurt all over and his left testicle hung lower than normal. It had been internally damaged, something that affected the rest of his life. His head hurt, but it did not hurt nearly as much as his pride. Somehow he felt that he had failed as a soldier because he had been injured, nearly killed, but *he* had not been able to kill the enemy on that battlefield. Slingshot was so angry that he wanted to find the enemy right then and there, to kill the VC without mercy!

Slingshot's frustration mounted over the months as the VC attacked, and then just disappeared like ghosts! It was very difficult just to find the VC, much less kill them. *Because he was frustrated by the tactics employed by both the VC and the American units, he felt more and more like a failure.* He later realized that just being in Southeast Asia, on that battlefield, trying to do his best to get a negotiated peace with North Vietnam and its allies of China and the USSR, was something to be proud of. The Cold War *had* to be won! It just had to be!

With the entire Pacific basin at risk of becoming controlled by the Communist, the stand in Vietnam meant the US could now negotiate trade and peace agreements to ensure *free enterprise* with all the Asian countries. Because of Vietnam, the US was finally in a position to *negotiate* access to the Asian raw materials. The U.S. agreements eventually made with the Communists in the early seventies, especially with China, guaranteed world peace and free trade for many years to come. It did not happen without a high price paid by both sides, but the "Bamboo Curtain" was finally lifted, and the door opened to China as a result. Additionally, bargaining from a position of military resolve, the "Strategic Arms Limitation Talks" (SALT) with the USSR began to lift the "Iron Curtain" dividing Europe between the East and the West.

Slingshot did not know at the time that the injury to his testicles would require an operation some months later, and that his injury would affect his ability to have children! His injuries that faithful day had changed his life forever! It took months, even years before Slingshot knew to what extent he would suffer from the wounds of the war effort both physically, and *especially emotionally.*

It took many more years for Slingshot to realize that he had not *failed* at anything! He had carried himself honorably on the battlefield, and his efforts had helped to eventually win the Cold War. If only he could just find peace within himself everything would be alright!

CHAPTER SIX

Okinawa

By November 1966 "First Amtrac Battalion" had taken a tremendous beating on the battlefield. To be sure, the unit had won every battle, but not without cost. Several men of Slingshot's unit had been killed. The damage to the equipment was so extensive they were ordered, after about nine months of continuous operations in the field, to Okinawa to refit or replace the vehicles. The Marines loaded their amtracs with supplies, formed a long column, and started their advance toward Da Nang.

On Highway 1 through Da Nang, the road was cluttered with people on scooters, bikes, old buses, and Vietnamese people walking to and fro. There seemed to be no order in the way people hurried about in *Dog Patch*. They chattered and waved as the Marines passed by. The amtrac column slowed to a crawl as they entered the congested area. Slingshot's amtrac was located about midway in the column. He was in the driver's seat watching the activities and talking with his crew chief through the intercom. Suddenly, a jeep traveling at a high rate of speed was trying to pass the long column. The driver, an American soldier, hit a Vietnamese man riding a bicycle head on. The man went flying through the air from the impact of the collision, and landed head first onto the concrete, right next to Slingshot's amtrac. He saw and heard his skull crush as the Vietnamese hit the road. The man curled up and died immediately. The jeep swirled off the road and hit a pole. The driver slumped over, probably dead also.

Death from the unexpected was a common occurrence in Vietnam!

The amtrac column continued toward the "Red Beach" area of debarkation. There they waited for the ships to arrive. When the ships arrived, they anchored at least a mile from the shore. Slingshot checked the hull plugs along the bottom of his amtrac to make sure there were no leaks. It was a dirty job because he had to crawl underneath the amtrac, which was parked on the damp sand of the beach. All the marines were required to check the hull plugs.

After the marines entered the water via the amtracs, they steered toward the ships anchored off shore. The sea was a little rough that day. The waves smashed into the amtracs with a terrific crash, like when you dive into a wave rushing toward shore. About half way to the ship, one of the amtracs started taking on water from the rough sea. It sank within moments, dumping the crew into the sea. The crew had to be rescued! No one drowned, but the platoon records sunk to the bottom of the sea along with the amtrac and all of its equipment. It was dangerous in the South China Sea!

Slingshot drove his amtrac into the bowls of the ship that was waiting for him in the South China Sea without further incident. The USS Gungston Hall was to be passage to some well needed and well earned rest and recuperation.

The marines disembarked from the LSD early in the morning with the land of the "Rising Sun" before them. Slingshot guided his amtrac straight toward the Hagushi Beaches that were used during WWII for the invasion of Okinawa, and he made a perfect landing. Each amtrac was landed as required. The marines formed a column and headed for their base near Kadena Airfield and Camp Hansen.

The marines were severely fatigued from the efforts of war. They had been under continuous stress for months. Some called the condition of the marines as having "Combat Fatigue." Others from the WWII era called it "Shell Shock." Still others called the symptoms associated with the experience of the war as "War Neurosis." The marines were drained of all of their strength and energy, all emotions were numbed, and their eyes seemed to be staring into empty space. Later, the Vietnam soldier's reaction to the constant stress of the war would be termed "Post Traumatic Stress Disorder," or PTSD. The after effects of PTSD would show up much later in the soldiers life, as Slingshot was to find out!

At Okinawa, the medical attention was badly needed to put the marines back into top fighting condition. Slingshot got immunization shots, his teeth repaired, good food, plenty of regular sleep, and showers, all of which was not to be had in the field *in country* (Vietnam).

The marines also got liberty! While on leave in Okinawa, it was like everyone was itching for a fight. The marines were told to go on leave in groups to avoid being caught alone because some of the Japanese were still hostile about WWII. So they explored the town, including the red light districts where many a fight took place over the women.

The native drink was rice wine, called *Sake*. It tasted awful the first two or three sips, but after that it went down smoothly. It was kind of like the moonshine produced in the hills of Kentucky, except rice was the produce used to distill the liquor instead of corn. It was a clear liquid that produced a sudden knock out punch, the kind that just sneaks up on you. One moment you are drinking the Sake like water with no apparent results, and then suddenly you are out of your mind, literally hallucinating from the impact.

Slingshot saw soldiers crawling through the barracks on their hand and knees, completely out of their mind from over dosing on Sake. He also saw several fights and even participated in a couple himself! The marines were men who had lived under extreme war conditions, on the front lines of battle for months, conditioned to fight everyday for their very survival, now in another hostile environment, with liberty to let loose. The result is not hard to understand. The marines kept the MPs busy with the bar fights and challenged each other for the primitive right to have a particular Japanese girl. The marines ran wild on the weekends, but it was because they knew they were going back to Vietnam where their chances for survival was slim. "Why not enjoy the last days of our lives?" exclaimed Slingshot's companions!

So it was that Slingshot's attitude had reached that uncontrollable state. "Live for the moment for tomorrow I will die," Slingshot believed. Fortunately, he did have a reason to live. He had Loretta. Loretta with all of her faults still gave him hope! Also, Slingshot really did not enjoy drinking all that much. He needed to escape the horrible images of war, the charred and mutilated bodies, the sounds of rifle fire and explosions, the roar of the war machines, so he drank. He needed relief from the impact of the extreme conditions of heat and dust and monsoon rains on his exposed body, day after day, and night after night, so he drank. The fatigue had worn him down, and the constant adrenaline rush had effected his mind psychologically, tearing at his very soul; the fears, and perhaps the most difficult thing of all, the horror of living with himself when and if he survived! He needed to escape the horror of war to survive for another day! So Slingshot danced and sang the night away under the influence of the Sake, to forgot about everything that pained him on that God forsaken island called Okinawa.

During the day the marines worked very hard on their amtracs. The amtracs were based at *Camp Schwab*. They replaced the worn heavy steel track with new track. They oiled and greased every bearing, and painted the hulls with fresh olive drab green paint. They gathered supplies and stored it on each individual amtrac. They were preparing for *round two* of the war effort.

After a few weeks the marines took physical tests to ensure their bodies were conditioned and ready for what they already knew was required. They even trained in the mountainous jungle of northern Okinawa.

Jungle Training

Slingshot thought it an ironic twist of fate that while he was stationed in Okinawa, the Marines were required to go to "Jungle Warfare School," to learn how to survive in a jungle warfare environment. After Vietnam, where jungle warfare was the norm, it seemed ridiculous to try to teach the Marines the theories of jungle warfare. The Marines already knew that the enemy used every kind of device imaginable to cripple or maim them, devices made from the jungle itself! Pungee stakes were common. These were bamboo sticks with pointed sharp ends that had been infected with poison or bacteria for maximum affect. Often a hole was dug and the pointed stakes were placed at the bottom of the pit, where they waited for one of the exhausted marines to *fall* to his death. The Marines already knew that the enemy could place explosives in trees with trip wires for a trigger or other swinging devices designed to stab them at a moments notice. The Marines already knew that their enemy was the world's most experienced jungle warrior on the face of the earth, and that the VC had taught them, from the marines own mistakes, about how deadly his techniques were. The Marines already knew about the variety of land mines and how affective they were against their foot soldiers and the armored vehicles. The Marines already knew about the ghost like appearances that seemed to vanish in thin air after the VC had attacked them, and Charlie's ability to blend into the forest and hide in underground bases. Slingshot also believed that the VC was being trained by the Chinese since the VC used Moa Tse Tung tactics, also known as Mao Zedong's *Peoples War*. The Chinese perfected the use of guerilla war tactics in rural areas as a means of promoting revolution for world domination as Communists.

The "Jungle Warfare School" was designed for someone who had never experienced these things, and many other things not mentioned here. The Marines already knew about the snipers and how they could strike anytime from any distance. They also already knew what it was like to spend the night in *the bush*; to be *ambushed*. The Marines therefore, looked at the school as not a necessity, but as a continuation of their misery. Training was "make believe," and hard to learn because it focused on what was *expected*. In Vietnam everything the Marines had been taught about war fell apart. Logic became illogical, and reason was unreasonable. Nothing was as expected! *The only thing they could expect, was the unexpected!* Logic and reason didn't work! What worked, unfortunately, was usually illogical and unreasonable. That is what reality taught the Marines and no school could change that.

The day the marines left for the jungle school, Slingshot had a very bad head cold. It was also a rainy, cloudy, miserable day. The marines had to ride in back of a six-by to the other side of the island to get into the mountainous range where the jungle was the thickest. The column headed south from the base to Naha where they caught Highway 1. Highway 1 ran north along the coast from Naha to the Motobu Peninsula where the USMC training took place.

Slingshot felt so bad he did not think he was going to survive the ordeal, but he had come prepared to complete the school. He had slipped a bottle of *Sake* in with his gear, along with a can of orange juice. After they were on their way, he took the bottle out of his gear bag and he asked the guys if they would like a drink, along with a chaser. Everyone took a drink or two and all of them were delighted with the party, as if they were heading to a grand celebration. The marines laughed, and they joked their troubles away. Slingshot had thought the Sake would simply numb his headache, but it must have had an affect on the virus. Slingshot had drunk just enough of the Sake and orange juice to put him sound asleep. When he awoke, he felt much better. The head cold was gone and everyone was in a good mood!

It had taken about six hours to arrive at the training site. The platoon was in the middle of the mountainous jungle for sure. Since it had been raining all day, the ground was a muddy mess and moisture continued to drip from the rain forest. Everything was wet including the marines as soon as they departed the truck. The marines pitched their tents, the small bivouac type that only allowed them enough room to sleep. The cloud cover was so thick that no light was able to shine through the night sky. With the rain coming down, Slingshot slept in his dark tent alone, not sure of what to expect the next day.

The next day the marines mounted up for a long walk through the jungle. They walked along side a river. Slingshot felt uneasy even though this was Okinawa, not Vietnam. The river wound itself into a deep valley. The platoon worked their way down into the valley where they crossed the river several times as it wound through the valley. Slingshot could not help but to think he would not want to be in this situation in Vietnam, where the enemy could ambush them from the high ground. But what did he know? He was just a corporal in training, right? The brass acted as if they forgot that he was a veteran of jungle warfare. He began to believe the whole exercise was more for *their* training than his. The platoon just formed their patrol quietly observing their leaders mistakes.

Everyone knew the Marines would do things differently in

Vietnam. There the platoon would not bunch up for conversation like the brass did to exalt their authority, and the patrol would be much more staggered with a good distance between each man. Done properly one grenade would not get them all. The officers would not wear their brass on their collar, and they would not stay together just to talk. In training they walked and talked together giving their rank and position away, which would have made them the first casualties in Vietnam! Additionally they talked about booby traps but did not do what was necessary to reduce the risk. They choose to walk the path of least resistance and the most likely place for a booby trap. The officers were usually inexperienced in Vietnam battle, having usually been in Vietnam less than six months. *They* had to be trained by the enlisted men on how to survive the next day! The sting of battle changed all the rules and the training in school did not prepare them for that. It therefore was hard for many of the marines to accept the leadership, knowing what the enlisted men had experienced from some of the officers in Vietnam. The training exercise was like returning to high school after you were already established in the work force.

The platoon walked all day far into the jungle. Observers were placed on the ridges of the valley the marines patrolled. The platoon was split up into squads. When night arrived, each squad from the platoon was told to use the compass to find their way out. The plan was to work their way out of the jungle and then they were to meet at a certain place for their walk back. The night was as black as a cave!

Slingshot literally could not see the guy standing next to him! The clouds and the jungle filtered out all the light. The compass barely glowed in the dark. Only one person had the compass. The rest of the squad had to follow the leader. It was so dark! They had to hold on to each other to stay in contact. The compass did not differentiate a good smooth path from a bad path. The squad had to follow that compass, with it pitch black across whatever path it led. Often it led the squad into ravines that they had to climb down into. The marines struggled to climb out of the ravines helping each other by instinct and feeling their way through the complete darkness.

After climbing from the ravines the marines had to climb through the thickest of brush and trees. It led them to the sides of mountains where they could with certainty fall to their death. It led them through water. It led them to places they had to swing on the vines to get to the other side. One false step would send them careening down a slope.

Slingshot stepped off a ridge that sent him and his equipment careening down a steep slope. The others heard Slingshot falling through the brush. Two marines tried to help. They reached the edge and they too stepped off the ridge and started falling through the brush and trees. It was just too dark to see!

Slingshot slid downward for what seemed like an eternity, having no idea how deep the ravine was. As he fell he grabbed for a branch or anything that would stop him from falling. Eventually he was able to slow his fall to a stop. Hanging on a branch for dear life he could not tell how far down the ravine he had fallen or how far it was to the bottom. He knew he had fallen and tumbled a long way before he managed to stop. No one could see him and he could not see anyone either. The marines could hear each other, so the other squad members stopped while those who fell slowly worked their way up the ravine side. They started crawling on their stomachs and they grabbed branches, rocks or anything that would hold them. It was a very steep climb that took every ounce of Slingshot's strength. When Slingshot reached the top he found someone to hold on to by calling out for help. After everyone was recovered the squad continued on their way.

Later on, as the ill fated night patrol continued, one guy fell into a 20 foot cavern! The squad leader lit a lighter to see what had happened. All that was heard was a thud, like someone falling off a building onto hard concrete. It was Slingshot's friend from South Carolina, Lance Corporal Carl. Slingshot thought Carl was hurt bad, and then he realized he had fallen on his head. "Nothing could crack his rock-hard head," mused Slingshot.

At first Carl did not move or say anything because he was knocked unconscious! After a few seconds he began to moan loudly. Slingshot climbed down to him, holding on to tree branches and rocks to reach him. Carl remained motionless for a few moments. Slingshot tried to talk to him. "Oh (expletive deleted)," Carl moaned. "Oh (expletive deleted), what happened?" For a few moments Carl did not know where he was or just what had happened. Slingshot helped Carl to his feet where he and Carl staggered to the wall of the hole. They leaned against the dirt wall for support. Slingshot checked Carl as best he could under the circumstances. He was in a deep hole on a mountain ridge deep within the jungle and he had to take care of Carl in the dark. "Are you OK?" asked Slingshot. It was determined that no bones had been broken and except for a bad headache, thanks to Carl's steel helmet, he was OK!

The rest of the squad, one by one, climbed down and past the cave-like ravine using lighters to allow them to see. They knew in 'Nam they could not use lighters, but a need to survive a situation sometimes requires whatever is available. By morning, after hours of struggling through the dark treacherous mountains and wet jungle, the squad had worked their way back to their main unit to link up as planned.

When the training was over the marines walked out of the jungle to where the trucks were waiting. The marines climbed aboard the trucks for their long ride through the mountainous terrain. They found the road that led out of the jungle. It seemed to be a lot farther to civilization than it was to the jungle, probably because Slingshot had slept for most of the way up. Eventually the Pacific Ocean could be seen from the mountain road that led to civilization.

Later that day the marines arrived at Camp Schwab. Slingshot was relieved to have the experience over. He had gained a whole new appreciation for what it took to take the island from the Japanese during WWII. The thick jungle canopy covered unending caves and deep canyons in the mountains. The many ridges along the mountains had provided a formidable obstacle to overcome, and it afforded the Japanese with a natural fortress. What the training had not taught Slingshot about jungle warfare was replaced by that deep appreciation gained for those who had come before him.

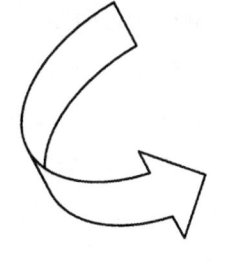

Liberty

The marines went on liberty almost every night while they were on Okinawa. The war had created bottled up tensions in all of them. They had been aboard ship for several days after they left Vietnam to go to Okinawa, Japan. The ship sailed through the Luzon Straight past Taiwan and the Philippines. With each passing day their anticipation increased. The young men were like coiled springs ready to explode from all the tension!

Slingshot went on liberty with a few of the guys just itching for adventure; maybe a fight with some of the sailors in one of the bars. He had a few drinks during the evening and after a lot of war stories and talk about women the guys decided to split up. Three of the marines took a cab to a village named Kochi which was near Naha.

About midnight Slingshot's buddies and he were just wondering around when they came upon a Japanese cathouse! Slingshot's buddies wanted to go in but Slingshot really did not care to. With their urging he decided to join them in the adventure fully expecting to just walk out after his buddies connected with their girl of the evening. Slingshot did not want them to think he was less a man by outright refusing to join them. Slingshot decided to play along with the macho act!

When they got inside a Japanese madam approached them and asked them if they wanted a girl for the evening. Slingshot's buddy immediately said yes, as Slingshot stood by to see what his other companions were going to do. He said nothing as the young marines looked at each other with a shrug of, why not? The madam led all three of the young men into a big parlor where the women were sitting all around inviting lustful attention; some looked real serious while others smiled as Slingshot made eye contact. All of the women were pretty in their own way. Some had gorgeous legs and others had pretty faces. The slanted eyes seemed both inviting, and yet somehow intimidating at the same time. Slingshot did not trust anyone by now, much less Orientals. That they were pretty women did not seem to touch him emotionally. He looked at them with a numb defensive caution!

Slingshot's buddies picked out their partners right away! They disappeared down a long hallway. Slingshot was drunk but he still was on guard from distrust and feared of being vulnerable. "No, I want to go!" said Slingshot. He started for the door, thinking he would just wait outside until his buddies were through.

A petite thin, very fair skinned Japanese girl approached him. She was young, no more than eighteen, and her hair was shinny black. It made her face stand out in a way that enhanced her dark slanting eyes and childlike smile. She reminded Slingshot of a ceramic doll that had no flaws. She started teasing him as she giggled in an almost child like way. She was cute but she could not speak English. "No! Slingshot said. "No!" She just smiled and giggled until she finally got his total attention. Slingshot was getting excited now, so there was no turning back! She took him to a room knowing she could have her way. After awhile the madam came to ask Slingshot if he wanted to stay all night, for an additional charge. Slingshot had only spent two dollars for the time with the girl! Still uncomfortable about being vulnerable to attack at any time and much shaken that he had gone along with the others this far, he said no. His buddies decided to stay the night!

When Slingshot stepped out into the darkness there was no one in sight at first. It was about 2:00 AM so the back alley street was empty. He stood there for a few moments trying to figure out what to do next. Suddenly out of the shadows stepped a Japanese man. Slingshot immediately got defensive and circled him as he *stared* to make sure the man was not armed with a knife or gun. To be defensive was an automatic response for him when he saw an Oriental.

Slingshot quickly sized him up. He slowly circled as he approached while the Japanese man reacted the same! There they were in the middle of the night, one man representing the U.S. and the other man representing Japan, squaring off for battle, *slowly* circling each other. Slingshot crouched low in a karate like stance moving his hands and staring the strange man in the eye. Slingshot did not want an incident in Okinawa so he really did not want to attack *unless* he was attacked first! It was apocalypse now!

Slingshot was ready for the Japanese man to make the first move while the Japanese man seemed to be waiting for Slingshot to make the first move! They circled each other two or three times, each waiting for the moment of attack. Since the Japanese man was not closing the circle, Slingshot slowly took a step back to indicate to him that he did not want to attack.

It was the Japanese man's move now. A step forward would mean he wanted to get it on. The two warriors stared at each other and Slingshot waited to see what the man was going to do; step forward or step back. The man very slowly stepped one step back. No one was around as the two men played out this confrontation in the middle of the night in front of the cathouse. Parasitic evil forces reminded them both about the horrors of past engagements between the two cultures.

After standing in the same spot for several seconds, Slingshot's fight or flight adrenaline was at its peak. He wanted to fight the man! He wanted the Japanese man to know he was the king of the hill. *The devil was trying hard to do his evil work!*

Slingshot knew it meant a court marshal if he was caught fighting the locals. Greatly tempted but aware of how senseless it would be, Slingshot very slowly took a step back to indicate he meant no harm. The Japanese man did the same! Without either one of them ever saying a word or losing face, they communicated to each other their stand-down intentions. Finally each man went his own way. A cataclysm was avoided as the evil forces were destroyed!

Slingshot felt like he had escaped a very bad situation. He knew he could have gotten busted for fighting a local as tensions between the U.S. and Japan was very high regarding the U.S. occupation of Okinawa. The Japanese people on the island did not want the Marines there and they showed it. A busted up Japanese man who complained to the authorities was enough to get Slingshot in deep trouble. Slingshot shook from the adrenaline rush for several hours after the standoff. He thanked God he did not have to fight the man, knowing God's will did prevail!

Slingshot left the cathouse feeling pretty mixed up. He had broken his vows to Loretta! He was ashamed of himself! Slingshot rationalized that he was going to die before he ever saw Loretta again anyway. The visit to the cathouse bothered him tremendously during the nights to follow. *His guardian angels made sure of that.*

On December 25, 1966 the whole experience of being away from home came to a head. Slingshot had just turned 20 years old. It was Christmas, with no loved ones around. He was completely isolated from any loved ones on a foreign island, where the Japanese really did not much care for him. He knew it was a special day, but it was hard to appreciate it. Almost everyone went into town for the evening, searching for some reason to exist. In Vietnam, at least there was the "Bob Hope Christmas Show" for homesick relief! On Okinawa, the best Slingshot could do was to place a small silver Christmas tree in his bunk area, and dream of better times.

Slingshot placed the tree on a box and wrote "Merry Christmas 1st Platoon" on the front of the box. Most of the guys really appreciated it. As they walked by, some said, "Merry Christmas" even though they weren't in a very merry situation. Other guys just looked at the tree with sort of a blank stare as they walked by. Some said, "Merry Christmas, see you in the 'Nam for a Happy New Year!" Slingshot felt good about at least sharing the tree with them.

In town things got a little crazy as well as a little emotional. Everyone was out to get drunk to take away the *pain* of loneliness. The future did not look too bright for any of the marines because they were about to go back to the 'Nam. Some drank and danced with each other because there were not a whole lot of girls around. Others sat around talking about home.

Slingshot wandered into a bar to just be around other people. He sat at the bar, ordered a drink, and tried to be friendly with the Japanese barkeep. The barkeep looked as if he was apprehensive around Slingshot and he did not talk or jester in a friendly way. Slingshot did not understand Japanese and the barkeep spoke only broken English, so they communicated with hand signals. After several awkward moments in which Slingshot did not feel at all welcomed, a young Japanese girl came from the back of the bar and stared at him in a curious way. The stare was not in a sweet shy way, but more in an angry way. Her eyes were dark brown and slanted. They seemed to stare right through Slingshot. She was short but well built in a womanly way, not too thin, and not too chunky. Her lips were big and soft looking like those of most of the traditional Japanese girls. Her hair was a long shiny black! She differed from the way Vietnamese girls looked because she was not as skinny. She looked to be about sixteen or seventeen years old.

      Slingshot was very lonely, so he tried to talk to her but their different languages made that very difficult. She did not seem to want to warm up to him, to be friendly in any way. Slingshot motioned for her to come. Slingshot spoke softly as he reached for her. She stood still as she spoke to him in Japanese. He did not understand. Slingshot went to her and gently pulled her to sit her down on the bar stool next to him. She sat for a few moments as they tried to communicate, then she got up and moved away; then she came back to sit, as if she was nervous around Slingshot. Slingshot asked, "What is your name?" She did not understand, so he decided that talking was not the way to communicate. Slingshot began using hand signals, to indicate to her to go for a walk with him. She was afraid to go with him. In his desperation for company he asked the barkeep, who appeared to be her father, if he could take her with him around town. He asked for five dollars! Although Slingshot did not want to pay for her company, he decided it was the easiest way to get on with the evening, so he gave the barkeep the money. He then spoke with her in Japanese. She seemed to argue with him about what was said. Finally, she grabbed Slingshot's hand and out the door they went.

Eventually they came upon a bar where some of Slingshot's platoon was. He went in with the girl and they all wanted to know where he found her. Slingshot explained that he just picked her up from the bar down the street. The party was in full swing before long. Everyone was drinking and dancing with the girl. Slingshot just wanted her company, but she seemed to enjoy all the guys. After a few drinks, and now for sure feeling very lonely, since she was obviously not interested in him, Slingshot began to cry. He missed Loretta, and here he was in the most terrible environment. Tears were streaming down his face as he thought of her and of his life back home. Some of the guys saw that he was *homesick* and they tried to comfort him. One brought Slingshot another drink.

After awhile Slingshot was ready to leave but the Japanese girl wanted to stay. She was having a good time as the guys bought her drinks. Slingshot started to leave and one of the guys smarted off to him. A scuffle ensued between Slingshot and a couple of the other marines, spurned by the emotional state of things. After the profane behavior began, Slingshot grabbed the girl by the hand and he left the bar in a huff shoving one marine out of the way, threatening to attack anyone else who got in his way. She was yelling at everyone in Japanese and Slingshot just wanted to return her to her dad. She was so drunk that he threw her over his shoulder and off they went to the bar where he had found her.

When Slingshot arrived, the girl's Dad was not there but her mom was. She motioned to Slingshot to lead the girl to her room. He took her to her room and her mom seemed like she wanted him to stay with the girl for the night. Slingshot was tempted as the girl sat up in the middle of her bed looking at him in a defiant way, giving her an uncanny sensuous look. Her mom was motioning for Slingshot to stay. "It's OK, you stay." Her mom talked to her in Japanese then turned to Slingshot to say again, "You stay!" Slingshot really did not want to stay with her, especially on Christmas and especially when he was married and homesick and missing Loretta. Slingshot was ashamed of himself for cheating on Loretta before. This time he was going to do the right thing!

The pretty Japanese girl looked at Slingshot with those not so innocent eyes in a defiant way, but Slingshot could tell that she wanted him to stay. She really looked no older than sixteen! It was kind of intoxicating that she was so young and feisty. Slingshot felt dizzy from the crying, fighting, and booze. He stood staring at her in the doorway for several minutes as she stared back! They quietly continued to look at each other for awhile longer until Slingshot finally turned away, feeling good about his decision to leave.

All the guys back at Camp Schwab did not believe Slingshot when he told them the next morning that he had not spent the night with the girl. They thought he was covering up because he was married. They teased him with, "Yeah right, you just left! Sure! Sure you did!" Slingshot just let them believe whatever they wanted. Some yelled, "Hey did you all hear about Slingshot? He got laid last night!" Slingshot just went along with it. His marine buddies continued to laugh and joke about what they had done on Christmas day of 1966. For Slingshot, his silence revealed that it was in fact the loneliest Christmas he ever had, and without a doubt the worst!

The next evening Slingshot went into town with his friend Sal. Sal was from Texas also. He was of Mexican descent and he was fun to be with. Homesick and depressed during the holiday season they went from bar to bar having a drink from each place they visited. In one bar, a Japanese girl sat at the table and asked Slingshot to buy her a drink. She was slim and athletically toned with a lot of energy. Her smile captured Slingshot's attention. He bought her a drink and began to size her up as they sat across from each other.

Slingshot was constantly looking around thinking the bar girl might be a setup for some muggers. Vietnam had made him ever so anxious. While his attention was on her he was afraid that someone might sneak up on him from behind or blow-up the bar with a grenade. After about three drinks, his uneasy feelings caught up with him. "She is up to something, I'm sure of it.," Slingshot sensed. Slingshot felt nervous and uncomfortable as he continued to anxiously look around. The pretty girl continued to talk in broken English as Slingshot tried to find out more about her.

As Slingshot began to come under the influence of the alcohol, he noticed the bar girl was not responding to her drink! As they talked, he reached across the table and took her drink. It was a cola *without* alcohol! Slingshot became furious about paying for alcohol that was not provided. He threw the girl's glass at the barkeep as he furiously yelled at the girl telling her off. The barkeep ducked behind the bar and the girl quickly ran out of the back door.

Slingshot was so mad for being taken he threatened to tear the bar apart as he slung his chair across the floor. In his tense condition from the beginning, he was ready. Sal pulled him away to calm him down telling Slingshot that the girl was gone, "Take it easy amigo. The *chica* is gone. The barkeep has offered us a free drink! Let's have another drink. Relax mi amigo." Slingshot clumsily sat down. He was still very angry about the situation even after he sat.

Sal had talked him into staying. They stayed there for the free drink as the other guys argued about what to do about Slingshot having been taken. Slingshot was still itching for a fight, but all the others just wanted him to leave. Finally with the help of the cooler heads of some of the marines present, Slingshot and Sal decided to leave the joint so they could enjoy the rest of the evening.

Slingshot and Sal did not go far before they found another bar. They entered the next bar with a hyper-adrenaline rush feeling very drunk by now. It did not take much to start a fight under the circumstances! As they entered the bar a scuffle broke out. Words were loudly exchanged! Some marines ran outside. Slingshot ran out into the street to see who was fighting. He saw his friend Sal was talking with someone and he thought Sal was in trouble. Having a lot of pent up frustration and tension from the previous months, Slingshot was *looking* for a fight, although he did not even know it.

In the street Sal was standing in front of a very tall marine looking up to him talking loudly. Slingshot, thinking that Sal was part of the scuffle, immediately came to his rescue. Slingshot reacted without thinking! He jumped into the air and kicked the unknown intruder in the face with his right foot. The marine fell to the ground out cold, but Slingshot having the killing instinct to survive, immediately delivered another kick to the side of his head. He stood over him as the other marines attacked their opponents.

The bar fight had ended up in the street with *everyone* swinging at anyone who opposed them. Slingshot threw one guy to the side when he ran at him, and in his drunken state Slingshot was yelling obscenities at everyone. He pushed or shoved anyone who came near him by throwing a karate type blow at them. The marine on the ground still had not moved. Slingshot had delivered a solid blow to his head at least twice. Slingshot was thinking during his confused state, "I hope I have not killed him!"

The barkeep must have gotten in touch with the MP's because they came roaring down the street in their jeep. By now another marine and Slingshot were exchanging blows and yelling those kinds of things designed to provoke someone to fight. The jeep screeched to a halt and two MP's jumped out. They immediately grabbed Slingshot and his opponent and they held them both from getting at each other. Blows were being thrown in the direction of each even as the MP's held them. Both of the marines were still screaming at each other as the MP's separated them. They managed to wrestle Slingshot into the jeep to take him to the MP station. He was put into the back seat and the other guy was placed into the front seat.

As the MP's drove away Slingshot saw two men picking up the marine he had knocked out. He was awake but it was obvious he still did not know what had hit him. The two MP's placed the dizzy marine between them; they placed his arms over their neck. They were carrying him through the street as Slingshot disappeared from the scene in a cloud of dust coming from the back of the jeep. All the marines in the fight had scattered! They had had enough fun!

The *Paddy Wagon* was full of other marines in the same shape as was Slingshot. They were all drunk, bruised and bleeding, mad, mean as hell, and itching to get back into the fight, which had actually broken up by then. The marines were taken to the *holding pen* where they were allowed to calm down and sober up with some coffee. One by one each marine was released. No one took their names or tried to make more out of it than it was. It was just a typical Marine bar fight to let off steam! No one had been seriously hurt!

The Return

The day came when the marines were ready to return to Vietnam. They had spent the previous several weeks training hard. They had perfected their specialty of "Ship to Shore" assault. The amphibious assaults became an automatic exercise since the Marines did them so much. The marines had finished the jungle warfare school and they were ready for the final tests.

Each marine took a "Physical Readiness Test," a specially designed test to see if they were physically ready for embarkation. Slingshot was still hung over from the previous evening but he managed to pass the test. After all the preparations were done, the marines were ready to return to Vietnam.

The marines drove their amtracs to the Okinawa beach, the same place they had landed a couple of months earlier from their LSD, and the same beach that U.S. forces had used during the battle for Okinawa during WWII. It was December 31, 1966. The marines boarded their LSD for their voyage back to Vietnam.

The ship, the "USS Point Defiance" tossed and pitched as Slingshot maneuvered his amtrac into position to enter the ship. The weather was rainy with rough seas. His steering was good as the amtrac entered for a perfect docking.

He was really feeling the movement of the ship this time. He was getting a little seasick, but he toughed it out for the five day trip that followed. Slingshot spent New Years day aboard the tossing ship feeling pretty bad. What a wonderful way to start the New Year!

CHAPTER SEVEN

Vietnam II

Slingshot arrived off the coast of Vietnam during the first week in January 1967. The South China Sea off the coast of Da Nang was calm. He exited the ship to form the approach to *Red Beach*, the same beach where the original landing took place by the 9th Marine Expeditionary Brigade on March 8, 1965 at the beginning of the war. Like the original landing, the marines landed unopposed by the enemy, formed into a column, and headed through Da Nang on their way to the base camp. Slingshot reflected on the fact that he had helped to start the main base when he left Chu Lai with the advanced party almost a year ago. Now he was returning to continue the fight. He was a bit nervous about traveling in his brand new amtrac down Highway 1. Slingshot was always concerned about an ambush and always concerned about mines. Da Nang air base had grown considerably since he first saw it. Supplies were visible from the route, and there was more stacked supplies than ever. It sure looked like the Americans were there to stay.

The marines arrived at the firebase without incident. It was not long before they left for operations out in the field. The field of operations assigned was in once again the "Arizona Territory." The VC mine fields greeted the marines with a welcome back! By mid January 1967, the platoon lost the newly fitted amtrac A-10 when it hit a mine and burst into flames. The marines hadn't fired a shot yet, but there lay several wounded and dying. "Welcome back to 'Nam!"

The Fights II

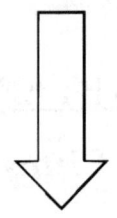

A Chinese General, Sun Tzu, author of "The Art of War," written in 600 BC, stated the basic philosophy used as the Viet Cong strategy. He wrote:

"All warfare is based on deception. Hence, when able to attack, we must seem unable; when using our forces, we must seem inactive; when we are near, we must make the enemy believe that we are away; when far away, we must make him believe we are near. Hold our baits to entice the enemy. Feign disorder, and crush him. If your opponent is of choleric temper, seek to irritate him. Pretend to be weak, that he may grow arrogant. If he is taking his ease, give him no rest. If his forces are united, separate them. Attack him where he is unprepared, appear where you are not expected. These military devices, leading to victory, must not be divulged beforehand."

The Viet Cong implemented their strategy by using three approaches:

The **first** they called "Dich Van" which meant "Action among the Enemy." The VC, through espionage, would organize propaganda networks amongst the villagers and provide misinformation. They would assassinate the leaders by using booby traps or bombings and sapper attacks. Others they would kidnap for interrogation.

The **second** approach was called "Binh Van," "Action among the military." The VC would infiltrate the ARVN or U.S. forces with the intent of causing dissention within the ranks of their enemies military. This approach caused many desertions, especially from the ARVN, and many ARVN troops also defected to the VC cause.

The **third** VC strategy was called "Dan Van," "Action among the People." The VC would win the hearts and minds of the villagers by providing care and training which led to the VC becoming village mangers. The village administration was controlled by the VC. The VC would recruit most of the young men for their service this way.

By 1968 the enemy could recruit approximately 300,000 troops a year! The VC were winning the war of attrition. They were also winning the hearts and souls of the South Vietnamese villagers as the U.S. search and destroy methods got out of control.

Whenever the U.S. forces approached a village to *sweep* through it on a *search and destroy* mission, the village administrators knew in advance from their sentries that the Americans were coming. They ordered the evacuation of the men of the village leaving only the woman and children to be searched. This administrative approach proved to be very successful for the VC. U.S. forces often took casualties from well placed booby traps the fleeing VC left behind. Because of it, out of frustration some U.S. units terrorized the women and children. The *hooch's* of the village were sometimes torched to ashes when munitions were found.

When the Americans left the village, the VC then returned without having received any casualties of their on. They then rendered aid and comfort to the villagers thus solidifying their hold.

On one of the Marine's *sweeps*, Slingshot was traveling in a column of amtracs, loaded with infantry supported by M-48 tanks, when his amtrac threw a track. The decision to leave his amtrac behind was not a popular one, but the decision was to leave slingshot and his crew to their fate while the column continued its mission.

There were five marines left with the disabled amtrac. They were in an area near the coast. The ground was very soft and sandy. It made it extremely difficult to lay the track out and to role the vehicle over it without the track shifting out of alignment. There was extreme tension in the air as the crew tried again and again to button up the track onto the sprocket of the right side of the vehicle. After the attempts, they were exhausted from the heat and heavy labor. They knew their lives depended upon finishing the track repair and rejoining the main column before dark.

The five marines were out in the open separated from the main column. They were a perfect target for the VC. They had food and ammunition aboard along with their weapons, which were very prized by the VC. The crew worked on the track and watched out for a VC unit or sniper to appear at anytime. They were scared, very scared! They were a unit separated from the main force in the open with their armored vehicle disabled and it was loaded with supplies. What a prize for the enemy to take advantage of! The VC did not disappoint them.

The crew of the disabled amtrac was soon spotted by the VC. Fortunately for the crew, there were only three lightly armed VC with small arms. They fired at the crew to harass them but soon fled when the marines returned fire!

Slingshot had a second problem to be concerned about. They needed the daylight to find their unit, which could be almost anywhere by now. Realizing that, Slingshot and his crew made a decision that probably saved their lives. They decided that if they were successful at repairing the broken track, they would not try to find the main force and rejoin the mission, although they wanted desperately to do that. They decided to try to find the field base instead. The field base designated as 1/1 was located some miles to the south of their location. They had to somehow find it from where they were before dark.

After dark, their chances of reading the terrain correctly to find the base would be greatly reduced. They had already been spotted by the VC so time was of the up most importance. The VC came out of there tunnels in *force* at night. Most of the firefights with them occurred at night, when the amtracs were stopped for the crew to rest. No one would be expecting the amtrac at the field base, because all available amtracs were committed to the mission. *The amtrac crew had to get the track repaired and they had to find the field base before dark.!* That was their only chance to survive! They were on their own.

To make matters worse, the area that they were operating in was known to be heavily mined. The VC controlled the mountains to the west. Their chances of getting the tract repaired before dark and then reaching the base without hitting a mine or being attacked was slim.

The crew tried again to button up the track. The track shifted out of alignment every time they tried to roll the vehicle on it. They had to figure out a way to keep the track from shifting. Slingshot had an idea! "Let's drag the track to a more even part of the ground using the single track of the vehicle to pull the vehicle and stretch the track all the way out." They had to drive the vehicle off all of the broken track to drag it to a different place; a risky move because the track was so heavy, the five of them could not possibly move it by hand to align it to the vehicle. To drag the track the driver had to lock the right sprocket by steering to the right. This allowed the left track to move the vehicle and to drag the track. Then they could pack sand on each side of the track to help hold it in place. Additionally, for as long as they could, they would stand on the track in a spread formation and place their steel leverage bars to use as locking bars between the sections of track. That way they could anchor the track, and they could back the vehicle onto it. Maybe, just maybe, they could feed the track through the torsion bar section over the wheels with the proper alignment to button up the track at the sprocket. It was getting late in the evening as the sun was setting behind the Annam Cordillera Mountain Range a few miles to the west. They had been disabled since about noon. Time was running out! This was their last chance to succeed!

Their last ditched effort to repair the track worked! They got the track buttoned up and started their journey to the field base. Never did one amtrac go anywhere without at least one other amtrac with it. It was standard operating procedure to operate in pairs. They had no choice this time. They were alone in very hostile territory as night began to blanket the area.

Slingshot traveled very cautiously, looking for signs of mines and avoiding anything that looked suspicious, such as grass that did not belong, soil that was damp or a different color than the surface, or a narrow path between trees that might be an obvious way to go if there was no such thing as land mines. He drove to avoid the land mines and he also drove away from likely ambush sites. Although time was now critical, it was about dark, Slingshot felt he had to be very careful. With a little good luck, they might just make it!

Slingshot pulled into the field base camp just after dark. Everyone was amazed that the crew had survived. They cheered as the repaired amtrac pulled to a stop. The marines were exhausted, but they had managed to live another day. The main unit arrived the next day. The mission had been a success and Slingshot rejoined his unit. They had a lot to talk about!

After several months in the field, First Amtrac Battalion was joined by the 26th Marines of the 5th Marine Division in the field at 1/1 (1st Battalion/1st Marine Division) where 1/3 (1st Amtrac Battalion/3rd Marine Division) gave operational support to 1/1.

Slingshot's amtrac unit returned to the main firebase near Da Nang. The firebase was located off highway 14 on a hill near Dai Loc, and also around an area the Vietnamese called Nui Kim Son. The rivers served as major supply routes for the VC as well as for commerce for the local peasants.

The *Kong River* originates from the Lancang River in China and becomes the *Mekong River* which flows south and forms a natural boundary between Laos and Thailand until it empties into the South China Sea through South Vietnam near Ho Chi Minh City (Saigon). The *Kong River* branches off the Mekong River and flows from the Annamin Mountains of Northern Laos and runs south through Vietnam toward Da Nang. Southwest of Da Nang the river splits to become the *Vu Gia River* while the *Thu Bon River* flows from the southwest mountains to empty into the Vu Gia. Both rivers merge to empty into the South China Sea at Hoi An. The rivers were natural shipping routes for the VC to re-supply, especially at night.

Slingshot was assigned to a three man outpost to monitor VC activity off the base along the Vu Gia River. It was a scary assignment to man the outpost. Several marines had previously perished on the assignment by VC commando attacks.

The three marines were loaded down with about 100 pounds of munitions each. The munitions for each marine included 4 hand grenades, about 10 magazines of M-14 rounds containing twenty rounds each, the M-14 rifle, and a backpack with food rations and sleeping gear. One marine carried a backpack radio, and a 45 caliber pistol with four ammo clips. Slingshot carried a 30 caliber machine gun with the ammo belts crisscrossed around his chest. The munitions made the outpost a prime target for the VC. The VC not only did not want to be observed; they wanted to kill the Marines just for the munitions.

There were *special forces* formally and separately trained for information gathering patrols. The long range patrols in the Marine Corps to gather *reconnaissance information* was done by the highly trained and skilled *Forced Recon*. In the 60's the Army called its elite, *LRRP*, (Pronounced Lurp) for *Long Range Reconnaissance Patrol*, or more commonly known by the American populace as *Rangers*. The special forces represented a better way of observing VC activities. Slingshot was just an ordinary marine trying to do a tough job in an exposed outpost. Slingshot wished the special forces were available.

From the main firebase, the three man patrol left the compound, to walk about 3 klicks to a position just north of the Vu Gia River. The walk took them past the village of Dai Loc about 3 clicks from the base, past a rice field, through the bush to the outpost location. Personnel mines had taken life and limb from many marines on the night patrols. Slingshot was so concerned about the mines, he stepped into what he thought was a small pond, to avoid the trail where a mine would most likely be. The side of the pond gave way under all the weight of his munitions, and he slid to a deep well in the center of the water pool. It happened so fast Slingshot could do nothing but yell at the others for help as he sank beneath the water. He was so weighted down, he could not even move as the well sucked him into its bowels and beneath the water. Slingshot gurgled as the cool water entered his lungs. The last thing Slingshot heard as he slipped beneath the water was his team leader hollering at the other marine to grab him. Slingshot literally held his breath for the last moment of his life.

Slingshot would have drowned right then and there, but his buddies grabbed him just in time to be able to pull him from the trap. Slingshot was severely shaken and very upset about how close such a stupid move almost cost his life. What a way to die in a war zone! That's the way it was in Vietnam though. The Marines would do their best to avoid being blown up or shot, only to find that they were in another unforeseen trap.

Slingshot was now soaked and wet from head to foot and it would have been very amusing under a different set of circumstances, but the marines were on a mission of a very serious matter. None of them laughed! They rescued Slingshot and they continued on, in a matter-of-fact manner without any noise or delay or loss of concentration of whom and where they were. The enemy could take advantage of a situation when the Marines let their guard down. They just remained focused and continued on with the mission. Inside though, for a brief moment, Slingshot felt so stupid! He quickly realized however, by the grace of God, that although his pride and ego had been bruised, he was still alive.

The marines of the patrol arrived at their destination just before dark. It was just a fox hole at the river's edge. No sand bags or bunker preparations, just a hole in the ground. Across the Vu Gia River was a jungle tree line. Just beyond the tree line there was a trail that ran along the riverside from the jungle to the village of Ky Lam. Their mission was to lie low, observe the river and the village activity in the tree line area, and to report back to the main base of any suspicious activity via the radio. The villages of An Hoa and nearby Ky Lam were noted for VC activity, and both were observed at times.

All was calm for most of the night. It had started to sprinkle rain at about midnight. It did not matter to Slingshot because he was already wet and chilled from his earlier misfortune. At about 2:00 AM, Slingshot noticed movement in the tree line just across the river. He asked the others if they had seen the movement. No one else noticed anything unusual. "I see someone moving along the trail!" Slingshot said. Since it was hard to clearly see what was going on, he decided to shoot a flare over the area. The dark night erupted into a dance of shadow and light. The parachute flare swayed back and forth as it floated toward the ground. Sure enough, the shadowy figures of the VC could be seen tip toeing through the jungle growth along the trail.

The primary mission of the outpost was to *observe* the enemy activity and to report back to the main base. The marines radioed the firebase and told headquarters they were observing VC *activity* across the Vu Gia River. Slingshot shot up another flare just before the first one went out. He could not help but to feel very vulnerable in the situation! The hole he was in allowed some protection from the front, but another tree line existed on his right flank about two hundred yards from the listening post. He feared the VC could easily put them in a crossfire from both the tree lines, one line of fire coming from about 100 yards across the river, and the other line of fire coming from the tree line about 200 yards to his right flank. Their situation seemed desperate to Slingshot. The enemy was all around them!

The marines could easily be outflanked. There were only three of them, and the enemy could decide when, and with how many, to hit them at anytime during the night. Slingshot began to believe that they were in that position because they were considered expendable, a necessary sacrifice for the protection of the firebase. Others had made the supreme sacrifice on such missions before. The primary purpose was to protect the firebase, even at the cost of their lives. Slingshot decided that they would give them a good fight before the VC got them. The forces the Marines could call to bear on the VC would win the battle, no matter what happened to Slingshot and his two comrades. Slingshot *expected* the worse.

There is a cliché said by soldiers in a fox hole: "There are no atheist in a fox hole when the shooting starts!" Slingshot began to pray. He knew they were vulnerable, so he decided not to open up on the VC. Headquarters was kept aware of what was going on. They ordered the listening post not to attack unless they were attacked first. It was reasoned that a later mission would be prepared to deal with the VC, and the village that was supporting the VC, at a time when the Marines were ready, and with a force that gave *the Marines* the advantage.

Later during the night Slingshot popped a couple of more flares to better observe what was going on. The enemy already knew where the listening post was, so stealth was not necessary. The trio of marines watched the VC scurry through the jungle across the river as the VC watched the marines all during the night. Finally morning arrived and the cat and mouse game was over.

With the nights work done, the listening post packed up their munitions and walked back to the base. The VC had returned to their under ground base sometime before daylight. Slingshot was aware that the patrol could still be killed by a booby trap or by an ambush on the return trip, but he really did not feel any real fear about it. He had lived in fear of his life all night! He was wet and cold and emotionally and physically exhausted. When he laid down to rest back at the main base, Slingshot somehow knew he could survive the war, because he no longer feared it! *He could now get on with the job of soldiering without fear, because he had learned to face fear head on.* This gave Slingshot a hard earned confidence.

The sun beat down relentlessly during the hot summer, creating desert-like conditions along the coast. While moving through the dirt fields, the amtrac column threw hot dry dust up in the air, like billows of smoke. The hot dust consumed everything for half a mile. The hot dust looked as if a wind storm was blowing across the land as the amtrac column passed. The sweat on Slingshot's face mixed with the dust, to create a cake of mud all over him. Slingshot wore a scarf to protect his eyes, sinuses, mouth, and lungs, from the treacherous wind storm. *The marines on top of the amtracs looked like masked ghosts obscured by lack of any definite dimensions, flying through a cloud, suspended as angels of death.*

It was just another hot, dry day! The infantry walked along side of the column of amtracs carrying their equipment while on the search and destroy mission. First Amtrac Platoon was in support of Charley Company, when they received incoming rounds from a village located in the valley just below . The village was on the right flank about 150 yards from the Marine infantry unit. Everyone hit the dirt and crawled for position as they returned fire. Everyone was pinned down from the attack.

Slingshot had just stopped his amtrac and had dropped the forward ramp when the fire fight began. He ran toward the infantry to join the fire fight. As he ran bullets were hitting at his feet and all around him. Slingshot had no chance of reaching the skirmish line so he quickly reversed his position and dove through the ramp opening back into the amtrac. The bullets chased him all the way, hitting the ramp as he cleared the opening. An all out fire fight was now taking place between the infantry and the VC. Slingshot raised the ramp of his amtrac and got it into position to return fire. The Marine commander gave the order to cease fire. The VC also ceased firing!

It appeared the action was over when a marine infantryman trying to flank the village, stepped on a personnel mine. Slingshot had just taken position on top of the amtrac where he had his M-14. He saw the infantryman get blown high into the air about 25 yards from his amtrac. The VC opened up again. The marines returned the fire until the shooting from the village stopped once again. The commanding officer, fearful of losing additional men, called in an air strike on the village. Two Phantom F-4 jet planes came roaring in dropping bombs and strafing the village while the marines continued the fire fight.

When the VC had been destroyed and the attack was over, a helicopter was called to rescue the wounded. The marines carried the wounded in a make-shift stretcher made from a Poncho to the dust-off chopper. His legs had been mangled, and his chance of survival was slim. With the enemy village destroyed, the marines continued on with the search and destroy mission. Several VC were dead. One marine suffered with fatal wounds. It was another very close call for Slingshot but he was miraculously unharmed!

The VC had sniper units around all of the bases. Slingshot was used to hearing the sound of the bullets as they passed overhead. He learned which rounds were close and which rounds were not, just from the pitch of the cracking sound as the bullet passed. The louder the cracking sound, and the less the duration of the snap, meant the bullet was within inches.

Slingshot had just driven into one of the tent field bases after a long patrol. He was very tired, drained from long days without much sleep and the hot sun that baked him. The steel of his amtrac was so hot he could not touch it but for a brief second. It acted like a furnace from which Slingshot had just emerged. Slingshot was looking forward to some Kool Aid that he knew was provided by the mess tent cooks. He wanted anything available to cool his hot body! He drove the amtrac until it came to a stop just inside of the compound where the tents were placed. He dropped the ramp of the amtrac and stepped out in front of it, walked about ten yards, when a bullet went cracking by his head. A sniper had Slingshot in his sights! His shot had just barely missed Slingshot! A second bullet, even closer this time, snapped by his head as he ducked low on the run. Slingshot dove into the Amtrac, started it up, and raised the ramp.

The sniper continued shooting into the compound. Slingshot's platoon sergeant, Sergeant Rickman, a salty Korean War veteran, ran toward Slingshot's amtrac dodging the incoming as he approached. Slingshot dropped the ramp to let him inside, then quickly raised the ramp as soon as Sergeant Rickman was inside. "Where the hell is he?" shouted Sergeant Rickman. "The SOB is shooting from the east side of the compound! The (expletive deleted) VC barely missed me!" shouted Slingshot. "He's got to be in one of the trees to get a clear view of us," yelled Slingshot over the roar of the amtrac engine. "Get over there!" yelled Sergeant Rickman.

Slingshot whirled the amtrac around and headed toward the east side of the compound. A sand dune completely surrounded the compound. At the sand dune's edge, the sniper was spotted in a tree about a hundred yards out. Slingshot pointed his amtrac straight toward the tree. "Halt!" Sergeant Rickman shouted. Slingshot brought the massive amtrac to a halt. Sergeant Rickman slowly raised his M-14, and without a scope, fired one shot. The sniper fell out of the tree. The VC that had tried to kill Slingshot and Sergeant Rickman was now dead!

Additional shots were being fired by the VC on the north side of the compound. Other marines had left the compound to pursue the VC on the north side. The firing continued from that direction as Slingshot drove the amtrac back to where the attack on him had started. Slingshot dropped the exit ramp of his amtrac. He grabbed his M-14 and ran to the aid of a marine that had been wounded in the leg. He saw two other marines who started carrying the wounded man. Slingshot joined the trio helping with the gear and guarding their rear as they carried the wounded to a tent.

With the firefight over Slingshot continued on with what he had intended to do in the first place as if nothing had happened. He wanted something cool to drink! After the adrenaline rush of the action subsided, Slingshot's legs felt like lead as he struggled to walk to the mess tent through the soft sand. The heat of the scorched earth continued to drain what little energy Slingshot had left. His steps were slow and labored, his body was numb from the action.

It was not unusual to get sniped at while the marines were trying to eat at the base. Today was no different! Slingshot took cover behind a boulder just outside of the mess hall. He was more upset that his meal was being interrupted than the fact that he was being shot at. He peeked around the boulder trying to find the sniper but he could not tell where the sniper was hiding. The bullets cracked overhead. Slingshot grumbled a few choice words. He was tired and hungry and the sniper was becoming a nuisance. To Slingshot it was as if the sniper had released a swarm of mosquitoes to annoy him while he was trying to eat. The perimeter guards returned fire. The sniper fled and Slingshot returned to the mess hall to eat. A marine sniper pursued the VC sniper. It was just another day in the 'Nam!

During the night the sounds of warfare were always present. Fire-fights took place outside of the base perimeter almost every night. Tracers lit the path of the bullets which created red and green streaks in the sky, flares popped up on the distant hillsides, and claymores mines announced the presence of hostility.

A burst of fire from the VC also announced the beginning of hostilities. Numerous weapons possessing tremendous fire power was available to the Marines to counter attack. A helicopter was sent from Da Nang airbase to deal with the enemy attack. An occasional burst from Puff-the-Magic-Dragon rained bullets on the enemy position as only a modern Gattling gun can. A solid red line of death pored from the sky like an angry dragon's breath. The boom of artillery echoed through the hills. The wop, wop, wop, of the helicopters could be heard for miles, and the roar of the Phantom F-4 jets from Da Nang airfield suddenly filled the air. The roar of the amtrac engines that gave pursuit, with their clanking tracks, sent chilling vibrations into the air. The mere sound of the amtracs struck fear into the VC. The rattling sounds of the equipment from the marines as they ran beat with a unique rhythm giving evidence of the action. After the fire-fight there was a strange silence which was replaced by the sounds of the base activity.

The hum of the diesel engine with the electric generator gave assurance that the huts the Seabees built were still well lit. The chatter of the men that gathered around the *NCO Club* gave evidence that the fighting spirit raged on. The sound of radio chatter from the men on patrol could be heard all during the night. Even the insects and the frogs added their familiar sounds! Everyone was use to it! Slingshot heard the sounds and wondered if he would ever forget. He was doomed not too!

While on a mission *in country*, the marines set up their defensive perimeter using their amtracs as sort of steel bunkers. Everyone tried to get some rest while the guards kept a watchful eye for VC activity. Slingshot had just completed his four hour night watch without incident. The night guard always remained on top of the amtrac behind a machine gun while everyone else slept inside of the amtrac. The amtrac was a good bunker. Just as Slingshot left the top and lay down in his bunk inside his amtrac, the VC attacked.

The VC opened up from the tree line directly behind Slingshot's amtrac and the guy who was on top had to scramble to keep from getting hit. A M-48 tank that was parked right next to Slingshot's amtrac returned fire with its 90 mm canon into the tree line where the shooting started. Slingshot grabbed his M-14 rifle to join the ruckus. After the shooting stopped, Slingshot decided that it might be safer to sleep just outside of the amtrac. Inside, Slingshot was literally sitting on top of 12 gasoline fuel cells, which when full contain 456 gallons of fuel. One well placed rocket into the amtrac and the whole thing would blow-up into flames. As he lay outside beside the track, the VC started shooting at him from the right flank. He rolled off the bunk and hit the dirt just as a flurry of tracer bullets flew within inches of his head. The marines returned fire and the VC broke contact and disappeared. Having just narrowly escaped death, Slingshot did not sleep all the rest of the night!

It was very hard to get *any* sleep in Vietnam. The enemy loved to attack at night and disrupt such a luxury. The Marines exchanged the courtesy with their own gunfire. The end result of the VC tactic meant that everyone was running on adrenaline. That meant that Slingshot went for days without sleep. He did not know that as a result he would find it hard to get sleep for the rest of his life.

After every mission, which lasted for several weeks, the Marines were walking zombies, since they were fighting both day and night. A return to the main base meant they might have the luxury of at least *some* sleep. After awhile Slingshot looked forward to the change to sooth his anger. At the base the smoky mist of the early morning hung over the Annam Cordillera Mountains to the west in defiance of his anger, calling for yet another patrol as soon as he awoke.

When night arrived it was time for the night patrol. On the night patrol outside of the base perimeter, Slingshot settled into the ambush position concealed in the brush like he always did. He had been watching the area in front of him for hours, when suddenly he saw a shadowy figure that seemed to approach him very slowly. Slingshot's heart began to literally pound against the inside of his chest. It was about 3:00 AM. The sky was dark with clouds moving across the moon every few seconds causing shadows on the ground. Slingshot was very sleepy and he was suffering from battle fatigue. He rubbed his eyes in disbelief. Was he imagining things? The shadow stopped moving and then disappeared for a few seconds. "Did I see someone, or was it just a bush moving in the breeze?" Slingshot unsure, anxiously thought. It was common for the men to imagine all sorts of unrealistic things during the night, and Slingshot did!

The shadow reappeared again, coming right at Slingshot's position. Slingshot clicked the safety off of his M-14. "If it is a VC, I must take him out," Slingshot reasoned. He squeezed the slack out of his trigger mechanism! Slingshot's heart was pounding uncontrollably now. "Fire now," he reasoned. "Fire your weapon! No, not yet! remember your training! He's probably the point man! Wait for the whole VC squad to enter the kill zone!" Slingshot's mind raced for the answer to respond. "Fire! He's almost on top of me! No, Hold it, hold it!" The man slowly passed Slingshot. The man could have reached down and touched Slingshot he was so close! "Why didn't the man see me? He didn't see me in my camouflaged, concealed position!" Slingshot reasoned. "Here comes the whole squad! I've got them now! Hold it, hold it!" Slingshot's heart raced so fast by now he heard it beating against his chest. He feared the thumping was going to reveal his position. "Why hasn't our ambush squad spotted the enemy point man? They should be opening up by now! My target is in my sites! Come on guys, let's blow them away, now!"

Slingshot very slowly turned toward the shadows, took aim at the shadowy figure now directly in front of him. With the safety off, he again took every bit of the slack out of the trigger. "Now squeeze, s-q-u-e-e-z-e the first round into the target," Slingshot nervously reasoned. With no slack left, Slingshot started the squeeze on the trigger that would release the bullet!

At that very moment Devine intervention occurred! One of the shadowy figures spoke! His English was perfect. His demeanor was serious, but calm. "It's alright man, it's only us!" he said. "What the hell? Who was that? What the?" said a confused Slingshot.

Slingshot froze in sheer terror! He knew instantly that because that man spoke, at precisely the moment that he did, that a terrible, terrible mistake was avoided! Only he knew how close it was to being a night of disaster, that by the grace of God many lives were spared an unfortunate death! Another Marine squad was returning from their patrol, a patrol that Slingshot did not know was out there! Slingshot, confused from the shadows of the night and the extreme fatigue had come, literally within a heart beat, of ambushing his own men!

Many mistakes occur in war. It is very easy to overreact when your life is on the line. It happened in Vietnam, it happened in Korea, it happened in WWII, it happened in the Gulf Wars, and it probably has happened in every war. Many soldiers get killed by friendly fire! It is a fact of war. Many suffer in the silence of their grief their entire lives.

Slingshot thanked God many times that that man spoke when he did! Had he chose not to say anything, at that very moment, had God not intervened to save many souls, Slingshot probably would have been killed along with many others from the fire-fight that would have occurred?

Tired and confused Slingshot shook for hours. He did not understand what was happening to him. It was not just this one night, but an accumulation of events that was affecting him. His *mind* was beginning to change without his awareness. His *behavior* was beginning to change. He only wanted to survive the moment, but unknown to him he needed to learn how to survive the future. Slingshot was *severely wounded* that night. He was wounded in a way that no one understood at the time, especially young Slingshot himself. In the silence of his nightmares he struggled with grief, anger, and depression. He also suffered from guilt. *His whole life Slingshot would never stop shaking at the thought of that moment long ago!*

The war continued, having had caused another psychological casualty without any notice or concern from anyone else, *especially* the very civilians back home who's freedom he was trying to preserve. *Slingshot was wounded and all alone now!* It would take many more years for the people back home to understand soldiers like him.

All the types of patrols; the ones that led to ambushes, foot patrols, armored patrols with tank support, amtrac patrols, night patrols, recon patrols, mine field detection patrols, sniper patrols, and search and destroy patrols, were extremely dangerous. However, the patrol that Slingshot felt most vulnerable on was the river patrols.

The Vu Gia River and the Thu Bon River flowed through the Marines primary area of operations of I Corps. Often the marines entered the river to patrol a short segment of it and then crossed over to the other side to continue the patrol on land. Chances were that they were going to run into something because the VC controlled the entire area. Slingshot was concerned about the vulnerability of the amtrac while it very slowly lumbered through the water.

Other times the marines entered the river to patrol westward toward the Annam Cordillera Mountain Range. The villagers signaled the approach of the marines to the VC who were in their main base area of the mountains. After driving his amtrac upriver and then ashore, Slingshot watched as the infantry dismounted the amtrac to checkout the villages. Then the VC either sniped at the marines, or they headed for the tunnels of their mountain hideouts so they were no where to be found. Slingshot often joined the search.

The women and children of the village cleverly acted friendly. They squatted to the ground and placed their hands in the praying position. They chattered and mumbled in Vietnamese as Slingshot searched for weapons or of any signs of the VC. The VC were experts at warning their men and covering their tracks. They knew where the marines were but the marines did not know where they were!

Slingshot felt like he was going to die without even knowing where the shot came from when he searched a village. He cautiously entered each thatched hut more worried about being shot in the back and booby traps than anything. Slingshot did not trust the villagers! When found inside a thatched hut, Slingshot ushered the Vietnamese out into the dirt jungle path that ran through the center of the village. The interpreters started immediately questioning the peasants. Their loud unfamiliar chatter created a mixture of chaos and high tempers. Blows were exchanged to maintain control of the most rebellious members of the crowd. Slingshot was unsure of the search tactic. It troubled him when things got out of control.

The Vietnamese merchants used the Vu Gia River as a major supply route. Small canoe like boats flowed up and down the river from village to village. The VC got their supplies that way! Slingshot saw the four to five Vietnamese dressed with their top pointed conical straw hats trying to maneuver their boat out of the way of his amtrac as he approached. They wore the same black silk pajamas and shirts that the VC were known to wear! They looked young and strong, and that alone made Slingshot nervous.

Slingshot's amtrac column headed straight for the small craft. Were they VC or merchants? They were sometimes one and the same. Most of the cargo was covered by straw mats and cloth. The Vietnamese bent over and faced away as if they were hiding something as the amtracs plowed low in the water toward them. The column of amtracs caused a strong wave that destabilized the small boats. "Unless we stop, how are we going to know the contents of the boat?" Slingshot rationalized.

The Vietnamese boats had to get out of the way! The Vietnamese furiously paddled their boats to the shore while the amtracs roared past. The huge steel amtracs looked monstrous as they one by one floated past the Vietnamese with their flimsy wooden boats. As Slingshot drove his amtrac past the small boats, he was very curious about their contents. A quick glance by one of his amtrac crewman revealed no evidence of VC supplies in the boat; just fish. It occurred to Slingshot that the fish were the supplies!

Slingshot just had a gut feeling that the Vietnamese were sneaking VC supplies into the area. Slingshot blurted out to his crewman, "Why aren't we checking these boats? What's going on?" No one cared to answer because no one knew the answer. The column just kept moving along. "We have VC right under our nose, mused Slingshot, and no one cares." He was suspicious of all Vietnamese. It did not make much sense to Slingshot that each boat was not checked as the column proceeded along. In Vietnam though, a lot of things just did not make sense. The political aims versus the military aims clouded all reason.

Two amtracs on a river patrol, far away from the main base, made a tempting target for the VC. A few marines could be easily ambushed from the shore where the VC could conceal themselves in the jungle growth. The two amtracs, part of Slingshot's unit, did not know they would be hit that day. The VC fired their Chinese made 57mm canon at the back of the amtrac, where the hull was the most vulnerable. The water immediately rushed into the engine department where the amtrac was the heaviest, and where the least buoyancy occurred. It took only a few seconds for the amtrac to sink. Slingshot's comrades, with their heavy equipment, were blown into the water from the fuel tank explosion. They struggled to swim as the VC opened up with their AK-47's. The VC literally shot the struggling marines like fish in a pond. The other amtrac crewmen returned fire, but the VC broke contact after having accomplished their goal of inflicting several casualties, and destroying the amtrac.

Slingshot never forgot the results of the ambush. Afterward he feared the river patrols day or night! His eyes told the story; that cold stare that was absent of any emotion. The numb feelings that produced the stare was fuel for isolation, and contempt for the living! He wanted to survive the day but at the same time he did not care if he didn't! He was a human being prepared to reap revenge on a merciless enemy. Death was the common denominator, and life was the division. Slingshot braced himself for the next patrol!

The next amtrac patrol lead the platoon deep into the jungle! The marines exited the river near some deep grass as Slingshot drove his amtrac through the formidable mud of the river bank with no idea of where their self made path would lead. A village appeared in the distance that they did not know was there, a village that had no name to Slingshot. Was it friendly or Foe? Was it a hot LZ far away from nowhere? The truth of the matter was there was no way to know unless the VC decided to attack!

The marine infantry platoon methodically dismounted the amtracs to do a search and destroy sweep of the area. They were expecting the worse but it was routine for them by now. One by one the marines cautiously entered the village searching for anyone suspected of aiding the VC. The point man signaled the directions. Slingshot remained on his amtrac watching everyone. Was the peasant looking at Slingshot a VC, a NVA Regular, or a friendly peasant? Slingshot was never sure!

Slingshot anxiously waited on his amtrac. He heard the marines shouting as they continued their search. Slingshot was lightly armed but he was ready for anything. With the rest of the platoon on the ground, that put him and the other two crewmen on their own to defend the amtrac. They had a 30 caliber machine gun mounted on the top of the amtrac, and they had their M-14s at the ready. A fox hole built out of sandbags surrounded the gun and protected Slingshot from incoming provided one well placed shot didn't get him first! They also had the usual infantry munitions of grenades and plenty of ammo. The steel armor of the amtrac offered good protection from the VC small arms fire, but it was little comfort for Slingshot since the amtrac was very vulnerable to the VC heavier weapons.

Slingshot was uncomfortable to be isolated from the infantry during the sweep, but he was glad he was *on* the amtrac. He was in his element aboard the amtrac! He very slowly drove through the village keeping close to the infantry. With each steer of the amtrac the tracks tore deep trenches in the soft jungle soil. The dirt flew from the spinning track in all directions as the villagers scrambled to get out of the way. Some of the dirt hit the pigs that roomed through the village causing them to squeal loudly adding to the drama taking place. The monstrous steel column of amtracs just kept rolling over whatever got in the way. It was a frightful sight for the simple villagers.

Slingshot skillfully used his driving experience to pick his path around the thatched huts facing the trail. His eyes scanned the area for booby traps and for any evidence of aggression from the villagers he saw. He knew the amtrac offered some protection but he also knew he was vulnerable. The ground was soft, especially near the village, where he could get stuck in the soft mud of the water drenched rice paddies. Rice paddies provided the village with food, and the wet fields encircled many villages. The amtrac tracks were known to throw the soft mud out from under them, causing the under belly of the amtrac to settle down on the mud. A helplessly stuck amtrac made a very tempting target for Charlie! Without the mobility usually afforded by the amtrac, the VC could easily assault them from any direction. Slingshot drove around and through the village locked and loaded.

Slingshot continued to carefully maneuver his amtrac through the village watching the infantry as they entered each thatched hut for the search. He waited as the marines gathered the VC suspects. Except for some yelling, the villagers offered no resistance. The marine riflemen forced the occupants of the houses to gather into the street. There the VC suspects were patiently loaded aboard the amtracs.

The villagers were hard looking men; men who knew no other life *but* hard times. They were farmers by definition, but guerilla fighters by necessity during the war. They cared neither for the South Vietnamese government ruled by President Thieu nor for the North Vietnamese Communist. They only cared for the survival of their families and they catered to whoever was there at the moment.

The VC suspects were transported to the marine base for interrogation. The village disappeared in the distance as the marines and Vietnamese aboard the column of amtracs left the area for the journey. The Vietnamese women and children began crying for their men, and their wailing could be heard in the distance even above the roar of the amtrac engines. No shots were fired during the search this time but the operation was just as nerve wrecking just the same. The sun disappeared below the mountains as the amtracs with their human cargo entered the base for the evening. Morning would bring on another patrol.

The amtrac was the *most* vulnerable to damage from the bottom. There twelve fuel cells which could contain as much as 456 gallons of gasoline when they were filled to capacity, waited to explode upon impact from munitions. The fuel cells themselves were like a preset bomb! The amtrac was designed to land the marines on the beach from the ship to the shore. The fuel cells were protected well under water while the amtrac was floating in the sea, but they were exposed and very vulnerable to land mines while operating on land. To protect the crew from the deadly fire which was usually caused by coming into contact with a mine, the bottom of the amtrac cargo space was lined with a layer of sandbags. The sandbags were there to absorb the initial impact of the explosive device, and also to help to snuff out the fire caused from the gasoline. The additional weight however, coupled with the sandy terrain, caused the steel track of the amtrac to fail prematurely. An amtrac with a thrown track was an easy target.

On patrol with two amtracs, Slingshot's amtrac was ambushed from a rice paddy that was directly across from the Thu Bon River. The VC looked as if they were working in a rice paddy, just like every farmer in Vietnam did all the time. When the two amtracs approached the rice paddy with Slingshot in the lead, the VC posing as farmers, suddenly opened up with rifle fire on Slingshot's amtrac. Two squads of infantry was sitting on top of the amtrac. They immediately returned fire and Slingshot drove the amtrac in pursuit of the VC. The VC bullets hit just inches from Slingshot's head, which was the only part of his body exposed while sitting in the driver's seat. Another bullet went right between the legs of the platoon sergeant, splattering sand into Slingshot's face! He was sitting on top of the sandbagged turret of the amtrac with his legs spread for support, like he was seated in a chair right at home. He looked at Slingshot and *smiled* as he returned fire. The calm platoon sergeant looked as if he was truly enjoying himself! On command everyone began shooting from the top of the amtrac. The sound of the weapons ranged from the thump-thump of the grenade launcher to the cracking of the M-14. The intense firepower coming from the marines broke the line of fire coming from the VC. The VC broke off contact as they began to flee. The formidable M-79 grenade launcher with each thump sent explosive bursts of shrapnel toward the VC, wounding several. The marines in hot pursuit fired their heavy caliber M-14 rifles into the field of brush surrounding the rice paddy where the VC were in full retreat!

The amtrac bounced and heaved as Slingshot roared toward the VC. The marines kept laying down a treacherous wall of lead as they blasted away at the running VC. The VC turned and knelt down long enough to return fire, then they ran for the tree-line in the distance. Slingshot could see them bobbing up and down in their black pajamas as they ran for cover. Slingshot steered right for them!

Unfortunately for the marines, the VC were on the other side of the river! At the river's edge, Slingshot paused as he looked down from a steep embankment high above the river. It appeared to him to be at least 60 feet down to the river, although it was probably less than that! A any rate, he was not sure the amtrac and its passengers could survive such a steep plunge! Still ducking the incoming everyone reacted quickly! It was time to react, not to think!

In the heat of the battle at the top of the embankment everyone via command from the platoon sergeant jumped through the hatches to the inside of the amtrac. It had been quickly decided that everyone might survive the dive to the river from the *inside* of the amtrac . Once inside, the amtrac was to be sealed by closing all of the hatches! Slingshot moved from his drivers seat to allow entry through the driver's hatch! During the switch Slingshot was caught outside of the amtrac as everyone else buttoned up the hatches from the inside. Someone had jumped into the driver's seat to take control, and the marine quickly closed the access hatch trapping Slingshot outside!

All along on top and completely exposed, Slingshot grabbed the turret handle of the amtrac as the amtrac lunged forward! He hugged his body tight against the turret. He literally held his breath as the amtrac dove through the air from the top of the steep embankment into the river. Slingshot closed his eyes, holding onto the top of the amtrac as it hit the water. The amtrac plunged completely underwater with Slingshot holding on for dear life! The muddy cool water of the river rushed over Slingshot's body as he submerged. Underwater he continued to hold onto the amtrac while it sank. "How deep am I going?" Will the amtrac bob up from beneath the river, or will it just sink to the bottom?" Slingshot had no way of knowing as he sank ever deeper beneath the water. "I'll hold on until I just can't hold my breath any longer," Slingshot reasoned! "If I let go I'll be shot like a fish in a pond! I must hold on!" He was sure the amtrac was going to get stuck on the bottom of the river after they had plunged from such a high embankment. "This is it! I'm done for!" Slingshot mumbled underwater, almost out of breath.

The VC now in full retreat was running from the rice paddy and was about to disappear into the tree-line. Amazingly, the amtrac *did* bob to the surface, and it began to slowly claw its way across the river to the other side. The hatches popped open to discover that Slingshot had made the plunge from the *outside* of the amtrac and that he was still aboard and alive. Until then it was thought he had been shot! Without saying a word he motioned to the other driver to switch! Slingshot methodically took control of the amtrac. He was much older now. He had aged many years in just those few chaotic minutes!

Everyone was unsure about what had just happened! How come Slingshot was left outside? Why had all of the hatches been closed without everyone inside? How could Slingshot have held on? Why hadn't he drown? Hadn't he been shot? Was he angry? Were the marines wrong to think he had been killed when he had not? What had happened? No one knew the answers about the events that had happened so fast. They were all amazed, surprised, and a little embarrassed that he was left for dead. The cold fact was, the reality of the war is what was happening!

Slingshot drove his amtrac toward a garden that was between him and the fleeing VC. As he started through the garden an old woman jumped in front of the amtrac and started screaming at the top of her lungs in Vietnamese. The platoon sergeant raised his arm to stop Slingshot. Slingshot stopped the amtrac in the middle of the garden. The tracks had already damaged the garden badly when the amtrac plowed through it. The woman kept screaming and crying! It did not take an interpreter to figure out that she was begging us not to destroy her garden!

The remaining VC had managed to run to their escape even before the amtrac got to the other side. The marines saw them disappear over the horizon into the safety of the tree-line. Since the

VC had scattered into the trees, the marines broke off their pursuit. Slingshot slowly began backing out of the garden! The Vietnamese woman cried while waving her arms and leaning on her hands and knees as she tried to piece her garden back together. Slingshot felt remorse with an uncanny sense of confusion. The infantry dismounted the amtrac to search the rice paddy and the surrounding area for wounded VC. There was plenty of blood on the ground but the VC had taken their dead and wounded with them as they fled.

    Slingshot had barely escaped death once again and the events of the day had caused him much confusion. The confused emotions that he felt tended to disrupt any immediate thoughts of valor. When the initial bullets of the VC had hit in front of his face while driving his amtrac, he could see the ricocheting fragments hit the sandbags as he escaped their deadly intent. The horrific battle, being left out, the near drowning, and the Vietnamese woman screaming, reminded him that it was one hell of a war. It began to affect his already fragile psych! He would never forget it! He would *forever* relive the experience in the silence of his unwanted nightmares!

Hong Kong

After several months of duty in the Asian theater of war, all of which was out in the field, Slingshot had earned one week of rest and recuperation. Slingshot could choose from a variety of places to go for R&R; Hawaii, Tokyo, Australia, Manila, Penang, Taipei, Kula Lumpur, and Singapore were offered. In Vietnam he could take R&R at Vung Tay or an area known as China Beach. Additionally he could go to Bangkok, Thailand; or he could go to Hong Kong, China, which in 1967 was still a British colony scheduled to be transferred to Chinese rule in 1999. Although he had heard that Bangkok was *the* place to go, it was too much like Vietnam for his taste, so he chose to go to Hong Kong. Besides he wanted to see a little of China because his dad had served in the CBI; China, Burma, India Campaign during WWII.

Slingshot was not disappointed. He was fascinated with Hong Kong. He was a little surprised at the wealth. To see young Chinese men dressed in nice suites going to work in high rise buildings that dotted the hillsides, and that overlooked the Hong Kong harbor, created an atmosphere far different than that he had experienced the last several months in Vietnam. To see wealthy Chinese instead of poor Vietnamese or poor Okinawa Japanese, changed his narrow perception of Orientals. His hotel was first class. The service was excellent. The servants spoke fluent English as well as Chinese so there was no problem with transactions.

The U.S. dollar was worth about ten times more than the Chinese dollar. Slingshot felt rich and privileged. It made shopping a lot of fun, because everything was inexpensive in U.S. dollars. The Japanese Akai reel to reel tape recorder was the state of the art in audio equipment at the time. Slingshot bought the tape recorder and two large speakers for a fraction of what it would have cost in the U.S. He did not care that he had to hand carry the heavy equipment back to Vietnam. War has its quirks!

The Rolling Stones, a rock and roll band, were a big deal for Slingshot's age group so he had their music, as well as some others, recorded on a large real of tape as part of the deal. The guys at the tent in 'Nam enjoyed "I Can't Get No Satisfaction" by the Rolling Stones in full stereo sound. It reminded everyone of better times back home in "the world."

Slingshot roamed the streets day and night around the hotel to see as much of the general area as he could. There were many shops with lots of goods all around. He also, being curious, entered a couple of the bars to enjoy the Chinese women with drink. Very lonely in a very strange place, he paid the bar for one of the pretty Chinese girls for the evening. She could speak English as well as Chinese. She was petite in stature but mean and aggressive in her manners. Slingshot had another drink trying to decide if he wanted to be with her. The hormone driven part of him did, but the small town boy in him did not. Eventually he gave in to his loneliness and took her to her house. It was located on one of the back streets just a couple of blocks from the hotel where he stayed.

Her room was upstairs over looking the street that led to the harbor. It was a majestic scene right out of a romance novel. A lot of people were busily scurrying about on the street. Rickshaws were everywhere and the people moved through the streets in rhythm with each other as if they were dancing to the beat of the noisy street. The boats in the harbor lit the night which provided a warm glow to the bouncing water already lit up by the evening moon. Still it made Slingshot feel uneasy seeing so many Chinese below. Hardened by the war Slingshot trusted no one, much less a Chinese woman in a strange place. He was uptight and on guard in spite of the beautiful scene below.

After she talked with Slingshot awhile she took him to her bedroom where she got ready to please him. She was a thin well toned woman that was in her late twenties, perhaps about five years older than Slingshot. Her face was cute and her body was attractive but she seemed all business with him. When she began to please him, Slingshot kept one eye on the door and listened to every sound coming from below.

Slingshot paid ten dollars for the girl's services. She then offered to spend all night and all the next day with him for an additional twenty dollars. Slingshot agreed to the deal but he told her he would have to go back to the hotel for the money. They got dressed and went back to the hotel where Slingshot got twenty dollars from the clerk's safe, and only twenty dollars! She seemed upset that he would not take it all. He knew she would take him for every last cent if he let her. They roamed the streets for awhile and Slingshot had a few more drinks. Then they went back to her room. It was about 2:00 AM. Slingshot was tired and drunk but he let her please him and then he tried to sleep. He could only half sleep, his survival instinct keeping his senses fully awake.

The next morning Slingshot arose to the sounds of the busy street below. He had a hangover and he was not in a good mood after being awake most of the night. The first thing the girl said was that she wanted more money. If Slingshot had agreed, the day might have turned out to be pleasant, but her business like approach and his bad mood turned him off to the idea. The more he thought about it the more he hated himself for being there! He took it out on her. She made him so mad arguing with him about the war and the Communist that he lashed out at her throwing things and cursing her for all she was worth. "You kill other people in Vietnam, now you want to kill me! She screamed. "You (expletive deleted) right I do! You're a (expletive deleted) Communist too! All you Chinese are Communists!" Slingshot, out of control now, screamed loudly. In his state of mine he wanted her to admit it so he could justify his actions! For all practical purposes he was back in Vietnam! His built up tension from the war was taking over his behavior. "You leave now," She said, as she took the twenty dollars from his billfold. By now she knew she could not get anymore money from him. Slingshot believed she was provoking him to madness on purpose to get rid of him. They continued to argue over the money even after the Chinese girl's parents, aroused by the commotion, came into the room.

It was a shock for Slingshot to see her parents there! They had been in the next room all night! It was a real culture shock to say the least. Her parents were actually accepting their daughter's sinful activities as a means of support! "What kind of people are they?" Slingshot thought. It was obvious to him by now that she was a *con artist* of the first degree. Slingshot told her father that his daughter took his money even though they were not going to spend the day together and that he was going to hurt her if she did not give it back.

The Chinese man stood quietly by his wife as Slingshot and the man's daughter continued their futile argument. Their cool appearance settled Slingshot down a little. They just stood there quietly and motioned for him to go. The slightest aggression from any of them would have caused Slingshot to attack! It was all he knew at the time. Wisdom was years away! They looked so meek in their old age and he knew by their concerned look that he was just as wrong as she was. He decided to leave without saying anything else. After all, he had spent the night with her so he figured it was best to just forget it.

Her father just stood there quietly with his hands behind his back. The Chinese girl was a tough gal; she just glared at Slingshot as he started for the door to leave. Slingshot turned to close the door where he saw them still quietly looking at him. Their manner confused Slingshot. Slingshot was use to being attacked! With no attack to react to, Slingshot was unsure of what to do next.

The Chinese girl looked pretty even in her anger but the parents looked real serious; then Slingshot noticed something that sent chills down his spine! The old man had brought a loaded revolver cleverly hidden in his hand behind his back. Slingshot was unarmed and the Chinese man could have killed him instantly had Slingshot actually struck their daughter or tried to harm them in any way! Slingshot would not have known what hit him!

Slingshot sighed a breath of relief as he entered the street. He was shaking now from the confrontation. *He realized immediately that he could have died in a most dishonorable way on a back street in Hong Kong!* He wondered if the old man was going to send a gang after him to put him in his place. Slingshot was much more guarded the rest of his visit. He thought how ridiculous it would be to be shot over a fight with a whore after all he had been through; shot because he no longer knew how to behave in a civilized society! Shot because of uncontrolled anger! Shot because he was afraid. Those thoughts were to haunt him all through the rest of the day and years beyond.

Much wiser now, Slingshot was sure glad she had not gotten *all* of his money the night before. Afterwards he did not find the bar women all that attractive anymore, knowing that they were out to just take his money. He never went back to any of the Hong Kong bars after the terrible experience!

Slingshot chose to tour the city during the day, for the rest of the week. It was a strange environment for him. Slingshot was just a small town Texas boy who literally grew up in the forest of East Texas, there locally known as the "sticks." Here was the Paris of Asia, Honk Kong, full of history and intrigued. Slingshot was amazed at seeing many Chinese driving Mercedes, dressed in fine silk suites, living the wealthy life he himself had never known. Others were living on the boats in the harbor, while others lived in sheer poverty in the allies that connected the main streets. Slingshot walked up the streets to the Nathan Road shopping district to view the abundance of goods that was packed into every store. He bought several items.

The Chinese mainland people came through a gate that was guarded by Chinese guards with AK-47 rifles. They directed the traffic coming from the mainland of China to Hong Kong and from Hong Kong to China. They were well dressed in their uniforms and Slingshot felt uneasy seeing them with rifles when he did not have his M-14. Slingshot started to approach the guard anyway to see if he could go deeper into mainland China. He walked up to the guard, looked at him for a moment and decided it was too risky for an American soldier to be in Communist China, especially for an unauthorized visit. The "Bamboo Curtain" descended over the door to mainland China, so Slingshot just walked away never taking his eye off the armed guards.

At night Slingshot rode the rickshaws through the streets

along the harbor. The Chinaman that pulled the rickshaw was a tall thin man that could run like the wind. He wore the traditional conical palm leaf hat, a top pointed straw hat made from palm straw. He had the traditional Chinese mustache and chin hair. His skin was dark from many years in the sun and wrinkled badly. He was not too friendly with Slingshot. His dislike for Americans was obvious, especially military Americans, and Slingshot did not trust him either.

The harbor traffic was right out of a romance novel, with the wooden *sampan* boats along the shore. The sampan is a typical Chinese boat propelled by a single scull over the stern, and provided with a roofing of mats. It is used for the transport of goods on all of the waterways of the Orient. Other ships had sails. Several of the boats were moored to the docks, where it appeared the occupants lived full time. These people looked like they lived a rough life. They viewed Slingshot with a non friendly stare, but made no sign of aggression either with their hands or with their body language.

Slingshot ventured dangerously into the back streets and allies of the city, where there were a lot of poor people, like the homeless in the big cities of the U.S. The smell of opium filled the air, emanating from the bamboo cane pipes that the alley dwellers smoked. Slingshot noticed that several men, either sat in open doorways, or lay in the alley with ragged dirty clothes for their only cover. Erie sounds echoed through the alley as cats and mice scurried through the rubbish. Kids could be heard crying in the door-less rooms next to the ally, while women chattered continuously in Chinese to anyone who would listen. The smell of urine and human waste filled the air with its sickening stench. A couple of astonished old men mumbled indecently at Slingshot as they picked their way through the rubbish. Slingshot held his breath for fear of disease.

Slingshot, seeing the Chinese version of back-ally life, realized how crazy he was for exploring the city from behind the glamour. Although somewhat shaken by what he was observing, he walked cautiously through the maze of trash and human suffering. It occurred to him that what he was going through in life, was not as bad as all of that. He quickly worked his way back to the main streets, knowing he was fortunate to have made it without being mugged for his money or possibly killed as a foreigner who lost his way.

Slingshot beckoned another rickshaw for a ride, whereby the astonished runner shook his head in disbelief that Slingshot had just emerged from the alley alive. The runner waved his hands at Slingshot in a frantic display of resentment. He must have thought that Slingshot was crazy for entering the no-mans-land alone at night! The runner angrily mumbled Chinese gibberish as he quickly ran down the street that led back to the hotel. Slingshot did not understand his flamboyant words but he knew that the Chinaman was calling him obscene names just from the angry tone.

As the runner vented his feelings about Slingshot's uncalled for and unnecessary stupidity, Slingshot sat in the rickshaw thinking about his misadventure there in China. The buildings flew by him like a blur as he searched his mind for answers to his unusual behavior. Slingshot unconsciously felt like he had just survived another night patrol in Vietnam. Why had he gone into the dangerous ally? Why did he take the risk?

The runner stopped the rickshaw in front of the hotel. Slingshot was relieved that he was safely there. He had gone into the dangerous area to purposely seek adventure because he had gotten a little bored of not being at risk! Vietnam had conditioned him to accept dangerous and risky situations as "normal" activity. He missed the adrenaline rush! He missed the excitement of danger! He *missed* living on the edge of life! He missed the need to overcome fear! He missed the power! He missed the extreme forces of nature he had faced! He missed the physical demands and the chaos that a war creates! Slingshot needed to reassure himself that he was not afraid of anything. Greatly satisfied after the challenge that he wasn't afraid of anyone or anything after all he had been through, Slingshot paid the runner a few American cents and quietly walked into the hotel for some uneasy rest.

While on leave in Hong Kong, after that first night, Slingshot called Loretta almost every night. He missed her, especially while he was in Hong Kong. Somehow his experience in Hong Kong had made him appreciate her more. On the phone Slingshot talked about her. They talked about *life* in general. They teased each other with sultry sexual innuendoes. They talked about "the world" back home. They talked about American life compared to Asian life. They talked about when he was coming home and what they would do for fun. They made serious plans. They made love with their voices. They shared their loneliness, and how they missed each other!

Just to talk with Loretta gave Slingshot a reason to survive! He had been living in fear of his life from day to day, thinking that each day he lived was the last day of his life. He promised Loretta that he would do his best to come home, but he reminded her that the whole situation was up to God. Slingshot found out later that his phone bill was well over $500.00! That was a lot of money in 1966! He missed Loretta so it did not really matter. To him it was worth every cent!

When the flight left Hong Kong, China to bring Slingshot back to Da Nang airfield in Vietnam, it was almost like he was coming home. He was on familiar turf now, so it somehow seemed less intimidating to him in Vietnam. The Cold War environment of China frightened him more. At least in Vietnam Slingshot was armed!

Along with some other items, Slingshot had bought a bulky Akai reel to reel tape recorder; it included some large speakers in separate boxes. He had to carry all the heavy items he had bought by hand from the air field tarmac at Da Nang airfield to Highway 1. He flagged down a six-by and managed to get all his stuff in the back of the truck. Slingshot climbed into the back of the truck and asked the driver for a rifle. He felt more secure with a rifle but the driver said he had one and for slingshot to sit down and to relax. Although uncomfortable about being unarmed, Slingshot rode in the back of the six-by from Da Nang airfield to the main base some twelve miles south. Slingshot wondered if the stuff he got in Hong Kong would survive the war. He did not think about whether or not he would survive the war anymore. He was numbed by months of fear so he was ready to accept his fate without care. To die meant nothing to him.

Slingshot always wrote his parents while he was in Vietnam. He was concerned about *their* welfare. His mom, in turn always wrote to keep him updated about their welfare. She would not tell Slingshot that she was having health problems or that they were suffering from difficult times. The family was not in trouble as far as Slingshot knew.

Slingshot's mom received the Western Union telegraph explaining that Slingshot had been wounded in Vietnam. "How bad is it?" she thought with the pain of a loving mother. "Will he be OK?" She was worried and anxious to hear from him to find out if he was OK. Slingshot did write his mom to let her know he was back in action. He told her not to worry but *he* knew that there was plenty to worry about.

Slingshot's mom always sent him care packages stocked full of candies, cookies, crackers, and other food stuffs. Slingshot always shared these things with the other guys who missed these niceties as much as he did. His mom reassured him in her letters that Loretta missed him too and that everyone was looking forward for him to return home. Although those things made Slingshot feel good momentarily, and it certainly gave him hope, he wasn't sure just where he wanted to call home. He had left Baytown thinking he would never return, and obviously nothing was the same to him now.

When Slingshot went to Vietnam, he was a very immature teenager. Because of his traumatic experiences, he was now aged beyond his years. He also knew that he still had two years left in the Marine Corps. He had originally joined the service for one tour. Now, he did not know if he was going to make a career out of the service, or return to civilian life. He was undecided about reenlistment, and he was a changed person after Vietnam. He was a warrior with a new kind of war to face! How could he fit into a civilian world?

Civilian concerns about everyday life now seemed trite and unimportant to Slingshot compared to the struggle of the life and death situations he had experienced in Vietnam. He found most of the activities that he encountered boring, and without any stimulation. It was like he was all alone wherever he went, and no one seemed to care! It was now hard to relate to the so called "ordinary" people back home. He was not prepared for what these changes in his psychic would mean to his future. Slingshot began to feel really confused about life, although he did not even know it at the time.

When it was time to rotate out of Vietnam, Slingshot thought very briefly about staying a little longer. If he had not been married, with the expectations of a good life back in the world, he probably would have extended his stay. However, when he added up how many times he had faced death during his tour, he realized that he should not continue to tempt fate. It was time to leave Vietnam.

Much of Slingshot's unit was being sent north for "Operation Prairie II," which officially had begun 2/1/67 and lasted until 3/18/67. The Marines were to confront the NVA 's 324th and 325th divisions building up around the DMZ. Slingshot rotated out of Vietnam in March of 1967 as his unit prepared for the northern deployment. The 1st Battalion Landing Team, the amphibian tractor battalion in which Slingshot served, had arrived in Vietnam in July 1965. During 1966 and 1967, his unit started the counteroffensives that lasted until 1969. His unit, with different personnel each year, remained in Vietnam until July 1969. Then they were deployed to Okinawa, Japan.

During Slingshot's tour of duty, he had earned the **Purple Heart**, the **Presidential Unit Citation**, the **Vietnamese Service Medal** with two stars, the **Vietnam Campaign Medal**, the **National Defense Medal,** and the **Vietnam Cross of Gallantry.** He later received the **Cold War Certificate signed by the Secretary of Defense.**

Slingshot was an ordinary corporal in the United States Marine Corps, and by **God's grace a survivor** of one of the most tumultuous periods in U.S. history.

Coming Home

The return home was swift via a 707 passenger plane. Slingshot hardly had time to reflect on what he had been through. He thought of the places he had seen his first year in the Marine Corps: California, Wake Island, Hawaii, Okinawa, Japan; Vietnam, Southeast Asia; and Hong Kong, China. Each place had been a new experience for him. It would take years to appreciate it all.

Slingshot got off the plane at El Toro marine airfield in California and literally got on his hands and knees to bend down and to kiss the ground he was standing on. He was in the United States, where *the world* existed. He was extremely excited emotionally but he was very reserved when it came to outward expression. The war did not end for him when he left Vietnam! In fact the war was *always* to be with him. Slingshot's whole life was changed as a result of Vietnam! He just did not know it at the time.

Slingshot didn't really think about it at the time but, he had changed. He had changed from a very innocent, small town, conservative, even bashful kid, to a man that had experienced much of life's basic dramas, before he even understood the affects of such traumatic experiences. The true affects of his experience did not show up until several years later. Psychiatrists would later define the pent up emotions of Vietnam Veterans as *Post Traumatic Stress Disorder*, or PTSD for short. Slingshot was a victim of the unknown curse.

Slingshot flew from Los Angeles, California to Houston, Texas the same day his bus arrived in LA from El Toro. The day before he was in the field of a war zone. His senses and emotions were tied to that environment. He reacted to the change in a state of mind that was acutely aware of everyone and everything around him. It required a lot of concentration, so he was not responding to the people around him in the relaxed and friendly way that was normal among the civilians. He was running on adrenaline mode, expecting to respond to the next move necessary to survive. When the stimulus for such reaction was not forthcoming, it really confused him emotionally and physically. He was like a race horse in the gate, struggling to control his desire to begin the race; the forces holding him back, an obstacle to be overcome!

Slingshot was home. It was as different as it was the same. To the people at home the war was far away, and to Slingshot's surprise an unpopular war. There were no marching bands in support of his return or any mention of the honorable sacrifices he had made. He was a validated war hero, but nobody cared! Wasn't it for them that he had laid his life on the line? Without the recognition or support from the society he served, the sacrifices suddenly seemed in vain. He was to find out over the years that many people did not care about what he had gone through, and that was the realization that hurt him the most for many years to come.

Slingshot was proud of his service. He still had a lot more to give. He began to realize that he had to get by on his own without the support of the public or its officials. He realized that he did not agree with society about a lot of things. His immediate love ones appreciated his efforts. To them he could do no wrong. For the moment that's all that mattered.

Slingshot had sent almost his entire combat pay home the whole time he was overseas. He had bought bonds, and Loretta had worked while he was gone, so they had some money. They used some of it to buy a brand new 1967 Camero. It was the hottest sports car on the market at the time for his age group. He was like a kid all over again, with a brand new toy. He had not driven a car in so long that it felt both really strange, but refreshing all at the same time. Loretta and he made the rounds about town. She had rented an upstairs garage apartment for them to have for awhile. There they tried to get reacquainted. Slingshot knew he would have to leave soon which made the leave home somewhat artificial to him. There was no chance to become too excited about it all. His leave was for a short thirty days.

  Slingshot's orders were to report to Camp Lejeune, North Carolina after his leave was over. Loretta and he decided that they would live in an apartment off base. They drove to North Carolina so that they could have their new car with them. They left Baytown early so that their trip could be an adventure. Although a bit rushed, they drove happily through all of the Southeastern states to get there unharmed. Since neither one of them had seen much of the United States, they enjoyed the long road trip.

CHAPTER EIGHT

Camp Lejeune

During WWII it became necessary to have a base area on the East Coast where troops could be trained and deployed to the European theater. During September 1941, the 1st Marine Division set up camp in the piney woods of North Carolina near the Atlantic ports of Morehead City and Wilmington. Marine barracks were soon established at New River, North Carolina. By the end of 1942, the base was named after the Commandant of the Marine Corps and Commanding General of the 2nd Army Division in WWI, Major General Lejeune.

General John A. Lejeune believed that a true leader serves for the welfare of others rather than being focused on self-serving motives. He established seven imperatives of leadership:

- Being morally worthy
- Being thoroughly responsible
- Being highly competitive
- Being an impeccable example
- Being dedicated to highest standards
- Being dedicated to noble service
- Being physically and morally courageous

It is fitting that the East Coast base was named after such an impeccable example of leadership. Camp Lejeune has grown to become the "Home of Marine Expeditionary Forces in Readiness."

Slingshot drove for two days to get to Camp Lejeune North Carolina. He was entering a new phase of his Marine Corps Experience. Camp Lejeune is located deep into the piney woods along the Atlantic east coast. He could not help but to notice that the area was not that much different from the piney woods of Eastern Texas, much like the Gulf Coast area where he grew up, except in North Carolina, the winters were much colder with snow and ice.

The couple got an apartment off base. It was a small apartment that was not exceptionally comfortable. It had one room that combined the bedroom and living room. The floor was concrete with a worn vinyl cover. The kitchen was small with tiny appliances. It was not much, but it was better than the way he had been living for the last several months. Loretta did not like it at all! Slingshot was only a corporal who did not make all that much money. It was about all he could afford. Loretta did not work at that time. They decided it was only temporary, so they could live with it, at least until he got promoted.

The base was to have a routine muster at 7:00 AM via a company formation at Courthouse Bay. Slingshot left the apartment at about 5:30 AM to drive the approximately twenty miles through the woods to get to the bay area that harbored the marine amtracs. He arrived at the camp about 6:15 AM. He talked with the sergeant major to find out what they would be doing for the day, and then he helped muster the marines that lived and slept in the barracks, to the company formation. After formation, after their orders were given for the day, the marines usually boarded the "cattle car," which was a truck pulled trailer designed to transport troops while standing, to make the trip to where the amtracs were parked on the other side of Courthouse Bay. At the camp, the marines worked on the amtracs all day. This included greasing all the fittings, changing or adding oil, fueling the amtrac, painting it, cleaning it, doing all sorts of preventative maintenance repairs, and working on or replacing the track. The marines were always prepared for an inspection. This ensured that the amtracs were being properly maintained. Some marines still had to be taught the importance of that. In Vietnam however, the maintenance was done automatically to survive! To do maintenance on the amtrac just for an officer to look at seemed much less important to Slingshot now. It insulted and intimidated him to think that some officer that had never even experienced combat would tell *him* how to maintain his amtrac! It was the thing about stateside duty that irritated Slingshot the most. To him stateside duty was for the inexperienced, and not for the combat veteran, unless his rank allowed leadership.

  The promotion came quickly. Slingshot was now a sergeant E-5. He was a *crew chief* of an amtrac. As such, he always made sure his amtrac was well maintained and ready for an inspection at any time. His crew and he always looked sharp from a Marine Corps prospective. They always got very high and favorable marks from the inspecting officers. He personally took pride in looking well groomed, and in having his crew and amtrac in a state of readiness. His "fatigues," a term used to describe the dark green military clothes that were used for combat and work, were always starched and pressed at the beginning of the day. Slingshot always shaved before leaving the apartment. He made sure that he had a military hair cut, and that his boots were shined. The brass buckle used on his web belt shined to perfection! His M-14 was spotless, each individual part, disassembled and cleaned before reassembly. He treated the standard issue of tools and equipment he carried on his amtrac the same way. Every item associated with his MOS (Military Occupation Specialty 1833) was ready for an unannounced inspection, right down to the finest detail. Slingshot felt stateside duty required him to look and be the best the military had to offer. He was a very proud Marine. He had to lead, or he would wilt from the mundane routine of stateside duty.

Stateside Duty

After the overseas assignments, the stateside duty was very routine and tedium in nature. It took a lot of discipline to adjust to what now seemed to be trivial activities. Gone was the threat of being killed at any moment. Gone was the *urgency* to react just to survive. Instead, the marines were to behave as if none of them had been through the war. Many marines simply could not readjust to the boring conditions now before them. Many drank themselves into a stupor night after night. Others just went about their duties as if nothing mattered anymore. Some just wanted to fight! Since there was no immediate enemy, many marines just fought each other. Many were demoted.

The need to have excitement was overwhelming. Some marines behaved in an overbearing way, shouting orders to each other, expressing an outward desire for perfection, while not trying to achieve perfection themselves. On stateside base, the veterans were race horses that were led to pasture in the prime of their lives. Many, especially the ones that had been drafted as a result of the Vietnam War, just wanted to get their discharge and get out. Nothing else mattered.

Slingshot was delighted when he found out that he was to join the FMFLANT (Fleet Marine Force Atlantic). He questioned it at first because Loretta and he had not been together very much since he had enlisted into the Marine Corps. They had only been in their little apartment a couple of months before he was to start training for the overseas assignment. Although he questioned it at first, he soon realized it to be an opportunity for an adventure of a life time.

The first basic change that took place was that the marines were required to *run* to work instead of to ride the cattle car. A trail through the heavy woods of Camp Lejeune led to the work area where the amtracs were maintained. The run was approximately four miles through deep, soft, uneven sand; sand that had been grinned through the tracks of many amtrac maneuvers.

Each morning after being briefed in a *company formation*, the amtrac platoon formed to make the run. Then the platoon ran to work in platoon formation, chanting phases such as: "Here we go, all the way, up the hill, down the hill; here we go, one, two, three, four; one, two, three, four."

Many times the drill sergeant, knowing they were in the woods far away from sensitive types, lead the platoon with a more creative growl, such as: "I know a girl dressed in red, she makes her living lying in bed; here we go, all the way." Or perhaps, "I know a girl that's dressed in black, she makes her living lying flat on her back."

The chants reflected the un-politically-correct times! There were no women in Slingshot's platoon to insult in the Marine military of the 60's. After the days work was done, the platoon ran back to the main barracks to complete the day. However, times were changing!

Med Training

Soon Slingshot started training for the Cold War between the U.S. and the USSR. The platoon prepared for inspection after inspection. All necessary equipment was issued as the men prepared for readiness for their duty overseas in the Mediterranean Sea. The USSR was there with their own fleet waiting for them. The marines knew they had to be ready for the confrontation, so they trained very hard.

Physical fitness training began in earnest. The Physical Readiness Test (PRT) was similar to boot camp basic training. Slingshot climbed high ropes with his combat equipment strapped to his back and hips. His arms and shoulders were very strong for his size. He could often shimmy up the knotted rope faster than the other guys, not even using his feet or the knots; using only his arms to pull him to the top. Everything was timed. The marines did step-ups to test the readiness of their legs. Slingshot maxed that! They did pushups, chin-ups, sit-ups, and squat thrusts. They ran through the woods with full combat equipment. They ran through the woods timed without full combat equipment. Slingshot got top score on the readiness test

The marines marched a lot from one part of the camp to another. They crawled through the mud and dirt like reptiles after their prey, firing pistols, rifles, and other weapons at various targets. They participated in war games company wide. Mock patrols were practiced. They practiced carrying each other on their backs over long distances. They threw hand grenades, or fired the M-79 grenade launcher through the doors and windows of "Combat City" as they assaulted the city structures. It was boot camp all over again, and much more! Although it was important and good training for the coming Cold War patrol at the flanks of Europe, it all seemed fun and games to Slingshot after Vietnam. He breezed right through the training in a matter-of-fact way as he continued to improve his skills. He had trained in California during staging for Vietnam after all of his basic training was complete. He was trained in Vietnam while on the job! He was trained in Okinawa. Now he was being trained at Camp Lejeune.

Field operations involving the amtracs were conducted. The marines trained with overnight operations in the woods. It was a strange feeling for Slingshot sense many operations in Vietnam were in the jungle and that experience in hostile territory had already taught Slingshot's platoon the tactics to operate under such conditions. In addition Slingshot's platoon went to Jungle Warfare School while stationed in Okinawa to become even better trained. Never-the-less the marines practiced the war game maneuvers and amphibious operations. They assaulted the makeshift towns. They trained at the "Vietnam Village," as if most of them had never seen one! They did search and destroy patrols where they looked for the enemy positions during the war games. Most of the trainers were surprised at just how quickly the Vietnam vets were able to achieve their objectives, while the new guys fumbled through the exercise.

Slingshot went to the firing range to again qualify with the M-14 rifle. The new M-16 had not yet gained the favor of his unit. He enjoyed shooting the more powerful M-14 rifle whenever he had the chance. Many times he practiced shooting off base in the back yard of his house, using no ammo and a technique called "snapping in." Slingshot always shot well enough to be given the *expert* rating. The marines practiced firefights using blanks as ammo. They trained as if none of them had ever seen action in a war zone like Vietnam. Most of the marines in Slingshot's outfit considered the training mere child's play after what they had already experienced. They had no trouble meeting the very strenuous standards required for the duty, because most of them were already experienced veterans, and well trained to boot. Slingshot knew from experience how important it was to be prepared. He took pride in his development as a marine, and he worked extremely hard.

    The Med patrol required a different approach to training than did the training for Vietnam. It was in reality a different assignment than Vietnam. Vietnam was a brutal "Hot War" and it called for difficult and brutal training. Europe was not technically in a Hot War, but it was a powder keg waiting to explode should the Cold War become hot.

    The Vietnam veterans understood the reality of a Hot War. They had been fighting the nations of the "Bamboo Curtain" in a hot spot of the Cold War for years. Although already experienced as combat veterans, they took the training very seriously knowing that it could very likely, given the Cold War tensions of the time, lead to combat in Europe. From experience, the leaders from WWII, the Korean War, and the Vietnam War prepared for the possibility.

    Slingshot was excited to be on the Med patrol with the Sixth Fleet, eye ball to eye ball with the USSR and its "Iron Curtain" allies. There he would be on the front lines of the action should the USSR or the Middle East erupt into war with the U.S. and its allied nations of the free world. He did not want WWIII to happen, but he certainly was ready to do his duty should it become necessary!

I-68 BLT 2/2

The finale inspection before the marines deployed to the Mediterranean Sea was the Commanding Generals Inspection. General E.B. Wheeler was the Commanding General of 2nd Battalion, 2nd Marines FMFLANT, as Atlantic Force Sixth Fleet I-68. The *Sixth Fleet* consisted of 25,000 sailors, manning 30 ships, serving in the Mediterranean Sea. Some of the ships of the fleet most closely associated with the Marines included the USS Fremont APA 44, USS Monrovia APA 31, USS Arneb AKA 56, USS Walworth Co. LST 1164, USS Ashland LSD 1, and the ship Slingshot was on, the USS Rushmore LSD 14. **Slingshot was assigned to 1st Platoon, C Company, 2nd Amtrac Battalion, 2nd Marine Division, FMF Atlantic.** The Atlantic Fleet Marine Force commonly known as the "Sixth Fleet."

BLT 2/2 was ready to embark. Slingshot rode the six-by troop trucks from Camp Lejeune, North Carolina to the beach at Morehead City. There he prepared his amtrac for the trip out to the ship. After he drove his amtrac through the surf, he steered through the Atlantic Ocean for the stern of LSD 14, knowing that a mistake in his maneuver could send his amtrac to the bottom of the Atlantic. The USS Rushmore was waiting for him about a mile from the shore. Slingshot made a perfect entry into the ship.

After everyone was safely aboard, the marines and sailors set sail across the Atlantic for the 4500 mile trip to the Mediterranean Sea. It was May 29, 1968. The fleet arrived in Gibraltar, the gateway to the Med, in late June to make turnover with BLT 1/2.

BABYBOOM DOOM

USS Rushmore

CHAPTER NINE

Rock Of Gibraltar

The *Straight of Gibraltar* is a channel that lies between Southern Spain and Northwestern Africa that connects the Mediterranean Sea with the Atlantic Ocean. It is 36 miles long and narrows to 8 miles in width between Point Marroqui (Spain) and Point Cires (Morocco). The straights western extreme is 27 miles wide between the capes of Trafalgar (north) and Spartel (south) and the eastern extreme is 14 miles wide between the *Pillars of Hercules*. The *Pillars of Hercules* have been identified as the *Rock of Gibraltar* (north) and Mount Hacho, just east of Ceuta, a Spanish enclave in Morocco (south). This water gap between the Atlas mountains of North Africa and the High Plateau of Spain has been used by Europeans as the main connection to the Atlantic and beyond for centuries. *Slingshot was once again on the front lines of the Cold War.*

The *Rock of Gibraltar* is a historical place where the Europeans have fought for centuries for control. Since Gibraltar controlled the entrance to the Mediterranean Sea (Med), for many years it had major significance as a fortress. It is a British Colony occupying a narrow peninsula of Spain's southern Mediterranean coast, just northeast of the "Straight of Gibraltar." The Spanish and others have built tunnels through the solid rock, wherein are placed cannons that guard the entrance. Slingshot walked through the tunnels and touched the centuries old cannons. He thought about how the ancient soldiers had worked and played behind the walls of this natural fortress; soldiers of the Roman Empire, or soldiers from Spain. In the 70's the British used the natural fort as an air and naval base. NATO used the port facilities and the Marines operated with their allies in NATO as they patrolled the Med with the Sixth Fleet.

From the summit of the island one could see the entire Sixth Fleet moored in the harbor. Slingshot could not help but to think about Pearl Harbor when he saw all those ships lined up that way. "Hadn't we learned anything?" Slingshot wondered with a frown.

On December the 7th, 1941, the U.S. Pacific fleet was all but destroyed by a Japanese air raid. There were close to 3000 U.S casualties from the attack! The Pacific fleet was moored in Pearl Harbor with the ships lined up just like what Slingshot was seeing below! The unprepared U.S. entered WWII and rallied behind the cry "Remember Pearl Harbor!" President Franklin Roosevelt declared December the 7th as "A day that will live in infamy!" Hadn't the loss of so many lives, and the loss of so many ships, taught the U.S. anything about a determined enemy? Wasn't the Marines now facing a determined enemy set on world domination? Wasn't the U.S. in a *Hot War* with the Communist in Asia, and at the same time a *Cold War* with the Communist of Europe? Slingshot worried with the nervousness of a veteran, "Shouldn't we be prepared for an attack on the Sixth Fleet by the Soviet Union?" Slingshot felt the fleet was not properly prepared as he viewed the very vulnerable fleet from the summit of Gibraltar. A cold chill ran down his spine as he shuttered to think about the consequences of such an attack!

The *Rock* was also occupied by *Barbary Apes*, a local monkey that roamed freely throughout the island. The Apes were as curious about Slingshot as he was about them. They squealed and jumped around and postured as if they were challenging Slingshot to a duel for the territory. They were not afraid as they wandered all around Slingshot. Slingshot tried to get a picture from the high vantage point overlooking the fleet. The monkeys constantly jumped in the way. After much fanfare, Slingshot took several pictures. With that done, he started the long climb down to the town.

The Town

The town was built with the buildings on every level imaginable. Slingshot noticed how narrow the streets were as they wound their way around the buildings on the steep inclines. The cars were also very small, especially when one considers the size of U.S. cars in the 60's. This was Slingshot's first impression of Europe. Everything seemed small, crowded, and it was old and outdated. He sort of liked the quaint appearance though.

The marines left, and sailed past the "Rock of Gibraltar" into the Mediterranean Sea where Slingshot observed the Barbary Coast of North Africa. This is the same coast line of the former Barbary States of Morocco, Algiers, Tunis, and Tripoli where pirates harassed Mediterranean trade. Now the U.S. fleet was being harassed by the Cold War tactics of the Soviet Union's ships and planes. The Med is a colorful dark blue, and the water danced beautifully with the spirit of the wind. The air smelled fresh as the fleet continued the journey. Slingshot studied the African coast to see if he could see anyone on shore. He could not distinguish anyone from where he was, but he could see the shore clearly. Spain was on the other side of the ship. That was to be his next destination.

CHAPTER TEN

Spain

The Sixth Fleet then sailed to Almeria, Spain where the marines coordinated with the navy a turn-away landing. This is a practice landing without *actually* landing. For the navy the first thing Slingshot heard was "Set condition 1-Alpha!" Then came the order "All boats to the rail!" Next came the order "All boats to water's edge!" Finally the order the marines were waiting for! "Land the landing force!" This meant the landing operation had started for the marines via the navy. When the intercom barked out "Boat Team 1-1 lay to Red One," it was time for the marines to go into action. This was the first time that the marines, not on the amtracs, went down the wet nets of the APA ships to board the navy landing craft.

The amtracs, loaded with troops were started, and with a roar one at a time, they exited the back of the ship. Outside they formed a circle, then on command turned to assault the beach. Slingshot drove his amtrac out the back of the ship, and circled to rendezvous with the rest of his platoon. This was not new to him because he had done this in actual operations in Vietnam. The marines had also trained to do this while in Okinawa. The *turn-away* landing went real well; just another day at the office for the Marines.

Barcelona

The fleet entered Barcelona, Spain for liberty. A friend of Slingshot's, SGT Ellis from Illinois, and he took leave together. They both were married, so they did not want to run with the groups that would be looking for the bar girls. They toured the shops and restaurants and sought out the tourist land marks. The statue of Christopher Columbus reminded Slingshot of the history associated with him. The beautiful fountains, which created a romantic touch, reminded him of home with their peaceful brook-like sound.

Barcelona is made up of three main zones. The old city (Ciutat Vella) lies between Placa de Catalunya and the port and breaks down into Rambla; the Barri Gotic (Gothic Quarter); the Barri de la Ribera (Waterfront Quarter); the Raval, or medieval "outskirts" west of the Rambia; and Barcelonete, the old fishing quarter. Slingshot explored the old city that lies off the port. The fountains and shops made him homesick and soon he was drinking to deal with the pain of loneliness.

Slingshot returned to the ship to find many others were sick and lonely as well. He found some comfort knowing that he was not alone in his grief. He missed Loretta but he tried to handle his mixed feelings by reading in his bunk. Others wept and whined about their position in life but Slingshot tried to disassociate from the pain. He was beginning to withdraw from the others. The isolation tended to make him even more lonely. He fell asleep in his bunk to face the nightmares of the Vietnam War all over again from his dreams. He suffered in the silence of the night without anyone even being aware.

The Dance

Slingshot decided to go on leave by himself one evening. After touring the various buildings and shops he wanted to get something to eat. The evening was comfortable, about seventy five degrees, with a slight breeze. The stars could be easily seen, and the moon offered a beautiful compliment to the evening. It was the kind of evening that made one homesick, especially whenever couples could be seen who obviously loved each other as they walked hand in hand. Many couples stopped to face each other, to hug and kiss in that special way that only loved ones can do. Slingshot noticed the Spanish women, who seemed to be very different from the Oriental woman he had seen for so many months in the Far East. Spanish woman carried themselves in almost an arrogant way. They did not even look at Slingshot as they walked by in a hurried manner, eyes looking straight ahead, or in any other direction. It was obvious the town people did not like the marines in their country. Slingshot really was not all that interested in any attention from them, but he thought a "Hello" even in Spanish would have been nice. Perhaps it was because Slingshot did not look all that friendly himself! After a short walk, he decided it was time to get something to eat.

Slingshot entered the restaurant thinking only of getting something to eat. He was led upstairs where he found the restaurant all but empty, probably because it was about 9:00 PM in the evening during the middle of the week. Male waiters formally dressed in black tuxes stood near the bar. One pulled the chair out from under one of the tables to offer Slingshot the seat. The table was set with a white table cloth and it had real "Silver" utensils all formally arranged in ceremonial order. The crystal glassware was filled with water immediately. Slingshot was not use to that kind of formality! He was in the military, aboard the USS Rushmore, where he had been at sea for several months. He was use to being served by sailors stationed behind a cafeteria type line on the mess deck where he carried his own food to a ship's small table, and that after he had waited in line for half an hour on a rock and roll footing. He was very astonished about all the formality. Additionally, he was young and inexperienced with that type of life to begin with. He had never had a *formal* dinner in his little town back home in rural Texas!

The waiter asked in Spanish if Slingshot wanted a drink. Through hand signals, Slingshot motioned that he understood. He brought out a bottle of wine. He popped the cork, poured a little of it into a glass, and handed it to Slingshot. Slingshot had seen in the movies where the guy smelled the wine as he swirled it around and observed the color. The actor would then take a small sip, smack his lips, move his jaw around, swirl the liquid inside his mouth, and then announce his approval. Slingshot acted like he knew what he was doing by re-enacting the ritual he had seen in the movies. He slowly nodded his head as if to say the wine was excellent. The waiter poured the wine into the glass until it was a little over half full. Slingshot liked that wine, although he would have liked any wine just the same. He began to sip the wine. The waiter left the table to stand by the bar.

A different waiter came over in a hurried way. He opened a silver cigarette case, and held it within easy reach of Slingshot's hand. The cigarettes were lined in the case all in a neat roll. Slingshot did not want to smoke because he had promised himself that he would never do so. He wanted to avoid the expensive and unhealthy habit at all costs because he did not want to get hooked on nicotine, nor to have everything around him smell like the smoke. He remembered the very unpleasant days in his parent's house when the room was filled with cigarette smoke as he choked for relief.

Up to that point Slingshot had behaved as if this was his everyday lifestyle. He hesitated while the waiter nudged the case toward him as if he were insisting that Slingshot try one of his cigarettes. Since the waiter was so insistent, out of politeness Slingshot took a cigarette from the case. He thought that he would just take one, and throw it away after the waiter left. As soon as Slingshot took the cigarette from the case, the waiter lit a lighter to light the cigarette! Slingshot handed the cigarette back to the waiter, and asked the waiter to light the cigarette for him. The waiter did so, and handed the lit cigarette back to Slingshot! "Now what?" Slingshot nervously thought! He had acted out this ritual never wanting the cigarette, but not wanting to refuse the kind waiter's service. Finally, Slingshot just smiled and accepted the lit cigarette to get rid of the waiter. He held it in his hand while he ordered the meal.

Slingshot wanted a "chicken fried steak" like the ones that he had had back home in Southeast Texas. This is a southern way of preparing steak by incrusting it with egg based flour, then frying it in hot grease to a crispy brown crust. When Slingshot felt that he had finally made the waiter understand what he wanted to eat, he sat back, cigarette in hand, and thoughtfully sipped the wine. Slingshot noticed the waiter would glance at him from his bar spot. When he did so, Slingshot raise his hand as if he was going to take a puff from the cigarette, then stopped short of doing so as the waiter looked the other way. Slingshot was acting like he was somebody important to live up to the unexpected sophistication presented to him. He had no problem accepting the wine refills as he waited for his meal.

When the meal arrived, Slingshot discarded the cigarette, never having smoked on it at all. He could not believe how the meal was prepared. It was a steak alright! He had gotten that much of his order understood. It was not, however, a southern chicken fried steak! On top of a slightly warmed piece of dark meat, not at all well done, was a fried egg! The yoke ran over the steak like gravy, giving the steak a slimy texture. At that time in Slingshot's life, this was a strange looking meal. He began to think that he should not eat the steak because it was not prepared the American way. He slowly bit into the meat wondering if he should scrape the egg entirely off the steak. The waiters kept watching him every minute it seemed. The waiters were just making sure that they were available for a motion of service, but Slingshot, was paranoid. He felt like he was being watched. Images of threatening circumstances danced in his mind!

Slingshot smiled a quick smile and pretended that nothing was wrong. The waiters were a little curious about him, but they were basically disinterested in Slingshot's unusual behavior. Slingshot, however was hyper-vigilant and watched every part of the place, thinking he was going to be attacked at any moment. The Vietnam War had made him that way, and survival dictated that he be alert!

Slingshot nervously devised a plan of attack. He would take out the nearest waiter first, then spring for the back door. He planned his escape in the silence of his paranoia. He was especially nervous about someone approaching him from the rear! Slingshot kept looking over his shoulder. He watched everyone who entered the restaurant, and he perspired as if the room was very hot, although the room was not. He ate some of the meal, but he could not finish it all, since it was not well done and not at all what he had expected. He was getting very tired from the hyper-vigilance, but he was use to it by now.

With the meal now over, Slingshot started to drink a cup of coffee, anxious to leave as soon as he was finished. Then it happened! The unexpected happened! Slingshot was startled as they entered the room. He jerked back in his chair from their sudden appearance.

A well groomed couple dressed in the traditional Spanish attire ran out onto the solid wood flooring and began to dance! With the castanets in hand they swirled around, arms overhead as their solid heel shoes clattered on the hard wood floors to the rhythm of the beat. At first, Slingshot thought they were after him!

Slingshot quickly looked around as if the couple was sent to distract him from being on guard. Slingshot took a deep breath, and after a sigh of relief, he realized that he was being "entertained" by real Spanish dancers in a safe restaurant setting in Barcelona, Spain! His spell broken, he realized that he was apparently in no immediate danger. The first dance was soon over, and it thrilled him beyond comprehension to have witnessed it. Slingshot watched the elegant couple as they prepared to continue their dance.

Her hair was solid black and wrapped tight in a knot at the rear of her head, giving her forehead a shinny black appearance that accented her dark complexion and dark brown eyes. She was tall and thin in stature, but she had a strong presence about her. The Spanish man looked much like a matador with his elegant stance, as his lovely partner danced around him in a circle with all the class of the elite. Slingshot was a little surprised that such elegant entertainment was taking place without the benefit of a very large crowd.

Slingshot felt strangely proud to have witnessed the traditional Spanish *dance*. He began to realize that the trip he was on was very special. He was seeing the sights and sounds of some of Europe's most historical places, and enjoying a culture filled with undeniable style. It was a once in a lifetime experience.

No one knew what kind of dance Slingshot had just experienced, least of all the professional dancers! He was tired, no exhausted, from his mental dance of stress for survival. He was physically in Spain, but the flashbacks triggered by the common circumstances surrounding him, put him mentally in survival mode, and for all practical purposes, back in Vietnam!

Slingshot was ready to move on to his next adventure in the hope that it would somehow bring him relief from his fateful anxiety! He desperately needed relief from the pain that danced inside his troubled mine. He had an anxiety problem that he, nor anyone else could possibly understand unless they shared the experiences that brought about the "Babyboom Doom." The dance of life continued.

CHAPTER ELEVEN

France

Toulon

Slingshot boarded ship, and his unit sailed for liberty at Toulon, France. After safely sailing into port, he enjoyed watching the French people. The French people strolled through the pigeons, past the fountains, romantically holding hands, laughing and walking, as if there was not a care in the world. It made Slingshot think of home, and he began to really miss Loretta.

Slingshot constantly compared the buildings and the people of France to those of America. He was interested in the French culture. The French, although not always in agreement with U.S. foreign policy, did help the colonist achieve their freedom against the English during the American revolutionary war. Slingshot respected that. He did not like the French reluctance to support the US in the Vietnam war. It was the French who refused to allow Vietnam independence after WWII and whose policies involved U.S. support.

He loved the French music, the fountains, and the artful statues. The statues displayed all the body parts in uninhibited fashion, genitals, breast, and all. This was *never* seen as art in Texas in the 60's. It made Slingshot feel real uncultured because the French did not see their art as an item for a puritanical message; therefore they were a lot more uninhibited as a culture.

Slingshot, feeling bored walked into a downtown movie. Although he could not understand the French language, he could relate to the actions. He was surprised to see bare breasted woman on the big screen. It would be years before America would do the same. In the 60's it was unheard of in the Bible belt of Southeast Texas. Slingshot was taken by surprise to see that kind of open and uninhibited expression for the first time.

In one store a local French lady saw that Slingshot was admiring the merchandise and that he was a Marine from America. She started talking to him in French. In broken English he heard her say, "American! American!" Slingshot said, "Wee, wee," or something like that to indicate yes. She pointed to the merchandise, and Slingshot nodded his approval. Then she said, "De Gaulle! De Gaulle!" Slingshot understood her to mean the French President since 1959. The U.S. government was upset with De Gaulle over deregulation of the gold standard and of the French reluctance to allow U.S. military uses of their bases. Just months before in 1966, De Gaulle had withdrawn French participation from the military arm of NATO.

Slingshot motioned to the French woman, in a moment of uninhibited reaction, by slashing his hand across his throat as if to say De Gaulle should be dealt with that way. She immediately bolted from the store waving her arms and pointing her finger at Slingshot, astonished that he did not think much of De Gaulle, and mumbling French words that Slingshot probably did not want to know the meaning. He knew he had made a *détente* mistake. Slingshot worried that it might be taken as an international incident should she tell the authorities, and it were to end up in the papers. Slingshot imagined the headline, "U.S. Marine insults the French!" Slingshot was sorry for the obscene gesture, and he vowed he would be more responsible from then on. It was necessary to be diplomatic whether you liked it or not. Slingshot had mixed feelings regarding French foreign policy.

The next day Elmo, a friend of Slingshot's, and Slingshot took liberty together. It was July 14, 1968! Someone motioned to get Slingshot's attention and yelled, "Bastille Day! Bastille Day!" France had started its revolution to gain its independence on July 14, 1789, when the people of Paris captured the old fortress of Bastille. In France the celebration of *Bastille Day* is cause for national rejoicing, with parades, music, and dancing in the streets.

Elements of the military had gathered from all over Europe to celebrate Bastille Day. Slingshot figured that the French were celebrating the liberation of Europe from *Nazism*! "It must be a celebration of the Allied victory in Europe during WWII," Slingshot thought with a sincere belief. Actually, it turned out to be the French Independence Day parade, equivalent to July 4 in the United States. All of Toulon was a party town! Slingshot was impressed!

The parade started through the streets where Elmo and Slingshot paused to watch. Slingshot felt he was in the parade as the people engulfed them in the street. The street filled with great marching bands that played European patriotic songs as they systematically passed by the crowd. Many groups of military looking personnel march smartly by in their traditional outfits and waved at everyone with friendly broad smiles. Slingshot mused, "When we Marines march on our parade grounds, our eyes are focused straight ahead, with each step choreographed with precision and snap." It seemed strange to Slingshot that the marchers smiled. Some of the marchers were dressed in all white, like the Alpine Skiers of WWII. They carried their skis over their shoulders like rifles. The skies swayed from side to side, to and fro with each step. Others marched by in their green dungaree like uniforms carrying rifles and chanting patriotic songs. Various military cannons pulled by horses also passed by Slingshot, with a clanking rattle. Various trucks and armored vehicles roared by, many mounted with a variety of machine guns. The French girls waived energetically, and they attracted Slingshot . The girls were of special interest to Slingshot. It was nice to see pretty girls after so long at sea. The girls really added to the excitement of the parade as they smiled and waved from the backseat of the jeep like trucks.

    At one point, since they were walking, and watching the parade all at the same time, Slingshot and Elmo came to a stone wall that ran parallel to the street. Although the wall was about five foot high, it appeared that the wall would offer a good vantage point from which to watch the rest of the parade. Just as Slingshot started to jump up to the top of the wall, a heavy set woman tried to do the same. She repeatedly tried to jump onto the wall so that she could get a good vantage point to see the never ending advances of the marchers. She could not jump high enough to get to the top of the wall. So after a lot of meaningless English and French verbiage, and with the use of hand motions and signaling, Slingshot made her understand that he wanted to assist her. It turned out to be a hilarious situation because the lady was laughing at the fact Slingshot could not easily lift her. He decided to grab her around the waist to lift her high enough to grab the top of the wall with her hands and arms. The jovial woman squealed and laughed because she could not pull herself over. Her waist seemed to collapse as Slingshot attempted to get a grip to lift her upward. Slingshot let go of her waist and turned his back to her feet so she could use his back to step on for leverage to the top of the wall. Slingshot pushed with his legs as she tried to clear the top. She slipped back and turned around so that her back was against the wall with her feet on Slingshot's back. Others saw what was happening. They began to laugh at the awkward position Slingshot found himself in, and the lady, who was laughing all the time, lying all over his back, seemed to be stuck on top of him! After much grunting and pushing Slingshot managed to lift her high enough to clear the top of the wall. Elmo jumped upon the hill the wall set against, and began to pull her by her arms as Slingshot pushed from below. The French woman, obviously enjoying the experience, finally rolled over to a sitting position on top of the wall over looking the parade. Unaware of the sideline excitement, the parade continued to march by, its music playing, as if the three disorganized characters were part of the proceedings. Slingshot could tell she was extremely grateful for the help as she indicated by her laughter and sincere gestures. Slingshot was a little embarrassed over his clumsiness, but he was glad he was able to do a good deed for the determined woman.

Everyone continued to watch the parade. Slingshot laughed and waved and even threw kisses. The marchers returned the jester with big broad smiles on their faces. Elmo stood up to wave, and he jumped around with the excitement of a young child, although his uniform indicated that he was all man. The parading soldiers seemed to recognize the Marine uniforms. While Slingshot was admiring the parade, the members of the parade seemed to be admiring and appreciating the marines. They acted honored that the two marines were there to watch them.

From the hill Slingshot had a marvelous view. His legs dangled over the wall as the parade marched directly in front and below him. What a view! Slingshot could almost touch the marchers as they passed. He shouted patriotically , "Viva La France! God bless America!" He yelled the Marine Corps motto, *Semper Fi*, Latin for *Always Faithful*, and jubilantly threw kisses. He was having a great time. He felt he was truly *bonding* with the locals, and all was well.

Back aboard ship tension was mounting amongst the marines. A gay man had been transferred to the USS Rushmore from one of the other ships in the fleet. The decision to put a known gay activist in the marine's sleeping quarters did not set well with a certain group of marines. Gay men amongst the Marines was very unacceptable in the military of the 1960's!

Slingshot was laying in his sleeping quarters in the ship rack, when he heard a commotion about 2:00 AM in the morning. A group of marines had just gotten off liberty, and they were entering the sleeping quarters. A marine Slingshot knew to be from Massachusetts was leading the group. He was yelling to the others that something needed to be done about the gay guy. Slingshot could tell that all the marines, there were at least five, had been drinking. Slingshot heard one say, "We can not allow any (expletive deleted) fagots in here!" Another said, "We've got to fix that (expletive deleted) queer!" The first one said, "Let's get rid of that (expletive deleted) fagot!" A third one said, "Let's "code red" the (expletive deleted) sissy!"

A "code red" was a technique Marines used to discipline each other without the *official* sanction of the leadership. Unofficially the leadership turned the other way as the men squared someone away. Slingshot could tell the marines hated the man that was lying in the bottom rack about three rolls down from him.

The incensed marines approached the gay guy lying in the

rack. Trying to be a little quieter, Slingshot heard the leader say, "Get the (expletive deleted) out of here you (expletive deleted) fagot!" The guy moaned, "Leave me along!" "I'll leave you alone alright, you (expletive deleted) misfit!" At that moment the marine gang grabbed a blanket and threw it over the helpless guy. They began to punch him all over! The gay guy started to holler. They muffled the screams as they continued to dish out the attack. The leader said, "I told you to get the (expletive deleted) out of here! Do you hear me you wasted piece of (expletive deleted)?" The gay guy began to moan and cry with an eerie helpless whine. Slingshot blurted out, "Hey guys, he's had enough!" "We're going to kill the (expletive deleted)," whispered one! They hit the gay guy some more and then got quiet for a few moments while they quietly discussed what they were going to do next. Slingshot interrupted the discussion. "Let him go, I said! He's not worth going to the brig or getting busted!" A couple of the other guys who heard Slingshot mumbled amongst themselves, as they decided what to do. Finally, after they all argued for a few moments they again slapped the gay guy held tightly wrapped in a blanket. The gay guy could not even move in the improvised straight jacket the marines had devised from the blanket. He was moaning concertedly with an unnerving chilling cry as he struggled under the blanket, as one guy held his mouth to muffle the sound. Although they pretended to ignore Slingshot's interference, they knew that they were being watched by someone who did not approve of their actions. They had decided to carry the defenseless gay guy wrapped up in the sleeping blanket out of the sleeping quarters.

    Slingshot felt he had broken their will to "kill" him by interrupting the attack. They were now interested only in getting him out. They were through beating him up! As they walked by, Slingshot took a big breath and sighed. One of the perpetrators looked at him very angrily as if to imply that Slingshot could be next. The others passed by Slingshot without much concern, since they were preoccupied with the extraction of the gay guy. One of the marines said very sternly as he passed by Slingshot, "He won't be coming back!" Slingshot quietly thought, "I know that's right!" He was concerned, but he did not interfere with the "code red" any further for fear he would be next. It was obvious that the five marines had decided to extract him without killing him, so Slingshot looked the other way. He wondered, "Should I report this?" "Am I wrong for not doing more?" Slingshot knew that the Marines have their way of doing things; to *improvise, adapt, and overcome!* Still, he felt they shouldn't kill the guy. The incident added fuel to his emotional *distress,* and he was becoming more and more uptight and tense day by day.

The marines carried the gay guy out to an area outside of the sleeping quarters where they dropped him in the hallway. They then returned to the sleeping racks where they one by one stopped talking about it. They soon fell asleep to sleep off the booze.

The next day Slingshot saw the gay guy very cautiously return to his sleeping quarters. He was busted up good. His nose looked broken; his eyes were black circles of depression, his cheeks black and blue, his neck and ears red and swollen. He was obviously very sore with bruises that covered virtually every part of his body. He gathered his belongings and left the ship never to return.

Slingshot asked the platoon sergeant what had happened to the guy. He said he the guy was transferred to another ship. Slingshot innocently said as if he didn't know, "Why?" "He's gay! It has been decided that he will not live long if he stays aboard this ship," the sergeant said. "A few of the guys wanted to kill him last night! If he is not transferred they will finish him off!" The drift was that everyone was glad to be rid of the misfit. Slingshot had witnessed enough death, so he was glad too.

Corsica

The next operation was no ordinary landing. It was *Fairgoer VI*, a joint French and American NATO operation on the island of Corsica. Corsica is the fourth largest island in the Mediterranean after Sicily, Sardinia, and Cyprus. It is situated 105 miles from France and 56 miles from Northwest Italy. Corsica is separated from Sardinia by the 7 mile Straight of Bonifacio. The island terrain is largely mountainous but the flowers of the Maquis produce a fragrance that has caused generations of sailors to refer to the island as *The Scented Isle*!

The landing went well as a coordinated effort, but one of the amtracs got stuck in the surf. Slingshot immediately ran to help. He entered the water to swim a rope over to the stranded amtrac. Although the amtrac was near the shore, the water was over his head. Slingshot grabbed the mooring bit and held on for dear life, because the surf was throwing him around, and the track was spinning right at his feet! If his leg got caught in the track or the front sprocket, it would rip his leg completely off. Slingshot held his feet and legs way up to avoid the injury the spinning sprocket might inflict; a very difficult effort in the surf. He placed the ropes on the mooring bits needed to pull the helpless amtrac out of the trap. Slingshot timed his jump away from the amtrac to coincide with the surge of the surf and swam back to shore. The tow vehicle began to pull the ropes tight just as Slingshot swam to the beach and just as he began to run away. He thought, "The rope is going to break and snap my head clean off! Don't they know that? Stop!" He could see that they were focused on getting the trapped amtrac out and that they were not aware of the danger he was facing, so he just ran as fast as he could to be out of reach of any recoil. The stretched ropes twanged into a tight line. One tightened rope did snap with a tremendous recoil. *It stopped within ten feet of Slingshot!*

It was good that Slingshot had run far enough and fast enough that the rope stopped a few feet short of hitting him; to be a casualty on a training exercise, when he had already survived the real thing, would be a tragic event for sure.

Slingshot sighed in relief after his heart quit pounding so hard he could hardly breath. "That was just too close for comfort," he angrily responded shaking his head. It *was* too close even for a veteran who was use to life threatening situations.

At the end of the day some "Little Ole Wine Makers" came from the village to sell some wine. Most Vietnam veterans trusted no one, especially someone holding a bottle that could just as well be filled with an explosive! One marine sergeant tossed stones at them to chase them away; he hit one of them in the face with a large rock. It bloodied the Frenchman's nose. The Frenchman reported the incident to the platoon commander. The irate marine's behavior could potently cause a big political mess of international proportions, especially since the locals did not like the Marines landing on their island to begin with. The last thing the Marines needed was an incident on the island with the locals; rules of engagement, and all that!

The marines were called out to formation and placed at attention so the injured man could view everyone for identification. Slingshot could see the Frenchman through the corner of his eye as he worked his way down the line of Marines, scrutinizing everyone with deliberant intentions. He stopped in front of Slingshot and studied him for several moments. Slingshot nervously thought, "Oh no, he's not going to blame me! I didn't do it!"

The Frenchman stared at him for what seemed like a long time; sweat began to trickle down Slingshot's face and his heart began to pound uncontrollably as the Frenchman stared at the features of his face. Slingshot's mind raced with the fear of being blamed for something he did not do. He had seen what had happened and he was in the area but he had nothing to do with it. Finally the Frenchman stepped away to go to the next marine in formation, but then suddenly he turned back to Slingshot to look at *him* again! Slingshot really became nervous then. The Frenchman studied Slingshot for a heart stopping several seconds more. Slingshot stood at attention not showing any emotion while the Frenchman stared straight at him. Slingshot tried to make eye contact with the Frenchman. Slingshot glanced at the Frenchman's eyes with a stern stare, just long enough to communicate with his eyes that he was not responsible. Finally the Frenchman turned to continue down the formation to study each man; he quickly looked and moved on. Slingshot wondered if the Frenchman had just picked him and whether he was just checking the others to be sure. When the Frenchman stepped over to talk to the platoon leaders, Slingshot's heart was beating so fast; he was certain he was to be blamed!

The Frenchman did identify the marine that was responsible. The marine that was identified was later called before the fleet commander aboard the command ship. Everyone knew the Frenchman had identified the right man. The commander knew what to do!

Slingshot was identified as a witness! He had to go alone with the boarding party because he had seen the incident happen.

Slingshot waited outside of the commander's door as the proceedings began. He heard the irate commander yelling at the marine at the top of his voice. Slingshot tried to control his adrenaline rush and wondered what to say should he be called in. Slingshot wanted no part of the whole matter, and he prayed that he did not have to be seen.

Slingshot was very glad that the commander decided not to see him. The other party members had provided enough evidence. The irresponsible marine was given a Marine Corps *verbal chewing* that could be heard not only in the hallway, but from almost anywhere on the ship. The irresponsible sergeant was *busted* to private, demoted as a leader, and sent back to duty. He became very bitter after that, and no one could get along with him.

Over the next several days Slingshot tried his best to stay away from the incensed marine. The busted marine yelled orders at everyone as if he were still a sergeant, and he took his anger out on everyone who came near him. Slingshot knew that a confrontation with the angry marine could lead to his own demotion. The angry marine did not care if someone else was busted because of him. In fact he thought that such an event might somehow give him vindication. Slingshot was smart enough to realize that.

CHAPTER TWELVE
Italy

Sardinia I

Fleet Atlantic Force I-68 sailed to the island of "Sardinia" about 120 miles off the coast of Italy. The Italian island of Sardinia is second in size to the island of Sicily and lies 120 miles north of Africa, and 7.5 miles south of the French island of Corsica. The island has been dominated throughout history by the Greeks, Carthaginians, Romans, Spanish, French, and Italians. The island is rich in minerals, especially zinc and lead, which are important military materials.

The Marines made their first actual lading at Aranci Bay, Sardinia; they affectionately called it "Raunchy" Bay. The landing was executed without a hitch. The task force landed the men and equipment ashore with the precision of a well trained Corps of experts. It showed why the Navy and its Marines are considered *the* experts at amphibious operations.

Once the marines were in position on the beach, they set up camp for the night. It was very romantic to be camped out on a beach of the Mediterranean Sea, the waves splashing ashore with a soothing rhythm, the stars shinning brightly above bringing peace of mine, and no sign of civilization, except the marines there. Slingshot and his comrades built fires and did all the things that Marines do when they gather. They talked, laughed, ate, played cards, sports, and explored the area along the beach. For the moment they had a good time.

The special night passed much too quickly. It was time to go back to work. With the special night over the marines prepared to practice more amphibious war maneuvers. Each amtrac was prepared to enter the ships from the shore. The training exercise ended successfully the next day.

Naples

The next port of call was Naples, Italy. Slingshot looked curiously at St. Elmo Castle as the fleet entered the beautiful port. The castle was built in the 1300's and served as a prison for many years. "A lot of history there," mused Slingshot as he took a deep breath. The city lies amid some of the most spectacular scenery in Europe. Low hills tower above the beautiful Bay of Naples. Mount Vesuvius could be seen in the distance. He could not wait to go on leave to see the sights.

While touring the city Slingshot got a little hungry. "How great it would be to have a real pizza from Italy," he reasoned with a growling stomach! He could have had spaghetti, macaroni, or noodles but he chose pizza for a very good reason.

Slingshot had a lot of trouble trying to explain in English to the Latin speaking waiter what he wanted. The waiter could not speak English and Slingshot could not speak Latin. Still the waiter managed to bring Slingshot a real Italian pizza. It was good but it was not what Slingshot was used to in America. Slingshot did not care. It satisfied his hunger in a special way. Slingshot knew that Naples is the birthplace of pizza where a baker at the royal palace invented it in the 1700's.

After the pizza, Slingshot enjoyed the streets of Naples, full of exciting festive people, with fountains that adorned every main intersection. Statues of Herculaneum adorned the buildings on the outside while mosaics added an artistic touch of quality to the inside of many buildings. The ancient Greeks settled Naples and eventually named the city *Neapolis*, which means "new city". The cities name in Italian is Napoli. Slingshot walked along the Riviera di Chiaia, a road that runs along the Bay of Naples. He momentarily thought about the contrast between the Mediterranean Sea paradise he was now experiencing, to the Southeast Asian rural areas he experienced just months before.

The ruins at Pompeii were an interesting place to visit. The ancient city disappeared after the eruption of Mount Vesuvius in A.D. 79. It lay buried for centuries until it was rediscovered in the 1500's and later in the 1700's. The city once attracted many wealthy Romans and now it was attracting Slingshot. It took him back to ancient times he never had known about before.

After a full day, Slingshot returned to the ship to sleep, looking forward to more days of liberty. Tensions had been mounting for everyone aboard ship, however, and those frustrations came to a head after liberty. Everyone had to do night watch sooner or later.

Slingshot had just been relieved from guard duty one night aboard ship when a disturbance erupted in his sleeping quarters. The area was nothing more than a long steel hallway lined with racks stacked about six high. The area was below the water line so he could hear the slush of the water against the hull adding to the discomfort of the very tight and hot quarters. The noises from the Marines stacked in these close quarters ranged from snoring, farting, moaning, abrupt yells from nightmares, to the squeaking sounds of the chains and racks as they rocked with the movement of the ship.

Slingshot climbed into his rack after being relieved from his post. His rack was at the very top of the stack, located about halfway into the corridor. Suddenly, one of the platoon sergeants came into the sleeping quarters carrying a crutch. He was upset about all the crap that had occurred over the last several months. He was a short stocky man with black hair and was strong for his size. Most of the guys liked him and respected his position of leadership. He yelled obscenities as he took the crutch into his hands, gripping it like a baseball bat.

Already one sergeant had been busted for throwing rocks and hitting a civilian on Corsica Island. Several fights had taken place like the one Slingshot would later have at Sardinia. The code red had taken place causing a great deal of tension and a cover up. The war games with the NATO allies had worn the marines thin as they assaulted beach after beach. The Soviet Union had been at sea observing the fleet. There was unrest in the Middle East between Israel and the Palestinians. Tensions had increased between the U.S. and North Korea. The Viet Cong were still in control of Vietnam. Demonstrations were taking place in the U.S. at the same time fellow Marines were dieing in Vietnam. The Marines were risking their lives for the freedoms of the civilians, and it made them feel unappreciated for civilians to demonstrate against the war. It actually made the marines even more angry. The cramped quarters added to the tension and kept everyone on edge. The liberty had failed to relieve all the pain and frustrations of the times. What now?

The old sergeant, full of tension, had been on liberty drinking all evening. He must have thought about all of the things that bothered him. He was wired tighter than a rubber band, and he was ready to snap. He started swinging the crutch at the marines lying in their racks, sometimes hitting a marine, and sometimes hitting just the chains that supported the racks. He furiously yelled at his platoon, "You call yourself Marines! Get up you lousy (expletive deleted)! You want to fight! Fight me! You yellow belly scum bags!" Slingshot observed the old Korean and Vietnam vet from his high position, thinking that the old sergeant had completely lost his mind. Not understanding his frustration, Slingshot began to feel resentful toward him. "One more swing," Slingshot thought. "I'll be on him like stink on (expletive deleted)!" Slingshot positioned himself to spring on the sergeant. He waited for the precise moment that the sergeant's swing of the crutch could not recover in time to hit him. Just as Slingshot jerked to spring, the old sergeant saw him. He stopped swinging at the others and focused on Slingshot. Slingshot said, "Sergeant, sergeant! Knock it off! Stop what you are doing or I swear I will write you up!" Slingshot was still posed to leap from his rack to stop him, when two other marines grabbed him from his blind side. Slingshot had distracted the irate sergeant enough so that the others could grab him from behind. The sergeant stared at Slingshot with a scornful, most hateful glare. Slingshot stared back at him intensely as the others ushered him off to the shower. Still upset, Slingshot wrote a graphic description in the night-post log book about the incident.

  The next morning a meeting took place in the ship conference room consisting just of Slingshot's platoon. The ones that had been assaulted wanted his blood. The other platoon sergeants, the staff sergeants and the gunny, wanted to cover the incident up and let it lie. Slingshot felt an obligation to speak up, since he was involved in the incident. He told the others they needed to stick together, but that the way the sergeant attacked people in their sleep was unacceptable. Slingshot said it must not be overlooked! He must not be allowed to do that! The leaders knew Slingshot was right about the attack, but under the circumstances, they did not want their friend to be busted for his outburst. They defended his actions. Part of the platoon agreed with the leaders, and part of the group agreed with Slingshot. The incident caused a big split within the platoon for several days.

Slingshot was now controversial. He felt real uncomfortable about the situation, and part of him wished he had never taken a stand on the matter. Some of the guys supported Slingshot as the conversations of the next couple of days showed. Some of the guys told Slingshot it would have been worse if he had jumped the well-liked sergeant. Slingshot heard a couple of the guys talking about how they saw him about to jump the old sergeant, and that that would have ended up bad for everyone. Others were unsure about the whole thing. Many felt the platoon had had enough misfortune already!

When Slingshot wanted to go on leave, the platoon leaders tried to keep him from going. As he tried to leave the ship one staff sergeant stepped in front of him. "You're not going anywhere sergeant! You're not leaving this ship," the staff sergeant informed Sergeant Slingshot. "There's no reason for me not to leave," Slingshot responded. "I have no intentions of going to the *man*." While the ships were in port, the colonel, known as *the man* by many, could be seen by any marine that had a legitimate reason.

Slingshot pulled the old crusty staff sergeant to the side, where they had a conversation between just the two of them. "What the platoon is worried about is that the platoon sergeant could get busted," said the angry staff sergeant. "It will look very bad for the platoon, especially since we have already had one sergeant busted, and that was enough to put us in bad standing with the colonel." Slingshot felt the staff sergeant really just wanted to take up for his friend, whom he always went on leave with. Still, Slingshot realized that the staff sergeant had a valid point, and he understood the serious ramifications. Slingshot put his face right in front of the staff sergeant's face. The stare Slingshot gave could kill. "I don't want to carry this any farther than the platoon," Slingshot growled back. "I just want it understood that this must not happen again! Do we understand each other sergeant?" The old staff sergeant smiled as he nodded his approval of the agreement. "Now, I'm going on leave weather you like it or not! Get out of my way!" With that understood, Slingshot departed the ship to enjoy Naples. He wondered if the platoon would accept him when he returned.

After that, the word was spread throughout the platoon to leave Slingshot along. Caught between his own value system, and the way things were, Slingshot needed some space anyway. With plenty of time to think, Slingshot made an effort to make peace with the incident. After much thought, he did. He made no additional attempt to pursue official disciplinary actions against the platoon sergeant. Enough had been done, and said about it, to express disagreement, and Slingshot felt the old sergeant would not do anything like that again.

The unfortunate incident eventually died down, and no one was demoted or attacked again. Respected and accepted by the platoon once more, Slingshot prepared to go on leave to Rome.

Rome

Slingshot was excited to have the opportunity to have the most interesting experience of his life. He was in Europe, in Italy, on the way to Rome! He wanted to visit the birthplace of Western civilization at the heart of the once great Roman Empire. Slingshot wanted to see the sites of history associated with Rome. He was aware that what began as a cluster of small farms around Rome expanded into an empire that stretched from much of Europe and the Middle East to the entire Mediterranean coast of Africa.

Rome is located on both sides of the Tiber River in central Italy about 17 miles from the Tyrrhenian Sea. The city is surrounded by several hills where the ruins of ancient buildings are located on the original sites on which ancient Rome was built. Rome is also one of the world's most important art centers. Slingshot started the adventure of his lifetime knowing that he may never get the chance to see such important and marvelous sights again.

Slingshot made arrangements to ride the train from Naples to Rome. He had never used a train for transportation so he was looking forward to the experience. The train stopped a lot, but it was a comfortable passenger train that wound its way through the mountains, offering a picture window view of the landscape. Sgt Elmo went with Slingshot to see Rome for himself. They both arrived just before dark at the hotel. The hotel was very nice! It had the typical Italian architecture that radiated warmth and romance. The room that Sgt Elmo and Slingshot received had two queen size beds made of fine cherry wood. There was a balcony that extended from the room. It overlooked a back street that gave a very nice view of Rome, especially when the night brought forth the radiance of the sky's magnificence, and mixed it with the lights of the city.

Slingshot stepped out on the balcony just as a group of singers approached to form a choir below. Slingshot called Elmo over to see. The choir started singing in Latin below the balcony, looking up to serenade them as they waved and threw kisses. Slingshot didn't understand what was being sung, but the rhythm and beat of the instruments sounded great as they sang the songs. The sound was definitely European; neither did Slingshot understand why the choir was singing to them! Slingshot said with astonishment, "Elmo, they are *singing* to us!" "Yeah, they must either like Marines, or Americans, or both!" he said, as he choked back his surprise. "Maybe they think we are rich," Slingshot said in a joking manner! "Seriously, I wonder why they are doing this," Elmo laughingly said. "I don't know, but it sure is fun," Slingshot responded, as he threw a deliberate kiss their way with a slow swing of his arm. Elmo laughed and Slingshot smiled as the choir sang several more songs. "I wonder if we are supposed to throw money or something to them," Slingshot suggested. "No, I don't think so," Elmo quibbled. The choir began to walk away, so Slingshot and Elmo, having been duly blessed, went back inside.

Slingshot and Elmo argued a moment about who was to get which bed. One bed was against the wall in the corner, and the other was near the balcony. Elmo was from Illinois, so at moments like that Slingshot called him *Yank*, short for a *Northern Yankee*, and Elmo called Slingshot *Reb*, short for a *Southern Rebel*. Slingshot hastily pointed out, "You Yanks never could whip us Texans at anything!" "Is that what they teach you Johnny Rebs down in that desert you call Texas?" Elmo laughingly remarked. "Why we're so big in Texas, we use states like Illinois for parking lots!" Slingshot bragged. Elmo laughed and said, "You Texans aren't the biggest state anymore; the Northern state of Alaska is!" "Yeah, just wait until the ice melts!" Slingshot said with a laugh. Elmo squirmed like he was defeated, then he smiled as he replied, "Well when the ice does melt it will flood the entire state of Texas!" "Oh yeah, it will drown all you Yanks living in Illinois first!" Slingshot fired back. After teasing back and forth Slingshot, tired from the exchange, lay on his bed of choice and Elmo lay on his bed of choice, so that both were happy. Slingshot could remember sleeping on the ground in Vietnam with the threat of being blown up at anytime. The serious thought changed his mood. The thought made the argument very trite, even though the exchange was done in fun.

With the mood change, Slingshot began to talk about how he wished his wife was there with him. The talked switched to family, loved ones, and the good times back home. They both got real serious in their thoughts as they realized how unfortunate it was that they couldn't share the experience with their loved ones.

Another choir came to the balcony and started to sing. "What another one," Slingshot in wonderment mused. Slingshot and Elmo immediately jumped up together as if they were on the same wave length, and ran to the window. In complete amazement they listened as they waved. Slingshot yelled down to the people below, "Why the celebration?" Slingshot turned his palms up on both hands to indicate he did not understand.

The two young marines had made the trip to Rome via a train sitting in a stateroom with people who could not speak English any better than they could speak Latin. In that situation Elmo and Slingshot just talked with each other and enjoyed the scenery. They were not able to find out from anyone there about any specifics about Rome. Slingshot and Elmo did not know why a celebration was happening just outside their window, but they reacted to the fun time with delight. The *choir* sang to them and they became more excited about being in Rome. The singers added a real nice touch to their stay at the hotel.

The next day was Sunday. Elmo and Slingshot went to Vatican City to attend church. The avenue that leads to the church is about 1 mile long coming from the Tiber River to the *Piazza di San Pietro*. Stores, and strangely even bars, lined the avenue's approach to the church. The large open space in front of the church contained two fountains, and two colonnades arranged in semicircles on opposite sides of the piazza. A red granite *obelisk* stood 85 feet high in the piazza's center. Slingshot later learned that it was brought to Rome from Egypt about A.D. 37, and was moved to the piazza in 1586. Slingshot was impressed to see such an historical site!

As Slingshot entered Sistine Chapel, he saw what appeared to be ivy-like leaves of gold that protruded from planter boxes. The boxes formed a large square area in the middle of the foyer. Slingshot, being excited and very curious, decided to touch the leaves to see what they were made of. Guards came running over, saying that the area was off limits. The large area of planters were filled with plants made of *gold* leafs! The inside of the church had marvelous mosaic paintings on the walls, with *real gold* ornaments everywhere.

Slingshot marveled at the extensive art and sculptures that adorned the chapel. On the wall above the altar *The Last Judgment* shows the souls of mankind rising on one side of the alter and falling on the other. At the top Christ controls them like a puppet master. At the bottom, tombs open and the dead are rowed across a river.

On the ceiling of the Sistine Chapel he noticed there are nine scenes from the Old Testament showing God creating the world, the story of Adam and Eve, and Noah and the flood. Other larger than life paintings of Old Testament prophets and classical prophetic women surround the scenes, all of which were completed by 1512. Slingshot knew the brilliant artists of the early Renaissance used their skill to tell the story of the history of the creation of the world, the fall of humanity, and the story of the great flood. He never imagined that he would ever be able to see the original art in all of its magnificence for real.

Slingshot's neck strained as he looked up toward the dome and the Sistine Chapel's ceiling. He marveled at "The Creation of Adam" by Michelangelo completed in 1511. It shows God moving on a cloud among many angels. God extends his finger toward Adam who represents the first human being. Adam raises his arm to receive the spark of life. Slingshot could feel the electricity surge through his body from viewing the magnificent art piece and its message.

At St. Peters Church, the largest Christian church in the world, Slingshot saw Michelangelo's *Pieta*. He called Elmo over to help him interpret the meaning. This marble statue shows the Virgin Mary cradling the dead Jesus after the Crucifixion, sculptured in 1499. Slingshot believed that it shows Mary's love for Jesus and the unfortunate loss of her beloved son. He felt it represented the loss of Jesus' flesh, but the salvation of mankind through Jesus' love and sacrifice.

Slingshot approached the high alter that dominates the center of the church. It is located under a large bronze Baldacchino (canopy) designed by the famous Italian sculptor Gian Lorenzo Bernini. Bernini also designed papal tombs and monuments for the church chapels that lined the walls. Slingshot showed his respect by quietly observing the ceremony taking place there.

After marveling at the church interior, Michelangelo's and Bernini's work, Slingshot joined the others as the Italians finished their service, and began to walk from the church to the courtyard outside. The usher motioned to Slingshot as if he was trying to tell him something. Slingshot just followed the congregation to the outside unsure of what the usher was trying to tell him. When Slingshot reached the outside, most of the people were on their hands and knees in the courtyard, bowing and praying.

Slingshot and Elmo stood at the doorway, while everyone else proceeded to acquire the praying position in the piazza. The usher again tried to get their attention. He pointed to the balcony to the young marine's left, and uttered, "Pope!" "Pope!" There the *Pope* was on the balcony; Pope Paul VI speaking Latin and praying to the crowd! Slingshot finally understood what the usher was trying to point out. He was amazed at actually *seeing* the *Pope* during the ceremony. Since Slingshot was from the Bible belt of the US, a Southern Baptist and a Protestant since birth, he did not realize just how exceptional the experience was at the time.

Slingshot and Elmo did not kneel down to pray, but prayed just standing there. Later, after Slingshot absorbed the experience, he really began to realize that he had had one of those one-in-a life-time experiences. He had wanted to see Vatican City and the Sistine Chapel of the Church of St. Peter. He never expected to see the Pope as well. What an unexpected moment of delight!

Elmo and Slingshot spent at least a couple of days touring the ruins of Rome. They had seen Vatican City! The next great experience was the Roman Coliseum! Slingshot wondered about the types of animals that must have been involved in the activities. Slingshot looked up to see if he could see the ghost of Julius Caesar looking down at him. Slingshot imagined he was a Roman soldier waiting for the command from just one wave of Caesar's politically powerful arm. Slingshot could hear in his imagination the roar of the crowd as he stopped to listen to the wind blowing the ghost's of the past through the majestic columns. His heart pounded with excitement as he stood still to listen to the echoes. Adrenaline flowed through his arteries as if his body was preparing him for the next great battle to emerge from below. Slingshot ran from one location of the coliseum to another, looking for signs of the great gladiators that had fought for their very survival there. "Was I even half the warrior they were?" Slingshot wondered. "How many battles could I win?" His thoughts then wandered to how magnificent the coliseum must have been with features to admire for their efficiency even centuries later!

The next structure the young marines viewed was the great *Arc of Constantine* as they passed through it on the way to one of the ruins of the Roman Forum. The forums were the centers of ancient Roman life where public meetings were held. The *Via Sacra*, the main street made of lava, crossed the Roman Forum where victorious generals once paraded before government officials. Beautiful marble buildings helped to make the forums the most important places to be. The rulers of Rome built forums of their own.

Slingshot had to see the opening in the center of the dome of the Pantheon. He walked into this ancient building trying his best to imagine its importance to wealthy Romans. He then preceded to Trajan's Column, and many other sites throughout the city.

In Rome the marines visited every church they could find.

Slingshot and Elmo marveled at the great paintings by Leonardo De Vinci and Michelangelo and the churches with large domed ceilings. Many marvelous buildings were built with rolls of large Roman columns; buildings like those of St. Peter's Square.

They had seen the biggest church in Rome, which was the Basilica, where the grave of St. Peter was found. He learned the church was built by the emperor Constantine in the 16th century. Over the years the Basilica was enhanced with sculptures, frescos, funeral monuments, and furniture. Inside Slingshot had marveled at Michelangelo's magnificent dome, and his statue of the Pieta. The most significant artist of the Basilica however was Gian Lorenzo Bernini during the 17th century. His funeral monument of Pope Urban VIII, the Baldacchino placed above the tomb of St. Peter, the colonnades of St Peter's square, and the bronze Basilica Chair of St. Peter are examples of his work that stood out to Slingshot.

Slingshot marveled at the exceptional engineering of the many aqueducts. In addition, miles and miles of ancient Roman ruins were explored bringing to mind the great civilization that was the forerunner of the Western civilization of the United States. In his own way he imagined how he must be a descendant of the Great Roman Empire! After all, his ancestors were from Europe, and now he was from the great Western civilization of the United States, a U.S. Marine, and the modern physical equivalent of the gladiators that had lived there centuries before!

To operate in the European theater during the Cold War was a dangerous assignment. The Marines main objective was to be ready to go into battle anywhere, anytime, but in Europe, the NATO operations were paramount. As a Marine Expeditionary Force they were prepared to attack the enemy; Soviet Union or Middle East!

Sardinia II

After their leave in Rome, the fleet set sail for Aranci Bay, Sardinia where they made another *Raunchy* landing. While on the beach, one of Slingshot's crewmen threw some rocks at someone in a playful manner. The rocks hit Slingshot in the face! To defend himself, and without thinking he grabbed his crewman, threw him in the open Amtrac, and began to give him a lesson typical of an irate Marine. No one saw the two fighting. Slingshot punched him in the mouth two or three times, threw him around and punched him in the stomach! The careless marine threw some punches Slingshot's way, and Slingshot blocked most of them. They scuffled and yelled at each other until they had come to an understanding, and then they stopped. After the scuffle, Slingshot realized that he was really keyed up, because he felt he overreacted to the situation. Slingshot had cut his left hand to the bone as a result of the fight! The tendon was damaged, and it took months to heal. The other marine lost his front teeth! Cold War tensions continued!

Later that evening, a couple other guys and Slingshot started to wrestle in the sand. Slingshot took both of them on to prove to himself he could handle them. Once he was sure he could get the best of them anytime he wanted, he let them get the advantage of him. They liked to have twisted his arm off! Slingshot screamed bloody murder, partly in fun and partly because they were giving him payback. They even squeezed his bandaged right hand to inflict a kind of sadistic pain. Slingshot then got rough himself, the others ran, and the tough play was over.

The next day some of the guys played tackle football on the beach. Since they were young and tough as nails, the fact that they had no pads didn't bother them one bit. Slingshot was determined to score a touchdown as a running back. The sand was very soft and deep, so it really slowed everyone down. Never the less, Slingshot scored eventually, even though he wasn't the fastest guy there.

Each amtrac was like an individual apartment in a downtown complex. They offered compartments of privacy that allowed everyone to do something different. Several of the guys played high stakes poker. Someone mumbled, "Hit Me!" Another said, "raise you ten," "I call," came the reply as Slingshot slowly walked by. Several guys laughed and told jokes. "Did you hear the one about...?" Others laid in the racks, sound asleep, another marine played a radio, and another strummed a guitar. The marines trained hard, but they had fun when they could, whenever they weren't fighting.

CHAPTER THIRTEEN

Cold War Tensions

Russian Trawlers

With the NATO operations over, the fleet set sail across the Mediterranean on patrol. The Russian trawlers, vessels of the Soviet Union electronically equipped to spy, were always within site of the fleet. Slingshot often saw them near his ship, the USS Rushmore. He wondered why the captain did not try to get rid of them. Of course the trawlers had a right to be there in the open sea. Without a war, the trawlers were like parasites, attaching themselves to the host for an information feeding frenzy. The U.S. fleet was eyeball to eyeball with the Soviet Union! Any mistake could lead to a confrontation!

The marines and the navy personnel *prepared* for a confrontation with the Soviet Union by having many training *drills*. Slingshot was impressed with the navy guys ability. They scurried to their battle stations with the precision of a well tuned watch. It was an automatic response for them when the navy conducted the "All Hands to Battle Stations" exercises. Each man knew the fastest way to go to his battle station. The ship's crew ran to the mighty 20mm and 40mm cannons which they fired at imaginary targets in the sea. Many fired hand guns from the sides of the ship. Slingshot and his comrades setup the machine guns and fired them expertly from the rear of the ship. The sound of the weapons was deafening! Anti aircraft weapons, small arms fire, and automatic machine guns all firing at once, aroused full excitement from the marines and sailors.

Slingshot grabbed his M-14. He knew his infantry rifle inside and out. He could assemble and disassemble it with a blindfold on; an exercise the marines practiced many times. He aimed his rifle at a target placed in the sea, and then fired accurately into it in spite of the up and down movement of the ship. He then took his turn on the machine gun firing rapidly at the makeshift target being towed behind the ship. Later he relaxed and watched the maneuvers of the ships as they practiced pursuit and evasive movements.

The communication lights flashed to coordinate with the other ships in the fleet that also participated in the war game. All the ships of the fleet responded with maneuvers, hard lefts and hard rights, and complete circles were done in complete coordination with the other ships. Jet planes from the aircraft carriers did flybys overhead. Submarines monitored the activities

Given the level of tension between the U.S. and the Soviet Union, the exercises were necessary to keep the navy sharp. The war games prepared the navy for *any* possible confrontation. A confrontation with the Soviet Union was most likely to occur at this time in the Cold War because the Soviet Union had built and prepared a large fleet to challenge the U.S. dominance of the high seas.

The Soviet Union considered the Mediterranean Sea their first line of defense from U.S. aggression. The U.S. was there to protect Western Europe from Soviet aggression. Each was poised with unprecedented strength to strike the other! This was the front lines of the Cold War and each power knew that a war could erupt at any time.

During the Cold War, many war games were conducted at the doorstep of Eastern Europe to send a strong defiant message to the Soviet Union and its allies; the US Navy was ready!

Harassment

On one occasion during an ordinary day at sea in the Med, Slingshot was standing on the helicopter deck when from above two Russian Migs, their red star clearly visible on each wing, dove straight down toward the ship. They came down really fast, their sites clearly on the ship with Slingshot standing in the middle of the top deck! Slingshot hollered, "What the (expletive deleted)!" Although he knew he was dead if they opened up with their cannons, Slingshot stood in defiance right there in the middle of the deck. Calmly he lifted his right arm into the sky. When Slingshot saw the pilot, he looked him right in the eye.! Now Slingshot and the pilot were eyeball to eyeball with each other. Just as the Mig was at the bottom of its dive, Slingshot in direct defiance to the commie pilot, shot him *the bird*, an obscene hand jester. Slingshot stood firmly, standing like a stone wall, never running or dodging as the two planes approached! Although the Migs could have easily strafed the deck with their 20mm canons, instantly killing Slingshot, they pulled their planes up at the last possible moment. Slingshot steadfastly stood his position as they came around for a second pass. The roar of the jet engines became louder as the pilots accelerated the jets toward the ship again. Secretly, Slingshot was praying the Russians would not fire their weapons, but he was willing to die if necessary, rather than run from them like a scared rabbit! The Hot War in Vietnam had made him that way! He was a Cold War warrior now standing his ground in defiance of their superiority of firepower over him. Not running meant he could live with himself afterwards should he survive the harassment. The jets dove toward the ship, swerved away, and then disappeared.

The North Koreans

The containment of Communism in the 1950's manifested itself into a Hot War when North Korea invaded South Korea. Slingshot was still a small boy of four years when the world crisis resulted in the U.S. entering the war. Vietnam and North Korea were recognized as adversaries to a western struggle against Communism. China and the Soviet Union were aiding both countries, and the U.S. was committed to the defense of Western Europe through the "North Atlantic Treaty Organization," also known as NATO. To stop the military aggression of the Communist in North Korea would send a clear message to the Communist that the U.S. would support its favored allies, and would stand against any Communist military aggression in the world. Strategically, South Korea offered a good base of operations against Communist aggression throughout the region.

At the same time the U.S. was giving the South Koreans military aid, it was also giving South Vietnam aid by funding the French war effort there against Ho Chi Minh's Democratic Republic of Vietnam. France was viewed as key to the NATO defense of Western Europe from Soviet Union imperialism. The "Marshall Plan" was directed at freeing up French resources going to Vietnam so that those resources could go to NATO, while the U.S. rebuilt Germany and the rest of Western Europe. Phasing out the French commitment, both militarily and economically, to Vietnam would strengthen the NATO position in Western Europe. The redeployment of French power into Western Europe, therefore strengthened U.S. policies against the Soviet Union during the Cold War.

The Babyboom Doom

At four years old the stage was set for Slingshot's direct involvement into military action against North Vietnam, China, and the Soviet Union. *As a Baby boomer, his future was doomed to a war with the Communist from the policies following WWII, even before he was old enough to know anything about it!* Things were happening that would shape his future. Policies to contain the Communist were already taking place. The formation of NATO demonstrated that. NATO after WWII, started out as just a piece of paper. Only one division of U.S. troops was initially stationed in Europe, until General Eisenhower strengthened the U.S. position there to six divisions.

By 1968, Slingshot's previous unit was fighting the Viet Cong and NVA in the Provincial Capital of Vietnam known as *Hue* in the Thua Thien Province just north of Da Nang. Viet Cong and NVA infiltration had increased from the North and through Laos near the DMZ area of *I Corps*, in preparation for the Communist *TET* Offensive. Slingshot had no doubts his old unit would take the fight to the enemy. He was twenty-one years old now and after having already fought the Viet Cong himself, he was now a veteran Marine. He was continuing the fight in the Med, right at the doorstep of the Soviet Union; directly involved with NATO.

Slingshot felt that he had aged a hundred fold the last couple of years. *He was no longer an innocent teenager seeking glory or honor.* He was a *veteran* ready to fight the Communists in Europe! He was poised to strike like a mad Texas rattlesnake at the heart of Communism with the least provocation.

Slingshot was just one person of the Baby boomer generation facing the threat of impending doom via nuclear annihilation. The physical threat was obvious, and very real. The arms race certified that.! The psychological threat, brought about from continuous abnormal stress, was less obvious, but just as real.

A hostile North Korea loomed in the distance divided by a cease fire armistice at the 38th parallel. The Vietnam War continued with no end in sight. Nuclear missiles targeted the existence of mankind. Within the scope of the Med patrol, aid to Israel was necessary to secure oil reserves in the Middle East. Radical terrorist there planned for continuous destruction within many nations of the world. Slingshot's Med patrol was nearing the end! He still had a few months of military experience left. It was October 9, 1968, only his twenty second birthday! Doom-da-doom-doom still loomed in the not so distant future.

The Russian Migs continued to fly over the fleet, and the Russian Trawlers followed closely with open ears as the fleet approached the *Rock of Gibraltar*. The fleet did not stop as it passed the huge peaceful majestic rock. It was a beautiful site fading in the distance as Slingshot left the Mediterranean Sea to enter the Atlantic Ocean.

CHAPTER FOURTEEN
The Atlantic

The trip across the Atlantic was to take about a month to six weeks. The old salt sailors took delight in harassing the Marines about delays. Some sailors spread the news that the rudder on the USS Rushmore had been damaged. The sailors announced that they had been sailing in a circle for about a week, and that they would continue to do so while the work was being done to repair it. "We are having a lot of trouble getting the parts necessary to repair the rudder!" one sailor exclaimed, as he chuckled with his head slightly turned away. "It might take a month, maybe two, before we can finally head straight away!" The harassment only served to remind Slingshot of just how anxious he was to return home.

Another rumor the sailors spread was that the fleet had to turn around during the night to sail back into the Med because the Palestine in the Middle East was threatening war with Israel again. Slingshot's heart fell as he envisioned that probably he had been training to invade the Middle East all along! Although it was true that he had been training for such an assault, which leant credence to the rumor, the fleet had no official orders for embarkation to the Middle East. The Sailors just took delight in seeing the Marines squirm about not being able to go home as soon as possible.

The fleet navigators plotted their course and headed west across the vast and restless ocean. Slingshot expected the trip across the Atlantic to be non eventual. He was wrong!

The Storm

About half way home, the Sixth Fleet ran into a bad storm in the middle of the Atlantic. Slingshot knew the ship was being tossed about as he held tightly to his rack in the sleeping quarters below, but he did not know how strong the wind was, or how much it was raining. He was being tossed from one side of his rack to the other. He tried to change positions to anchor himself from rolling around. He was sleepy but he could not sleep well under the circumstances. He decided to go to the *head* to relieve his bladder. He worked his way down from the high top rack swinging from the chain supports like a monkey on a limb. Once Slingshot was on the *deck* he literally was being thrown from one end of the *bulkhead* to the other. He had to go up a stairway to the deck above to enter the head. He tried to anchor himself in front of the urinal as he swayed from side to side. His stream of urine was moving side to side as he swayed, some of it going into the urinal, some of it hitting the deck, and some of it finding the top of his bare feet. Slingshot rubbed his eyes. They were still blurry from not being fully awake. His eyelids seemed to dangle half open or half closed, depending on the rhythm of his slow breathing pattern. After the mess he made, he decided he needed a shower.

To shower aboard a military ship in the sixties was an exercise of deliberate conservation. The marines took *navy* showers! A navy shower required you to enter the shower with the water off. Once you were inside, the idea was to turn the water on, usually cold water, just enough to wet your body. You then were required to immediately turn the water off while you stood there chilled and wet.

On a day when the seas were rough, it was especially difficult to hold on while you slide back and forth. You would then take a single bar of soap to work up a lather all over your body. After you were completely covered with soap, only then would you turn the water on just long enough to rinse the lather away. The idea was to conserve as much water as possible, since the water was stored in holding tanks. Most ships of the 60's were without the benefit of having fresh water processed from the sea water.

With his shower done, Slingshot returned to his rack area on the deck below to finish getting ready for the day. After he dressed he went to the topside deck of the ship. He opened the door that led to the outside. The wind was blowing, and it was raining so there was no one around. Out of curiosity, using the *swabby stagger* he danced to the open deck area, which was about ten feet from the entrance to the ship conference room. Slingshot wanted to see the other ships in the convoy for just a moment because the seas were so rough they would be bouncing all around in the water. At the precise moment Slingshot stepped outside, the ship heaved up, and then bounced like some wild Texas bronco. A strong wind blew across the deck like a raging twister had grabbed the ship for its own. The whole side of the ship turned toward the water, throwing Slingshot completely off his feet. He was on the very top deck sliding out of control toward the stairwell that led to the next deck below! It happened so fast that he did not have time to grab any part of the stair railing. He plunged through the opening and landed on the deck below on his shoulder, and rolled into sort of a fetus position for just a moment. The ship continued to twist and heave in the violent sea. The deck was wet and very slick.

As Slingshot slid across the deck he grabbed for anything he could hold on to. There was nothing to grab but the slick deck, unmercifully angled downward toward the sea. A huge wave splashed over the deck and completely soaked him as he gave out a prehistoric yell. He tried to dig his fingers into the hard cold wet steel that presented *nothing* to hold on to. A life boat was hanging about five feet above the deck at the side of the ship that faced the open sea. The railing under the life boat had been removed! This was to allow the lifeboat to be swung over the side of the ship so it could be lowered unhindered into the water. Slingshot slid toward the opening out of control!

In an instant he was terrified! He thought in that brief moment, "I'm going to be tossed under the life boat into the open sea without anyone knowing that I have fallen over board!" There was nothing at all between Slingshot and the open sea; nothing to grab, nothing to stop him from plunging right over the edge as he slid toward the opening under the life boat.

His whole life flashed before him, his childhood, his teenage days, Vietnam, Okinawa, Loretta; instantaneous flashes of memories that covered areas of his life long forgotten. He even briefly imagined in that fraction of a second, "How can I die like this after all I have been through? How?" His hands strained as his fingers tried to dig into the cold wet deck that slid beneath him. The wet deck was now a slide toward certain death. He could see it all. "U.S. Marine Lost Overboard!" What would the paper report?

The paper read, "Early this morning, Marine Sergeant Casey "Slingshot" Trainer was found missing while serving aboard the USS Rushmore with the Sixth Fleet. The Sixth Fleet was on routine patrol somewhere in the Atlantic Ocean, when it was discovered after morning roll call that he was missing. A thorough search of the ship revealed that Sgt Trainer was not anywhere to be found. He is missing and assumed dead from drowning after he apparently fell overboard sometime during the night."

Slingshot's heart raced like it had not done since his tour in Vietnam. His body stiffened as he slid toward the opening, every muscle grasped for his very life, and his life flashed before him to meet his maker. Just when he was right at the edge of certain death, with nothing between him and the sea but open air, the ship gave a mighty heave, reared up in the stormy sea, and pitched him like a rag doll toward the latter leading up to the top deck. Slingshot grabbed that latter like it was his very best friend, and hugged it literally for dear life. He hugged it and hugged it , not wanting to let go! The ship, like a wild Texas stallion, continued to buck and jump around on the ocean surface. The ship acted like a cork in a washing machine. Slingshot held firmly onto his unexpected life saver as the water rolled over the deck, soaking him each time with a mighty splash. The ordeal had drained him of all his strength. Soaked and wet, he tried to regain his composure and his strength as the ship continued to roll around in the Atlantic storm. The waves mercilessly rose above the ship and then disappeared below it.

When Slingshot finally caught his breath and he felt that he had the strength to work his way up the stairwell, he began a very deliberate climb back to the deck from which he fell. When he reached the top he had to let go of any support long enough to make it to the entrance. It took tremendous courage because he had just nearly been tossed to his death from the same spot. "If I stay where I am to wait for help, maybe someone will find me," Slingshot thought as he shook from the fear that controlled his every move.

It was the childhood slide all over again! The storm was blowing even harder now. He was soaked to the bone from the blowing rain, and severely chilled by the fifty mile an hour wind blowing across the deck. Slingshot was bruised and sore, although grateful he was still alive. He decided he must try to make it to the entrance because no one else would be foolish enough to come outside for hours. He tried to get a sense of the timing between large waves and the swaying of the ship. He decided that he would let go of the stair rail when the ship leaned in a way that would *throw* him toward the door.

Slingshot very frightened by now prayed, "Lord help me, *please* help me now." Slingshot watched as the ship rocked him first away from the door, then toward the door. When he was sure of the timing, he let go at the exact moment he could be thrown toward the door, which led to safety inside the cabin of the ship. He then grabbed the entrance latch and waited for the ship to roll the opposite way. He could not open the door against the wind! His strength was so drained he could barely hang on. He waited so that the door would open with the force of the roll when he turned the latch. Once the door was forced open he had to quickly jump through the opening before the steel door slammed shut from the force of the wind and waves. Slingshot knew that if he did not time his entrance right, the force of the heavy, large steel door slamming shut would crush him to death, or at the very least break his leg or arm. He timed his entrance perfectly until he was safely inside, very shaken and wet from head to foot, but alive for another day.

No one saw Slingshot go through the horrifying experience of nearly being tossed out to sea. He had been so traumatized by now that he began to withdraw from the others. PTSD was manifesting itself. He did not intentionally do so, but the trip over the Atlantic back to Camp Lejeune was a lonely experience as a result. He wrote letters, and he began to play solitary cards in hidden away places. He played games with a string he had made to run designs and patterns through his hands. He was suffering from *all* the traumatic experiences he had been through the last several months. Outwardly he tried to maintain a normal existence, but inside he had died a thousand deaths, and it was getting harder to cope.

PTSD BEHAVIOR

Someone aboard the USS Rushmore came down with appendicitis. The USS Rushmore did not have any doctor aboard, so arrangements were made with the USS Freemont to have the soldier transferred over to it.

Slingshot was topside when the two ships came within twenty yards of each other side by side. A special gun launched the ropes across the water to the USS Freemont. Slingshot quickly ran down to his sleeping quarters to get his camera. As he approached the area a couple of marines were mopping the floor right next to his locker where his camera was stored. Slingshot politely asked them to let him through and one of the two said OK. Slingshot grabbed his camera and hurriedly started out of the area to get topside. The other marine stepped in front of him to say Slingshot could not pass. The marine complained that Slingshot had spotted his floor. He said, "Where do you think you're going (expletive deleted)?" Slingshot was in a hurry to get topside so he was in no mood to be bullied. Slingshot immediately exploded into a rage and grabbed the guy by the shirt, in one swift move he lifted the marine off his feet and threw him against the steel bulkhead. Slingshot got right in his face while he had him pinned against the bulkhead. Eyeball to eyeball, Slingshot said, "Anywhere I want to you (expletive deleted) idiot!" He threw him down and hurried to the topside deck spitting mad and cussing worse than any sailor ever thought about. With his adrenaline flowing uncontrollably he was fighting to control his temper when the platoon sergeant saw him. The sergeant could see Slingshot was very angry. He asked Slingshot what was wrong. Slingshot said, "I had to teach someone downstairs a lesson! I rather you hear it from me than from someone else." The platoon sergeant went downstairs to see if any real harm had been done. He knew that all marines are quick tempered, and that they both were just tense from the extreme conditions associated with military life. Slingshot never heard anything more about it. The rest of the platoon realized that Slingshot was not the type to back down from a fight. They generally left him alone after that!

At that time the term PTSD had not been developed. Slingshot was unaware that he was even suffering from it. The symptoms of self withdrawal which manifested itself into depression and the constant anger that he internalized, were already present. *The symptoms were just the beginning of his internal pain.*

The Final Landing

Slingshot could see the U.S. North Carolina shore through the haze of the morning fog from the USS Rushmore as the ship approached the anchor point just offshore. The piney woods and the beach beckoned the marines to make their final landing from ship to shore. They were all very excited about making their final landing. The mission complete, the patrol over, they were back at their homeport.

During the last several months, the Marines had faced the Communist of the Soviet Union in their own backyard. They had demonstrated time and time again that they were capable of attacking with great force from the sea. The NATO operations in the Mediterranean Sea had provided them with valuable experience as a deterrent force. In addition they had visited many European countries, and they had become very familiar with that fragile part of the world.

No parade or formal recognition from the civilian population awaited Slingshot's return. No news cameras or media coverage of any type awaited his unit. No CNN or History Channel to explain the importance! The Mediterranean Sea was a prime theater of U.S./Soviet rivalry during the entire Cold War. Bordering countries were the scenes of major confrontations, yet few Americans appreciated the U.S. military role in the region. It was NATO's Southern flank, and of major strategic importance to U.S. foreign policy. Just like in the Pacific where the marines had fought the Communist in Southeast Asia, their Atlantic patrol was treated as either non eventual or by distain by most Americans. The marines of I-68 were the unsung heroes of their day! They had done their duty to preserve the traditions and hard earned freedoms that the U.S. is privileged to enjoy.

The real hard part was just beginning! Slingshot had made sacrifices to do his duty. The sacrifice had changed him forever. He and his fellow marines now had to learn to deal with a large segment of the public that disagreed with their creed of honor, and at times the returning soldiers reacted poorly to the indifference.

Slingshot had learned from Vietnam that the media did not help to give the soldiers a welcome home, but they were quick to discredit any troubled soldier with their inflammatory stories. Where were they when the marines returned home from Vietnam? Where were they now? The soldiers saw that the civilians were perfectly willing to let others do their fighting while they sat back and criticized their efforts. Slingshot felt that those who were disrespectful were the ones who really did not deserve respect.

For the moment it felt good to be home because now he could at least be with his loved ones. *The final landing from his height of honor was to be the most difficult period of his life.* He found that not even loved ones understood him anymore, and he did not understand their attitude either.

The marines had trained hard to become very good at making ship to shore landings. Slingshot's final ship to shore landing was at Morehead City, North Carolina in November 1968, where he had embarked some months before. Unknown to Slingshot his most difficult landing would not occur until many years later. It was a *mental* landing to ground zero called PTSD!

CHAPTER FIFTEEN
Camp Lejeune II

Reserve Training

The return to Camp Lejeune was to change Slingshot's life forever. He had suffered for months from pain associated with his war experiences and his service related conditions. At Camp Lejeune he could start to address the many physical problems he now had. His back was in constant pain from the Vietnam experience and his testicles continued to bother him from the mine explosion. He was too proud to admit to most of his mental and physical disabilities, but he could not ignore the latter. He still had six months of active duty to serve, and he was determined to do the best job he could for the Corps in spite of his shaky condition.

The next assignment of his service was to determine the feasibility of adapting a new Amphibious Assault Vehicle (AAV) for the Marine Corps. It needed to be faster, more maneuverable, more economical, better armed, and more reliable than previous landing craft. Slingshot began testing the new LVT in December, 1968. There was two prototypes to test on the East Coast, and there was two other prototypes to be tested on the West Coast. The Marine officers called the test vehicle the "LVTPX-12" for "Landing Vehicle Tracked Personnel Carrier Experimental."

Test Program

The LVTP5 had served the Marine Corps well as an Armored Personnel Carrier and an Amphibious Landing Craft. It had met the needs of the Marine Corps for about fifteen years. It was time to upgrade to the new technology that was available.

The new craft was made of an aluminum alloy instead of steel. It was powered by a more economical diesel engine instead of a volatile gasoline engine. It also had *jets* to propel it through the water instead of track cups for propulsion. The track was much lighter! It had rubber pads to use on paved roadways instead of heavy steel sections. The vehicle was lighter, faster, and more maneuverable, both on land and in the sea. It was controlled by a steering wheel using the latest hydraulic technology instead of a mechanical stick. It was capable of carrying the latest armament and a platoon of combat equipped Marines. The question was: Would the new Amtrac hold up mechanically under the stressful conditions of combat?

Slingshot's job as the crew chief of one of the two experimental vehicles, was to find out what the capabilities and limitations of the amtrac was under *intentional* stress loads. Did it live up to the specifications and expectations that it was designed for? Slingshot was anxious to find out!

The program was set up to test the LVTPX12 by running it 24 hours a day. It was to be run for twelve hours with one crew, and then to be run another twelve hours by another crew , without even being shut down. It was to be tested for speed, both on land and in water. The maneuverability, climbing ability, and endurance of the new amtrac was to be thoroughly tested.

The program had some advantages for Slingshot. It allowed him to have stable hours with routine functioning. He lived off base and came to work, and then did it all over again the next day. This was a luxury he had not known for years! It was like a routine job! He was excited and grateful for the opportunity to be on the testing program. It gave him a purpose.

The program of testing the LVTPX12 was a serious matter. A lot of engineers, officials, businessmen, and political leaders were involved with the program, and all had a lot at stake. The program was being watched with considerable interest by all concerned. Engineers and photographers were often in the field to monitor the results of the daily test.

After the crew exchange, the day began by running the vehicle on a test track. It was the *official* test track that had been laid out by the officers in charge. The track was a dirt track that ran around a wooded area in more or less a circular fashion. There were many straight-a-ways that allowed the vehicle to reach top speeds. Slingshot had a lot of fun drag racing the two vehicles, pitting one against the other for top speed and best driving performance. The crews took great pride in being the winner of these races. When that got boring, after they tested each others skills by competing with each other, they whipped the amtrac into doughnuts and sharp turns to see who could make the tightest and quickest turnaround. The dirt tract went for miles, and they had it all to themselves! A teenager's delight! Some places had hills and deep holes to maneuver through. It was a challenge for the LVTPX12 and for the drivers to make it through the well designed course.

For the most part the officials were most interested in seeing how long the LVTPX12 would last, by running it hour after hour on the track rather than putting it through exaggerated movements. The drivers were told to just stay on the track and run the vehicle hour after hour to determine normal wear and tear.

All of the crew members of both vehicles on the testing program had been in combat. They all had been to Vietnam where the terrain severely tested the endurance of man and machine. It did not take long for them to want to put the LVTPX12 through the kind of situations they had actually experienced in combat!

Slingshot began to experiment beyond the normal wear and tear situations. He left the beaten path to go deep into the woods where he could maneuver around trees and swamps, and downshift or up-shift to climb hills. He took delight in spinning the track over loose logs and soft terrain. In Vietnam the LVTP5 often broke down because of wear and tear on the track system. Slingshot wanted to know if the suspension and track system of the new vehicle was any better.

On one occasion his driver came upon a steep hill that over looked a swamp area. They could go around the area to avoid trouble, but Slingshot decided to order him to go right through the difficult area. Could this machine do what the LVTP5 could do? Slingshot's driver was in real doubt about the decision. He was not sure they could not make it. Slingshot said softly as they set at the top of the hill over looking the swamp, "We are here to test the capabilities of this machine, aren't we?" His driver, Cpl Timmons said, "Yeah but we might get stuck!" Slingshot said without hesitating, "Let's test it!"

Down the hill the amtrac plunged toward the swamp below. The amtrac hit the water with a big splash and the LVTPX12 lunged forward as it forced its way through the mud and water. With the engine roaring loudly the amtrac pushed through the sludge. When the driver thought he was almost to the other side, the vehicle suddenly wobbled, and nearly threw him and Slingshot out of their seats! "What happened?" Slingshot screamed! No one including Slingshot knew what had happened! The driver continued to drive the amtrac to the other side of the swamp. To Slingshot's delight the amtrac had passed that part of the test. "Stop the vehicle," Slingshot demanded! Slingshot and Timmons climbed out of the amtrac onto hard ground. Slingshot walked around it to see if the tract had broken, or if a piece of the suspension had given way. Then he discovered a very big hole was in the right floatation pontoon! *Slingshot immediately realized that they had hit a stump below the water line and the pontoon had given way!*

Slingshot stared at the damage in disbelief. An LVTP5 would have just bounced off that stomp. His mind raced as he began to think. He thought out loud, "Man, we are not even supposed to be back here, this deep in the woods, much less going through swamp areas similar to Vietnam!" Slingshot began to sweat! He just knew his Marine Corps career was about to come to an abrupt end. How could he explain the mishap? Slingshot just shook his head. He believed he was busted for sure!

The dignitaries gathered around the LVTPX12 and discussed the damage amongst each other. They asked Slingshot a bunch of questions that he was sure was designed to bust him back to PVT. He could not sleep. He worried and waited for the fatal decision for days. Then one day he was called into the warrant officers office to explain his conduct. He was very nervous as he tried to explain his actions. After a few demeaning and insulting remarks about not following

following orders and all that, Slingshot was so mad he did not even care what was going to happen to him. The warrant officer then calmed down and told Slingshot that higher ups had decided that Slingshot had discovered a weakness in the amtrac design. They were pleased the engineering default was discovered! The officials said that Slingshot had discovered a defect in the design that could be corrected, and that his actions would probably save some marine's life along the way. Slingshot was actually to be congratulated for his desire to *really* test the endurance of the LVTPX12. Consequently, there was to be a design change to increase the strength of the pontoons. Additional individual internal support sections would be added to each pontoon.

Slingshot left the office still shaking from the fear that he felt when he entered the office. After a couple of deep breaths, he became overjoyed that he had been redeemed for trying to do the right job. The other guys welcomed him back and they all worked together on the one remaining prototype.

Shortly after Slingshot lost his vehicle to repairs he began putting the other LVTPX12 through its paces. One mourning he was driving the vehicle when he decided to take it back into the woods off the beaten path. Once more, Slingshot was trying to see how fast he could maneuver through the woods and back onto the beaten path to a predetermined starting point. He had made a couple of timed passes with each one faster than the one before. Slingshot was going to set the record on this one particular pass. The path from the woods led into an open field where the official test track circled around. As Slingshot came out of the tree line he was surprised to see standing in the field ahead, just off the beaten path, a number of officers who had come out to view the testing procedures. Slingshot track! Now they have caught me again!"

    Slingshot headed straight for the group of officers that had gathered in the field. He was wide open as he headed for them, and he knew they would be impressed with the speed at which the LVTPX12 could move. As he got near them, Slingshot took his foot off of the accelerator, but the accelerator did not come up! The accelerator was stuck to the floor in the wide open position! Slingshot reached to the floor and tried to pull the accelerator up, but it was stuck solidly to the floor. When he popped his head up, he was about to run over the officers, and they began to scatter in all directions. Had the situation not been so serious it was a hilarious scene watching those officers run for their lives! Slingshot made a hard right turn at a very fast speed and slammed on the breaks. The vehicle did a fishtail slide in the loose soil throwing dirt out from under the track in the direction of where the officers had scattered. The vehicle slid to a stop, and Slingshot threw the transmission into neutral. The engine screamed at the highest RPMs possible, and it roared with the strain of the maximum internal power tearing at its insides. The officers regrouped and ran toward Slingshot screaming and hollowing at the top of their lungs. Slingshot screamed, "Run away engine, run away engine!" The engineer of the designing company was with the officers. He and another mechanic came aboard to try to shut the engine down. It would not shut off! They pulled the engine cover and tried to move the accelerator linkage. It would not budge. Finally Slingshot put his foot on the brake as the company rep forced the transmission into gear. The engine struggled to keep running, but choked to a stop when Slingshot threw the vehicle hydraulic steering into a full turn. Slingshot was once again standing in front of the warrant officer responsible for the program operations. Slingshot figured this was the last straw; the straw that broke the camels back; off the beaten path, going full speed, scattering the officers and company staff to run for their lives! "Just call me Pvt Pile," thought Slingshot with a silly boyish frown.

The officer in charge just stared at Slingshot for what seemed like an eternity. Slingshot was too embarrassed to speak and was fully expecting the worst. Finally the warrant officer said, "You're lucky no one was hurt!" "Yes Sir," Slingshot managed to mumble. The officer said, "You obviously have a heavy foot!" "Yes Sir," Slingshot again struggled to say. Then the officer more or less explained, using very colloquial Marine Corps jargon, that the entire right bank of fuel injectors had frozen in the open position causing the engine to lock into the wide open position at full throttle. *Had Slingshot not reacted quickly the engine would probably have exploded!* He explained that Slingshot's discovery of the engine design defect would be duly noted, and the necessary corrections would be made. "Yes Sir," Slingshot said excitedly! "Both vehicles will be down for a couple of weeks," the officer continued. "We'll have to replace the engine as soon as we receive another one! We will have both vehicles running as soon as possible." Slingshot turned to walk away when the officer in charge said, "By the way, Sgt Leadfoot!" Slingshot turned to respond, but before he could the officer grinned and spurted out, "Sgt Leadfoot, get out of my office!" Smiling, Slingshot proudly did so!

Slingshot's war injuries were bothering him so he sought help. His left testicle had been hanging very much lower than his right ever since the land mine incident. It hurt inside as it bounced against his leg. Slingshot decided that it was a good time to have it corrected. While the testing program was at a standstill, Slingshot checked into the hospital at Camp Lejeune to have a Varicocele operation. Some of the tubules of his testicles were removed to repair the internal damage and to draw the testicle up into a normal position. Slingshot spent a week in the hospital and a period of recovery of about two weeks. The operation caused sterility to occur, and it forever doomed him to not being able to have children of his own. This caused him a great deal of emotional trauma, and it lowered his self esteem as a man. The physical condition was corrected to the extent that the pain was much less, but Slingshot would struggle the rest of his life trying to come to terms with his loss.

Slingshot's back continued to bother him following the explosion from the mine in Vietnam. It was now being treated at Camp Lejeune. Slingshot was beginning to feel the results of the VC attack emotionally, and it showed. PTSD was very obvious to those around him, even if he did not understand the symptoms any better than they did.

The testing program for the LVTPX12 resumed. Slingshot yelled at his crew a lot, and treated his wife with distain. The marines ran the LVTPX12 more on the test track now that the test was about to be completed. A big hole near the test track offered a tempting excursion, so the drivers attempted to drive the vehicle down into it to see if it would have the power to pull out of it. Luckily, both vehicles were able to pull out of the deep hole and they went down into it without toppling over. One attempt failed however. The driver approached the hole from an angle that was so close to the edge of the hole that the soft earth gave way and the vehicle ended up falling into the hole, standing it straight up on its nose! With no tracks touching the ground it was stuck solidly in the hole on its nose! It took some heavy duty retrievers to remove the amtrac from the hole. Slingshot was glad he was not driving that vehicle.

The next phase of the test program required amphibious

operations. Slingshot considered the ship to shore operations a lot of fun. He was glad to test the LVTPX12 for its amphibious capabilities.

On one test, Slingshot discovered that the nose of the PX-12 would dip beneath the surface when at full throttle. This would flood the open driver's compartment and cause the vehicle to take on enough water to sink. A new balance had to be designed into the vehicle to prevent the "nose dive" at full throttle.

The shore to ship and ship to shore tests proved the vehicle was very maneuverable with its jet propulsion. Years later jet skies would hit the recreation market with the same type of basic propulsion design. The vehicle could turn on a dime. The wet rubber tracks had a tendency to slip upon entering the ramp of the old style LST, but at full throttle it entered all the ships without incident. The exits were a little scary because of the nose heavy design but Slingshot knew that it would be corrected.

The LVTPX12 was eventually accepted by the Marine Corps after the flaws were worked out, as its basic Amphibious Assault Vehicle. Slingshot was glad to have been on the testing program. He felt like he had contributed a great deal to the successful design that came out of the tests. He was also very proud to see the same type of AAV being used in Operation Desert Storm in 1991 and in Operation Iraqi Freedom in 2002.

Undecided About Reenlistment

Slingshot joined the Marine Corps in March of 1965 and went active on July 1, 1965. He fully expected to be active until July 1, 1969. By 1969 the Marine Corps was downsizing as the U.S. decreased its involvement in Vietnam.

With the LVTPX12 test program finished by March of 1969, his day consisted of working at the amtrac park at New River doing routine maintenance. He painted the interior of the LVTP5, changed oils, fuel filters, replaced tools, replaced bad sections of track, ran it in the field, and did all the things necessary to keep the vehicle in top running condition. He also trained the reserves, who he referred to as *weekend warriors*. They were given instructions on the basic operation of the LVTP5 then allowed to drive it on the test track.

Slingshot was up for promotion from Sergeant E-5 to Staff Sergeant E-6. He was well liked by the leaders of the company because he was dedicated. He always looked sharp and took care of business. Slingshot felt he owed the Corps no less. Slingshot was told that if he re-upped, and continued his active service for another four years, he was guaranteed the additional stripe, plus a large monetary bonus.

After Vietnam things were changing. Slingshot was undecided about reenlistment. He felt he had experienced the ultimate that the military could offer because he was a decorated war time veteran. With no war to fight the daily routine was a let down of sorts. He was already suffering from PTSD. What that meant was that Slingshot needed more excitement than routine base life could offer. He just meant was that Slingshot needed more excitement than the routine could offer. He needed more of a challenge than being a base soldier could offer.

Slingshot considered becoming an officer! Now that would be a challenge! He asked around the base about the opportunity to become an officer. He was told that the Corps needed its NCOs, Non Commissioned Officers, to stay NCOs. Slingshot checked with some of the base leaders, and he was told that the best he could hope for was to become a technical warrant officer, a position that was sort of between a Commissioned Officer and a Non Commissioned Officer. That was not the same thing in his mind at the time. Slingshot realized that what he would need to become an officer was to have more education. He was already educated in the technical aspects of the Corps, but what he would need is a formal education, a degree. Slingshot checked around the base for a school that would allow him to stay in and at the same time to pursue the education he needed to become an officer. He was young and all alone when it came to a support system from family and friends. He had none because of PTSD. His efforts were not successful in finding the avenue of progression he was interested in. Slingshot was still married, and that influenced him to become a civilian because military life for his wife was difficult. She wanted to be with her family and friends. Slingshot was still leaning toward staying in if he could become an officer, but he soon realized that he did not know how to go about that. He began to think that one must be giving the opportunity up front before one joined the Corps. This was the 60s and attitudes and opportunities were different than modern times would later provide.

Many NCOs had a drinking problem, and Slingshot did not

want to end up that way. He could see himself reaching the top of the NCOs ranks, but he could not see where he would command the same respect that being an officer would allow. He was very troubled about what to do. Meanwhile the NCOs were encouraging him to stay in and to get the additional stripe. Slingshot talked with his fellow marines that he worked with everyday. Most of them wanted to complete their tour and to just get out; most thought because of Slingshot's dedicated attitude, that he would stay in for sure!

Slingshot did not know what he would do for a living if he got out of the Marine Corps. He was from the oil refinery town of Baytown, Texas, so he thought that maybe he could work in one. Slingshot had worked construction before he went into the Marine Corps, so he knew a little about that. He had acquired the "can do" attitude of a marine. Nothing was beyond his capabilities he believed! Slingshot was a lost soul, unfortunately a Baby boomer totally confused about many things associated with his life. The likely hood of having children and a normal family life was something he held on to, even though he had been told that the operation on his testicles made it unlikely that he would ever be able to have children. Slingshot was in denial of that for many years to come.

The day came when he had to make a decision sooner than he expected. Since the Marine Corps was downsizing for the post Vietnam era, all Marines were offered an early release from active duty. Slingshot's early release date was just a month away! He could be released on April 23, 1969 from active duty in the U.S. Marine Corps. He would be a civilian, and he could put the horror of war behind him. With little known opportunity to grow in the way that he wanted to grow in the Marine Corps, he reluctantly decided to take the early release. Slingshot had served his country honorably, was time for him to leave. On April 23, 1969 he was released from active duty to serve his mandatory two years of inactive reserve. On April 1, 1970 he received his temporary E-6 Staff Sergeant stripe while still in the reserves. With the mandatory reserve period over in 1971, that phase of his obligation to military service was over too. Slingshot became a civilian!

CHAPTER SIXTEEN

Civilian Life

Slingshot left the Marine Corps to become a civilian! He had lost his innocence while he was in the service, and now he had no idea what being a civilian meant, or how he was to support himself, dress, or act.

Slingshot thought at the time that it did not matter, that he would dig ditches if he had to, or do just about anything to distance himself from the stateside duty that was the military. He had been in combat, and that experience had changed him forever! He was still "in Country" (Vietnam) mentally even though he had returned to the "Land of the big PX" (U.S.) physically. Slingshot was excited inside, but very stoic outwardly. He was also very irritable, didn't sleep well, and subject to violent outburst, although he was unaware of the abnormal behavior in a conscious way.

After the Marine Corps, Slingshot was no longer referred to as *Slingshot*. He was once again just *Casey Lee Trainer* from the rural area of Texas. It took some getting use to not to be called sergeant or Slingshot. He actually felt strange not having the clout of discipline over him required to function in the Marine Corps. The change made him feel insecure since he had to have a new identity as a civilian. He was military through and through so it was going to take some time before he could even remotely relate to the civilian world. He felt second rate as a civilian, stripped of his rank, and confused.

The Trip Home

Loretta and Casey left Camp Lejeune April 23, 1969 about 1:00 PM. She was excited, and Casey was very tired.

They had been living in a small wooden house on the edge of the North Carolina piney woods for several months. It was a square house with one bedroom, a small bath, a living room, and a kitchen that joined into the living room. The water came from a well out back. It was very brackish and unfit to drink. They always had to get water from other places to bring to the back-woods house. The house was located about twenty miles from the Amtrac base. He would get up real early, about 4:00 AM, and then drive a route that took him literally through the woods where only the wild life lived. Casey once was ticketed by a base MP, for driving 70 MPH in the wide open stretch of road through the uninhabited woods. He had to go to a "Safety Class" to be exonerated from his sin.

Loretta did not work while Casey was in the military at Camp Lejeune. Casey could only imagine how boring and lonely she must have felt living in such an isolated environment. She stayed home all day while Casey was on base or working at night. They owned only one car. It was a two door 1968 Pontiac with a gas guzzling V8 engine which he drove to the base. Loretta stayed home without transportation to even go to the store! The nearest store was in town, about twenty miles north of their house. Loretta looked forward to going to town for supplies just to get out to go somewhere.

Casey worked in the military, and he moonlighted for

months by working in a meat processing plant at night. The effort left him with little sleep and needless to say, much energy for anything else. Casey did have sex a lot! Loretta wanted a child, but he soon realized that something was truly wrong. Casey got checked at the medical facility on base for sterility. Sure enough something was wrong! He was sterile! Loretta's dream of a family of her own was shattered.

They tried everything the doctors suggested. Casey had an operation at the base hospital that was supposed to increase his chances of having children by altering the critical temperature that sperm needs to survive. The Varicocele operation he had while in the military failed to correct the situation. The land mine incident in Vietnam had much more far reaching effect than he could imagine at the time. It seems the contusion to the testicles had caused unforeseen damage to his reproductive capabilities! Even more devastating was the mental after shock of such realization.

With this burden to bear, and with Casey in denial about his sterility, they didn't go out much and mostly dreamed of the day when his tour of duty would be over. They continued to try to have children for years to come, hoping beyond hope that the doctors were wrong. Casey really believed at the time that the doctors were wrong.

Loretta missed her family a lot more than Casey missed his. She was ready to go home! They didn't own all that much of material things, a few furnishings that they had bought at Sears and other places. The military paid for the eighteen wheeler used to transport their belongings from North Carolina to Baytown, Texas. They loaded a few of their clothes into the car and started out for Texas. He drove for about an hour until he just could not hold his eyes open any longer. Loretta took over and drove, while Casey slept well into the evening.

    The young couple didn't have much money so they decided to make the 1500 mile trip non-stop. They only stopped for restroom breaks and fuel. Casey drove all during the night. He was very tired by morning. He could barely hold his eyes open. Casey was speeding dangerously and taking unnecessary risks. Casey felt it was urgent to get home quickly since they had no money. It was as if the whole ordeal would be over if they just got home. Miraculously, they arrived into Baytown early in the afternoon, tired but unhurt from any accident. They had been driving for twenty four hours straight!

Baytown, Texas

Everyone that Casey had known as a civilian before the service was strangely different. He looked at everyone differently and they looked at him differently. Casey looked at them with an uneasy distrust, and they looked at him as if he had just arrived from another planet!

Most people had a contorted look in their face, which they hid behind giggles and strained smiles, as if they were struggling to hide the mounting discomfort they felt when they faced a real Vietnam Veteran. Many people had an uncomfortable feeling about being around someone they knew had been trained to kill and there was a subdued fearful look in their face; mixed with anxiety and pity that somehow forced them to take a look at themselves. They thought Casey was crazy to be willing to die for a particular way of life. *Casey thought civilians to be foolish to expect freedom to be a given without sacrifice.* He realized real quick that bravery is not endowed in everyone! Reasons for not serving their country ran rampant from going to school to free love. Casey had honorably served his country when it called for his service and now he had to live among those who had not! It was a shock Casey had not prepared for.

Casey did not realize right away that he was so much different from those who had not been in the military, much less war. He did begin to notice that everyone else seemed *childish* in their behavior to him, with their mundane and really trivial concerns. Casey had spent four years of service, first in Asia, then in Europe, being concerned about life and death situations. He was still mentally *keyed up* for action requiring survival. The majority of people he now met were only concerned about such trivial things as being late to a ball game or party, or that their brand new auto was dirty! Many people seemed more concerned about their possessions than anything else. Others were more concerned about their hairdo than that his unit was still fighting to the death in Vietnam. Casey felt angry and irritated about that. He felt very uncomfortable just listening to their conversations and observing their unabashed egos. He could see through their fallacy of over confidence and unchallenged life. They seemed totally unaware that their good fortune stemmed from the blood and sweat of others, or did not care, and he could not relate to their shallow behavior without scorn or distain.

Casey wanted to somehow adjust to being a civilian, even if that meant being a different kind of civilian. With his citizen soldier obligation over, that *adjustment* was far more than he had bargained for!

Baytown had not changed all that much from a physical standpoint. It was still a small town with small town values and the people were a breed apart from the international flavor of people Casey was used too. Many of the rice fields were now shut down and farming was giving way to the Petro-Chemical industry. Humble Oil & Refinery was still the best prize for work. Anybody that was anybody worked for the refinery! There seemed to be an unqualified air of superiority that existed among those who worked for the refinery versus elsewhere. The bank clerks treated you differently, the car dealerships treated you differently, the churches gave you leadership, the sports community and schools all catered to you, and your unearned respect extended to the politicians who ran the town on the contributions stemming from the refinery. Life in Baytown still centered on the refineries of Humble Oil.

It was therefore Casey's goal to become a refinery hand, although he had no network of friends or relatives to provide a lot of support. He had been absent from Baytown for four years, and although Baytown had not changed all that much, Casey had! He did not accept help easily, having been through so much in Vietnam that required a self reliant attitude. Help for veterans was largely unavailable anyway and veterans were not hired as quickly as non veterans during the Vietnam War era. Vietnam veterans were considered *difficult* to control!

Casey's father was of the greatest help to get him work. He worked for F.A. Richards as a carpenter craftsman building homes in the Baytown area. Casey's dad was building homes in Eva Maud Subdivision at the time, and he and Mr. Richards offered him a job as a carpenter helper. Casey did not get paid very much, about a dollar and half an hour, but it was work.

Loretta also looked for work. Her parents let the poor couple stay with them a couple of months until they could find a place of their own. She put in an application to work for General Telephone Company and Casey put in an application to work for Humble Oil & Refinery. After about six months, the refinery announced that they were testing for employment. Casey passed the tests, and he was hired by the refinery as a Process Technician, a shift-work position that paid two dollars and thirty-eight cents an hour. That was top wages in the area at the time. Loretta went to work for General Telephone Company. Their financial woes were over. They were making more money than they ever had seen!

Casey bought one of the first houses in Chaparral Village,

completely furnished it, and began to live the American dream.

Casey started Lee College to become an educated Petro-Chemical refinery hand, and Loretta worked just because she wanted to. Life on the surface seemed good as he enjoyed the fruits of the upper middle class, but beneath it all he was very troubled.

CHAPTER SEVENTEEN
PTSD Defined

Most of us go through life behaving a certain way but we really do not understand why. So it was with Casey for many years. He took his life for granted and like everyone else felt that his way was and is the best way. That's the self centered part of all of us!

Casey took going to school for granted, growing up in a rural area for granted, going to college in the big city for granted, becoming a professional for granted, serving in the military for granted, and living the American dream; all for granted!

Life is a *journey* through a certain time in a certain space and Casey's journey was a bumpy ride of highs and lows. His journey will end someday just as yours will. What he learned from his experience, good or bad, needs to be shared with others so that their journey can be a smoother ride than otherwise. Casey had some unanswered questions about his life. He asked:

What is Post Traumatic Stress Disorder or PTSD? You only have to be a survivor of some traumatic event! This event must involve some type of actual or threatened physical injury or assault. This could mean a car accident, rape, or war!

How does it happen that some individuals are effected and others or not? When confronted with a life threatening event the body reacts with a "fight or flight" response and certain physiological changes take place in the body. Certain hormones surge; this causes the senses to be hyper alert to the danger. The hormone levels ordinarily return to normal when the danger has passed. It can be argued that to *fight* is more stressful than to *flight* because the danger is more intense. For what ever reason, in the case of PTSD sufferers the hormones remain high. In Vietnam, like the Middle East conflict, the stress was consistent enough so that the hormone levels remained high. The terror of those moments takes up permanent residence in the mind even though the events were from the past. Trauma *survivors* find themselves re-experiencing the trauma in their mind. They can't control this or stop it from occurring. The consequences may include many symptoms such as:

- **Flashbacks:** feelings that the trauma is happening again
- **Nightmares:** reliving the events during sleep
- **Startle Response:** being started by loud noises or by someone unexpectedly coming up to them from behind
- **Anxiety:** fear or feeling of being in danger again
- **Numbness**: emotional shutdown of feelings; love, strong emotions
- **Nervousness**: a shaky feeling or unusual sweatiness
- **High Blood Pressure**: pounding heart or trouble breathing
- **Emotions**: trouble controlling anger, anxiety, when reminded of the trauma by triggers such as: something seen, felt, smelled or tasted
- **Concentration:** difficulty concentrating or thinking clearly

- **Sleep:** difficulty falling or staying asleep
- **Hyper vigilance:** being agitated from constantly looking out for danger
- **Surroundings:** the feeling that surroundings are strange or unreal
- **Memory:** trouble remembering important parts that happened during the trauma
- **Loss of Interest:** in things that were previously enjoyable
- **Disconnected:** a feeling of being disconnected from the world around you and the things happening to you

What can be done for a sufferer of PTSD?

- **Encourage the sufferer**-understand that the trauma sufferer is not *deliberately* over reacting or being difficult; because of anger, anxiety, or emotional numbness he or she may not be able to respond as you wish

The sufferer needs to recognize and avoid unwise coping strategies that cause further harm: self destructive behavior such as over eating, drugs, alcohol, social isolation, workaholic, uncontrolled anger, and anorexia

- **Strive to maintain a spiritual awareness:** pray a lot to God and go to His church to receive His love and uplifting; read God's word

- **Ask for help:** through the VA Hospital or numerous Vet Centers throughout the Country

How does PTSD differ from other mental illnesses?

- **PTSD is an Anxiety disorder:** it causes a great deal of discomfort to the sufferer but it does not mean that the individual is *crazy* or mentally ill in the same way that a schizophrenic behaves; there are no audio or visual messages *telling* the individual how to behave

- **PTSD symptoms are *triggered* by sights and sounds or feelings that remind him or her of the *trauma*:** it feels like they are in danger and must behave in a way that allows them to survive, even though there is no real danger; the individual becomes nervous, has violent outbursts, or becomes irritable unnecessarily for the circumstances; has very sensitive feelings

The Symptoms Begin

Casey was excited to be working for a large company at first. Humble Oil & Refinery was growing. It later evolved into a company known as Exxon, and much later as Exxon/Mobil. Casey quickly mastered the three year apprentice program. It consisted of written work modules with on the job training. He made straight A's in the program and finished it in a year and a half.

Casey spent his spare time on the shift tracing pipe lines, learning where the valves were, the pumps, and the controls. He began to know the units very well.

Casey worked in the Lubes Department. There were five units that made up the lubes department in 1970; the Propane De-Waxing Unit, the MEK Unit, the Asphalt Unit, the Phenol Extraction Unit, and the Clay Treating Unit. There was the Propane De-Waxing Unit that produced a wax that could be used in a variety of products, such as milk cartons or other such containers. It was a process that froze the wax out of a filtered solution.

The MEK Unit used a different technique to extract wax from oil. Methyl Ethyl Keytone (MEK) solvent was used to extract the wax by washing it out of the oil in huge filters. Both units were effective processes but required much routine maintenance. On a cold winters night it was not very desirable to have to go to the filters to work because the filters were mounted high in the pipe racks where the north wind would seem to cut right through you. The valves would be covered in ice and your only thought was to find relief from the bitter cold.

The Asphalt unit was difficult and dirty to work on, especially in the summer when the fumes would rise from the pumps to choke your lungs and cause dizzy spells from the kerosene that was used to flush the pumps. The thick gooey asphalt clogged the pumps and pipes which required cleaning with kerosene. The tar stuck to your shoes and clothing, not to mention to your skin, and it was impossible to remove the smell of kerosene and tar for the remainder of the shift. Casey changed coveralls just to not smell like fuel oil but it somehow remained in his hair and skin, even after a shower.

The Phenol Extraction Unit was the most dangerous unit to work on. Phenol is a very potent acid that can cause death if it is concentrated on the skin in just small amounts. Many pipes and pumps leaked at the seal joints and the whole unit smelled of the acrid phenol. It too would get in your skin and make you feel sick from allergic type reactions. A lot of time was spent washing the spills from the concrete flooring under the unit. Large filters had to be periodically cleaned with steam water. The very fumes would literally cause your skin to tinkle and your body would go numb from the fumes seeping through your clothing. Protective clothing did help but it did not prevent at least some exposure to the deadly solvent. Casey had many physical reactions to the solvents but he was trying to just do the job required. Casey protected himself as much as possible but exposure everyday began to eventually affect his health. Casey's first reaction was to avoid contact and to treat his problems with medicine provided by the Physicians after work. Soon he seemed to always feel miserable from the rotating shift and the exposure to the chemicals.

The Clay Treatment Unit was the easiest to work on except when the unit received clay from the train clay cars. Often the transport auger type screw, which acted like an earth pump, got bogged down with clay and stalled the electric motor that drove the auger screw. It was a hot treacherous job to climb into the clay receiving bin and dig the clay out of the clogged up auger screw by hand using a shovel. Casey worked hard to clear the bog down.

During the day the shift bustled with activity with managers, engineers, and maintenance crews repairing equipment. The equipment that was being worked on had to be isolated by the Process Technicians and tagged out for safety. Since this procedure was so important for the safety of all involved Casey was always very cautious around the equipment to ensure that all valves were properly sealed.

In the beginning each unit had four to five people on shift. Each man worked an eight hour shift that rotated from days to evenings to nights once a week. At first the shift did not bother Casey, but within three years he began to regret having to shift. He enjoyed the people, especially when there were several people per shift, but he was usually the only Vietnam Veteran on shift. Casey's ability to relate to the non veterans was difficult at best so he stayed to himself a lot.

During an emergency excitement ran high. Casey seemed to thrive on that aspect of the job. He would jump and run to any alarm that required the action of a Process Technician. Many others would just stroll over to the problem area. Casey was usually there first because in Vietnam his immediate response could mean the difference between life and death. Casey expected the other technicians to be as responsive, but of course they were not. Some even thought it humorous how Casey jumped and ran to respond to an alarm.

During normal operations the routine consisted of checking and maintaining the equipment and monitoring the temperature, pressure, and flow rate through the various vessels and pipes that made up the unit. This was done via a control board in a building for each unit. Pneumatic air was used to control the network of valves throughout the unit. The response from a control change was slow and much time was spent monitoring the effect of control changes.

The normal routine was very boring to Casey. Each shift seemed to drag on forever. It wasn't long before it began to affect his attitude. He also began to have problems associated with his combat experience. During the night shift he would often have flashbacks about being on patrol. Casey would see shadows and automatically duck behind cover. He would always be looking for suspicious areas that could be used to conceal someone waiting in ambush. At times Casey would position himself behind some peace of equipment to be in a position to achieve surprise as if he was waiting for someone to ambush! Often he jumped, startled from the sound of a steam trap releasing pressure. The steam trap made a sudden hissing sound that caused Casey to grab a pipe wrench from his pocket and swing around into a defensive position. Sometimes he even threw his pipe wrench in the direction of the noise before he even knew he had. Other times he swung around as he threw his fist in the direction of the sound; any sound that provoked a startle.

Casey's temper had a short fuse backed up by very profane language and excellent physical fitness left over from his military training. He did not understand the other technicians so he was often in controversy with them. Sometimes this even manifested itself into fights. Casey was use to fighting. It was a way of survival overseas.

College

Casey wanted to succeed as a civilian so he started Lee College, a technical college in Baytown, in September of 1970. He wanted to be the best he could be as a Process Technician. Casey took the core courses first, and then concentrated on the Petroleum and Chemical process courses. He wanted to not only complete the apprentice program provided by the company, but he also wanted to earn a *degree* in Petro-Chem Processing. He went part time at first carrying only six hours. Since he was working an average of 60 hours a week it was difficult to find time to study. The only time he could was by finding a place on night shift; a tool shed hid behind the unit or a vacant building used for lab tests provided a retreat. If he could sneak away from the others long enough, he could manage some study time. It wasn't long before he started loading up on courses. He had money from his work, plus money provided by the government for college. He had the drive to succeed!

The company changed its name to Exxon and began to reduce man power. Each unit was now controlled in a central computerized control room instead of at each unit. The technicians all worked very hard making the change over from pneumatic to the electro-pneumatic controls. There were unit upsets to be sure, but all considered, the change over progressed well. Most of the early problems centered on the computer or was caused by malfunctioning valves. The changes caused a lot of overtime, many sixteen hour shifts, leaving very little time for Casey to study during his pursuit of a college education. Still, he was determined to earn his degree!

Having been in the military for four years taught Casey something about discipline. He needed a lot of discipline to get his sleep, which he often did not! He needed a lot of discipline to work the long hours! He needed a lot of discipline just to trade shifts in order to make his classes! The courses were offered either at night or during the day. If he worked the night shift, he stayed up most of the day to get to the classes offered during the day. Then he stayed up all night only to repeat the situation the next day. If he took evening classes at school he traded his evening shift for the more difficult day shift in order to make the classes. Casey did this for five years!

College Physical Education (PE) classes were not required for credit if you had been in the military. Casey's neighbors had gotten into *scuba diving* and encouraged him to take the basic course offered by Mr. Robins at Lee College. Mr. Robins had a good reputation for being a top notch teacher and instructor.

Casey refused to take the course at first because of his military deferral, but soon he became interested because of the peer pressure. He wanted to fit in with his civilian associates even though he was having a difficult time doing so. Perhaps it was important that he *try* to fit in to avoid the internal loneliness he felt. Eventually he took the basic scuba course to find an outlet for his pent up feelings.

Scuba

Suddenly Casey had a brand new interest that he soon realized would bring him untold adventure! The adventure offered by the military was something he was really missing in his new life as a civilian. The new found sport, taught and trained in a para- military way at the time, really challenged Casey; that served to fill a void. Casey really did not have time for any additional endeavor, but it soon became all consuming to him. He took the advanced course and every course he could until he became an instructor himself!

In December of 1973 Casey graduated from Lee College with an Associate of Science degree in Petro-Chemical Processing. He had not seen much of Loretta during this period. She did not care for scuba diving. He and his friends were always going on trips to scuba dive. Lake Travis in Austin was one of his favorite places to go. The water was clear, and the surrounding hills made great places to camp for the night. Casey missed the stars he viewed in Vietnam. At Lake Travis, when the conditions were right, he could find a flat boulder to lay on by the lake and look up to see the sky filled with beautiful dancing and shooting stars. It reminded Casey of when he was on guard at night in Vietnam, although in Vietnam the frogs added their charm with rhythmic croaks to the magnificent sight.

Casey took his first open water dives at Lake Travis under the watchful eye of his instructor, David Robins. Mr. Robins was a big man, but he had a special sort of patience and gentleness coupled with a sly since of humor that made you naturally like him.

Casey had not been as motivated to do something since his military service. Up until he discovered scuba he had felt like he just existed for no reason. The first sight of the lake hooked him forever on the sport. He could not wait to go down!

Located in the rolling hills of central Texas the scene was majestic. The water was an emerald green and so clear you could see fifty feet down. Hugh boulders lay around the lake which added to the beautiful roughness of the adventure.

There was no fear because Casey had practiced what he was going to do over and over. He was confident of his equipment and of his abilities. Casey just wanted to complete the requirements for certification as quickly as possible so he could be on his own. Casey wanted all the adventure and gusto the sport could bring: exploring the unknown, travel to far off destinations, underwater spear fishing, underwater wreck diving and treasure hunting, underwater photography, cave diving and collecting of species to study. He even enjoyed the technical detail of how each piece of equipment worked.

Casey had found an interest in Island life while practicing maneuvers in the Pacific and the Mediterranean. With scuba he could explore many islands that were new to him. Just off the Gulf Coast of Texas the Caribbean Sea offered a treasure of adventure. He was excited to say the least! He was getting bored being a civilian because he was used to adventure coupled with some danger. He had to add danger to his existence although he did not realize that some form of risk taking would always be a prominent way of life for him.

Casey explored every lake and water hole he could find in the hill country of Texas. One such lake, know as Canyon Lake; near New Braunsfel became a regular for additional training, along with Lake Travis near Austin. Casey took every course he could to improve and joined a diving club called the *Kingfins*. Casey stayed in shape by participating on an Underwater Hockey team and diving every chance he got!

Soon Casey was challenging other teams with his brand of underwater hockey. Each University, such as Rice, the University of Houston, Lamar and others, had teams to challenge. Casey's team took it to them many times but they also lost to some very good teams. The Kingfins enjoyed it tremendously! Each player had to dive beneath the water on a single breath and move the puck forward as far as he could against the defending opponent. The next player on offense would take a breath and dive to continue the advance while the other player grabbed a breath on the surface only to re-dive to continue on offense. It kept them in shape for their sport to say the least.

It wasn't long before the Kingfins were taking on the mighty Gulf of Mexico as a regular diving destination. The Gulf of Mexico becomes very clear about fifty miles offshore. Dotted all along the Gulf Coast are numerous oil and gas platforms. These mammoth steel *rigs* create a haven for marine wild life and they became a major scuba diving destination for Casey and his diving associates.

The trip could be long and rough through the typical four to six foot swells, and the divers would go as far as one hundred miles offshore. Open ocean diving required advanced skills to handle the extremely strong current, which could grab a diver and take him or her far away from the dive site.

Casey learned how to use the strong current to his advantage. He used a compass to position himself below the surface so that the current carried him back to the boat.

The possibility of encountering sharks or other very large creatures in the open ocean was a given. Casey encountered his first shark at a natural reef that lies about a hundred miles south of Freeport, TX called the "Flower Gardens." The weather was perfect for the trip, although he always struggled with sea sickness to one degree or another. For Casey the most critical time was when the boat arrived and dropped anchor. That sudden change of motion caused him to feel sick, and he could not wait to hit the water. Once he slipped beneath the wave action the sick feeling went away.

As his buddy and Casey started down, he was excited about the clear water. He began to scan the entire area as he had done many times on previous dives. At about eighty feet, Casey was checking his gauges when suddenly he spotted three sharks coming right at him. Casey's buddy did not see them. Casey was a scuba instructor by now, and he was very confident of his abilities. He knew how to react! He was very concerned as his heart rate increased to near panic pulsations. Casey's body was preparing him for the inevitable. His military training was paying off as he maintained his cool even under the extreme new danger. He watched as the prehistoric creatures seemed to be zeroed in on him. Casey took his finger and tapped on his buddy's face mask. His buddy was still staring at his gauges. Casey pointed to the approaching sharks. The startled divers eyes filled his facemask as they seemed to pop right out of his head! He jumped behind Casey and grabbed Casey's tank to ensure Casey remained in the forefront. His breathing tripled as he approached full fledged panic. Casey remained motionless as the sharks swam right up to him. Here Casey was face to face with one of the deadliest creatures of the sea, on the front line of attack, with a panicked buddy behind him. It reminded him of some of his experiences in Vietnam! In the next few seconds Casey was to live or die according to his destiny!

Casey stared the shark right in the eye as it did the same with him. Casey had no weapon capable of injuring the shark, only the peace that comes when you're ready to die. The shark stared at him as it continued its approach, and like two warriors ready to do battle they faced off. Casey continued to stare at the shark as if he would kill it if he got the chance. At the very last instant, within inches of Casey's face, the lead shark turned to swim past him, and the two other sharks followed as they glanced his way. Casey's buddy immediately let go of Casey's tank and shot to the surface to get out of the water, never desiring to dive in the Gulf again! Casey watched his buddy climb back aboard the ship. Casey kept a watchful eye on him and on the sharks. They did not circle to come back and Casey watched them as they disappeared into the bleakness.

Having just survived the most dangerous of confrontations for scuba divers, Casey felt there was nothing else to fear. He continued his dive by finding another partner. No one else had even seen the sharks so they were unaffected. The ships crew later caught a shark and hung it up for all to see. Casey approached the shark as if it was a defeated enemy. He began to dissect the creature with his knife just as many VC had met their end!

As Casey's scuba adventures heightened he began to get *really* bored at work. He could not see himself caught up in the cooperate grind to become rich at the sacrifice of not having his freedom to adventure. He struggled for months with the issue of making money versus doing what he really enjoyed.

As a learned instructor he felt he could go into business for himself. His marriage was beginning to fall apart as he became more and more confused about his future. He began to think in terms of opening a retail store. Casey's students would become his first customers. Many trips were made to the Caribbean where he toyed with the idea of working and living on the islands he so loved. Loretta did not share his dreams and they began to drift apart. Casey became interested in other women in this period of confusion but he did not understand he was suffering from PTSD at the time. The war had shaped his future behavior, and it was not going to be nice.

Loretta and Casey were divorced in 1973. It was an equitable divorce financially. They had spent about fourteen years together when you include their teenage days and their marriage of eight years. During that time they had earned their independence from their parents. They had acquired a lovely home, and they were blessed with the best cars and many material things. Casey's retirement fund was well on its way to securing them a good future, but all was not well.

Casey was restless and he wanted to be more than a shift worker that earned good money. He needed to find his place in the world and he felt the best way to do that was to go to school full time. Casey went with his feelings and he threw all Loretta and he had done together away; to pursue his dream of a four year college education and a business of his own.

Casey eventually quit Exxon to follow his dream since trying to change shifts to make his classes proved to be too much. For awhile he was happy even though he had lost everything he had earned before and was now without money. The desire to grow drew him into the unknown, and he was scared to death to take the risk.

What Casey regretted most of all about the loss of Loretta and the good job was that she was there for him during his Vietnam experience, when he really needed someone to care, and now they were splitting because of irreconcilable differences complicated by him being a *civilian suffering from PTSD*.

In 1974 Casey became a National Underwater Association of Instructors member, NAUI pronounced (Now-we). He began to teach scuba lessons at night in order to continue his goal of finishing school. Casey continued to dive every chance he got. He left the Kingfins Diving Club and joined the Houston Underwater Club to further his goals as an instructor. There he met some prominent people in the sport's business. It seemed for awhile that everything was on track for him to reach his goal. Casey had worked hard for two years, and he was a well known instructor with contacts.

The Houston Underwater Club arranged many trips both to the Caribbean and to the Gulf of Mexico. On one trip to a ship wreck, known to locals as the VA Fog, Casey's buddy Keith and he decided to go spear fishing. Casey thought it would be neat to photograph the exact moment the fish was speared. His buddy took the spear gun, and Casey took the movie camera. They found a big sea bass to spear. Keith's shot hit the fish solid, but it was not a kill shot. The sea bass took off toward the bottom where it ran into the deck of the wrecked ship. Casey handed his camera to Keith, and off he went to capture the injured fish. Casey grabbed his knife and thrust it into the tough side of the fish. Its scales were too strong to allow the knife to penetrate its body. Casey stabbed again and again, but the fish was unharmed from his attempts. Casey grabbed for the dangling line of the spear gun while the fish pulled him toward the bottom along the slanting deck of the ship wreck. Just when he thought he was going to lose the fish, Casey decided to ram the knife through its throat and out the front of its mouth! With one hand below its jaw and the other hand on the blade sticking out of its mouth, Casey gained control of the fish. He started pulling the big fish toward the surface. Casey was exhausted! When he surfaced he was about fifty yards from the ship.

Casey began to swim toward the ship pulling the six foot sea bass, weighing close to a hundred pounds. The equipment he was wearing was not like the later equipment designed for buoyancy control. It was a tiny vest designed to inflate orally from a small tube near your cheek. The tiny vest was barely able to keep your head above water when fully inflated, and it would not float additional weight. The Gulf was very choppy that day with four to six foot seas so the swim towing the large fish was extremely difficult. About half way to the ship, Casey lost his grip on the fish, and it slowly slipped beneath the water. Casey's buddy saw what was happening and grabbed the fish and between the both of them, and the ship's crew, they managed to get the fish aboard the ship. Keith and Casey cleaned the large fish and divided it between them. They had fish steaks for months and a fish *tale* to remember forever.

Casey often ventured to the oil rigs to spear fish or to photograph the marine life under the rigs. Sometimes the weather was perfect when he entered the water, then it would suddenly change from a black cloud that appeared out of nowhere. The Gulf of Mexico is known for sudden storms. The water suddenly became like a washing machine from the wind throwing the water and boat around the rig. Water spouts dipped from the cloud so close that Casey was sure the next one was going to explode the boat. The boaters had to high tail it out of there just ahead of the danger!

On one spear fishing day, smooth seas and clear weather, Casey decided to go to the oil rigs that lie about 30 miles south of the Galveston jetties to spear a catch of *ling*. Ling are fish that are about as large as a small shark and look similar to shark, except for the tail. They are good eating! There were four divers in a twenty-seven foot

Sea Ray boat. They tied off down current from the rig. Two divers stayed aboard while two dived. Casey stayed aboard the first dive. His buddies went down and the Ling were in! They speared two each and brought them to Casey to heave aboard the boat. They were nice size fish, about four to five feet in length. Casey couldn't wait to try his luck, so he hit the water as soon as the others were aboard. He swam to the rig and dove to about 40 feet down when he saw only one ling in the distance. Casey's spear gun was cocked and ready, but the ling was too far away. He very slowly inched his way toward the fish as it circled him in a downward pattern. At about 60 feet the fish came within about five feet of Casey as it passed. Casey waited as the big fish became curious about him. It inched up to about three feet below Casey's fins! Casey spread his legs widely and took a shot at the ling as it swam under him. Casey's shot hit the ling on the side of its head instead of dead center. A dead center shot would have killed the ling instantly. The side shot caused the ling to spiral down toward the bottom, pulling Casey along with it. The bottom was very murky at about 70 feet, and the ling was pulling him toward it. The fish was too strong for him to pull against it as Casey tried with all his might to swim in the opposite direction. He was still being pulled down! The spear had lodged into the fish deep enough that it held as Casey descended with it toward the bottom. Seeing that he could not keep it from spiraling to the very bottom, Casey decided to reach out and grab hold of one of the rigs cross members. The ling strained against his hold and he was sure that he had it now. "All I have to do is hold on until the fish tires," Casey reasoned. After about a minute the line went limp! The strong fish apparently spiraled loose from the spear. Casey's heart was pounding with excitement, but he was disappointed to say the least. Casey's buddies didn't believe he had even seen a Ling, much less speared one. They laughed very playfully.

Casey's diving experience took him to such far off places as the Pacific Ocean off the northern coast of the State of Washington to the island Keys of Southern Florida. Casey traveled to several islands in the Caribbean Sea, some many times. These included Grand Cayman, BWI, Cozumel, MX, Roi Tan, Hondurance, Belize, Hondurance, Bonaire, Aruba, and Carucia of the Netherlands Antilles. The Bahamas and Jamaica offered other experiences as well as the U.S Virgin Islands. The Gulf of Mexico offered Liberty Ships that had been sunk as reefs, the Flower Gardens, and many oil platforms.

Each experience offered Casey something new and exciting! From beautiful rain forests to volcanic mountains he ventured. He explored them all.

A subtle benefit of his travels to the different countries he visited was that it made him realize what it meant to be an American. As *Slingshot* Casey had fought for freedom and now he was enjoying the fruits of that effort in ways he never thought possible before. He enjoyed freedom! He enjoyed the experience more than anything!

CHAPTER EIGHTEEN

Free Spirit

Casey never seemed to have any trouble attracting the ladies during this period of his life. Casey was a genuine *free spirit* with good looks, charm, and a sense of humor. His students liked him because he was very good at teaching firmly without being too overbearing. Casey had gained the respect of the industry by being dedicated to teaching safety. His students performed exceptionally well in open water, and other instructors could see that. It was hard for him to study with all the attention, and his grades were not the best he could do.

Casey met a girl named Jennie from Canada that was as much a free spirit as he. They became an item in the industry for about three years. Their counter culture life style was filled with good fun, travel overseas, and exciting adventure. He loved to photograph her underwater along with the coral reefs and other marine life. His photos were winning awards by now, and everyone in the Houston Underwater Club knew him.

Jennie was so spirited that she triggered Casey's PTSD symptoms constantly. This led to many fights, and he could be terrible with his language, and extremely abusive to anyone that challenged him verbally or physically.

During the good times they thought of marriage, but during the bad times they could barely stand each other. The seesaw relationship lasted for three years until one too many fights ended it.

Casey continued to teach scuba in the evenings and to go to the University of Houston at the central campus. He was now certified as an instructor for both NAUI and PADI. The Professional Association of Diving Instructors, PADI, was gaining in popularity with some of the scuba retail stores. He began to teach through both of the associations, depending on the scuba retail outlets preference.

His strength really lay in the technical arena but he needed some business courses to reach his goal. He found that he did not do well with the business courses because he was not interested in the very foundation he needed to have his own business. Realistically he was broke all the time with barely enough money to eat during any given day. School was expensive and it took all he made to continue. He began to loose interest in the business even as he struggled to prepare for it.

Casey advertised on campus to attract students to his class and many did take his course. One student, originally from California, took his class. Casey could not get her out of his mind. She was attractive, with long blonde hair, blue eyes and a nice figure. She seemed interested in Casey, and soon they were together as a couple. Her name was Lora. With her Casey was sure he had met his soul mate. They were both college students on the verge of new frontiers and the way to go was up. Casey and Lora became an item and they did a lot of scuba diving together. She was a wonderful model and easy to work with underwater. She helped Casey achieve much better photos with her co-operative style and her overall support.

Being from California, Lora had a different outlook on life than did Casey from Texas. Their cultures clashed! She wanted her education and career with no children or marriage. Casey wanted an education and a career within a married framework. She wanted to be a psychologist, or perhaps a Doctor of Psychiatry. She was interested in Casey's military experiences, perhaps as a study. For whatever reason she was the first person Casey ever shared the intimate information about his war experiences, which so shaped his behavior. That made them close at first, but later it became the primary conflict within their relationship. They eventually got married, although for financial opportunities more than any long term relationship. Casey bought a house, and he and Lora started to live in it as a convenience. Lora was restless! She soon wanted to move out! She hated the small town! Casey hated his job of shift work, therefore they both were miserable. She wanted to correct what she felt was a terrible mistake. Casey sensed the loss and grew violent.

With her, Casey's feelings were more intense, therefore his outbursts were even more heated than they were with Jennie. They argued terribly, to the point that they both felt they were a danger to each other! It had to end, so it did! She walked out on Casey. Casey was devastated, but he knew they needed to part. It was the hardest thing he ever faced. He loved her in spite of it all, so he found it hard let go! Trying to face the situation he became emotionally disturbed.

The months that followed triggered all of his built up hatred! He just wanted to die! Because of his loss he was failing at school. He could not focus on *anything*, much less studying. His scuba classes were interrupted as he struck out on his own, splitting with the retail outlet that he had taught through. He dropped out of school for a couple of semesters to earn money, and to regroup. He only worked hard so that he could return to school to finish his degree.

He hated women for their power to hurt him emotionally, and he seemed to take that frustration out on them sexually. Women became just sexual conquests for him, absent of any mindful love!

Casey had many pickups for one night stands. He was out of control! By now he had few male friends, and he was suffering from loss of sleep, nightmares, and hyper-vigilance. He was coming apart!

Casey became desperate and homeless! He just roamed from associate to associate totally inept for life. He began to drink a lot! He slept in vacant buildings and under trees. He was in the middle of a tragic nervous breakdown. *At the time it was impossible for one to admit to having an emotional breakdown.* Society tended to label you as crazy as a result of making it known. Casey had no one to turn to for fear of the repercussions that would be placed on him from society. He struggled to maintain his dignity as he slipped into a deep depression.

Casey still had just enough dignity left to finish school, but it was the hardest year of his civilian life. Broke, unloved and unable to love, he roamed around completely lost. Finally he realized that his dream of owning his own business was not to be anytime soon. He needed help, but like so many who are in trouble he was unable to receive it. In desperation Casey decided to leave the country.

Casey needed to regroup. He left for Grand Cayman Island in the B.W.I. where he struggled to become a *resort* instructor and a tour guide. He had earned his Bachelor of Science degree in Business Technology but he had not developed a network to find work outside of the scuba business. In Cayman he felt he could gather underwater photos for use later in books. He wanted to stay in Grand Cayman for about a year to pursue his love of underwater exploration and photography.

Casey worked hard photographing the reefs. The pictures had to be developed in the states so he accumulated about thirty rolls, which represented a wealth of photo material. Unknown to him a wire on his camera failed to synchronize the strobe light. When he finally got the film developed, he was shocked to find that the film was all black! Everyone of the pictures was black; all those dives and all that effort down the drain. It was the straw that broke the camel's back. It seemed Casey could not succeed at anything! Frustrated and deeply depressed Casey left the island and returned to Houston expecting to give up scuba diving forever.

A completely broken man, emotionally and physically exhausted from working seven days a week in Grand Cayman for several months, Casey had little energy to find other work. After several days rest, Casey did manage to find an apartment. There he tried to assess his abilities to figure out what he could do next.

After many lonely nights of music and reflection through the use of the bottle, Casey decided that he had to change from teaching scuba to something else. He reached way back, to a time that seemed prehistoric in nature to him by now, to find some ideal of means to support himself. He remembered working with his dad building homes when he was a teenager. "Why not use my technical background of building homes to *sell* homes?" reasoned an unsure of himself Casey. The idea had merit because there is a lot of selling that takes place in scuba activities.

Casey, having found a direction for his life, began to sell homes with a renewed spirit for success. He became a workaholic instead of an alcoholic. He was still trying to cope with the war and all of his failures but he was working toward *something*.

The change was a serious challenge for Casey because he was at the end of his rope psychologically. With very low self-esteem, he had to give up what he *loved* to do for something he *had* to do.

In spite of his depression Casey started making good money selling homes. He had his mood swings, but he became a finalist for the coveted *Prism Award*. He became known in the home industry as a good closer. He had decided to give up his scuba activities as a business, but he still wanted to pursue the sport as a diver.

While selling homes Casey met a Mexican girl named Glorietta who was very attractive. She had a beautiful smile and a good figure. They flirted for awhile then they began to date. After awhile Casey asked he out. It seemed strange to him to be involved with someone whom he had not met via scuba. She was different in her culture, and she did not want to scuba dive. Eventually Casey married wife number three. Glorietta seemed happy.

Things were fine for several months. They rented a house together for awhile; then they bought a house. Unfortunately Casey lost his job soon afterwards, and he had to let the house go.

The stress of having to find work put Casey over the edge as they began to argue a lot. It led to another divorce. Casey moved to San Antonio to sell homes. He missed her there and after several months requested she join him there. They made up and eventually remarried. They rented a house but the pressure of trying to make ends meet on a commission basis kept Casey on edge. His PTSD symptoms did not allow him to rest. The nightmares were horrible! He became irritable with Glorietta, and the fights came often and got worse and worse. Finally they divorced again after a brief effort at reconciliation. Casey eventually moved back to Houston to find work. *Casey knew something was terribly wrong with him but he did not understand what!* It was obvious to him that he had no joy in his life!

The divorce, and the loss of work intensified his PTSD.

Casey seemed to be getting worse each year, and everything he tried ended in failure; he failed at marriage, jobs, and schoolwork, and the stress caused him to have low self-esteem. He had severe bouts of depression. Sometimes he was near giving up on life! He went to work for another home builder in Dallas where his closing ability really paid off for awhile. He was selling homes and making money professionally, but his private life was a living hell.

The only thing that he thrived at was *work*. He hated to go home to an apartment that was empty, and he did not find it easy to make friends. With no friends or family and nothing to look forward too, he returned to Houston, Texas. He was *nothing* without work! Soon he found work in Houston and continued to live the life of a *workaholic!*

Then Casey met Sandra who was much younger than him. She seemed exciting to Casey at a time when he was very, very lonely. He got involved, and he married wife number four for his fifth marriage. Sandra reminded Casey of his Aunt Odell from Brenham, only much younger. She was fun to be with, and she really excited Casey. Casey was an older man, and he and the young woman had some good times, but of course with Casey's problems the relationship became strained. After awhile, sex was the only thing holding the odd couple together.

When the home building industry collapsed in the 1980's from high inflation and high interest rates, Casey was without a source of continuous income once again. After several months of unemployment Casey was again desperate! He needed work, and his past source of income was no longer available because of an economic recession he had nothing to do with. Homeless and hungry, he hit the road to drive an eighteen wheeler truck.

Truck Driving

The mighty international diesel engine roared to life as Casey began his first training on how to drive an eighteen wheeler. The school was a fly-by-night outfit called The National Driving School of Houston. There he learned the basics of truck driving using a verity of trucks and trailers. The cab-over design allowed for better mobility for parking the huge rig; better than the front nose design. So it was a good rig to train on in the beginning. With seven forward gears, the big truck and van trailer slowly came up to speed. Casey eased the shift into high gear. Shifting through the lower gears was rough for him in the beginning. He grinded the gears, and selected the wrong gear for the situation at first. The truck jumped jerkily forward and stalled with a selection of too high a gear. He practiced day after day to get the basic shifting down to a smooth movement. Still Casey was unsure of his new endeavor.

Parking the big rig required excellent driving skills. With the size of the rig such that it did not easily fit just anywhere, the skill to back straight with a trailer, good side or blind side, was and is an absolute necessity. Many loading docks required nothing less than perfection to properly park the trailer, with the back door open toward the dock and aligned correctly between the bumper pads. Casey went through the school's test of the skills without any problem. He was use to handling heavy equipment from the USMC, and the common sense he learned while driving an amtrac loaded with troops in the USMC made him a natural driver. Observing was a natural behavior to him. He wanted to know the condition of the truck and trailer at all times. Casey learned in the service that the condition of his equipment could mean the difference between life and death. He did not want an injury to someone to be the result of *his* negligence! He took the inspections seriously.

Casey hooked the trailer to the big truck. He was becoming very good at hooking up the trailer to the truck, and then unhooking it when necessary. The hook requires good alignment of the truck while backing toward the trailer. A slight tug on the trailer with the truck indicated to Casey he had made a good lock on the hook. He could *feel* the trailer catch snap the lock. The legs of the trailer must be raised after a good connection is made.

Casey got out of the truck to complete the hookup. He connected the air hoses as well as the lighting wire and raised the trailer legs. After checking all around his rig, especially the lights and the tires, Casey was ready to recheck his truck.

Casey got back into the truck and gave a quick look at his gauges. Everything still looked good; oil pressure, air pressure, battery, temperature, fuel. Before pulling away Casey always liked to check his trailer brakes. He applied only the trailer brakes while he gave another firm tug with the truck. He felt the truck engine strain as the trailer held firm in place. Having already checked his CB radio, his fuel cards, his tax receipts, and his paper work Casey was sure everything was in order. His Bill of Laden he picked up from the trailer pouch listed what was in his trailer and the origin and delivery point of his cargo. "Have I checked to make sure the trailer doors are properly sealed?" he asked himself. "Have I noted any damage done to the trailer before I arrived and am I sure that I am picking up the right trailer as indicated by its number and location?" He Had!

At the end four weeks Casey had completed the road testing on city, county, and interstate roads and highways. The course had to be successfully completed with written and road certifications along with testing for a class A commercial driving license (CDL). Casey made a safe delivery which was his last road test before certification. He only needed to pass his written tests to finish the school.

Casey completed the other basic things covered in the school; DOT rules and regulations, logs, yard training, dispatching, shipping and receiving, warehousing, loading and unloading, and weight distribution. He was ready to hit the road from coast to coast.

Casey completed the school in 1982. He retrained with JB Hunt Trucking in 1985 for an additional diploma. He was to use his new skills all through his truck driving experience.

Although he had earned a Bachelor of Science degree from the University of Houston in Business Technology, which included distribution, and he could have earned more money by working in a warehouse as a manager, Casey *sought* the adventure of the open road. The economy was in a slump in the 1980's and jobs were hard to find. Most companies were down sizing as opposed to hiring anyway.

Casey did not want to seriously drive over the road for ever but it was a skill he knew he could use if needed. He drove vans and tankers off and on throughout the eighties and late nineties and he enjoyed the adventure of seeing the U.S.A.

Casey's first dispatch was to the East coast. He loaded the van from a warehouse in Houston and headed east on I-10. He was already familiar with the east coast as far as North Carolina because he had driven from Camp Lejeune to Texas several times while in the Marine Corps.

The truck driving for the eastern route took him much farther north to Boston, Massachusetts near Portsmouth, Maine and then westward to Chicago, Illinois. Casey picked up and delivered cargo that was dispatched in a circle that included all the eastern states as far north as Detroit, Michigan and as far south as Miami, Florida. The Appalachian Mountains and the Great Smokey Mountains offered beautiful scenery and was particularly interesting to him when he saw them for the first time. The routes through the mountains however challenged the best of drivers as one went into deep valleys, then climbed and circled through the steep grades that burnt the brakes until they were red hot. Casey saw many drivers lose control in the mountains and crash to their deaths due to soft breaks.

From Texas Casey drove east through the southern states and north to Tennessee and Kentucky where he viewed the Cumberland Mountains. He thought about the Cumberland Gap where civil war soldiers traveled through the mountains to gain position on each other. It was hard to imagine how theses beautiful mountains looked while walking through them. Casey wished he could have seen them that way.

The Allegheny Mountains of Pennsylvania and West Virginia provided a scenic backdrop to the yellow and golden leaves of the trees, offered by the fall season. Casey had never seen a more beautiful site during the fall. He felt blessed to be witnessing such a beautiful morning at a time when he was very depressed about his failures. It allowed him to forget about his troubles for a few minutes as he tried to replace the mind troubling mistakes and numb, angry, feelings with the hope of the future, using the simple but magnificent art of nature.

On one back road of Ohio, Casey noticed a buggy up ahead. He could not believe that a buggy was being used in his era of technology. Here he was in his great big tractor trailer rig, following a horse drawn buggy on a narrow country road, with farm fields on either side. "What a picture this would make!" Casey muttered to himself. It was a place where modern technology was *behind* the old way of travel, where two strangers slowly lumbered alone in modes of transportation from times of two different eras. They were on a rural country road with no one in site but the two of them traveling west, a horse drawn buggy in front, with the eighteen wheeler right behind it. After about fifteen minutes of following the horse drawn buggy through the hills and valleys, and around the farm fields, Casey was eventually able to slowly pass.

There was a single driver in the buggy, a slim, sun tanned man that looked older than his stout frame indicated. He had a long, light reddish brown beard, and narrow eyes that glared at Casey for a long look. His skin was light and freckled, but burnt red from exposure to long hours in the sun. "He *must* be a farmer," Casey reasoned. On his head was a top hat made of black material, while his clothing was all low keyed colors of earth tone browns.

After about ten minutes of driving, Casey entered a small town. He was getting hungry so he decided to stop. He parked the rig on a back street to look for a café to have lunch. After a brief walk, Casey found a small café, entered it and sat down. At a table near the window of the café there were three other apparent farmers that looked much like the one Casey had passed on the road. Their accent was foreign to him as they chattered about their day. Casey must have looked foreign to them also, dressed in his boots and Texas style clothes. The men glanced at Casey often as if they were sizing him up.

After a few minutes as Casey was eating his lunch, another man entered. It was the same man Casey had passed on the road earlier who had been driving the buggy. He sat down with the others, and the conversation got livelier amongst the group. They were talking about a harvest about to take place and the needs of their community. Casey sat quietly observing them, hyper-vigilant as always. He was afraid that as a group they might start to harass him like some of the rednecks back south. They did not speak to Casey or pay much attention to his appearance although they glanced at him occasionally with a quick look. Casey ate his lunch slowly, slightly amused by this encounter of a clash of cultures. "Who are they?" Casey thought to himself. They appear to be living in the 18th century instead of the 20th century! The café owner told Casey that the men were *Amish Farmers* that chose to rebel against the fast paced changes brought about by technology. They live a simple, but harsh life similar to the pioneers who settled the country long ago. Casey was not able to trust anyone, so he did not chose to talk to them. Later he thought how wonderful it would have been to have sat with them in conversation to learn more about their way of life. It was not in him to do that, suffering from PTSD. He did relish the experience of observing them though, and he did learn some things about their values.

As with all of Casey's travels each section of the country had its home grown ways that differed slightly from other areas. The way people spoke, the way people dressed, the way people jested, the way people treated each other, all were as different as the location dictated. Mountain people are different than plains people. River people are different in their behavior than coastal people. City people are different from country people. Each state offered a different variation of culture. How astonishing that so many diverse cultures could come together to be Americans in a single country. "How wonderful that the Amish people are free to live as they wish," reflected Casey. Casey was glad he had helped to secure the American way of life by serving his country. He was proud to have done so in spite of the situation that he now had to bear. Truck driving is a very enlightening experience. He would never regret it. He was learning so much about himself and others throughout the journey.

Casey was excited to pass through the North Folk Virginia Navy Yard which could be seen from I-64 running south along Chesapeake Bay to U.S. Highway 13. He could see several U.S. war ships in the harbor. It was a comfort to him to know they were there. He slowed the truck to a crawl so that he could see as much of the harbor as he could. Then he spotted a couple of nuclear submarines! As an ex military man his heart raced with excitement knowing the subs to be a very destructive weapons. He could not believe his eyes. "We really do have them," Casey thought out loud. "This is the real thing, not a movie scene!" The site of the subs made Casey shake. Seeing the atomic subs triggered his anxiety about the Cold War with the USSR. He remembered how China and Vietnam had succeeded in the spread of Communism. He literally shook for hours as the irritability brought on by PTSD took control.

Driving to Missouri, Casey marveled at the site of the big arch of St Louis. He had seen pictures of the arch in books but it was even more magnificent than he thought, with its shinny exterior, beautifully crafted of smooth stainless steel as it curved and rose from the ground toward the sky, and then curved back down to the ground. "What a work of art!" Casey thought as he passed it by.

After driving for some time, Casey was tired and hungry, and in need of a break. He had not had much sleep for several days. He rubbed his swollen eyes, looking for a place to rest. He passed a couple of promising places, but he opted to wait until he found a facility that had some amenities. Soon he found a good truck stop.

Casey pulled into the truck stop after receiving a new dispatch, to use the scales to weigh his load. The weight of the load had to be fairly equal on all of the axials so Casey made a practice of weighing each new load, to show the DOT (Department of Transportation) that he was within the law when he first loaded. When entering each state the load was re-weighed. While on the scale another truck driver pulled up behind Casey. Casey took longer than the other driver wanted him too. He opened his door, stood up over it and started yelling obscenities at Casey. Casey was getting upset! Casey gave the man a cold stare without saying a word as he drove the truck and trailer to a parking spot. Casey was studying the situation and the man to see if he was armed. Casey felt he would get him in the truck stop! There was a long line to pay for fuel so Casey stood there waiting for the man to come in. Casey was tired and angry which does not mix well with patience. Casey was dressed in his brown cowboy outfit with his hat and boots. He was ready to put his boot right between the rude man's legs when he came in. There were a lot of guys standing around. The driver walked in with two other guys but Casey still confronted him. "Are you the one that was making such a fuss on the scale?" Casey blurted out. "You need to watch your mouth," Casey said! The man was shorter than Casey. Casey thought for such a small punk he had a big mouth. Casey sized the man up! The man was young and inexperienced. Casey told him, "one more word like that and we'll settle the score outside." The young man became really nervous while Casey waited for his next move. Casey knew the man had to make the first move so that Casey could claim self defense. Casey was ready to get it on but the man left the line shaking. Casey stayed in the line to pay for the fuel. Casey stepped into the bathroom. The man wasn't there, but his two buddies were. They looked at each other as Casey sized them up fully expecting to take *them* on. They could see Casey wasn't bluffing. To Casey's surprise, after a moment of tense staring, they said, " We'll talk to *him*." Casey very calmly but in a firm manner said, "You do that!" Casey, very alert to ambush walked out watching out for the other driver, but he kept his eye on the other two as well. Was the man hiding with a tire tool behind the corner, ready to nail Casey from behind? Casey was on full alert as he felt the same adrenaline rush he had experienced time and again in Vietnam.

Casey set down to eat his meal and to drink his coffee. He sat with his back to the wall where he had full view of anyone approaching. Casey trusted no one! When Casey finished his meal he watched everything as he approached his truck. Casey figured the three of them might try to ambush him behind his truck. It was not easy to ambush Casey. He was aware of every trick. To Casey's surprise he never saw the three men again.

It always took Casey a long time to relax after he was angered. Casey started his truck and headed down the road to make his delivery. He eventually unwound from the incident.

Experiences of everyday living like that confrontation with the drivers triggered Casey's PTSD symptoms. He became irritable and nervous as he was startled with every sound or shadow. The experience aroused *flashbacks* that kept him awake at night. He could not sleep well as he remembered the battles from his past. The effort it took to be constantly alert drained his energy level to such a degree that he found no interest in things that use to be of interest to him. Casey had an empty stare as he was numb to the existing world and of any emotion. He existed in a world of his own not feeling any connection to the outside world. He was running around the country as if he was looking for peace somewhere in the distance, just over the next hill.

Interstate 95 (I-95) took Casey through Washington DC at night, and he could see the Capitol and some of the monuments lit up. He vowed that one day he would return for a visit to see Washington DC up close. For the moment it was pleasing just to know it was real and not just a picture in a book.

It was 1984. It would be twenty years later before Casey could realize that return trip up close. He passed through DC several times while making deliveries to neighboring states. Each time he wished he could visit the monuments. Casey headed east with thoughts of the future.

New Jersey, Philadelphia, and New York were a lot different from East Texas. On the Pennsylvania Turnpike from Chicago, Illinois to Philadelphia, Pennsylvania you could not exit just anywhere because it went for miles without an exit. Also the New Jersey Turnpike did not have a lot of stops just anywhere, but it had oasis occasionally where you could stop for food and restrooms.

There were no truck stops, but the oasis had large enough parking lots that truckers used them as truck stops. Casey thought his bladder would explode before he found a stop, and he learned to take advantage of the opportunity to stop when he could. The next stop might be far down the road.

Tunnels that cut right through the mountains were much larger than Casey expected. He was able to drive his large eighteen wheeler right through many of them. Casey noticed they were well lit!

On I-95 northbound through New York City, a traffic jam before and after the George Washington Bridge allowed Casey to witness a New York gang in action. A southbound vehicle stalled on I-95 near the Bronx River Parkway so the driver left the car to find help. There were no cell phones then, so Casey expected he was trying to get to a phone. As soon as the driver disappeared from sight, a small gang of guys descended from the Bronx apartments above, down into the underpass area where the car stalled. The car looked fairly new. The northbound traffic was still stopped completely. Casey watched in amazement while the gang posted a lookout. The others began to strip the car of everything they could carry! The CB radios began to chatter about the event as several other eighteen wheelers were in the jam also. Some tried to notify the police but got no response. Most of the drivers talking were from out of town, but the New York City drivers indicated that it was a common occurrence. They knew that the police would not get there soon enough to do any good. The thieves boldly continued to strip the car even after the northbound traffic started to move. Everyone stayed with their own vehicles thinking it was best to take care of it instead of the abandoned car. A couple of days later Casey passed through that area southbound, and he saw that that new car was still in the same pace, although it had been striped to nothing but a shell! Casey did not like the behavior he saw, and he decided that Texas was a better place to live. He had seen cars broken down on Texas highways, and no one would bother them for days. Horse thieves were hung in Texas at one time so the traditional behavior of leaving ones transportation along continued into at least the beginning of the 21st century, and the problem was not as serious as elsewhere. Thief rings were organized for stealing cars to smuggle across the border into Mexico, but the common folks never bothered anyone else's car. The police were quick to catch the car thieves in Texas most of the time. Casey thought the New York gang should be hung without mercy.

Casey enjoy seeing the Empire State Building and the rest of New York's skyline, as well as the Hudson River area as he crossed over the George Washington Bridge. The bridge has two freeways, an upper and lower level. Casey had never seen anything like that before. He was impressed with the largest city in the U.S. and valued the experience of seeing it.

On another dispatch into the New York area Casey was again stuck in traffic before crossing the George Washington Bridge. He looked at the map and saw that the Palisades Interstate Parkway headed north along the Hudson River. To bypass the traffic jam he decided to turn north before the bridge to take the parkway. The scenery from the parkway was majestic so he slowed to observe the Hudson River from the high vantage point. He thought it was a beautiful sight so he thought about stopping for a better view. About halfway through the route a police car pulled him over! Casey knew he had not been speeding and he wondered why he was being pulled over. After the preliminaries of checking Casey's license and bill of laden the policeman told him he needed to turn around. Casey didn't understand , so he asked, "why?" The policeman said, "The parkway is off limits to eighteen wheelers. You must turn around and go back to I-95 to the George Washington Bridge." Casey did not want to go back so he argued. "According to the map I'm closer to an exit up the road than if I return back to the bridge." The policeman more firmly told Casey to turn the rig around. Casey eventually did so feeling upset that he had lost so much time by trying to *save* time. The view was worth the drive and the time it took, so Casey did not stay upsct for very long.

The Boston, Massachusetts area had no truck stops for the big rigs. Casey was exhausted from his driving, and it was getting late.

Casey ended up in Boston without finding a safe spot to pull over. He found a construction site near downtown across from the Charles River. The construction crew was about to close the fence gate when Casey approached the foreman to ask if it was OK to park his rig to spend the night in the construction parking area. The foreman said it was OK with him so Casey slept in the truck about a block from an expensive hotel over looking the Charles River.

Casey awoke the next morning to find joggers running along the river. It made him a little homesick to see the walkers and joggers enjoying the early morning sunrise along the river. He decided to have breakfast at the hotel just to feel important for a few moments in Boston. The walk was about a block. Casey wore a cowboy hat to cover his messy hair, not thinking it was not a common thing to do in Boston. He was met by a couple of waitresses that were curious about him. They were also less friendly than the waitresses back home. With their Boston accent they seemed all business and not all that friendly. After a few seconds one waitress seated him at a table. Another couple came in and then some others. After a few minuets Casey was asked to move to another table away from all the others. Casey found that to be humiliating; the Boston home grown prejudice of class distinction Casey thought.

Cowboy outfits are not the norm in Boston! With his light brown shirt and dark brown pants, his cowboy hat and boots, a large shiny buckle, and his unshaven face, Casey knew he did not look like them; he thought they could have been a little more understanding. Everyone seemed to stare at Casey as if he was from another country! Strictly speaking Texas *is* a different country from Massachusetts. Dressing western is common in the wide open areas of Texas! Casey didn't concern himself with social skills. He just wanted breakfast!

Casey ate breakfast and left there feeling that he was an embarrassment to them and an unwelcome guest. Casey had been on the road for weeks so he was exhausted. Fatigue will make anyone look unfriendly. Casey apparently gave the waitress an unfriendly feeling with his ruffled clothes and hard, tired look. Moving him around was upsetting to him. He disliked her bossy stand-offish attitude. She spoke fast in an unconnected way. Casey needed someone to appreciate him, not only for the hard work he was now doing, but for his service to his country. He felt very unappreciated.

With PTSD he was the one who was numb to good feelings and very sensitive about what others said about him! He trusted no one so he was on guard all the time which increased his sensitivity. The increased stress level caused him to want to avoid crowds. It is just too tiring to mentally be on alert all the time. While others were talking small talk, Casey was totally disinterested, because he was on guard subconsciously for any sign from others that they were a threat to him. He expected others to behave in an abusive way so he was abusive first! To relieve the stress he often just left a party to be alone. The hyper-vigilance made him so very tired it increased his emotional numbness. He just wanted to get away! *His comfort zone became the loneliness!*

In Cleveland, Ohio Casey needed to find a phone to call for directions to the delivery dock. He was heading south on I-90 looking for an exit from the freeway. He saw a corner store at the top of the exit of the freeway so he took the exit. There was very little room to park the eighteen wheeler at the store, but he managed to park it anyway. Casey asked to use the phone, but the store keeper said there was no phone in the store but that there was one behind the store about a block down the street. Casey started walking toward the pay phone located down the street. Casey started walking toward the phone location carrying his information book. It was very dark. He began to flashback to the night patrols in Vietnam as the hyper-vigilance set in.

In the distance Casey spotted two shadows standing across the street. He continued toward the phone booth watching everything as he approached. A street light dimly lit the phone booth in the distance. As his figure came into the light the two dark shadows began to shout profane insults to him, and Casey knew they were thinking of mugging him. Casey lifted his chest and picked up his pace toward them, his adrenaline rushing to his head for the fight he expected to encounter. His boots made a clunking sound as if he was marching in step in a column in the Marine Corps! He heard music as he marched. He held his padded notebook under his arm. Not showing any sign of fear, Casey kept going toward the two figures. They began to change their tone as Casey got closer. He was in that state of mind where you go numb from pain or fear, and his whole body was keyed up for the battle with the big mouth muggers. Moments before he was about to attack them for their insults, they sensed he was not afraid. Fear began to overcome them! One shouted, "He must have a gun! Let's get out of here!" They broke and ran into the darkness. One ran to the left while the other ran to the right. Casey figured they were going to get help from a gang to circle him. He would be enveloped from all sides; a common VC tactic. Casey made the important phone call watching the darkness every second as if his conversation was just a dream. With his emotions at its height he braced for a counterattack thinking he was going to die on a city street of Cleveland, Ohio. After all he'd through in Southeast Asia it seemed a ridicules and useless way to die. He watched the shadows, and he heard every sound as he walked on guard back toward the truck. It seemed like it took a life time to enter the relatively safety of the truck. He climbed into the truck cab, still angry. He began to shake uncontrollably as the adrenaline high took over. Was he afraid? Probably! Did fear control him? No! He was taught to ignore fear, and to just react.

Casey began to have flashbacks seeing VC running around for a flanking position to get at him. The experience triggered his symptoms of PTSD in a way that left him again irritable and angry. He had nightmares which interfered with his sleep which is very dangerous when you are driving a big rig. Now he realized that he was stupid to take the chance of using the pay phone located in a dark area so far from anyone. At that point in his life he only knew how to fight for survival. *Fear was a weapon to use for survival.* Casey actually enjoyed the adrenaline rush! It was Hong Kong all over again.

Entering Chicago from the east Casey could see the Sears building from a long way off. It appeared to be right in the middle of the freeway when viewed from a distance going westbound on I-90. "The tallest building in the world," whispered Casey! "Man what a sight. Someday I will visit it inside," he mused. Casey liked Chicago, built right on the Chicago River and the shore of Lake Michigan. "I could live here," Casey retorted with astonishment.

In Detroit, Michigan Casey crossed over into Canada by mistake trying to deliver auto parts to Ford Motor Company! Unknown to him he was supposed to drop the trailer in Detroit to be shuttled over to Ford later. His Bill of Laden indicated to deliver to Ford in Canada. He took it literally, not knowing of the shuttle arrangement for customs. Customs pulled him to the side to check his load and to make the appropriate phone calls to clear his entry.

Casey entered Canada surprised to find the streets to be very narrow. The streets were not suited for the big rig he was driving so the turns were very tight and tricky. Casey managed to find the delivery warehouse after a few miles where his trailer was emptied.

Casey felt the little town was quaint. The people were not in a hurry like the people were in the states. He liked the relaxed atmosphere they showed. He even envied it because he always felt anxious and stressed with his lifestyle. Everything had to take place now! The load had to be there on time. Never be late! Hurry, hurry, hurry! No time to relax. He even felt *guilty* to stop for rest. The anxious feeling fed his adrenaline and hormonal rush as long as he was moving. When he stopped moving, the downside caused extreme depression. Loneliness was a way of life, not needing anyone but his independent self. He even disliked having to deal with the warehouse people! He just wanted to be left alone!

During the winter in Milwaukee, Wisconsin Casey was waiting at the dock for the next morning to unload. He decided to walk over to the river. The Milwaukee River was flowing fast with huge chunks of ice roaring down the river. It was a natural phenomenon the likes of which Casey had never seen. He was curious, but he was also afraid because he knew that if he slipped into the river he would be swept away within the ice, never to be heard of again. An eerie discomfort was aroused in him as he sensed the danger! He became nervous and jumpy. It was about 3:00 AM with a night chill covering the snow. Not a sole was stirring. Casey imagined the river surging from its banks and grabbing him within its jaws of ice and crushing him as he disappeared beneath the water. The still of the night seemed to increase the flow of the river! He remembered the river patrols in Vietnam and sensed the same feelings of danger.

Casey watched every shadow as if he were about to be ambushed by some unknown power emerging from the misty fog. His heart raced as if he had been running. It was his self generated anxiety to survive the next day. He had experienced the feeling many times in Vietnam. *In the grasp of fear he became alert as his senses tuned into everything.*

Fighting his emotions, emotions conditioned by his combat experience, he became extremely stressed; alertly tuned into every sight, sound, or even his own thoughts! The longer he felt stressed the more violent his thoughts became.

It was the same kind of unrecognized stress in his life that at times made him violent towards others. He did not even realize he had the vicious emotional cycle of ups and downs. Anger and distrust caused him to be more stressed. The more stressed he became, the angrier he became, and the more he wanted to be left alone.

Returning to his truck Casey tried to gather himself. Inside of the truck he felt safe. There he did not have to deal with the senseless authority expressed by imagined civilians. He distrusted authority figures, and he hated to take orders from managers, who in his opinion were less qualified than him to be in charge. Casey scuffed at authority with contempt as he sat in the truck all alone fighting his fearful thoughts. He could not sleep!

Casey's next dispatch was to the west where he first enjoyed the Interior Planes and the Great Planes of North Dakota, South Dakota, Nebraska, Kansas, Oklahoma, Texas, Idaho, Minnesota, and Missouri. The desert stretched for mile after mile where a trucker could hammer down with relative safety. Smokey the bear (Highway Patrol) was always monitored by all the truckers, reporting their location on the CB radio. This is *Cuda* westbound on I-94. Anybody got your ears on westbound?" "You got the *Hammer Head* here, come on!" "*Hammer Head* this is your good buddy *Cuda*!" Casey used *Cuda* as his radio handle, short for Barracuda, a long fast fish with sharp dog like teeth that can strike a prey faster than you can wink! "What's your twenty?" "You got the *Hammer Head* here, *Cuda*," about mile maker 278. "What's your Twenty, come back?" "Cuda here, I just passed mile marker 280, I'm about two kicks behind you. How's my front door, come back?" "You just follow ole *Hammer Head*, the ole salt of this dried up sea. I'll take care of you *Cuda*. Smokey's taking a siesta at Momma's Cafe! You have an open door all the way to the state line, so hammer down, and I'll see you at the next stop!" "Ten-Four *Hammer Head* See you then. Thanks for the info good Buddy. Have a safe sail. *Cuda* out!"

In Kansas, Casey felt excited to be in the "Land of Oz" where the "Wizard of Oz" from his favorite childhood movie, made his requests to Dorothy to bring him the slippers of the wicked witch of the North. Casey looked for Dorothy "Somewhere over the Rainbow" as he hummed the most famous tune. It brought him back to a time of innocence long ago when he was a child in Brenham, Texas and of growing up in rural Texas. Casey remembered the carousels, and Fireman's Park, and his grandma, and his parents and cousins. It seemed like a dream of a long, long, time ago in a world far, far away; not at all as real as fact; a time of innocence lost long ago for he had lost all that was innocent in Vietnam, never to be the same again!

Casey grew up watching westerns on TV where the good guys always wore white hats and won, while the bad guys wore black hats and lost. The bad guys always took to the hills. In North Dakota, Casey saw the Black Hills used in many westerns, as their outlaw hideout. One has a lot of time to think while driving for hours; about the past and about the present. Casey only lived for each day, while he tried to understand how he got to as lonely as a traveling maverick.

As Casey traveled to Wyoming he saw the area where General Custer made his last stand near the Little Big Horn. The Big Horn Mountains were visible in the distance. Casey thought of the battle where all of the 7th Calvary perished, and he somehow knew how they felt just before death was imminent because there were times in his experience in Vietnam that he felt he would not survive. He wished he could have walked the battlefield close up, but he had a job to do that was time dependent. Casey thought of the deaths that have been lost due to war and wondered if anyone really cared. "*When I returned home it seemed no one cared then,*" Casey angrily remembered. Casey cared for the soldiers that *gave all*, whether it was to open up the west for settlers or to defeat Fascism, contain Communism to Asia, or to defeat terrorism in the Middle East. To Casey all soldiers are heroes regardless of whether they are recognized by the government with a chest full of metals. Metals are issued for political ambitions as much as for bravery, and many deserving soldiers are not given metals even though they fight just as hard as the next guy. General Custer's men gave their lives so that everyone could travel the road that now can be driven on, without being threatened by a band of hostile terrorist.

In Idaho, Casey viewed the Bitterroot Mountains with their snow caps shimmering brightly in the sky like a soft white collar around ones neck. It gave him comfort observing the environment in its natural state. Casey thought, "How foolish humans are, thinking they can win their goals by blowing away the earth with hydrogen or atomic bombs! If we destroy the world to save it, what have we gained?" The philosophical thinking did not take Casey's mind off of his troubled past.

Casey was enjoying his experiences traveling throughout all of the states. He enjoyed making deliveries throughout California and northward to Oregon and Washington. At San Diego Casey reflected on his training at Camp Pendleton where he first experienced the site of the Pacific Ocean. He remembered the difficult training in the foothills of the Laguna Mountains. He remembered the Watts race riots of Los Angeles and how his unit in the USMC was put on alert should the riot develop into a full fledged revolt. He recalled how relieved he was when the order came to *stand down* because he did not want to fight his fellow Americans at home. He wanted to fight the Communist revolutions! When he saw the Golden Gate Bridge for the first time he marveled at the American engineering feat; a valued icon of the industrial revolution. San Francisco Bay sparkled below the coastal range of mountains. It reminded him of something out of a story book.

One of the scariest drives through California involved climbing Breckinridge Mountain at Bakersfield. With a full load in the trailer and the truck in the lowest gear, with the fuel pedal to the floor Casey started the climb of nearly 2.5 miles to the top. The big rig shuttered under the strain of 80,000 lbs, and he could hear sounds like the vehicle was *moaning,* as it gave all it had to keep going up. Slowly, about 5 MPH the rig reached for the top, but the top was still a long way up. For 30 minutes the big rig struggled with the whine of the diesel sounding like it was about to explode any minute while the metal parts of the trailer and truck cracked with the sound of the twisting medal. The wheels grabbed for the pavement with each turn as if the rig was holding on for dear life. One slip, one moment of lost traction, or an engine stall would cause the rig to start rolling backwards. Probably the breaks would hold if the emergency knob was quickly pulled out. With a maximum load on a steep incline like the Grapevine at Bakersfield, Casey did not want to lose control.

Casey kelp the pedal to the medal as the heavy rig inched its way up. Although the truck was doing all the work, the anxiety of it all made Casey a nervous wreck. He was sweating a great deal although the temperature was 75 degrees Fahrenheit. He was shaking as he gripped the steering wheel with a death hold as if he was holding onto a tree limb hanging over a cliff. Casey's leg shook as he kept pressure on the pedal trying to drive it against the floor, as if he could gain speed the harder he pressed. The truck would not go any faster no matter what he tried. Casey shifted up just once to see if he could gain speed but the truck bogged down immediately so he got back into the granny gear. Slowly the truck and trailer weighing nearly 80,000 pounds inched its way up the unforgiving mountain.

When the heavy rig reached the top, a rest area provided a place to check the truck for safety. Casey felt exhausted after the 30 minute climb so he needed the rest to regroup. He checked the brake pads, tires, all other connections, and took a deep breaths as he rotated his arms and upper body to loosen up the tight muscles caused from the stress of the climb. The real challenge was about to come. He had to get the load down the mountain without melting the breaks!

After about thirty minutes Casey was ready to make the drive that could end up being his last if the breaks failed. He climbed into the rig, took a deep breath, and shoved the gear shift to low gear to start the journey down the mountain. It was necessary to use the low gear to hold back the weight because his rig had no "Jake Break" designed into the engine. The only way to get down the mountain was to go slow, use low gears, and lightly use the breaks when the rig began to gain too much speed. If the breaks were held solidly the heat would melt them before the rig reached the bottom. So he used them, let off them to cool, then used them again to slow the rig, then released to cool in a very slow descent. Some drivers chose to let their rigs go as fast as they would go. One driver got on the CB and said, "Look out, I'm coming through," as he passed Casey at about 100 mph. "He must have run this mountain before," Casey thought very concerned. "He surely must know what lies ahead." This was Casey's first trip down the *Grapevine* so he was being very cautious! He watched the other rigs to try to judge his speed with theirs, and most of the other drivers were going down just as slowly as he.

When he reached the bottom the road took a sharp turn around a curve. His first trip down the mountain was one he will never forget. Many trucks in years past had not been able to slow down enough to make the curve because their brakes were too hot! After the experience up and down the *Grapevine*, Casey could handle the mountains with respect. He controlled the *fear* of the consequences. The most important lesson he learned was that you have to respect the danger, and like war, channel the fear to use it as a source of energy.

One early morning, about 2:30 AM, Casey entered the Bitterroot Mountains coming from Butte, Montana, west toward Spokane, Washington. The night was very cold, especially traveling through the Rocky Mountains. Casey was tired because he had been pulling cargo for weeks through all kinds of foul weather. This winter night it was snowing as he entered the mountain range. The trucks had slowed to a crawl as he approached the curves knowing that any mistake would cause the rig to slide off the mountain to the valley below. The column of trucks slowly weaving around the mountains reminded Casey of a military caravan. One set of trucks could view the other set of trucks below, as the column circled the mountain to enter the pass. It was especially eerie with the ice and snow but also strange to see nothing but eighteen wheelers with no cars in sight. Here Casey went down into sharp curves with valleys below and up around the curves, as the truck grabbed for traction on the ice covered road. The windshield wipers slapped through the slush leaving a smear that fogged his vision, as if being tired and droopy eyed wasn't enough. "Anyone with any sense at all should take cover for the night," growled Casey. He heard his partner snoring in the bunk behind him.

Casey wondered if his partner realized how dangerous the conditions were. Casey did not worry, until he reached one sharp curve that tilted the truck forward and to the right as he approached the valley. The decline was so steep it rolled his buddy right out of the bunk! His partner stuck his head through the curtain after being jarred awake. "What's going on," he stated. Casey said, "We're in the Rocky Mountains and the weather is awful." "Are you OK?" he asked. Not wanting to frighten him or to admit he was stressed over the precise driving required, Casey said, "Its pretty bad but I think we'll be through it soon!" "I'll be glad to drive if you want," Casey's drive partner said. Casey knew his partner did not really want to drive. He realized that his partner was just being kind. His partner was still half asleep as he sat up to analyze the conditions. "Boy its snowing bad out there," he said in a stupor as he took a deep yawn. "Yeah, its been sleeting and snowing since I entered the ridge about an hour ago," Casey said with conviction. "We'll be out of it soon! Go back to sleep and get your rest. You'll need to drive in the morning for sure." He grunted and with an underserved faith in Casey he shut the curtain and went back to sleep. The CB was cracking with conversation about the conditions and warnings of the icy curves. One truck slid off the road and landed against the mountain! Casey held his breath as he rounded the next curve, a little angry about his partner's lack of concern, but proud he trusted his life with him. In the military Casey was often required to execute dangerous missions. His mission now was to get the cargo through the snow covered mountains without going over the edge. As he rounded the next curve and started down the steep grade, the rig slid on the road to the right.

It frightened Casey as he peered over the bottomless edge. Thinking he was going over the edge Casey down shifted and only lightly used the brakes. The rig slowed and regained traction as it curved around the edge of the mountain narrowly escaping the fall.

When morning arrived Casey was safely through the mountains. He knew from the CB that others had not made it. He was exhausted as he arrived at a truck stop below the mountain. He climbed into the bunk with no interest in spending time in the store! Casey thanked God that the night was over and that *He* had been with him throughout the night. Casey went sound asleep immediately knowing that once again, by the grace of God, he had been spared from injury while doing a dangerous mission.

Out west Casey got a partner that he could not get along with. Casey was experienced enough to correct his own mistakes but the other man thought only he could drive expertly! After hours of the man's insults Casey was getting mad. His partner finally shut up and went to the bunk. Casey was glad to get rid of him! After several miles through the Great Sierra Desert of New Mexico, Casey decided that he needed a break. Very tired he pulled into a truck stop. Casey's partner stuck his head around the curtain covering the bunk area and growled, "What the hell are you doing?" Casey, upset with his attitude said, "I'm taking a break. I'll be right back!" The man seemed mentally distraught that Casey stopped. He angrily cussed Casey for stopping and whipped the curtain open to get out of the bunk. He wanted to use the restroom. Casey had parked away from all the other trucks to stay clear of them. He just wanted to stop for a few minutes and leave without having to park the rig in a tight spot. That meant Casey had to walk about 25 yards to the store. It started to rain as he approached the store. The insulting man was cussing and grumbling about what Casey was doing. As Casey approached the store he was at the point where he had had enough of the abuse.

When they got near the store the man pushed Casey's shoulder. Already upset over the abuse, Casey grabbed him by the shirt collar and threw him against the building so hard it knocked the breath out of him. Seeing that he was done Casey stuck his fist in the man's face! Casey shouted, "Stop abusing me! I'm going to beat you if you don't shut your big mouth." Casey meant it! He slammed the man against the wall again then threw him to the ground. Startled the other driver just backed away, and said no more.

Casey went into the store still fuming with outrage. The store keepers had seen him attack the man, not knowing Casey was just defending himself. They looked frightened as Casey walked pass them. They were not aware of the abuse Casey had put up with for hours mile after mile. After physically confronting him the man stopped bullying Casey. Casey couldn't really sleep but he got into the bunk. Casey did not want to sit in the cab with *him*!

That angry outburst was a common reaction by Casey to others who let their mouth over ride their good sense. *He did not understand that PTSD is a chronic condition that includes verbal and physical abuse from the sufferer.* Casey just *reacted* like he had been trained to do many years before.

All that is needed to trigger the symptoms of a PTSD sufferer is a stressful situation. It would be years before Casey was diagnosed with PTSD or to receive treatments for his anxiety . Casey suffered an entire life time before he received help! How wonderful it would have been for others to know and to recognize the problems of combat veterans right from the start. *PTSD sufferers can receive help through therapy and medication that can help to control the symptoms.* After the Vietnam War it took years before the Vietnam veterans received the help they needed. That man did not realize that Casey was like a time bomb ready to explode. Neither did Casey!

At the next truck stop Casey called the office and told the dispatcher he wanted off the truck with the abusive man before they had any more confrontations of a more serious matter. The dispatcher agreed, and Casey got his own truck soon afterwards. Casey still trusted no one so it was difficult for him to work on a team on the road. He decided that driving solo was best for him!

In Knoxville, Tennessee after being on the road for several weeks, Casey was lonely. He pulled into the truck stop for a routine fuel stop, some food, and a shower. His clothes always looked rumpled because they were folded in a suitcase. Casey put on clean wrinkled western clothes and topped them off with his cowboy hat. Being young, trim and slim, his boots made him look two inches taller. On the way back from the shower a nice looking Tennessee woman saw him and followed him to the truck. Casey climbed into the truck to find her standing by his door. She asked if Casey could use some company. Always cautious, Casey said no, but he was intrigued by her southern beauty. She reminded Casey of the Texas girls back home. She was slim built but filled out in all the right places. Her blond hair and slightly freckled light skin caused her blue eyes to shine like a beacon. Casey believed she was in her twenties just like him. Casey talked with her a few minutes as he lay his upper body on the open window frame of the cab of the truck. She shifted from side to side and the more she talked the more Casey began to change his mind about having company. Finally she said she felt uncomfortable about standing outside to talk, so Casey said for her to come into the cab and sit down. Her southern draw was music to his ears after traveling back and forth in the northern states for weeks. She talked *slow* like the girls back home, not at all like the quick northern talk. She explained she was born and raised in Tennessee and she was stranded for the night. They both talked about their respective states and of their upbringing. She said she had no children. She talked and talked but finally she got tired so she asked Casey if she could lay down in the bunk to rest. Casey said yes but that he needed some rest also. She said he could join her in the bunk and lay with her. Lying next to her excited Casey, and she picked up on it. The two young strangers responded to each other immediately. Casey was lonely, and she wanted his company for sure. They made love and held each other for awhile. Suddenly she began to cry. Casey could not understand. He had treated her kindly and she had willingly responded by giving herself to him. Now she was upset emotionally. Casey asked, "What's wrong?" She cried, not wanting to tell him. She told Casey that she had told her *husband* she was going out and that she didn't mean to have sex with me; she was sorry for betraying her husband. Casey did not even know she was married until she began to cry and explain. Casey comforted her, wondering about what had just happened. She said she had to go. Casey, sensing her desperation, gave her some money. Casey sadly watched her disappear into the busy town. "Who was she?" Casey often wondered. "Was she some desperate, lonely confused girl on the road, or a local girl in an unhappy marriage? "One more adventure for the road," mused Casey. He never saw her again.

Casey was glad to be back to the East Coast for awhile, except for the ice and snow! While driving through Hartford, Connecticut Casey was about to have one of his most frightening experiences. On that night Casey and his team partner loaded their tanker with an oil additive to be delivered out west. Tankers drive the most dangerous of the semis. Casey was driving a straight bore tanker. Many tankers Casey drove were straight bore, a tanker without any baffles inside to soften the movement of the liquid through the tank. That meant that every time he came to a stop, the liquid load would surge forward causing the tanker trailer to push the *truck* forward with a loud, hard, bang. Casey had to break very softly to reduce the surge. When he accelerated forward the liquid load would surge backward, pulling the entire rig backward. He learned to time the shifting between the surges to catch the gear as the load surged forward or backward, to nullify the impact of the liquid on the tank. By its very nature the entire rig was unstable on icy roads.

It was very early in the morning, just before dawn when Casey was loaded and ready to make delivery. His partner was asleep in the bunk while he started driving southwest along I-84. The weather was cold but clear until he reached the hills near Hartford. There it began snowing hard. The snow covered the freeway hiding anyway to distinguish it from the surrounding ground. With snow on top and ice below the snow the freeway was very slick. As Casey started up one of the rolling hills the liquid rolled backwards, putting the weight of the load on the rear of the trailer. Casey slowly climbed the hill following the tracks other vehicles had made in the snow. When he reached the top of the hill and over, the rig began to accelerate down the hill. The speed reached about 40 MPH when the downward surge of the liquid caused the trailer wheels to slide. Casey steered slightly to keep control of the sliding trailer. Having felt the trailer slide, Casey told his partner to get out of the bunk. He was entering very bad conditions and the unstable rig was in danger of losing traction. They decided they needed to get off the road. They agreed to drive to the next truck stop about five miles ahead and then shut down until the weather improved.

On the next hill Casey downshifted to slow the rig as he started down the steep grade. He dared not use the brakes as the rig would certainly lose traction on the slippery road. With visibility to near zero Casey headed for the safety of the truck stop. About a quarter of a mile from the bottom of the hill the sloshing load caused the trailer wheels to again lose traction. Casey looked into the mirror and was horrified to see the rear of his trailer fishtailing toward him! . Casey knew he had only a fraction of a second to react or the jackknifed rig would squeeze him and his partner to death in a crumbled mass of metal. To use the brakes would have meant certain death because the trailer would have accelerated even faster around the rig increasing the force of the impact. In a flash Casey realized the jackknifed rig was being forced toward the center railing of the freeway. He knew the trailer was about to hit the cement railing and they were about to be crushed by the tangled truck.

Casey instinctually reacted as he had been trained to do in Green Bay, Wisconsin a year before. Without hitting the brakes he turned the steering wheel fast and hard to the right. The tractor immediately swung right, out of the jackknife! As one unit the entire rig made a complete circle in the middle of the snow covered freeway. Fortunately for Casey there were no other vehicles around. The back of the trailer hit the barricade. The jolt broke the trailer lose from the truck! The trailer turned over on its side and continued to slide down the hill in the middle of the freeway. It came to a stop about twenty-five yards from the truck. The truck, with Casey and his partner still inside, made a second clockwise spin until it stopped facing opposite the trailer. Shaken, but unhurt, they both bolted out of the truck to prevent a spill of the liquid load by tightening the hatch bolts and looking for leaks. Fortunately the cargo was intact!

Casey was surprised they weren't dead! He wasn't sure at first! It took him a few seconds to realize what had happened. By the grace of God they had escaped the accident with their lives and unhurt! The trailer and the tractor both were badly damaged but the liquid cargo had not spilled. The snow kept coming down heavily as the two shaken drivers worked to secure the liquid. They were concerned about a fire or explosion from sparks. Ironically the wet conditions reduced the risk of fire.

Casey was totally convinced they both would have died had he hit the brakes and not *steered* out of the fishtailing rig. At the very least they would have been badly injured. He felt his life was worth more than the damaged equipment. His guardian angels frowned.

An investigation followed. Casey was exonerated from any wrong doing giving the conditions and the type of hazardous load. With no safe place to pull over and stop, the decision to stop at the next truck stop was considered reasonable and prudent. Casey was giving credit for reacting in a way that saved their lives from injury or death.

During that day several other vehicles lost control in the very same spot and the news had it all on TV. The snow- covered black ice was the primary cause. The road crews worked to cover the ice with sand and salt as Casey rested in a hotel room that day. He thanked

God for saving him once again. His guardian angels wondered what he was going to do next!

Casey's truck driving took him from coast to coast where he managed to see every state but Alaska. He could not feel warmth for others and being alone suited him just fine. The travel gave him time to think and it filled an empty void. Casey enjoyed the adventure of the road, of seeing the west coast and the east coast and all the states both north and south, but the hours were long and the pay was short.

Although his marriage with Sandra was failing, he sent most of what he made to her to pay their bills. She had joined Casey on a previous trip and much to his surprise seemed to enjoy the travel. Then she met a young man while they were on the road and spent some time with him while Casey was laid up sick for a couple of days.

Casey began to realize that he was just a fling for her when he came back from a six week trip and found that she had moved out of their house and was spending the money he had sent home on others. Casey divorced her soon after. Divorce number five!

Broke and depressed Casey hit the road again for several months until he was so tired he needed help just to think. He had to get off the road to take care of his problems. He realized that in a fateful way.

One night Casey looked up to the stars and spoke to God. He asked God what it was that *He* expected of him. "What can I do? I've been such a sinner!" he prayed. The answer was clear! Casey asked Jesus into his heart and asked him to forgive him of his sins. A spine tingling feeling came over him as God spoke to him with conviction. *He* said, "Go Home! Go Home! Repent of your sins. Go home!" Casey had not thought of going home since he had left there many years ago. "Why go home now?" Casey thought. "There is no one there that cares for me, except maybe my parents." *Casey trusted no one! How could he trust Jesus now?"* He realized right then that he was to stop running all over the country and to just go home! Casey needed to turn his troubles over to *Him* because only *He* knew how desperate Casey was. Casey had found the answer of what to do through his faith in an all forgiving God! Casey finally trusted someone; Jesus!

Casey completed his tour of duty in the truck. He had some unfinished business with Sandra to finish his divorce so he remained in contact with her for a couple of months. Casey's parent's health was failing so he tried to help them the best way he could. Casey went to work selling cars. Casey had little reason to live because his failures had all but finished him. With his spirit broken he struggled on.

The danger and excitement he had previously sought, to keep him going, was fading away. He no longer needed it as much to work through his problems. Casey started attending a Baptist church in Baytown regularly, and found for the first time in his life there was someone he could depend on to be there for him. His name is Jesus Christ! Yes, he could be trusted.

Casey began to help his parents and to let go of the hatred of his past. He began to pray a lot. He had become a complete financial failure with no future retirement but that was the least of his problems. "I can't have children so I can't have a family," cried Casey. No one will ever love me except Jesus.

Casey's relationship with God was the beginning of a new life for him as he tried to find work that was meaningful. He avoided the loose women because he knew that fulfillment could not be found there. He stopped running around and drinking just to seek excitement. He tried to find meaningful work! He began to worship and to live a Godly life as best he knew. Then the miracle of miracles happened!

One evening a lady walked up to Casey in church and introduced herself. She was pretty with a smile that invited conversation. Casey had prayed that a good moral Christian woman would walk into his life someday. "Do I know you? She said with a warm smile. You look so familiar?" "Could she be *the* person for me?" Casey wondered. She was dressed in a sophisticated way, not too flashy like many woman Casey had known before, but more of a smart *nice* clean look. Her figure was thin and well proportioned. Her face radiated a beauty that can only come from knowing God! Her demeanor was peaceful but full of energy. Casey introduced himself. She said, "My name is Beth." She was born and raised in Casey's hometown where God had directed him to go!

Casey was not *expecting* anyone to become a part of his life after all that he had been through. His self esteem was shattered, and he did not feel worthy of her attention. Still, she was nice enough to invite him to her house for a social after church. Casey was sure he would not fit in, but he decided that it would be interesting. He learned she had been divorced from her husband of seventeen years and that she had two children from that relationship, a son named Brian, who was twelve years old, and a daughter named Elizabeth, who was ten years old. They were very nice kids and she was so gentle that he was immediately sure this was a lady of good moral character. Her small house showed good taste but she was not a rich person financially. She worked in a local hospital in the radiology department to support her family. She had planned for her comfort well and she was trying to give her children the best care she could afford. Her friends were very nice, and she had a large loving family.

Casey immediately felt she was a sweet person, but he was convinced that he would most likely never hear from her again after the evening was over. To his surprise she did call him. They talked and Casey asked her out. Casey took her to dinner to a restaurant near the port of Houston called *Shanghais Reds*. It was a romantic place with its low lighting and a view of the harbor. Casey learned more about her family. She has five brothers, Ray, Chuck, Lewis, James, and John all of whom live in the Houston area. Beth has a sister named June who is much older and who has established a large family from her marriage with Jake. Beth's dad had gone to be with the Lord, but her mom was still going strong in her late eighties at the time. Casey talked and they laughed as they got to know each other. Casey tried to explain that he was struggling, in a way that was genuine, without really crying about it, and without letting his *problems* dominate the evening. Casey was more interested about her than himself. After dinner he drove her home. When he tried to kiss her goodbye she was unaffectionate. Of course, Casey thought she did not like him.

Casey felt an unusual peace with her that evening but he knew that he could not provide for her in his situation. "If only the timing was different," Casey thought! "When I worked for Exxon I could afford anything a working man would want. I could have provided a good life for her then. She could have been there for me and maybe my life would have turned out different! But now! How can I even come close to being a good provider?" She knew the answer! God works in mysterious ways. *It's called unconditional love!*

Casey and Beth dated several times. One evening he knew for sure that she was the person that God had chosen for him. All the others did not compare! Casey asked her to marry him that night in a strange way. The setting was perfect! The place was a restaurant in northwest Houston called *Vargos*. Outside the restaurant was a lovely garden pond, complete with beautiful white swans. A large gazebo dominated the landscape, and the walking paths that led through beautiful flowers were romantically lit The evening was a little cool, but the moonlight reflected beams of approval from the pond. The sounds of the birds could be heard as if they were singing just for them. They spent several minutes outside holding hands as they walked, feeling as if nothing else mattered but how they felt for the moment. Inside the restaurant a staircase led down to a floor where live piano music filled the air. The music was perfect for someone feeling in love. The fire in the fireplace cracked explosive bursts as it consumed the wood. The laughter of her friends could be heard in the next room. Beth looked gorgeous, and the smell of sweet flowers from the tables added a nice touch. They sat on a couch near the fireplace. Casey took a sip of wine to gain a little courage. He was so unsure of himself that he needed all the courage he could muster.

Feeling certain of his feelings for her and sure of her feelings for him he stared at her in awe and stated, "Would you like to get married, *or not?*" The "or not" part was there because he expected to be turned down! "Who would want a failure like me?" Casey secretly thought? With the "or not" he had an out. To Casey's surprise she smiled a big beautiful smile and said, yes, *yes!*

With that unexpected answer Casey hesitated a moment and then quietly said, OK! Casey had not planned or expected to ask her that evening. He knew it had to be God inspired and therefore the right thing to do. He did not even have a ring! He could tell she was disappointed about that. It didn't matter! She knew Casey could not afford one anyway! She could tell by the sincere look in his eyes he was seriously in love with her. Casey's guardian angels smiled with relief. They had filled Beth's spirit with the acceptance of the moment, and they knew she would now make their job much easier.

The wedding was a simple ceremony that was done in the living room of Beth's small house in Baytown. His parent's were there. His cousin Lee and his wife were there and one of Beth's best friends, Janis Janis' father performed the ceremony while Beth's nephew, Jake Jr. recorded the exchange of vows. Brian and Elizabeth got in line and everyone shuffled as Elizabeth took her spot. The shuffle was particularly funny because Beth had a broken leg and had to use crutches just to stand up. On a date the month before Casey had a car accident that happened while they were going to an exclusive shopping center in Houston called the *Galleria*. They went ahead with the wedding anyway! There was gifts and cakes and a room full of love.

As they left the house to go on their honeymoon, rice was thrown as Casey helped Beth to get into their new car. Her leg would not bend so it took some doing to fit her in. Jake continued to film as a pop-sickle truck came around the corner. It was playing the tune "Pop Goes the Weasel!"

No one gave Casey and Beth a chance of having a good marriage. Her family felt she deserved a stable, successful financial man that could provide her with the best. Her friends thought she was crazy because she and Casey had not known each other very long. Some were certain it was just a fling and a passing affair.

Casey lived in fear of that very thing for months, fully expecting his behavior to ruin it sooner or later. Casey vowed that he would not be the one to leave, that he would stick it out for better or worse. Casey began to treat her like all the others at first. He had violent outburst of pent up anger. His temper was often out of control. His suspicious nature and insecurity complicated the relationship. It looked like their marriage was going to fail for sure!

Casey had to change to have a fulfilling life, even if it meant seeking professional help. He thought about therapy, but he could not afford it. His history of job instability and violent outburst had to stop! He struggled to keep work. He hit the road once again.

After several months over the road he began to really miss Beth so he decided that he wanted to drive *locally.* For about a year Casey drove the tanker rigs in the Houston area from refinery to refinery. It became routine as he visited the same places over and over. Many of the loads were received late at night and then delivered early the next morning. Casey still had no social life or consistency in his routine. He could do very little with Beth either during the week or on the weekends. Many of his loads were delivered on the weekend.

Casey decided he needed to find a job with *normal* hours. He went to work for the refinery industry as a lab technician for about three years. He had better hours at first but then he had to work a shift. Casey hated shift work, even more now than from the earlier years, so he was about to change jobs again when he landed a day position in the lab. Unfortunately, tension was mounting in the refinery as the leaders struggled to gain a market in the polymers product line. A bad truckload of product was delivered to a new customer. Casey was the only one blamed for the bad batch of product because he had tested *some* of it without detecting any flaws. He was fired to make an example of the refineries commitment to satisfy its customers, even though all the people involved with the production were at fault for making a bad batch. A strict delivery time had been established and the pressure to deliver it on a tight time schedule clouded everyone's judgment. Once again devastated, Casey returned to truck driving.

The rigs had grown larger; fifty-three foot trailers was the norm. The trucks also were more comfortable with larger sleeping quarters. Casey went through the motions of learning about the new rig, but having Beth at home had changed his desire to roam, and he felt it was bad for a relationship to be gone all the time. Casey feared he would lose Beth if he seriously stayed with truck driving. He drove for about six months through the northern states. His partner received a dedicated run from El Paso, Texas through the northern states to Indiana. It snowed a lot and it seemed Casey never could keep warm up north. One evening they stopped to fuel when the cold wind just took Casey's breath away. He was only in the cold for about ten minutes. He hurried to finish fueling. He then climbed into the warmth of the cab of the truck. After getting into the cab he felt bad. Bad went to worse, and Casey became very ill within hours with pneumonia. His lungs filled with fluid as his condition deteriorated. The coughing and fever grew worse. His partner lived in El Paso, Texas where Casey reported his illness to dispatch who shut him down for a few days.

The experience was made more difficult because his partners house was located near the Mexican border. It smelled like a rural Mexican dwelling, and it looked like a country place, complete with chickens in the yard and unused junk. His partner's wife was very nice to Casey by allowing him to stay in a small spare room that contained a bunk. With no money to see a doctor all he could do was rest. She fed him during the evening when she came home from work. During the day Casey watched a two station TV until he fell asleep.

Casey's partner saw that he was getting worst and he asked what he could do. Casey told him that he needed medicine, probably penicillin but that he could not afford it. His partner said he would take Casey to Mexico where one can buy medicine over the counter cheap. Casey was not familiar with Mexican rules to cross the border or if it was legal to bring prescription type drugs across the border. He said he would take Casey to Mexico and that it would be OK to buy penicillin there.

With his wife and two children they all climbed into a small car to go to Juarez, Mexico. Casey's fever had him dizzy as if he was in a dream. He felt so bad he did not care about living. Casey *felt* like he was dying. Casey's partner drove to his grandmother's house in Mexico where they all visited for awhile. The building was stucco with two rooms. It contained very old furniture, none of which matched with its dull pastel colors. They all communicated in Spanish as Casey looked around the room to see a couple of old pictures gathering dust. He had no idea what they were talking about but he nodded every now and then to show respect. Occasionally Casey's concerned partner would explain the drift of the conversation. Eventually, Casey and his partner got into the car to drive to a pharmacy. Casey could make out the street scenes although his mind was working in slow motion.

After a short drive through the town where no rules of driving that Casey was familiar with were followed, they arrived in a haphazard way to a corner where Casey's partner said, " Let's walk!" Casey responded, "Walk! Walk Where?" Casey was suspicious of everyone although he was in no condition to argue. The two men walked to a store that was fully equipped with shelf after shelf of medicine in a narrow path straight back. Casey's partner told the clerk in Spanish that he needed penicillin. The clerk handed Casey a bottle labeled in Spanish. It was penicillin and Casey handed him ten dollars; no doctor's fee or high prescription cost or prescription needed!

Casey's partner returned to pick up his family and then

proceeded to the check point that took them into El Paso, Texas. Casey hid the pills under his shirt, still not sure it was OK to have them. As the guard looked into the back window Casey began to grow weak at the thought of being searched where the guard would find the pills. His partner spoke to him in Spanish while Casey sweated from the fever and stress. Casey was relieved when the Mexican guard waived them through the gate. They drove past some vehicles that were being searched with all their possessions outside the car; their items still setting on the ground.

After a miserable week for Casey they were dispatched to do a load from El Paso to Dallas to Indiana again. Although Casey was weak he drove the 600 miles to Dallas nonstop. For ten hours he thought about his situation. He knew that he had changed. He no longer needed to run. Peace was to be found through his faith in God and the love he received at home. He decided that he was going to get off the truck in Dallas and return to Houston. There Casey decided to use his driving skills to drive the city *buses* in Houston.

After being unemployed for three months, Casey went to work driving for METRO, the Houston city busses. Although deeply depressed he managed to do the job well. The hours were long but the pay was enough to keep he and Beth going.

Casey's life changing break came when a friend of Beth's suggested that he go to work for Harris County as a Senior Citizen Bus driver. Casey admits, "*I had to swallow my pride to except such a low paying job, even less pay than METRO in the beginning.*" Casey, however had learned to live on a low income after so many failures, so he reluctantly accepted his status, although his feelings were really hurting.

Feeling depressed about life in general, Casey went through the motions of the day. He had difficulty getting along with some of the other drivers, and his PTSD symptoms were destroying his health.

Casey learned that the Veterans Administration needed a driver for the Harris County VA Program. Casey applied, and by the grace of God, was transferred to drive for the VA. This turned out to be a life saving blessing in disguise! At the VA Hospital, Casey learned that help is available for veterans that have service connected disabilities and the resulting mental problems. Casey's problems were directly connected to his service so he sought help for his depression. Casey entered the Trauma Recovery Program offered through the hospital and began individual and group therapy. The doctors put Casey on antidepressant medication and started treating his inability to get sleep. They gave him a very complete mental and physical examination and started to treat him for his headaches, back problem, high blood pressure, high cholesterol, ringing in the ears, and allergy related sinus problems. Most importantly they started treating his PTSD, his life destroying Post Traumatic Stress Disorder.

They started treating his hatred for the government's failure to see the Vietnam War to a successful political end, and they started treating his contempt for a society that did not even care enough to welcome the Vietnam soldier home. Those who had served in military combat needed desperately to be appreciated. They were not appreciated at the time, and in some circles they were even cruelly despised!

Casey discovered in therapy that he was not alone in his inability to form close friendships. He learned that most combat veterans have been traumatized in one way or another and that they too behave the same way. In combat , soldiers do not typically want to make close friends. The pain of loss of that friend is just an additional weight to bear, which quite literally could cost his own life. Casey could not sleep with the demons of his traumatic past.

Others too had trouble sleeping, and when they did sleep they were awakened by horrible nightmares from the war. Being alert and irritable all the time was the result of having to survive without sleep for days and having to deal with an attack at anytime.

Hearing the others tell of their experiences made Casey realize that he felt the same way as they do, and that unlike the civilians that had not experienced combat, these veterans understood what he was going through. Casey soon realized that he could open up to them because they understood what civilians did not.

When civilians like to gather for socials the attending veteran feels uncomfortable in the crowd because he or she was taught to disperse and watch everyone. *To gather meant that one grenade would get you all!* In Vietnam a seemingly civilian in a crowd might turn out to be a VC. Everyone had to be watched at all times, so crowds were avoided.

To be hyper-vigilant is an energy sapping, emotional whirlwind that causes you to only half listen to someone else talking while you keep alert of your surroundings. You constantly scan the area around you and are prepared to react instantly. The other person has no idea what you are doing mentally as they are self absorbed in conversation. Many times you don't hear what they are saying or remember the complete conversation because your mind is alert elsewhere.

Some people bring out the worst in you when you are suffering from PTSD; those who are puffed up with success, or who are so selfish that you see right through their intentions, or those that challenge you on everything to submit you to their self appointed authority. The anger and hatred bottled up in you is triggered, and an angry outburst, or violent reaction is the result because you know that they are full of themselves. You actually resent their innocence, because you have lost yours during the "reality" of traumatic events. Many times you just want to get away from them because you know your reaction to them will be bad for everyone concerned. Casey withdrew a lot into activities that removed the social hypocrisy from the equation. Being lonely in a crowd is a given for a veteran of combat. Being alone is often the result!

It is the small things that trigger the symptoms. A certain smell, like the rotting flesh or site of road kill; a certain sound like firecrackers; a certain sight that creates a *flashback* to an event long ago that is trapped in the memory as if it happened yesterday!

Casey learned that stress is a draining demon that takes your energy away bit by bit until there is nothing left for you to emotionally give. You become numb and unattached to others, and your only thought is to survive the day. Veterans find *comfort* from the emotional pain, by becoming numb in their *feelings*. Many try anything to become numb for the day; alcohol, drugs, a fight, an argument, lashing out at others, dangerous activities; activities that only lead to feeding the monster that has control of them.

Stress management is essential to a positive way to treat a veteran's dilemma, and treatment is available at the VA Hospital for the mood changes caused by *stress*. Casey learned that understanding and recognizing you have an injury to your brain is the first step to seeking help! *You are not a failure or a weakling if you seek help!* You are not alone! The help must be by those who understand your combat experience and your particular disease. Many civilian psychiatrists are not schooled in the particular problems of the combat veterans.

Choose wisely who you want to help you, seek that help, and you will not regret it. Casey chose the "Trauma Recovery Program" at the VA Medical Center in Houston, Texas. (713-791-1414)

Many veterans have learned to survive on their own. They are survivors! The restlessness, job loses, marriage failures, financial setbacks, drug addition, alcohol abuse, and countless other failures have made them wise beyond most as they grow older. The cost of surviving the next day was unnecessarily a tremendous effort for some veterans. Most often self destructive approaches were chosen, such as drugs or alcohol, because they knew of no other way to survive the pain! Casey is a survivor of the era he calls the *Babyboom Doom*! You can

It is up to veterans and civilians alike to help the new generation of veterans who must face some of the same problems the Vietnam veteran faced. It is up to society as a whole to give all veterans a better direction than the Vietnam veterans initially had. Casey dedicates his story to that effort. He is committed to helping all victims of trauma, military or otherwise, to know that help is available!

Most recently, P.L. 109-114, the 2006 "Military Quality of Life and Veterans Appropriations Act," signed November 30, 2005 provides 2.2 billion for specialty mental health care. Additional increases in the VA budget will be allotted for Afghanistan and Iraq vets. Funding is being reviewed for the future as needed.

The 24-hour toll-free information and referral telephone number for "Military One Source" includes resources dealing with PTSD. (1-800-342-9647) Web site (www.militaryonesource.com)

Success

Casey's life is good now. His *success* is defined, not by an accumulation of wealth, but by his ability to *survive* a very troubled period in his life. Money accumulation is some people's *only* definition of success in America. Casey learned that *real* character is built by learning from your trials and tribulations, your mistakes, as well as your successes.

What *is* success? Real success to Casey is feeling comfortable with who you are and content with what you have. Casey's wife taught him that by demonstrating her unconditional love for him! Casey is thankful to her and to God almighty for her.

Casey started this book defining his childhood as he remembered it. He thinks his childhood was good, and he grew up as innocent as the next person. The Vietnam War changed all that was innocent for Casey as he faced the reality of human existence through that violent conflict. He suffered beyond the conflict for many years in ways that proved to be self destructive. If he can save one person from the many hardships he suffered as a result of war and trauma, then God has surely used him for His purpose, and his journey through life has ultimately been as a delayed witness for the Lord.

There will always be wars that young men and women will have to fight. It is society's responsibility to see to it that the veterans that actually fight the wars are not treated with distain, but are giving the love they deserve for their sacrifice. Calvin Coolidge said in the 1930's, "A nation that forgets it veterans will also soon be forgotten." Abraham Lincoln said in the 1860's that it is our responsibility, "To care for him who shall have borne the battle and for his widow and his orphan…" Civilians must know in their heart that they must care for the four-tenths of 1% of U.S. citizens that wear a military uniform amidst a world full of terrorism. For his sacrifice, the universal prayer of every warrior is: "Just don't forget me!"

No matter the politics, the soldiers job is simply to sacrifice himself for the good of society, and whether he lives a good life afterwards, or dies as a disgraced being is in large part the responsibility of that society.

CHAPTER NINETEEN
Survival

Casey gets up in the morning knowing that he has *sinned* as a young man, and that he has behaved abnormally as a civilian. His participation in the war conflicted greatly with his spiritual and religious values. He began to question a God that would allow such horror to go unchecked.

He began to question the upbringing values that his parents had taught him. Everything he had learned about logic, order, or reason fell apart in Vietnam. He could not reason why the expected did not happen. He could not understand the fact that "no rules" applied when it came to survival, or that unreasonable behavior might develop. *Death became the only true reality*, and the paranoia that developed to survive death or injury, by being constantly stressed and alert, took its toll. The greater the exposure to combat the greater the severity of the PTSD. Casey reflected:

"As young teenagers it is the time of life when we put our identities together. This means finding gainful employment, learning our sex role, and discovering our commitments that leads to a normal identity. War disrupts this process by creating a diffusion of identity! How? The stress of war disrupts the process by changing how you *see* yourself. Many veterans say that after they experience combat, that they are a *different* person, that they are *changed*, that they feel *old*, or that they just don't *fit* in with others." In addition Casey felt that he was spiritually empty, and he knew he was in moral pain after he left

Vietnam. He realized the "Thou Shall Not Kill" rule was made an exception by our government to defend its existence. An exception is made to the same rule to defend even our religious faith! So governments and religions make exceptions to the rule. To handle his guilty feelings, he rationalized:"Why not me?" Casey withdrew emotionally to come to terms with his values, and he found it hard to except changing values, even as he struggled with his own value system.

In Vietnam the *enemy* was not clearly defined. The military *goals* were not clearly defined, especially to civilians. Officers were inexperienced because they were rotated every six months. Egos aside, each new officer initially had to be taught by his men how to survive, therefore the official leadership was compromised. This eventually led to a breakdown in disciple and morale for many units.

After Casey returned from Vietnam there was no warm homecoming; no homecoming at all! It was as if society did not care about him at all. He was called a baby killer, misfit, war monger, spit at, and treated with disdain everywhere he went. He put on civilian clothes and stopped telling anyone that he had been to war. He just never talked about it to associates. The rare times he mentioned it to someone they immediately treated him differently, like he was a criminal to society instead of a patriot of his country. So he just stopped trying to explain, and he held his pain inside.

Trauma impairs the strongest of men, and Casey was no exception. He went through life feeling like he had a heavy burden to carry with no one to turn to. He had been traumatized, both by the war itself, *and* the lack of societal absolution. Keeping the experience bottled up inside of him for years caused the so called delayed *response* attributed to PTSD. Finally, someone explained to *him* that PTSD is a "normal" reaction to an "abnormal" amount of stress. For years he believed what society was saying about him! His self-esteem thus shattered, he just didn't care about what happened to him anymore, and he had many episodes of depression. Casey reflected some more:

"The problem with depression is that it is rage turned inward! Like a slow cancer it saps your energy for life and ruins your physical body bit by bit until you not only have mental problems, but also physical problems that are out of control. Obesity from trying to find love and nurturing through too much food ruins your cardiovascular system with high blood pressure and cholesterol. Alcohol or drugs destroys the body by replacing it with too little desire for food, with more and more a desire for the drug. One must learn to *recognize* their problems and be willing to systematically change their behavior.

One sociology counselor at the VAMC explained to him that you cannot be *thankful and angry at the same time*. To replace either violent outburst of anger, or anger turned inward you need to focus on the things that you can be 'thankful' for." Casey now replaces angry thoughts with thankful thoughts, to help control his unsociable behavior. It takes a concentrated effort to change your behavior, but that effort pays off when you combine it with good physical habits, proper medication, and spiritual faith. For years, without a desire to change his behavior he began to mimic his depression, to accept it as normal, and nothing mattered, not even to "survive" another day. His behavior was ruining his ability to love, and to *hate* everyone and everything slowly destroyed any reason to live. To say the disease began to be life threatening is an unequivocal understatement!

Casey can never forget his experiences so he doesn't even try! What he has done is to make "peace" with his past by embracing it, good or bad. With the help of the VAMC Houston, and his wife's understanding and emotional support, he is learning to deal with his PTSD in a positive way. Casey knows that he will never be cured from the *anxiety disorder*, but he is now able to learn coping strategies that make his life more enjoyable. The journey continues today.

BABYBOOM DOOM

Washington DC

Washington DC

Over the years Casey's scuba connection with the sea kept him going to far away places to explore and photograph the undersea environment. His love for the sea was obvious, a true marine.

Casey found a degree of peace under the sea, a peace that he had sought all of his life. To photograph the sea one has to develop an intimacy with the animals under the sea. The sea animals must *trust* you and begin to accept you as a their friend. Casey worked hard to show the animals of the foreign environment that he was not there to harm them. This paid off with the subjects approaching him with curiosity, allowing him to photograph them without having to chase them. The approach he used manifested itself into a very good photographic record of the life that makes up the coral reefs.

Ironically he found it much more difficult to trust *people* whom he felt were more likely to harm him than sharks or other under sea animals. Part of the anxiety disorder that he acquired during the Vietnam War just did not allow him to trust people. Additionally he felt guilty for surviving the war because many of his companions did not survive. He needed to pray for the families that lost their loved ones, and to pay tribute to his lost comrades by visiting the Vietnam Wall. Casey finally skipped a Caribbean Sea trip to go to Washington DC. It was May 20th, 2004! He had lived with the pain and quilt of surviving Vietnam for 38 years. It was definitely time to stop running around trying to *find* peace. It was a belated time to seek healing!

Casey's first experience that contributed to his recovery efforts took place in the domed stadium in Houston, Texas., a place called the

Astro Dome. The local churches contributed to an all men "Promise Keepers" gathering in 1995 when he joined his church group to attend. He did not think the experience was going to effect him in the way that it did! The people in the stadium *recognized* the Vietnam veterans, by exploding into applause that lasted for several minutes. Casey still remembers the emotions that overcame him in those precious few minutes. Finally a group in society had shown an appreciation for the sacrifices that people like him, and his fallen comrades, had made during the Vietnam war. It meant more to him than he could explain. It also made him realize that he *had* to visit the Vietnam Memorial; "The Wall," as part of his healing attempts.

The day came when everything fell into place to make the visit. Beth decided to go with him when she realized how important it was for him. He was so grateful to have her by his side during the very *emotional experience*. She added a great deal of comfort to Casey as he shared the experiences he knew about those who had fallen.

Casey and Beth caught a flight out of Hobby Airport in Houston and flew to Reagan International Airport in Virginia located not far from the Potomac River and Washington DC. To get a good price on the hotel they decided to use the Governor Inn just northeast of Arlington Cemetery. From there they could catch a ride to Arlington Cemetery where they could catch a tour trolley to the mall area where many of the monuments are in DC. Casey will never forget the feelings that came over him as he viewed the Vietnam Wall from a distance as he approached the area.

Casey's heart began to pound hard, and he seemed a little out of breath, although he had not done any physical exertion to warrant it. The mere sight of *The Wall* took his breath away! They entered from the east end, and as he descended into the depths he began to look for the names he knew. After a brief orientation he found the panels that his unit names were on. Casey placed a flag at the foot of the panels and prayed for the families that had lost their loved ones. He asked God to forgive him of his sins so that he could live in peace the remaining years of his life. "To trust Jesus is easier said than done," re-

Casey, knowing he was doing just that. The next couple of days Casey toured the other monuments in the area where Casey silently paid his respects to other soldiers for their contribution to save freedom as a way of life. The WWII monument was now complete and was due to be formally presented to the public to honor WWII veterans on Memorial Day the next weekend. As Casey entered the memorial he thought of his dad's generation and particularly of his dad's experience in Burma. He spotted a stone section of granite that displayed the words "China Burma India" for that campaign. Casey thought of the stories his dad had shared with him about his experience fighting the Japanese for control of the Burma road.

The WWII Monument is magnificent, but it did not arouse the same emotionalism for Casey that the Vietnam Wall aroused. After touring the other monuments, Casey kept wanting to return to the wall. Each time he returned he began to tear up, and to get extremely emotional as he thought of the instances where his fellow Marines had perished. He struggled with the deep feelings that only someone involved with the era could truly understand.

Later, Casey was getting hungry, so they headed for the famous Union Station to both view it, and to get something to eat. Because of the WWII Memorial preparations for the official dedication, the station was decorated with many pictures that showed detail about WWII units. Viewing these he noticed a picture of his dad's unit boarding a ship as they walked on a flimsy pier with full packs. It completed his day to see what his dad had spoke of, in black and white where the caption indicated his units contribution.

The next day Casey and Beth visited Mount Vernon after a pleasant boat ride down the Potomac River. Casey thought of George Washington's life accomplishments, and of his contribution during the revolutionary war with Britain. The trip took all day as they explored both Mount Vernon, and Alexandria, Virginia. Mount Vernon stimulated Casey's desire to know more history about George Washington, whom so many have been named after, and for whom the U.S. Capitol is named. His plantation is located in a superb spot overlooking the Potomac River. As night approached, they boarded the boat for the trip up the Potomac River to return to Georgetown harbor. They caught a cab to go to the hotel, but on the way Casey just had to see the Vietnam Wall at night.

Casey stopped the cab driver and ran toward *The Wall*. It was not lit up as well as the other monuments in DC. The lights did, however offer a quite, serene experience to the monument at night, while the moon cast moving shadows from the ever changing clouds. Not another live person was around, only the ghosts of the fallen were there.

Perhaps it was the cool night air that caused Casey to shake as he stood all alone in front of *The Wall*. Perhaps it was because he knew he was in the presence of over 58,000 souls represented on the wall. Feeling chilled, as in the presence of the Lord, Casey began to pray. There he knelt all along, thinking of his comrades and of his troubled past. Casey searched within himself to find the strength to continue on with his emotional experience. He wept in the silence of the cool night with the fallen of *The Wall* towering over him. He found some names in the dark to pay a special tribute to those he knew. Afterwards he returned to the cab a step closer to understanding and accepting his past.

Casey's last visit to *The Wall* occurred the next day as Casey watched bus load after bus load of people file by *The Wall* to pay their respects. The people did not just file by disrespectfully! They stopped to take names from The Wall, and to leave respectful items to honor those who gave all. Casey felt very good about that, and he finally knew for sure that his experience in Vietnam had not been in vain.

Casey visited the Smithsonian Museum, which provided an overall look at the history of the development of the U.S. as a nation. On display at the flight museum there were various planes and rockets to observe. From the Wright brother's plane to the space stations, one can view enormous achievements through their association with the displays.

The trip to Washington DC provided unequaled healing by allowing Casey to pay direct respect to the fallen. It helped him to fill a void that he had lived with for years.; the void of *guilt* for surviving when so many others did not.

Now the void of not loving himself is being filled through his family of Beth, Elizabeth, and Brian who show their love each day. Elizabeth has married a fine young man named Wesley and Brian married a sweet young lady named Denise. Brian and Denise have been blessed with their daughter named Elise.

The first grand child is a blessing to Casey in many ways because he could not conceive his own children. To see her grow up is a loving experience for him. She visits Beth and Casey quite often and they are there for her and the family.

Brian served his country in the U.S. NAVY where he did a tour at sea during the Cold War. He served honorably and is working hard to provide for his family as he faces the beginning of the 21st century.

Elizabeth is working hard and is earning her degree at the University of Houston. She and Brian have been a true blessing, for they provide the best reason to heal the wounds of the past. Casey loves them all!

Epilogue

Beth and Casey have a good life now. She loves Casey and he loves her unconditionally. From their difficult beginning in 1989, when Casey's PTSD behavior was acute, until now marks their sixteenth year together. It has been the happiest period in Casey's life. They have raised two wonderful children together and they are enjoying the American dream as never before. They are comfortable with their material things, but they both realize that material things alone can't provide happiness. *It takes love to make a house a home!*

They attend church regularly, and Casey's relationship with God has never been better. His self-esteem restored, he is looking forward to growing old with Beth, and when they die they will take their place with the Lord. Casey will have come full circle as one of God's beings! By the grace of God he is saved!

Casey still loves to scuba dive so in recent years Beth and he have visited many islands via cruise ships where she loves to shop and he loves to scuba dive. Maybe he'll see you in the U.S. Virgin Islands one day!

It is his hope that his story will help to save many lost and troubled souls, and help future generations understand the era of the Baby Boom Generation. It is a generation subjected to a period of chaotic social change coupled with civil unrest, brutal warfare, and Cold War hysteria; chaos unequaled in the U.S. since the Civil War. From war, to anti-war protests, to social changes Babyboomers made a difference! From military confrontation to political resolution, Babyboomers made a difference. They *survived* the Babyboom Doom, became professionals, and raised good families in spite of it all!

There is nothing Casey ever experienced as exhilarating as the sting of battle; nor the complete depression he experienced all the rest of his living being! From war to peace, it has been a journey full of adventure!

Casey learned that success is not an accumulation of material things or power, but a condition of being content with *who* you are. Afterwards you are always a success because you do not *fear* the future.

A boy becomes a man only after he has gained wisdom through his mistakes. The baby boom generation gained much wisdom throughout the chaotic changes they were all a part of in the second half of the twentieth century. These changes were brought about by war and peace. Each Baby Boomer has their on story. This has been Casey's.

As Casey grows old and reflects on his life he remembers what a great soldier said:

"The spirit of man springs from divinity. It is the God-like quality in man and through its workings in his heart a transformation is wrought; buoyancy, courage, determination, forgetfulness of self, and love for comrades, his country and the organization to which he belongs dominates his whole being. In after life, he remembers that period of unselfishness and exaltation. It becomes the most sacred part of his life and he glories in the hardship and the suffering he endured, the dangers he faced, the difficulties he overcame, the sacrifices he made, the courage he displayed. In these memories, and in these only, lie "the glory of war."

-Gen John A. Lejeune

Casey believes the spirit of man is derived from God-like qualities also! God knows he has had to go through a transformation from his early childhood, to teenage warrior, to a man with faith in God, to find peace with his past. Casey has had to *embrace* the past because he can never *forget* it as long as he is healthy enough to remember. *By embracing his past Casey has learned and matured from his mistakes, and you can too! God Bless America!*

CHAPTER TWENTY

Reflections

Thank You, *Jesus, for answering me when I called on you to save me. (*Romans 10:13*)*

Thank You, *Father, for blotting out my transgressions and remembering my sins no more. (*Isaiah 43:25*)*

Thank You , *Father, that I am strong in the Lord and in the power of His might. (*Ephesians 6:10*)*

Thank You, *Father, for doing a new work in my life. Thank you for making a way in the wilderness and rivers in the desert. (*Isaiah 43:19*)*

Thank You, *Father, that no weapon formed against me shall prosper. (*Isaiah 54:17*)*

Thank You, *Father, that you are taking what the enemy meant for bad and working it out for my good and for your glory. (*Genesis 50:20*)*

Thank You, *Jesus, that You have set an open door before me that no one can shut.* (Revelation 3:8)

Thank You, *Father, that You have good plans for my future.* (Jeremiah 29:11)

Thank You, *Father, that You are able to do exceedingly abundantly above all that I ask or think.* (Ephesians 3:20)

Thank You, *Jesus, that You will never leave me nor forsake me.* (Hebrews 13:5)

               From the Author, Thank You

Marion Wehmeyer

Be glad that your life has been full and complete,

Be glad that you've tasted the bitter and sweet,

Be glad that you've walked in Sun and rain,

Be glad that you've felt both Pleasure and pain,

Be glad for the comfort that you've found in prayer,

Be glad for God's blessings, His love, and His Care.

Helen Steiner Rice

SELECT BIBLIOGROPHY

Kerrigan, Evans E., *American War Medals and Decorations*, A Studio Book, The Viking Press, NY p. 45, (1964, 1969, 1971)

Tregaskis, Richard, *Vietnam Dairy*, Holt, Rinehart and Winston, NY, Chicago, San Franciscop. 1-2 9 (1963)

Torrey, E. Fullex, MD, *Surviving Schizophrenia*, A manual for families, consumers, and Providers, Fourth Edition Quill, an imprint of Harper, Collins Publishers p. 101, (2001)

Whitney, David C. and Robin Vaugh Whitney, *The American Presidents*, 8th edition, Readers Digest Association, New York/Montreal, p. 323-327, (1968, 1965, 1991, 1972, 1973, 1975)

Maclear, Michael, *The Ten Thousand Day War, Vietnam 1945-1975*, p. 30-33, (1981)

Duncan, David Douglas, *War Without Heroes*, Harper and Row Publishers, New York and Evanston, p. 8

Stanton, Shelby L., *Vietnam Order of Battle*, U.S. News Books, Washington DC, p. 259 (1961-1971)

Millett, Alan R. and Peter Maslowki, *For the Common Defense*, The Free Press, p. 474-477, p. 553, (1984)

Olson, James S., *Dictionary of the Vietnam War*, Greenwood Press. (1988)

Doyle, Edward, Terrance Maitland, and the Editors of Boston Publishing Company, (1985)

Matsakis, Aphrodite PHD, *Vietnam Wives*, Woodbine House, p. 1-15, (1981),

Moor, John E., Captain, edited, *Janes Fighting Ships*, Franklin Watts inc., NY, NY p. 383, p. 466, (1974-1975)

Olendorf, Donna, Christine Jeryan, and Karen Boyden, Editors Vol. 4, *The Gale Encyclopedia of Medicine*, Mary K. Fyke, Associate Editor, Gale Detroit London, p. 2331-2332, (1999)

Horne, A.D., Editor, A Washington Post Book, *The Wounded Generation/America After Vietnam*, Prentice Hall, Inc. Englewood Cliffs, New Jersey 07632, p. 215-224 (1981)

CHRONOLOGY

This is a chronology of the American involvement in Vietnam, adapted from a study prepared by the Congressional Research Service of the Library of Congress, the staff of the Senate Foreign Relations Committee, and **Casey's** experience. *These historical events sentenced the Babyboom generation to an adverse fate or destiny unknown sense the civil war. It was an unwanted fixed sentence that sealed the Babyboom Doom.* We faced these events with courage and accepted a Peace With Honor in the end that left us unfulfilled and confused about our future destiny as a well meaning society. This is how it happened:

1955

January 1: United States begins direct aid to government of South Vietnam.

February 12: U.S. Military Assistance Advisory Group (MAAG) takes over training of South Vietnamese Army from the French. *Casey is eight years old!*

February 19: Southeast Asia Collective Defense Treaty (SEATO) comes into force.

October 26: Republic of Vietnam is proclaimed, with Ngo Dinh Diem as first president.

1956

July 6: Vice President Richard M. Nixon visits Saigon, carrying letter from President Eisenhower to President Diem. *Casey is nine years old in elementary school.*

1957

May 11: President Diem visits Washington, issues joint communiqué with President Eisenhower declaring that both countries will work toward "Peaceful Unification" of North and South Vietnam.

October 22: U.S. MAAG and U.S. Information Service installations in Saigon are bombed; U.S. personnel injured.

1959

May: U.S. Pacific Command directs U.S. advisers be provided to South Vietnamese infantry regiments and artillery, armored and Marine battalions.

July 8: Communist guerrillas attack Vietnamese base at Bien Hoa, killing two U.S. military advisers.

1960

February 5: South Vietnam asks United States to double MAAG strength to 685.

May 5: United States announces MAAG will be doubled by year's end.

May 30: U.S. Special Forces team arrives in Vietnam to conduct training.

June-October: Communist guerrilla activities in south Vietnam increase.

November 11-12: Military coup attempt fails to overthrow President Diem.

1961

January 29: Radio Hanoi announces establishment in December 1960 of National Front for Liberation of South Vietnam.

March 10: National front announces guerrilla offensive to prevent presidential elections scheduled for April.

April 3: U.S. South Vietnamese Treaty of Amity and Economic Relations signed in Saigon.

May 5: President Kennedy warns that U.S. combat forces may have to be used to save South Vietnam from communism.

May 13: Joint U.S. South Vietnamese communiqué issued during visit to Saigon by Vice President Lyndon B. Johnson pledges additional U.S. military and economic aid.

October 11: President Kennedy sends his military adviser, Gen. Maxwell Taylor, to investigate military situation in South Vietnam.

October 18: President Diem declares state of emergency in South Vietnam.

December 14: President Kennedy pledges increased aid to South Vietnam.

1962

February 7: Two U.S. Army air support companies arrive in Saigon, increasing total of U.S. military personnel in South Vietnam to 4,000.

February 8: U.S. Military assistance Command, Vietnam (MACV) established in Saigon, under Gen. Paul D. Harkins.

September 12: Gen. Maxwell Taylor visits Central Highlands where U.S. Special Forces are training *Montagnards* for war against Viet Cong guerrillas. *Casey enters high school.*

December 29: Saigon announces that 39% of South Vietnam's population is now living in fortified "strategic hamlets."

1963

January 2-3: Three Americans killed as Viet Cong guerrillas defeat Vietnamese Army units at Ap Bac in Mekong Delta.

May 8: Twelve persons killed in riot in Hue during celebration of Buddha's birthday, touching off months of rioting and antigovernment demonstrations throughout South Vietnam.

August 26: Henry Cabot Lodge arrives in Saigon as U.S. ambassador, replacing Frederick Nolting.

September 2: President Kennedy declares in CBS television interview that the war cannot be won without support of South Vietnamese people "and, in my opinion in the last two months, the government has gotten out of touch with the people."

September 24-October 1: Secretary of Defense Robert S. Mc Namara and Gen. Maxwell Taylor visit South Vietnam to review war effort, report U.S. will continue support.

November 1: Military coup overthrows Diem government. Diem and his brother, Ngo Dinh Nhu, assassinated.

November 4: United States recognizes new government in Saigon.

November 22: President Kennedy assassinated.

November 24: President Lyndon Johnson announces U.S. will continue support of South Vietnam.

1964

January 30: Saigon government overthrown in military coup.

February 4-6: Viet Cong launch offensive in Tay Ninh province and Mekong Delta.

June 20: Gen. William C. Westmoreland takes command of MACV.

June 23: Gen Maxwell Taylor is named ambassador to Saigon.

August 2: U.S. destroyer Maddox attacked in Gulf of Tonkin by North Vietnamese torpedo boats.

August 4: The Maddox and a second destroyer, USS C. Turner Joy, report another PT boat attack. President Johnson orders retaliatory air raids against North Vietnamese bases.

August 7: Congress passes Gulf of Tonkin Resolution supporting presidential authority to repel attacks against U.S. forces and declaring that U.S. will provide assistance in national defense to any SEATO member state that requests aid. Vote is 88 to 2 in Senate, 416 to 0 in house. *Casey is eighteen in high school.*

December 31: First North Vietnamese Army regulars enter south Vietnam. U.S. military strength reaches 23,000.

1965

February 7: Eight Americans killed, 109 wounded in Viet Cong mortar attack on base at Pleiku. President Johnson orders bombing of North Vietnam.

February 10: Viet Cong blow up U.S. barracks at Qui Nhon; 23 Americans killed.

February 28: U.S. and South Vietnam announce bombing of North Vietnam will continue in order to bring a negotiated settlement.

March 8: First American combat units (3,500 Marines) land at Da Nang. *Casey joins Marine Corps.*

March 19: First U.S. Army battalion arrives.

March 24: First college teach-in on the war held at University of Michigan.

April 7: President Johnson, in speech at Johns Hopkins University, proposes negotiations to end war, offers $1 billion in aid for Southeast Asia.

April 8: North Vietnam denounces Johnson speech, offers own four-point plan to end war.

May 4: President Johnson asks $700 million in additional defense funds for Vietnam. Bill is passed by House, 408 to 7, and by Senate, 88 to 3.

May 15: National teach-in against the war held in Washington and on college campuses.

June 7: U.S. troop level passes 50,000.

June 8: State Department spokesman says U.S. command has authority to send American troops into combat.

June 27: 173rd Airborne Brigade opens first major U.S. combat offensive.

July 8: White House announces resignation of Gen. Maxwell Taylor as ambassador to Saigon, to be replaced by Henry Cabot Lodge.

October 14: Defensive Department announces December draft call of 45,224 men, largest since Korean War.

October 15-16: Antiwar demonstrations held in U.S. cities.

October 23: U.S. troop strength reaches 148,300.

December 1: Casey completes basic, infantry, and amphibious warfare training in USMC, goes home on leave.

December 15: Air Force planes destroy North Vietnamese power plant in first bomb raid on major industrial target.

1966

March 2: U.S. troop strength 215,000. *Casey arrives in Vietnam.*

April 12: B52s from Guam bomb North Vietnam for the first time.

June 12: Casey wounded by 155mm shell bomb during preparations for Operation Hastings while driving through Que Son Valley.

June 29: Hanoi and Haiphong oil installations bombed for first time.

November 1: Casey goes to Okinawa with his platoon.

1967

January 7: Casey returns to Vietnam via LSD USS Point Defiance.

January 25: Defense Department estimates Vietnam spending for fiscal year ending June 30 at $19.4 billion.

March 15: Nomination of Ellsworth Bunker to replace Henry Cabot Lodge as ambassador to Saigon announced by President Johnson.

March 30: Casey rotates out of Vietnam. Troop strength 389,000.

April 15: Antiwar demonstrations held in New York and San Francisco.

July 15: Viet Cong mortar attack on U.S. air base at Da Nang kills 13 Americans, wounds 150, representing one of many attacks on the air base.

August 3: President Johnson announces maximum limit on U.S. troops in Vietnam has been raised to 525,000.

August 17: Under Secretary of State Nicholas Katzenbach tells Senate that 1964 Gulf of Tonkin resolution gave president authority to commit troops without formal declaration of war.

September 3: South Vietnam holds presidential elections. Gen. Nguyen Van Thieu wins presidency with about 35% of the vote.

September 7: Defense Secretary McNamara announces U.S. will build anti-infiltration barrier along demilitarized zone between North and South Vietnam.

September 29: President Johnson, in San Antonio speech, announces U.S. will stop bombing North Vietnam "when this will lead promptly to productive discussions."

October 16: Public burning of 50 draft cards in Boston.

October 21: Antiwar demonstrators march on the Pentagon.

December 31: U.S. troops killed in combat during year total 9,378.

1968

January: North Vietnamese troops surround Marine base at Khe Sanh.

January 30-31: Communist launch Tet Offensive with attacks on major cities and province capitals. Viet Cong invade U.S. Embassy grounds in Saigon.

February 24: South Vietnamese recapture royal palace at Hue after 25 days of fighting.

March 16: U.S. troops report killing 128 enemy in hamlet called My Lai 4.

March 31: President Johnson orders partial halt of bombing of North Vietnam above 20th parallel, and announces he will not run for reelection.

April 3: North Vietnam offers to discuss starting peace talks.

April 6: Relief forces reach Khe Sanh, ending 77-day siege.

April 10: Gen. Creighton Abrams named to replace Gen. Westmoreland as U.S. commander in Vietnam.

May 13: First negotiating session between U.S. and North Vietnam held in Paris. *Casey sails for Mediterranean Sea for NATO operations.*

August 8: Republican Party nominates Richard Nixon for president. Platform calls for "progressive de-Americanization" of the war and "a fair and equitable settlement."

August 28: Democrats nominate Vice President Hubert Humphrey for president, after Chicago convention marked by demonstrations and rioting in streets.

October 31: President Johnson announces total halt of bombing of North Vietnam.

November 1: North Vietnam announces Paris peace talks will be expanded to include South Vietnam and National Liberation Front on Nov. 6.

November 2: President Thieu says South Vietnam will not attend Paris peace talks.

November 6: Richard Nixon elected president. *Casey returns to U.S. with the Sixth Fleet. Makes final landing at North Carolina.*

December 31: U.S. troops killed in combat during year total 14,592.

1969

January 5: Henry Cabot Lodge named chief negotiator to Paris talks, replacing Averell Harriman. *Casey is stationed at Camp Lejeune.*

February 23-24: Communist forces launch mortar and rocket attacks on 115 targets in South Vietnam.

April 23: Casey honorably discharged from USMC. Enters reserves.

May 12-13: Communist launch more than 200 attacks against military and civilian targets.

May 14: President Nixon offers eight-point formula for peace.

June 8: Presidents Nixon and Thieu meet on Midway Island. Nixon announces first U.S. troop withdrawal of 25,000 men.

September 16: President Nixon announces second U.S. troop withdrawal of 35,000 men by December 15.

October 4: Gallup Poll reports 58% of Americans polled feel U.S. involvement in war is a mistake.

October 15: Vietnam Moratorium demonstrations held across United States.

November 11: Veterans Day rallies held to support government policy on war.

November 12: Army announces it is investigating charges that Lt. William Calley shot more than 100 civilians at My Lai in March 1968.

November 14-15: Largest antiwar demonstration held in Washington.

December 31: U.S. troop strength down to 474,400. U.S. troops killed in combat during 1969 total 9,414.

1970

April 20: President Nixon announces another 150,000 U.S. troops to be withdrawn by spring of 1971. *Casey is temporarily promoted to E-6.*

April 29: U.S. and South Vietnamese troops launch attack against North Vietnamese and Viet Cong sanctuaries across Cambodian border. White House says operation will take six to eight weeks.

May 2: First major bombing raids against North Vietnam since November 1968.

May 2: Demonstrations against Cambodian operation held on college campuses.

May 4: Four students killed by Ohio National Guard soldiers at Kent State University.

May 9: Protests against Cambodian operation held in Washington, New York, and other cities. More than 200 colleges closed.

June 24: Senate votes 81 to 10 to repeal 1964 Gulf of Tonkin resolution.

June 29: All U.S. forces withdraw from Cambodia.

June 30: Senate adopts Cooper-Church amendment barring U.S. military personnel from Cambodia.

October 7: President Nixon makes new five-point peace proposal based on cease-fire in place throughout Indochina.

December 22: Congress gives finale approval to Cooper-Church amendment.

December 31: Congress gives final approval to repeal of Gulf of Tonkin resolution.

1971

February 8: South Vietnamese forces enter Laos to attack North Vietnamese supply lines.

April 7: President Nixon says another 100,000 U.S. troops will be withdrawn by end of year. *Casey's USMC reserve duty completed.*

May 3-5: Mayday demonstrations held in Washington; more than 10,000 arrested.

June 13: The New York Times begins publication of the Pentagon Papers on the war.

October: U.S. drops opposition to China admittance to the UN.

December 26-30: American planes stage heavy bombing of military targets in North Vietnam.

1972

January 13: President Nixon announces that U.S. troops will be reduced to 69,000 by May 1.

January 25: President Nixon reveals secret Paris peace talks held by his national security advisor, Henry Kissinger, since August 1969.

February: **Nixon initiates normalization of relations** with China. Trade agreements signed, and cultural exchanges planned. Nixon announces "Generation of Peace" plan.

March 30: North Vietnamese troops launch spring offensive across DMZ and attack South Vietnamese bases throughout country.

April 16: B-52 raids resume around Hanoi and Haiphong.

April 22: Antiwar demonstrators in U.S. cities protest bombings.

May 8: President Nixon orders mining of North Vietnamese harbors.

August 12: Last U.S. ground combat troops leave Vietnam. About 43,500 service personnel, advisers and pilots remain.

October 10: Democratic presidential candidate George McGovern announces plan to end all bombing and withdraw all forces.

October 26: Hanoi radio announces breakthrough in Paris peace talks. Henry Kissinger says "peace is at hand."

November 1: President Thieu, in radio speech, objects to terms of peace agreement.

November 7: President Nixon is rejected.

November 20: Kissinger and North Vietnamese negotiator Le Duc Tho resume private talks.

December 13: Paris talks end without agreement.

December 18: Full bombing and mining of North Vietnam resumed.

December 30: Bombing halted above 20th parallel. Paris talks scheduled to resume in January.

1973

January 15: White House announces total halt of bombing and mining of North Vietnam based on progress in Paris talks.

January 23: President Nixon announces agreement has been reached for "peace with honor." *Casey feels unfulfilled.* The lost of 58,000 comrades seems to have been in vain since the Communist still held the field of battle.

January 27: Cease-fire begins.

February 12: First group of American POWs released by North Vietnam and Viet Cong. Soon the last U.S. troops leave on 3/29.

1975

April 30: Saigon surrendered to Communist! Remaining Americans evacuated. *Casey weeps when he hears the Communist tanks have entered Saigon!* All pain in vain? It would take years to heal!

INDEX

Amtracs: 97-101, 210, 211, 223, 228, 247
Atlantic: 304-310
Baby boom: 12, 302, 422, 423
Barcelona: 261-267
Base Life: 132-136
Beth: 398, 401
Berlin Airlift: 110
BLT 2/2: 254-259
Baytown: 333-336
Brown, L/CLP: 163
Camp Lejeune: 245-253, 315-328
California: 81, 90, 104
Carrousel: 16
Castro, Fidel: 74
Change: 26-35
Chapter 1: 12
Chapter 2: 36
Chapter 3: 63
Chapter 4: 79
Chapter 5: 115
Chapter 6: 175
Chapter 7: 199
Chapter 8: 245
Chapter 9: 256
Chapter 10: 260
Chapter 11: 268
Chapter 12: 280

Chapter 13: 298
Chapter 14: 304
Chapter 15: 315
Chapter 16: 329
Chapter 17: 337
Chapter 18: 357
Chapter 19: 412
Chapter 20: 425
Charlotte: 66
Childhood: 12-51
China: 52, 107, 200, 230-239
Christmas: 191-197
Chronology: 430
Chu Lai: 122-129
Civilian: 329-332,
Code Red: 273
Cold War: 37, 52-55, 103, 108, 109, 298, 299
College: 345-346
Coming Home: 242-244
Communists: 36, 52-55, 74, 79, 80, 106, 107, 111, 112, 118, 136, 181, 301-303
Containment: 108-113
Cousins: 13, 16, 32, 33, 55-60
Corsica: 276-445
Cuba Missile Crisis: 112

Dad Trainer: 20, 31, 38, 73, 76

Da Nang: 121, 130-136

Dance: 262-267

Divorce: 352, 358, 362, 363, 396

Drill Instructor: 85, 86, 92, 93

Elementary: 36-44

Elmo, Sgt.: 288

Elvis: 51, 65
Epilogue: 422-424

Exxon Mobile: 64

F.A. Richards: 335

Fights: 137-174

Fights II: 200-229

Final Landing: 313-314

Fireman's Park: 13

Flexible Response: 108-109

Forest: 55, 57

Forward Collective Defense: 109

France: 268-275

Free Spirit: 357

Friends: 64-78

Final Landing: 313, 314
Fireman's Park: 13
Flexible Response: 108, 109
Forest: 55, 57
Forward Collective Defense: 109
France: 268-275

Friends: 64-73
Glorietta: 362
Grandpa: 22-25
Grandma Stevens: 10-14
Grandma Trainer: 30
Gulf: 26
Gunny Sergeant: 80
Harassment: 300
Heists: 66
Herman: 31
High School: 74, 75
Home: 242-244, 330
Hong Kong, 230-241
Humble Oil & Refinery: 26, 64
I Corps: 219, 302
Index: 446
Infantry: 90-96
Italy: 280-297
Jennie: 357
Johnson Brothers: 66
Jungle Training: 108-186
L.A. Airport: 102
Lewis: 65-69
Liberty: 187-197
Lora: 358
Loretta: 66, 73, 77, 78, 81, 126, 190, 307, 330
LSD: 99
LST: 99
LVTA1P5: 97-101, 157, 173, 319
LVTPX12: 316-324
Los Angeles: 102, 103
M-14: 88, 206

Marine Corps: 79, 89, 122, 123, 130, 132, 133, 137, 175, 187, 198, 199, 200, 205, 245, 247, 249-255, 259-261, 268, 269, 276-279, 288, 296, 298, 300, 304, 305, 313, 328
Mary: 54
McCarthy: 53
Med Training: 251
Mickey: 64, 65, 67, 68, 70
Military MOS: 97-101
Mom: 12-21
Naples: 282-287
NATO: 110, 259-261, 268, 269, 276-279, 284, 288, 296, 297, 298, 300, 301, 302, 304, 305, 313, 328
North Koreans: 36, 301
Okinawa: 119, 75-197
Operation Hastings: 165
Operation Prairie: 165
Operation Prairie II: 165
Pacification: 139
Partner: 389, 390
Pond: 45-51
Pope: 293
President Kennedy: 112
PTSD: 153, 177, 311, 312, 314, 337-344, 373, 378, 391, 407, 413
Que Son Valley: 142
Reenlistment: 325-328
Reflections: 425-427
Reserves: 315
Return: 198-199
Robert E. Lee: 62, 75
Rock of Gibraltar: 256-258
Rome: 288-295
Russian Trawlers: 298
Sal: 194-196

Sardinia I: 280
Sardinia II: 296-297
SETO: 112
SCUBA: 347-356
Second Marine Division: 254
Segregation: 61
Spain: 260-267
Sputnik: 112
Slingshot: 125, 126
Smithsonian: 420
Storm: 305, 310
Stress: 408
Success: 410, 411
Survival: 412-415
Symptoms Begin: 341
Sonny: 54
Soviet Union: 36, 52, 74, 110, 112, 259, 298,-301
Stateside Duty: 249-253
Stevens, Dorothy: 22-25
Stevens, Leslie Swain: 22
Tom: 16-19
Teenager: 63
Test Program: 316-324
Third Marine Division: 134
Threat: 52-55
Thu Bon River: 205
Tom: 15-19
Toulon: 268-275
Town: 259
Trip Home: 330

Truck: 364-411
Trainer, Casey: 12-424
Trainer, Dad: 31, 35
Trainer, Herman: 31, 32
Trainer, Herschel "Buddy:" 33
Trainer, Kathryn: 32
Trainer:, Lane: 33
Trainer, Mary Lee: 13
Trainer, Rubin: 58-60
Trainer, Walter: 32
Trainer: 12, 30, 32, 35, 126, 329
Trawlers: 298, 299
Truck: 364-411
University: 345
USS Point Defiance: 198
USS Gungston Hall: 176
USS Rushmore: 298, 313
USS Point Defiance: 198
USS Gungston Hall: 176
USS Rushmore: 298, 313
VA: 405, 406, 408
Vargos: 399
Viet Cong: 111, 117, 118, 137-174, 199, 200-229
Vietnam: 113-174
Vietnam II: 95, 110, 199-229

Vu Gia River: 205, 219

Washington DC: 417-421

Work: 76, 78